The Arts of Logistics

Post 45

Loren Glass and Kate Marshall, Editors
Post•45 Group, Editorial Committee

The Arts of Logistics

Artistic Production in Supply Chain Capitalism

Michael Shane Boyle

Stanford University Press
Stanford, California

Stanford University Press
Stanford, California

Printed in the United States of America on acid-free, archival-quality paper.

ISBN 978-1-5036-4004-7 (cloth)
ISBN 978-1-5036-4043-6 (paperback)
ISBN 978-1-5036-4044-3 (electronic)

Library of Congress Control Number: 2024016227

Library of Congress Cataloging-in-Publication Data available upon request.

Cover design: Bob Aufuldish, Aufuldish & Warinner
Typeset by Newgen in 10/15 Minion Pro

For Lyle

Strategy is to war what plot is to the play. Tactics is represented by the role of the players. Logistics furnishes the stage management, accessories, and maintenance. The audience, thrilled by the action of the play and the art of the performers, overlooks all of the cleverly hidden details of stage management.

—LIEUTENANT COLONEL GEORGE C. THORPE, *Pure Logistics: The Science of War Preparation*, 1917[1]

Contents

Acknowledgments xi

Prologue: Ties That Bind xv

Introduction: Part and Parcel 1

1 The Ship: Salvage Spectacles 39

2 The Oil Barrel: Supply Chain Pipedreams 86

3 The Shipping Container: Levers of Dispossession 126

4 The Drone: Last-Mile Gimmicks 165

Epilogue: The Blockade 193

Notes 207

Index 263

Acknowledgments

IT'S TRUE WHAT THEY SAY about infrastructure, that it's impossible to acknowledge or properly appreciate all the ways a person is supported. This hits close to home right now, as I seek to give an account of all those who have sustained me in the decade it has taken to write this book. I will try.

Morgan Wadsworth-Boyle read every single word of *The Arts of Logistics*, in wooly draft form no less, while in a van couriering an artwork from England to Germany. That's hardly an ounce of all that she has added to this book and scarcely an inch of how far she has gone out of her way to help me write it. For this and for everything, thank you Morgan.

I wrote this book while working in the School of English and Drama at Queen Mary University of London. My colleagues here have endured years of me talking about shipping containers and shipwrecks, topics that seem to have nothing to do with either English or drama, yet I am fortunate to work with people who are too kind to tell me to stop. For their goodwill and especially their patience, my deepest thanks go to Faisal Abul, Mojisola Adebayo, Swati Arora, Sita Balani, Jaswinder Blackwell-Pal, Jonathan Boffey, Andrea Brady, Bridget Escolme, Lara Fothergill, Eszter Gillay, Patricia Hamilton, Jen Harvie, Dominic Johnson, Caoimhe McAvinchey, Sam McBean, Scott McCracken, Michael McKinnie, Aoife Monks, Martin O'Brien, Nicholas Ridout, Beverley Stewart, Martin Welton, and Tessa Whitehouse. Catherine Silverstone was there with this project from the very start, and remains so. While researching, writing, and revising, I had the privilege of learning astonishing things from the following people as they researched, wrote, and revised their

PhD theses: Eve Dickson, Lucy Freedman, Tatjana Kijaniza, Sebastian Mylly, Olivia Schaaf, Hanife Schulte, Karen Tomlin, Sofia Vranou, and Charlotte Young. And for all those in my union branch who labor to make hospitable this place we call work, I am exceedingly grateful—Zara Dinnen especially.

Too many people have had a hand in the pages that follow to mention here. If your name is missing, I owe you something, like a drink. Among those who offered tips, cheering words, or food: Naima Abed, Adam Alston, Timothy Attanucci, Sarah Bartley, Scott Brandos, Justine Chaney, Matt Cornish, Harriet Curtis, Amy De'Ath, Kay Dickinson, Adriana Eysler, Catriona Fallow, Ruth Fletcher, Katy Fox-Hodess, Faisal Hamadah, Shannon Jackson, Anton Kaes, Nick Kardahji, Alasdair King, Eero Laine, Callie Maidhof, Lynne McCarthy, Caoimhe Mader McGuinness, Hillary Miller, Sarah Mullan, Sean O'Brien, Daniel Oliver, Louise Owen, Joanne Rosenthal, David Shulman, Alessandro Simari, Shannon Steen, Myka Tucker-Abramson, Clio Unger, Philip Watkinson, Brandon Woolf, and Martin Young. Elyssa Livergant gets her own sentence but deserves much more. This book would have been completed earlier were it not for Limehouse Town Hall, so I am pleased that this book is coming out now. I am particularly obliged to Lewis Dryburgh and Sam Valiant.

I shared research that became parts of this book in talks at Leeds University, Queen Mary University of London, the Royal Central School of Speech and Drama, the University of Glasgow, the University of Roehampton London, York St John University, and also at annual conferences of the American Society for Theatre Research, Historical Materialism London, and Performance Studies international. I am appreciative for each of these opportunities and invitations—the hospitality of both Eirini Nedelkopoulou and Tom Six was especially warm. A turning point for this book came in 2016, when, with ally walsh, I convened the conference "The Arts of Logistics" at Queen Mary University of London. The conversations and excitement of those two days are the cornerstone of this book. Thanks especially to Deborah Cowen and Alberto Toscano for their keynotes. This book has its roots in Oakland. It's been a minute, but to all my friends from those heady days, I wrote much of this with you on my mind: Mattie Armstrong-Price, Cooper Bethea, Matt Bonal, Brandon Chalk, Joshua Clover, Mandy Cohen, Alex Dubilet, Joe Engelke, Amy Hale, Bernhard Haux, Jessie Hock, Zachary Levenson, Jessica Smith, and Jessica Taal—I'll have to stop there.

With the editorial team at Stanford University Press, I lucked out. Truly. From the start, Erica Wetter and Caroline McKusick have been nothing but heartening. I thank them and the Post•45 series editors Kate Marshall and Loren Glass for their steady hands and considerable care. And to the two anonymous readers who agreed to read an early draft, your feedback was buoying. I am still amazed by all those who took the time to be interviewed for this project and who, years later, patiently set right what I got wrong about their work: Anne Bean, Walead Beshty, Sokari Douglas Camp, John Fox, Frits Janus, Ton Janus, John McKenna, Lydia Ourahmane, Frauke Requardt, David Rosenberg, Nida Sinnokrot, and Richard Wilson. Matthias Koddenberg on behalf of the Christo and Jeanne-Claude Foundation, Mel Yimeng Chu at the Cai Guo-Qiang Archives, and Sally Stein and Ina Steiner for the Allan Sekula Studio were particularly helpful, willing not only to give image permissions but also to check my facts. Still many others helped source pictures and confirm details and are duly credited within the text that follows. Staff at the Getty Research Institute, Los Angeles, and the University of Bristol Theatre Collection provided the most welcoming of archives to carry out research—I suggest finding an excuse to spend time at both of those places. A part of Chapter 3 is adapted from an article titled "Container Aesthetics: The Infrastructural Politics of Shunt's *The Boy Who Climbed Out of His Face*" that was published in *Theatre Journal* 68, no. 1 (March 2016): 57–77 and appears here with permission. This essay benefited from the editorial work (and friendship) of Jennifer Parker-Starbuck. Antoinette Johnson helped immensely with the research for Chapter 1, as funded by an Undergraduate Research Bursary from Queen Mary University of London.

To the friends who read drafts and gave comments on chapters along the way, I cannot thank you enough for your candor, your kindness, and above all your time: Joshua Clover, Kay Dickinson, Zara Dinnen, Faisal Hamadah, Elyssa Livergant, Michael McKinnie, and ally walsh.

I would not have been able to write this book without the care of Pam Boyle, Mike Boyle, Stacey Schiavo, Carole Wadsworth, and Joe Wadsworth. Oh, and I almost forgot Syd—no, I could never forget Syd.

This book is for Lyle. The rumors that his first words were "shipping container" are false, though not far from the truth. Lyle: may you salvage the most brilliant things from the wreckages of this world.

PROLOGUE
Ties That Bind

NOVEMBER 2, 2011. WE ARRIVED at the Port of Oakland in the afternoon, some 25,000 of us having made our way there from a demonstration downtown. The short journey to the waterfront had been set in motion a week earlier when hundreds of cops attacked the Occupy Oakland encampment, soaking the city in tear gas and shooting a protestor in the head. That violence triggered calls for a general strike, and November 2 began as rallies, marches, and flying pickets rumbled across the Bay Area, culminating in the planned blockade. Many who stormed the port that day were wageless or underemployed. Those with jobs skipped them to be there. Teachers called in sick, and students cut class. Longshoremen stood down. Most of us had known the port only from a distance, a backyard logistical landscape that rose into view when driving across the Bay Bridge to San Francisco, its gargantuan container cranes briefly jostling for attention with the city's skyline before fading out of sight and mind. The port was hard to miss but, for all its enormity, easy to forget.

Situated on the eastern shore of the San Francisco Bay, the Port of Oakland ranks as the fifth largest for container shipping in the United States, though its historical significance for global supply chains far outstrips any current standing on domestic league tables. It was here in the 1960s that the shipping container locked into place as the linchpin of the capitalist world-system, just a stone's throw from the neighborhoods where Black Panthers were organizing against the police and American empire. Oakland had been a pivotal transport hub since the city's founding in 1852, serving first as the western terminus of the transcontinental railroad and later, during World War II, as a major site for shipbuilding, the jobs on offer there helping to draw the second wave of the Great Migration for Black Americans westward. The world's first shipping container crane was installed in Alameda in 1959, though it would be the port next door in Oakland that private capital, conspiring with local and federal government, picked to be the world's laboratory for containerization. Investment gushed into Oakland's port in the early 1960s, deepening the harbor, enlarging its berths, and delivering an array of novel equipment for handling shipping containers.

However unassuming these steel boxes may have seemed at first, the innovation's arrival in Oakland proved to be far more disruptive than anyone could have dreamed, like an Alka-Seltzer tablet dropped into a bottle of Coke. Commercial traffic exploded mid-decade when the American military ramped up its war in Vietnam, turning to Oakland and its intermodal containers for shipping supplies. Between 1965 and 1968, the port's throughput quadrupled to 1.5 million tons, doubling again the very next year, as cargo ships returning from Southeast Asia began making stops in Japan to fill their empty containers with commodities. By the decade's end, Oakland was handling as many shipping containers as Europe's top three ports combined. This early success in the East Bay launched a wave of capital investment that flooded ports up and down the West Coast, from Los Angeles and Long Beach to Seattle and Vancouver. Within decades, containerization would pull the axis of global trade from the Atlantic to the Pacific.[2]

Few who marched on Oakland's waterfront that day knew much of this history. But even lacking specifics, we could intuit the port's social function. Most of us had at least a vague idea that much of what we wore, used, and ate moved through littoral spaces like this one: that these goods arrived to such ports from somewhere overseas where they got made by people working under likely abysmal conditions; that this port connected us to those places and to those people; that these connections manifested as a seemingly unceasing flow of things; that we could cut this flow off by assembling together here in this port; and that the effects of such an action could ripple outward. The Port of Oakland was a common ground through which we could channel our shared discontent. And so, like lava we poured in without resistance, and there our collective presence hardened to ensure there would be no further movement of goods that day. When not wandering a landscape of metal and machinery left idle, we danced on railroad tracks and climbed atop shipping containers. It felt like a day outside of time.

A few years later, in 2014, I moved from Oakland to London for a job. Shortly after arriving in England, a new colleague, learning of my interest in logistics, invited me to join her for a performance staged inside several shipping containers that had been specially installed for the purpose in the city's former docklands. Sure, I said, motivated less by my enthusiasm for theater than by a need to make friends in my new home. The performance we saw that night left me mystified (you can read about it in Chapter 3), yet even more bewildering was the constellation of world-historical circumstances that had made it possible: the global spread of containerization, the replacement of inner-city docks with vast logistical hinterlands, the industrial decline of overdeveloped capitalist countries offset by supply chains wrapping across the so-called Global South. It was dizzying to ponder.

By then, I was familiar with a range of ways that logistics appears in art, from earnest documentaries that aspire to map supply chains to the ideological symptoms mushrooming in popular culture—think, for instance, of all the shipping containers that saturate superhero films. But what I encountered that evening on the River Thames seemed to be of a different order: the performance was not so much a representation of logistics as it was a repurposing of actual supply chain infrastructure. The shipping containers through which we traipsed were themselves stranded logistical assets converted into means of artistic production. I soon discovered that this performance was not unique and that there were many works of art built from and with transportation technologies. Besides shipping containers, the art world is peppered with freight trucks, gantry cranes, railroad tracks, oil barrels, pipelines, wooden pallets, forklifts, merchant ships, drones, and much else. What's more, the artistic technique of repurposing tools designed for transporting commodities has a history dating back to at least the 1950s. When considered in isolation, these artworks might seem like novelties or quirks, but when gathered together they cohere into a revelatory infrastructural form that points to commodity circulation as a factor in the shifting history of artistic form. As academics are wont to do, I gave this phenomenon a name: the logistical mode of artistic production.

What follows is a book about contemporary art, but it is also a book about how logistics came to be. *The Arts of Logistics* has two main tasks: (1) to track how the reorganization of capitalist production through global supply chains has impacted the production of art, and (2) to chart the role that art has played in giving form to the logistical infrastructure that supply chain capitalism relies on today. Some readers might find a book with such intents to be surprising, if not also unnecessary, and have valid reasons for their skepticism. After all, when it comes to logistics, there are unquestionably more pressing topics to address than art, not the least being the consequences of supply chain restructuring for workers globally, the dispossession that results from expanding logistical infrastructures like pipelines on Indigenous lands, or the ecocidal tendencies of the grossly polluting global shipping industry. Without wanting to exaggerate the significance of art to supply chain capitalism, I wrote this book as a contribution to the critical study of logistics, as one attempt among many to assess the costs of building this world-encompassing infrastructure for circulating goods. Art, specifically artworks produced using logistical tools and techniques, has things to tell us about the extent to which supply chains are now embedded in social life.

Recognizing the role that art plays in logistics is not the same as endorsing it. This is because logistics, in my understanding, is something other than the neutral management science for getting things to the right places at the right times that it is so often presumed to be. Rather, logistics constitutes a capitalist infrastructure geared to sustaining profits, regardless of the escalating harm to human and nonhuman life. It has been constructed not to produce the things we need to live, but to scatter their production across vast planetary supply chains. Building on the work of scholars such as Charmaine Chua, Joshua Clover, Deborah Cowen, Stefano Harney, Laleh Khalili, and Fred Moten, I present logistics as inseparable from the violence on which the circulation of capital depends.

The narrative I provide about logistics is less one of flow than of friction. It is a story that highlights how historical logics of racialized dispossession and worker exploitation persist into the present, encoded in logistical infrastructure. Instead of wading into debates about the "value added" by supply chains, this book zeroes in on the losses that capital accumulation demands, which requires beginning, as I do in Chapter 1, with the transatlantic trade of enslaved people. Many of the artworks and performances you will encounter in the following chapters offer opportunities for viewing logistics otherwise, with some providing situated perspectives on the violence inherent to circulation. I chose art as my entry point for studying supply chain capitalism because I am interested in what artworks repurposed from logistical technologies can reveal about the limited horizon for putting this planetary infrastructure to other uses. In this regard, *The Arts of Logistics* should serve not so much as a handbook for what can be done with logistics but more as a cautionary tale about what is to come should we naively assume there to be liberating affordances baked into capitalist infrastructure, just waiting to be discovered.

I have opened this book by recounting two of the experiences that motivated my research, and that highlight, respectively, the antinomies that bind *The Arts of Logistics* together: blockade and reconfiguration. Common sense might suggest that the latter term implies an attempt to find other uses in infrastructure beyond its designed purpose, whereas the former reflects a desire to render such infrastructure of no use at all. I return to and trouble these oppositions throughout this book. For now, though, I want to abandon any scholarly pretense of objectivity. As interested as I am in how the world of art is entangled in logistical infrastructure, I have written *The Arts of Logistics* in solidarity with struggles against supply chain capitalism. From Oakland to London to Ogoniland to Palestine to Shanghai, and with many stops along the way, this book follows the global circuit of capital but always travels with its antagonists.

INTRODUCTION
Part and Parcel

SINCE THE 1950S, CAPITALISM HAS come to rely, increasingly, on logistics. So too has art. With the astounding rise of the international art market and gallery system, more paintings, sculptures, and performances circle the globe than ever before. Art might not be a commodity like any other, but it certainly can move like one. The connection with logistics extends beyond the widening scale of art's circulation, as circulation has become a factor in the very production of art itself, dictating and delimiting what gets made and how—not to mention where, when, and by whom. Many are the ways that art is entangled in supply chain capitalism.[1] To take stock of them is this book's promise.

The term "logistics" was coined two centuries ago by military theorists to recognize how victory on the Napoleonic battlefield hinged as much on getting supplies to armies as it did on the strategizing of generals. Logistical thinking leapt from the war room to the boardroom in the 1950s, taking root in corporate plans to cut the costs of transporting and handling goods. The ensuing *logistics revolution* set the stage for the supply chain to supersede the assembly line as the exemplary organizing form of commodity production. Today, manufacturing in the capitalist world-system tends to be dispersed across a shifting patchwork of factories strategically arranged to minimize total costs. Stretching production across the planet in this manner required more than just a management science for getting the right thing to the right place at the right time. Supply chain capitalism has demanded building out a world-enveloping physical infrastructure for moving commodities, one composed of mega-ports and distribution centers, highways and railroads, shipping containers and pipelines, bulk carriers and big rigs, barcodes and RFID (radio frequency identification) tags, and a barrage of other disruptive innovations. This colossal construction project has helped businesses weather a half century of diminishing returns on capital investment in manufacturing, with global supply chains bolstering profit rates during the "long downturn."[2] The expense has been as immense as the undertaking itself. Supply chain capitalism entails, at its stem, a tortuous regime of global labor arbitrage that frees capital to scour the earth for ever-cheaper workers. The plummeting price for moving goods across long distances has made it cost-effective for companies to produce and assemble such commodities far from where they are eventually consumed. Enabled by logistical infrastructure and fueled by the relentless extraction of resources, land, and lives, capitalist production processes now wrap around the globe. For billions of people dispossessed and rendered surplus by the algorithmic imperatives of supply chain capitalism, logistics is not the life-sustaining management science heralded by business consultants and financial journalists, but rather a form of infrastructural violence exacted disproportionately across the planet.

As capitalism has embraced logistics, art has followed suit, and, in some cases, even helped to pave the way. Take, as a first example, the art of Walead Beshty. In 2007, strapped for cash but needing to produce work for an exhibition in Berlin, the Los Angeles–based artist requisitioned his gallery's FedEx account and began a project, still ongoing, of shipping shatterproof glass cubes made to fit precisely inside the courier's standardized boxes. Upon arriving at their destination, Beshty exhibits these sculptures removed from their packaging, the cracks and chipped glass accrued becoming a record of transit, as if a company hired to transport something by the artist Donald Judd had botched the job. The *FedEx* glass works (Figure 1), as this project came to be called, puts the damage from shipping on full display, making Beshty's endeavor a pristine example of what I call *the logistical mode of artistic production*, wherein systems and technologies designed to move commodities are retooled to make art. This mode is logistical insofar as it foregrounds the integral role of transport and handling in artistic production, analogous to the way that commodity production over the past half century has been molded by the demands of distribution. But the logistical link connecting art to capitalist production is also often more than analogy or metaphor. As we shall see, art made in the logistical mode

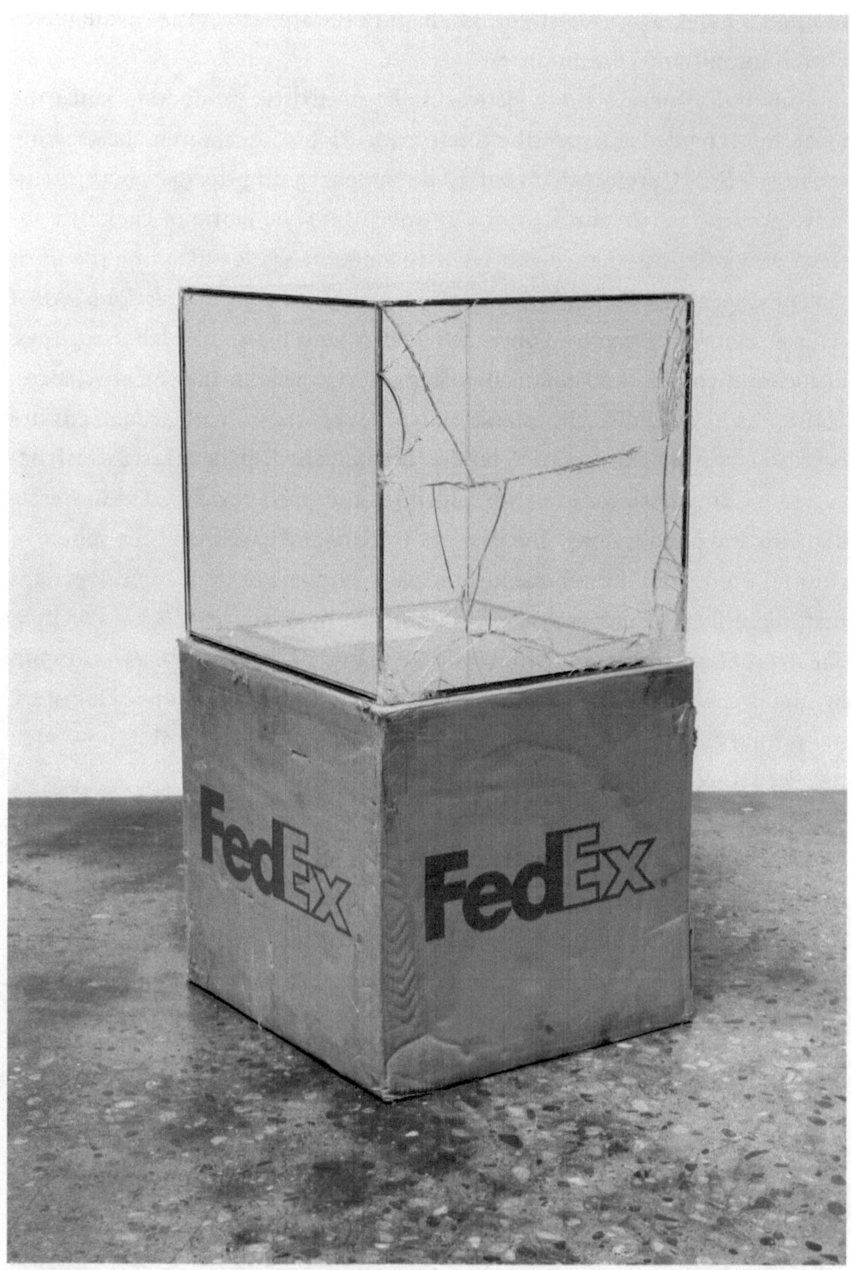

FIGURE 1. Walead Beshty's *FedEx® Large Kraft Box ©2008 FEDEX 330510 REV 6/08 GP, International Priority, Los Angeles–Tokyo trk#778608484821, March 9–13, 2017, International Priority, Tokyo–Los Angeles trk#805795452126, July 13–14, 2017,* 2017. *Photo*: Robert Acklen © Walead Beshty, courtesy the artist and Regen Projects, Los Angeles.

has had a hand, however slight, in shaping the infrastructure available to capital for moving commodities.

This book surveys the logistical mode of artistic production since the 1950s. It is intended as a contribution to critical logistics research, the growing interdisciplinary project that charts how supply chain priorities, both calculative and infrastructural, have been woven into the fabric of capitalist society, providing sustenance and security for some while offloading the most violent externalities onto, largely, racialized and surplus populations.[3] Most critical logistics research—concerned as it is with topics like labor regimes, histories of empire, and political ecology—originates in the social sciences. Those who have studied the intersection of supply chains with art and culture have, so far, principally focused on the "aesthetic life" of logistical infrastructure, analyzing how, for instance, pipelines and ports are depicted in media like film and photography. The best of this scholarship searches the sphere of cultural production for telltale ideological symptoms or even cognitive maps that might help us navigate a world upturned by offshoring.[4] I have written *The Arts of Logistics* out of a similar desire to find my bearings in a world spun by supply chains. But instead of combing through representations of logistics, my primary method for getting oriented has entailed examining how such infrastructure is used to produce art.

Scholars have seldom explored the extent to which artistic production relies on logistics, and even less how art shapes the fate of logistical infrastructure itself. A film critic might wryly observe that the climactic battle scene in *Iron Man 3* unfolds in a shipping container yard, but not stop to ask how business in the Port of Wilmington was impacted by shooting the scene on location. My book, by contrast, proceeds from the premise that art often does more than just represent logistics. One of my goals is to shine a spotlight on the varied supports that artists provide to supply chain capitalism, particularly when producing art in the logistical mode. To be clear, *The Arts of Logistics* is not an industry history of art transportation and storage, nor does it profile the globality of the art market or gallery system.[5] Instead, I try to explain why so much art since the 1950s has been made with logistical instruments designed to physically move goods. This book examines how art repurposed from transport technologies—such as merchant ships, oil barrels, shipping containers, and drones—while capable of revealing much about the shifting historical role of circulation in capitalist production, has also played an active part in this history.

To claim that art has helped give form to logistics does not mean avowing or celebrating what such art has done or still might do for supply chain capitalism. Many artists working in the logistical mode do not critically reflect or even comment on the infrastructure they use. More often than not, artists turn to specific transport technologies for practical or opportunistic reasons, be it because oil barrels and shipping containers are easy to obtain or because logistics companies invite them to experiment with delivery drones or to sail on cargo ships. Instead of contesting the violence done through logistics, most of the art considered in this book could be said, in some way, to reinforce it.

However much I am concerned with tracing the supports that artistic production provides to supply chain capitalism, *The Arts of Logistics* also simmers with examples of resistance and antagonism. Usually these will bubble up in the familiar forms of polemic or critique, with artworks providing opportunities for viewing logistics otherwise, as something contingent, abrasive, and harmful, a far cry from what parades in business schools as a life-supporting science of flow. Less common, but for that reason all the more worth noting, are those artists working in the logistical mode who have shown themselves to be exceedingly well positioned to engage in other, more direct, types of struggle. The ways that artists are tangled up in logistics are many, and so are the bracing lessons that can be learned from what they produce.

In this opening chapter, I propose that logistics is a missing puzzle piece in the picture that scholars have assembled to explain transformations in aesthetic form during capitalism's long downturn, privileging, as they tend to, the rise of financialization and the service sector. After first recounting how logistics has assumed an expanded role in capitalist production since the 1950s, I illustrate some of the varied ways that logistics has, during this same period, come to support artistic production. While remaining attentive to what art draws from logistics, my aim here is to outline a methodology for examining this relationship as a recursive one. To do so will require me to explain in more detail what I understand logistics to be. "It is not altogether clear," as Charmaine Chua points out, "how one should define the vast behemoth that has come to be known as 'logistics.'"[6] Some present it as a technocratic management science, while others view it as a specific industry of distribution.

For my part, I contend, in line with Chua and others, that logistics cannot be separated from the global capitalist infrastructure that has been built, at grave expense, for physically transporting and handling commodities. This infrastructure sustains much of human life as we know it today, albeit not as an end in itself but as a means. In the words of Søren Mau, "Logistics and the infrastructure on which it relies are essentially methods for carving the logic of capital into the crust of the earth."[7] However blunted it may be, art produced in the logistical mode remains one tool that capitalism deploys in this scarring operation, and it deserves to be judged as such. Here we arrive at this book's central task: to scrutinize how art has become part and parcel of logistics.

A Logistics Revolution

The history of artists making art from tools designed to circulate commodities stretches back centuries. At the early dawn of the capitalist world-system in fifteenth-century Venice, for instance, canvas sailcloth became a favored surface of Renaissance painters. The material was abundant in the merchant city, and using it made paintings easy to roll up and transport. In the nineteenth century, during the height of the British empire, the spectacular sets of London theaters were rigged with sturdy ropes bought from local ship chandlers.[8] Just as precedents for a logistical mode of artistic production can be found across the history of capitalism, what travels today under the name "logistics" also has origins that predate its so-called revolution in the 1950s. The early modern commerce of protocapitalist merchant powers like Venice and the transatlantic slave trade steered by Britain are just two historical projects that established pivotal technologies, trade routes, and calculative logics that allowed commercial capital to reduce anything to cargo, people included.

Despite these continuities, what sets our logistical present apart is that, today, the transportation and distribution of commodities has become a governing factor in the capitalist production process. Decisions on how, when, and where to produce the vast majority of commodities crucially hinge like never before on the cost of moving them. No longer an afterthought to production, the circulation of goods is vying to take the lead. Logistics might not be new to either art or capitalism, but its infrastructural significance for both has compounded since at least the 1950s.

No single or spectacular political event launched the postwar logistics revolution. No Bastille was stormed, and no chest of tea got dumped unceremoniously into the sea. As one executive for Pillsbury put it in 1960, the revolution then unfolding was more Copernican, in that it entailed shifting "the center of the business universe" from what it cost to make things to what it cost to move them.[9] Although robber barons like John D. Rockefeller had long since shown transport to be a source of competitive advantage, corporate wisdom throughout much of the twentieth century still regarded the movement of commodities to be a "necessary evil" of doing business.[10] This view changed in the wake of the American recession of 1957–58, when foreign competition began eroding the booming postwar profit rates of stateside businesses.[11] To keep pace with upstarts in West Germany and Japan, where labor was cheaper and technological investment higher, American firms started targeting distribution costs, spurred by studies that revealed handling and delivering goods accounted for anywhere between 10 and 30 percent of total expenses. As told in one early logistics textbook from 1968, the "profit squeeze" experienced by American businesses in the late 1950s acted as "a stimulant to logistical development" by showing that many industries had reached "the point of diminishing returns" in their efforts to improve profitability by intervening directly in production.[12]

In the 1960s, a corporate consensus emerged regarding the promise of logistical restructuring. This perspective was expressed most fervently by management consultants like Peter Drucker who spent the decade evangelizing in trade journals and at industry conferences, proclaiming distribution to be the "dark continent" of business, "the one big area in which something can still be done about costs."[13] Drucker's imperialist overtone would prove prescient. What began narrowly with managerial efforts to curb handling and outbound delivery costs eventually broadened into a new understanding of business, in which companies functioned as the levers to supply pipelines, managing a flow of products to consumers. This corporate pivot to a more holistic view of intrafirm activities led executives and consultants to search for profitable tradeoffs, wherein increasing costs in one division (like delivery) could be justified if it brought efficiencies elsewhere (such as in warehousing) that boosted overall profit margins. The advent of what's called "total cost analysis" helped transform distribution from a secondary role into an overriding consideration of manufacturing and assembly. This licensed all manner of once seemingly "counterintuitive decisions," such as relocating factories to distant locations to access cheaper workforces, or eliminating standing inventory altogether, as was the stated desire behind Toyota's just-in-time (JIT) production system.[14] While executives cast themselves as leaders of the logistics revolution, with managers serving as their lieutenants, in reality the true protagonist was the rapidly expanding logistical infrastructure that was making it all possible.

Recession in the 1950s kindled the logistical awakening of the 1960s, but this was just a provincial prelude to the full-blown international crisis of profitability that made landfall in the 1970s. The long downturn kicked off when a heady storm of factors—including overproduction, downward price pressures, and oil shocks—made it nigh impossible for companies in overly developed capitalist countries to achieve accustomed rates of profit from investments in the manufacturing sector.[15] To stay afloat in these choppy economic waters, firms scrambled into the twin lifeboats of finance and logistics. As Annie McClanahan describes it, while financialization provided a "temporal fix" that allowed companies and investors to borrow "from the profits of a hoped-for future production," logistics delivered a "spatial fix," as these same companies buoyed profitability by finding new markets for their goods and cheaper workers to make them.[16] The financial futures contract and the shipping container were patches cut from the same conjunctural cloth, stitched together by a general shift of investment away from production in the here and now. As capital flowed into hedge funds and speculative banking tools, huge amounts were also diverted into the construction projects that gifted the world an enormous physical infrastructure for moving goods around it.

Today, logistical infrastructure manifests as an assemblage of everything from port complexes and distribution centers to railway corridors and container ships. Yet, practically speaking, it functions more like a bolt cutter or crowbar, which capital uses to break into new consumer markets and untapped pools of labor-power. As early as the 1970s, the cost of shipping by intermodal container had dropped to a point where it became economically viable for firms in the Global North, whether through foreign direct investment or arms-length contracting, to begin relocating production to locales promising lower wages. And within decades, dismal pay, minimal workplace protections, racially stratified workforces, and draconian restrictions on labor organizing emerged as the common denominators of the supply chain regimes imposed by companies like Apple and Walmart.

Logistics furnishes the means through which capital has extended class war to a planetary scale, and constructing its requisite infrastructure has, fittingly, involved various forms of warfare. Key supply chain techniques and technologies—including JIT manufacturing, the shipping container, and the RFID tag—were tried and tested on American battlefields in Korea, Vietnam, and Afghanistan, respectively.[17] Furthermore, Cold War wrangling over trade conduits like the Suez Canal rejiggered the paths of world commerce and catalyzed the growth of bulk carriers and container ships. Less spectacular but no less consequential were the protracted trade wars that made offshoring production possible by eliminating tariffs and implementing structural adjustment programs, which gave corporations the green light to set up shop across the Global South. Logistics helped capitalism proletarianize citizens of newly decolonized countries, making it both the basis for a "revolution within capitalism" and a counterrevolutionary force for taming the world-system's mutinous peripheries.[18] More than merely a technocratic management science, "logistics is capital's art of war," whose essence is "exploitation in its rawest form."[19]

Make no mistake: capitalism has long been committed to building out its infrastructure for transporting commodities over lengthy distances. As I discuss in Chapter 1, scholars writing across the traditions of political Marxism, world-systems theory, and Black studies have, in their respective ways, warned against the lure of presentism in critical logistics research. "Modern logistics is founded with the first great movement of commodities, the ones that could speak," write Stefano Harney and Fred Moten, who point to the transatlantic slave trade as one source for the extractivist imperatives and racialized logics of contemporary supply chains.[20] Karl Marx, for his part, foresaw the importance of speeding up trade and improving its regularity, having observed that "cheap means of communication and transport [are] a condition for production based on capital."[21] Steam shipping, oceanic telegraph lines, continental railroads, and the Suez Canal were just some of the pivotal projects Marx himself witnessed during the nineteenth century. Yet the extended history of capital investment in building out logistical infrastructure does not necessarily mean, as some suggest, that "recent phenomena such as containerisation, intermodalism, and just-in-time production are nothing but contemporary incarnations of a dynamic as old as capitalism itself."[22] Recognizing the presence of logistics in the past is useful for anchoring supply chain capitalism within the world-system's violent *durée*, but it should not prevent us from discerning the novelty in this "new economic imperialism."[23] What, then, is historically specific about our logistical present?

Answering this question first requires distinguishing the circulation of capital from the distinctly logistical activities of transportation and distribution. In much recent social theory, "circulation" tends to function as a unifying metaphor that encompasses, however promiscuously, the flows that sustain various complex systems: bodies, cities, electrical grids, oceans, the internet, and so forth.[24] Compare this to a field like mainstream economics, where circulation is regarded as the bridge that connects the production of a commodity to its market. The definition of circulation I adopt in this book is more specific, deriving primarily from Marx's theory of the circuit of capital. Be it in the form of money or of commodities, capital must constantly circulate for wealth to grow, yet the law of capitalist accumulation requires that this circuit be interrupted so that new commodities can be produced, thereby allowing the lifeblood of surplus value to be injected into the system. Marx understood circulation to be a broad sphere of economic activity necessarily tangled up with production: simply stated, commodities are created in the latter and exchanged in the former. A commodity's value, generated by exploiting workers in the "hidden abode" of production, is realized as money only in the "noisy sphere" of circulation, where a market price for the commodity is set, and once purchased, said commodity changes hands to a new owner.[25] At the risk of stating the obvious, circulation is essential to the workings of capitalism across its history, regardless of how production and exchange are organized at any given point in time.

Even readers well versed in Marx's critique of political economy sometimes conflate circulation with the physical movement of goods, thereby downplaying a critical distinction between the two: a house, for example, need not be physically moved in order to be exchanged, but it must circulate on the market. Although circulation might call to mind delivery drivers and dockworkers, it is a far bigger tent that gathers beneath it all manner of jobs necessary for realizing a commodity's value on the market as profit, ranging from cashiers and security guards to accountants and lawyers—just as warehouse staff and truckers do not exhaust the ranks of those employed to manage the exchange of goods after production, nor is their work isolated to the sphere of circulation. Even in our supposedly dematerializing world, producing a commodity along industrial lines still requires that stock be pulled and parts be delivered for assembly. I leave to the endnotes the thorny Marxological debate over whether transport work can directly generate more value than the wages and overhead invested for it to happen.[26] Suffice it to say, I (like Marx) am skeptical of such a possibility.[27] All the more reason, then, why capitalists would want to limit the costs of logistical labor by disciplining workers, lowering wages, and implementing labor-saving technologies.

Yet the longstanding desire of individual businesses to reduce the price of moving goods does not, at least on its own, explain why an enormous and growing sum of capital has been spent since the 1950s on building out a world-encompassing logistical infrastructure. Even with the aid of containerization, there are inevitably cheaper routes for transporting an air conditioner than the one that stretches from a Guangdong factory to a ranch house in Texas. Nor, it should be said, is there anything to the usefulness of an air conditioner that means it must be assembled on the opposite side of the world from where it will be installed. For this planetary arrangement to be economically worthwhile, it must boost the overall profitability of producing air conditioners for a company, such as by giving it access to a cheaper workforce to run its assembly line. Capital investment has flooded into building logistical infrastructure over the past half century not to reduce total costs expended on transportation or even to achieve the lowest possible unit price for moving goods. Rather, the *raison d'être* of logistics today is, as Intan Suwandi puts it, "global labor arbitrage." Logistics frees capital to move across the globe to leverage local labor price differences in production, all while increasing economies of scale and decreasing the turnover time of investments.[28] Supply chains are the pattern that capital today follows when threading its way across the planet, and logistical infrastructure provides the loom.

To return to the question at hand about the historical specificity of our logistical present: the signal feature of supply chain capitalism is the astonishing shift of investment away from the direct production of commodities and into expanding the infrastructure for transporting them within and beyond the abode of production. "The massive finance-fueled build-out of global shipping and containerization" might just be, as Joshua Clover asserts, "the single most foundational project for capital" of the past half century.[29] If this logistical infrastructure is the means by which capital now pursues its longstanding imperial drive to annihilate "space by time," building it has only deepened the crisis that sent capital digging in the first place.[30] This is partly because much of the capital invested for the purpose has come from states themselves rather than the profiting firms. Supply chain imperatives pit the profits rates of individual companies against the value-productive capacity of the world-system as a whole, intensifying the very downturn in profitability and productivity that set the logistics revolution in motion. Making this endogenous crisis within capitalism even grimmer is the escalating ecological catastrophe now ripping across the planet, and in whose conditions the logistics sector has played more than a bit part. What the future might hold for capitalism I address in my closing chapters. But for now, having offered this potted account of supply chain capitalism's emergence and global expansion, I want to introduce how, from the very start of the logistics revolution, artists helped to give this infrastructure its form.

The Logistical Mode of Artistic Production

The world of contemporary art depends on capitalism's logistical infrastructure, not the least for transportation, delivery, and storage. How this came to be, though a fascinating read in its own right, is not the story *The Arts of Logistics* has to tell.[31] Instead, this book explores how logistics has become a means of artistic production. Artists today harness logistical infrastructure not just to move and store their art, but also to create it. To examine logistics as a means of artistic production entails something more than identifying supply chains as fashionable subject matter or a new wellspring of inspiration for art. Doing so requires scrutinizing the range of highly material ways that artists use logistical infrastructure when producing art, from partnering with shipping companies to repurposing transportation tools. The resulting art can provide a unique index for tracking the development of supply chain capitalism since the logistics revolution. But in addition to serving as an opportunity for chronicling this history, art produced in the logistical mode also furnishes scaffolding for logistics itself. To insist on this claim is not to imply the absurd idea that logistical infrastructure, let alone supply chain capitalism, would crumble without artists or their creations. Rather, my aim here is to underline art's deep entanglement in logistical infrastructure so as to understand better the extent to which logistics is embedded in social life.

For the purpose of illustration, we can move to a case example of what I have in mind, this one drawn from the formative years of the logistics revolution. In August 1961, the artists now known as Christo and Jeanne-Claude hired a crew of dockworkers in Cologne to build them several sculptures made from oil barrels and industrial rolls of paper found in the Rhenish port. This undertaking resulted in *Dockside Packages* (Figure 2) and *Stacked Oil Barrels*, two iconic artworks that are celebrated today for challenging what art could be, where it could be made, and who could be employed to make it. Viewed through a different lens, however, that of the logistics revolution then unfolding, Christo and Jeanne-Claude's artworks also challenged the existing organization of dock work. Just a year earlier, longshoremen on the West Coast of the United States, hoping to mitigate the looming consequences of

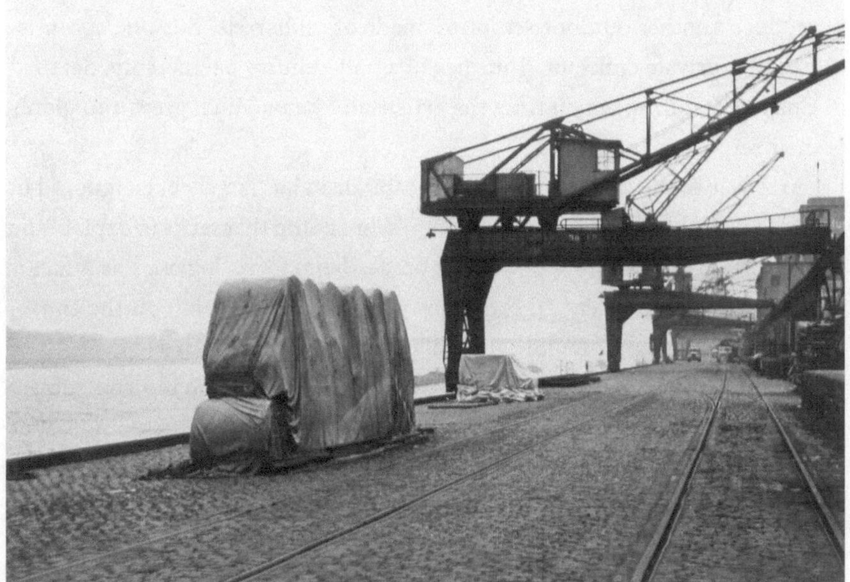

FIGURE 2. Christo and Jeanne-Claude's *Dockside Packages*, Cologne Harbor, 1961. *Photo:* Stefan Wewerka © Christo and Jeanne-Claude Foundation and ADAGP, Paris and DACS, London 2024. Reprinted with permission.

port automation, had signed a landmark deal with employers that did away with hard-won rules on work conditions and crew sizes. No sooner had the "Mechanization and Modernization Agreement" gone into effect in January 1961 than employers began overhauling the waterfront workplace by trimming breaks, increasing load limits, and introducing new labor-saving tools like shipping containers. This was the first stitch in a tapestry of automation and worker disciplining that rapidly blanketed logistics work across the capitalist world-system.

The fact that a pair of Parisian artists could, on a whim, employ idled German dockworkers to create art would seem to be evidence supporting the case made by employers at the time that there were "unnecessary men" working in ports around the world.[32] This included the inner-city Port of Cologne, which, by 1961, was already being consolidated and moved upriver. The gallery that hosted Christo and Jeanne-Claude's exhibition owed its existence to this restructuring, having just opened in the docks as part of the waterfront's gradual metamorphosis into a cultural district. In subsequent years, the two artists deepened their involvement with the logistics sector, first in 1966 by teaming up with a then-small Dutch packaging company called Janus Vaten to produce another outdoor sculpture made of oil barrels, this one commissioned by a private collector. Thus began a half-century partnership, detailed in Chapter 2, during which time the artists and Janus Vaten grew into giants of their respective industries.

Art's role in the rise of supply chain capitalism has largely been ignored in histories of both art and logistics. Even in scholarship that seeks to explain the impact of capitalism's long downturn on aesthetic form, logistics as a factor remains noticeably absent. There is now considerable research on the consequences of capitalism's "temporal fix" for art, with writers such as Max Haiven and Annie McClanahan having assessed how financialization informs subject matter and transforms artworks into market assets.[33] Others, including Jasper Bernes and Judith Hamera, have shown that late capitalist culture habituated people to the process of offshoring, with art even providing a template for newly flexible information and service-oriented workplaces. Illuminating as such research is, as far as accounts of the "spatial fix" go, they remain partial in many ways, largely limited to those countries that "deindustrialized" and leaving to the side the logistical restructuring that made offshoring possible.[34]

Even research, such as by Petrus Liu and Jisha Menon, that considers how contemporary art has been marshaled in service to global labor arbitrage in countries like China and India tends to give little time to the enabling infrastructural transformations in logistics.[35] Thus, the prevailing narrative told about art of the long downturn goes something like this: the art object's dematerialization coincided with the rise of service work and financialization in deindustrializing countries. Just as conceptual art and performance became newly prominent in the world of art, workplaces filled up with service jobs that resembled performance and financial markets made available novel opportunities for speculation. As a history of political economy over the past half century, this narrative, while accurate, remains incomplete insofar as it understates how global shifts in the division of labor and the ascent of financialization both relied on logistical restructuring.

We can watch the limitations of this narrative in action by turning to the critical discourse that surrounds Allan Kaprow's 1967 performance *Fluids: A Happening*, deemed by some to epitomize the deindustrial shift to a financialized service economy. According to Bernes and Helen Molesworth, echoing Jack Burnham before them, *Fluids* literally put the art object's dematerialization on display, with Kaprow enlisting dozens of volunteers to build large rectangular structures from blocks of ice, which were then left to melt in the Southern California sun. As the ice buildings liquefied, the artwork is said to have shifted into the realm of service, becoming the means for "the production of an experience."[36]

Let's pause for a moment on the frozen water used, and whose "very ephemerality" is presumed to make *Fluids* a "transitional" work of deindustrial culture.[37] This quality of ice—that it melts—makes it a notoriously tricky commodity to transport. Before ice could be industrially manufactured, it had to be extracted, moved, and stored, thus presenting a litany of logistical complications whose solutions spurred innovations in shipping and warehousing throughout the nineteenth and twentieth centuries. For a time, ice ranked as one of the most harvested crops by weight transported by train or ship in the United States, second only to cotton. And, like cotton, ice was a commodity of empire, typically shipped along colonial trade routes from North America and northern Europe to the West Indies and India.[38] The logistical demands of ice shaped *Fluids* in multiple ways. The project was a massive undertaking, unfolding not just once but in fifteen different outdoor locations spread across Los Angeles over three days. Each large structure used 650 blocks, which meant sourcing 405,000 pounds of frozen water from the Union Ice Company (Figure 3). Timing was critical to *Fluids* since the slow work of building had to be balanced by how quickly the ice would melt. Many deliveries were needed, and they had to be arranged for every two hours.[39] Attending to such logistical demands broadens the portrait of the kinds of work and workers *Fluids* required: alongside art school volunteers preparing to enter the service economy upon graduation, there were truck drivers earning a wage for their transport work.

The critical discourse on *Fluids* exemplifies a tendency in scholarship on art of the long downturn to overlook logistics. In addition to artists who sought to dematerialize the art object in the 1960s and 1970s, many also made art by moving objects, frequently working with trucking and delivery firms to do so. Even paragons of the dematerialization thesis created art using novel communication and information technologies integral to the logistics revolution, such as On Kawara's mail art projects and Nam June Paik's planetary

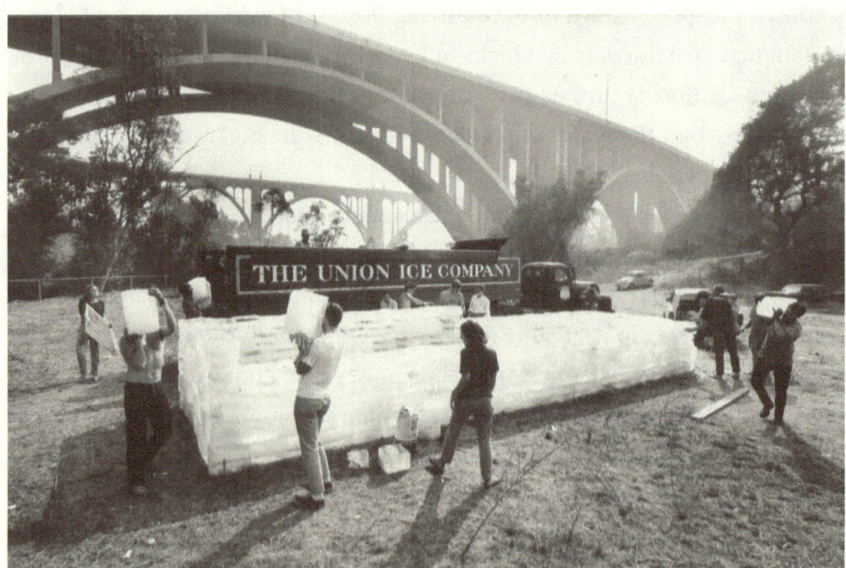

FIGURE 3. Allan Kaprow's *Fluids: A Happening* being built in Los Angeles, 1967. *Photo:* Julian Wasser © Julian Wasser, courtesy Julian Wasser Estate and the Getty Research Institute Los Angeles (980063).

explorations of telephone and satellite networks. The logistical mode of artistic production extended as well beyond the avant-garde and the capitalist core. As I discuss in Chapter 2, one of the most far-reaching examples emerged in Trinidad, where musicians invented the steel drum using oil barrels nicked from petroleum fields and American naval bases, yielding a musical instrument that welded histories of empire with the neocolonial rhythms of supply chain capitalism. Art's affinity for logistics has only intensified in recent decades, as artists salvage merchant ships to build sculptures, curators convert shipping containers into pop-up galleries, and e-commerce titans like Amazon orchestrate corporate spectacles to showcase their warehouse automation technology.

Detailing how logistics became a means of artistic production is just one task this book tackles. As I aim to show, art also plays a supporting role for logistics itself. In tracing this recursive relationship, my approach departs from how scholars typically study the connections between art and logistics. Usually this involves either reading *for logistics* in culture or reading *logistics for* its aesthetic qualities. It is not uncommon for scholars to pursue both ends at once, for instance, by examining how container ports are portrayed in photographs or by dissecting the ways novelists structure narratives around supply chains.[40] Such research tends to be motivated by at least one of two dovetailing desires: the first is to find artworks that can pierce the mystifying veneer of supply chain capitalism; the second is to practice a cultural criticism capable of doing the same. Due to its complexity and scale of operations, logistics lends itself to disorientation, a feature only compounded by the enormity of its built infrastructure, which includes sprawling container yards, gargantuan bulk carriers, and labyrinthine pipelines. In the face of this "logistical sublime,"[41] both art and the critic are thought to share the responsibility of orientating, whether it be through aesthetic techniques of cognitive mapping found in, for instance, the meticulous photography of Allan Sekula, or through methods of critical interpretation geared to unearthing a kernel of historicity in, say, the shipping container that Mel Gibson dropped on an Afrikaner mercenary's head at the end of *Lethal Weapon 2*.[42] This book began from a similar desire for orientation, and it also chooses culture for its point of dead reckoning. Yet, instead of turning to representations of logistical infrastructure, I find my bearings by looking at how artists use this infrastructure to make art.

To give a better sense of what this critical approach looks like in practice, consider again Walead Beshty's *FedEx* glass works. These sculptures are, inevitably, representations of FedEx, as they constantly refer to the courier company, both through their title and the branded packaging Beshty displays alongside them. In a statement that accompanies the series, the artist details how FedEx, founded in Arkansas in 1971, grew to become one of the planet's leading couriers, boasting an unrivaled airline fleet and clients that include the US military. Beshty directs our attention to the company's ravenous appetite for space, from the 35 million square feet it occupies in North America to the exclusive rights it holds over the specific volumes and dimensions of its cardboard boxes. We learn that FedEx secured privileges for the latter by obtaining Serial Shipping Container Codes from the international standards organization GS1, headquartered in Brussels. Best known for introducing the barcode to the world, GS1 operates in 150 countries and, with more than a million corporate members, has made rentier guideline agreements essential, if not invisible, cogs in global commodity circulation.[43] By documenting FedEx's multiple scales of operations, Beshty's damaged boxes aspire to be the kind of cartographic art that writers like Alberto Toscano and Jeff Kinkle, following Fredric Jameson, contend are needed to orient us to a world sent spinning by supply chains.[44]

The *FedEx* glass works could be compared to a considerably more famous representation of the courier company: the 2000 film *Cast Away*, starring Tom Hanks as a FedEx systems analyst who crash-lands on a desert island en route to Malaysia to solve a logistics problem. Like the cracks in Beshty's sculptures, the plane disaster in *Cast Away* would seem, at first glance, to challenge FedEx's customer-facing guarantee of smooth delivery. But whereas the *FedEx* glass works insist that harm is the necessary outcome of any logistical process, *Cast Away*'s heroic dramaturgy celebrates the company's resolve to overcome even the most harrowing of catastrophes. Despite the differences in their portrayals of FedEx, both the *FedEx* glass works and *Cast Away* were produced using the courier's shipping infrastructure. Beshty takes advantage of FedEx as, what he calls, a "readymade system" for making art.[45] *Cast Away*'s collaboration with the company was, by contrast, invited. In the words of one corporate spokesperson, FedEx agreed to be a "character" in the film because the script positively depicted the courier's "global reach and can-do spirit."[46] In lieu of a product placement fee, FedEx provided director Robert Zemeckis with access to its airplanes, trucks, and sortation centers in Memphis and Moscow, while marketing and systems specialists also worked as consultants, offering script advice and handling travel arrangements. Having grossed nearly half a billion dollars, *Cast Away* is one of the most profitable and mutually beneficial examples of the logistical mode of artistic production.

Art need not entail such a blatant or lucrative partnership for it to provide support to logistics. Other less egregious and even inadvertent examples abound. For as much as the *FedEx* glass works aspire to be a cognitive map, the series also exhibits hazards familiar to cartography. The wear and tear visible on each glass box would seem to promise a detailed portrait of circulation, only reinforced by Beshty's stipulation that, each time a sculpture is shipped, its title be extended to include the new destination, tracking number, and date.[47] While the accumulating cracks and lengthening title may provide a record of every move a box has made, like any map the sculptures necessarily leave out an enormous amount. For example, one learns nothing about the workers who handled the parcel, nor about how any of the damage came to be. Beshty's *FedEx* glass works exude an impossible desire to represent logistical operations in fine-grained detail, something even the most sophisticated supply chain software struggles to do. Admirable though this may be, such a strategy risks mistaking information for orientation, as if the more facts we know the better equipped we will be to comprehend and intervene in the workings of supply chain capitalism. In his initial theory of cognitive mapping, Jameson distinguished this aesthetic strategy from attempts at representing the totality of capitalism in all its particularity. The aim, he averred, should be to provide people with a "situational representation" through which they could define their "relationship to the totality"—knowledge that can be *used*.[48] A tracking number's utility, by contrast, is highly specific and is of little use to someone who encounters it in a gallery after delivery. In this regard, the *FedEx* glass works resemble what Larne Abse Gogarty calls "legibly political art," whose aim "to make things *visible*" runs the risk of reinforcing "capital's own fantasies of being too large, too complex and too *in*visible to smash."[49] The result is an aesthetic of information overload that may, for many viewers, compound mystification in the name of cutting through it.

Taken together, *Cast Away* and the *FedEx* glass works provide a sense of the wide range of ways that art and logistics support each other. Committed though I am to holding such infrastructural overlaps to account, in this book I also take care to give due credit to seeds of antagonism wherever they sprout. Whatever its limits as a cognitive map, Beshty's cracked boxes nonetheless exhibit a moving truth about supply chain capitalism: that damage is the logistical status quo.

On Management and Infrastructure

There is at least one further truth that the *FedEx* glass works put on display, one so obvious that it would seem like it need not be said, but, for exactly that reason and for the sake of not leaving unchecked any wayward assumptions, must be stated in no uncertain terms. At the core of Beshty's *FedEx* glass works is something that resembles an instruction or a command—let's call this an *order.* The sculptures can be shipped and reshipped so long as there is demand for them, so long as yet another gallery or museum places an order. And yet, the simple truth that the *FedEx* glass works declare is this: in much the same way that humans cannot live off ideas alone, goods cannot move on orders alone. Likewise, despite the work they do in ensuring that the right things get to the right places at the right times, instructions and commands—and with them, protocols, algorithms, and the like—cannot themselves do all of the work required for getting the things there. For all the talk of continuous flow in supply chain management, itself a variant of and contributor to the fallacy that we now live in a dematerialized society, the fact remains that where there is flow, there is friction. Rubber must hit the road sometime. Any flow requires support, be it a furrow or a canal or a pipeline, something to maintain its direction of travel; otherwise, all we are left with is a puddle.

Logistics is said to be many things: a supply chain management science, an industry unto itself, a cold logic of calculation that threatens to ingratiate itself far beyond the economic sphere of circulation.[50] Yet logistics is and does nothing without its tools, its workers, its built environments—let's call this *infrastructure.* Allow me to offer another definition of logistics, this one borrowed from Liam Campling and Alejandro Colás, who, with admirable lucidity, write that capitalist logistics entails "the *planned movement* of commodities across otherwise fragmented points of production and consumption."[51] This is right insofar as it clarifies that logistics enables the production and consumption of commodities across a particular geographic form, which today manifests as the supply chain. But for logistics to do this work, something that enables these enabling operations is also required. "Cheap means of communication and transport [are] a condition for production based on capital"—this sentence, quoted earlier, remains as true today as when Marx wrote it in the mid-nineteenth century; no, *truer.*[52] To fulfil its destiny, logistics needs more than managers armed with software or purchase orders issuing commands. Logistics needs materials, both those that will be moved and those that will do the moving. That we do not need art to be able to say this does not make the message that the *FedEx* glass works convey any less true.

This brings me then not to logistics per se, but to the infrastructure, including all the accessory equipment, on which logistics relies. Though a notoriously "slippery" term, "infrastructure" tends to denote that which enables.[53] To speak of infrastructure is to speak of something that gives support, or, when withdrawn, causes collapse. With etymological origins in nineteenth-century French civil engineering, the term has long evoked images of built environments like highways and bridges, though today infrastructure is also said to encompass knowledge, software, and all manner of work, be it administration, care, or maintenance.[54] Making the term only harder to pin down, the boundaries of any particular infrastructure are rarely obvious since systems often overlap and interrelate. Barely fixed or even stable, any given infrastructure is always relational and recursive, constantly shifting and evolving so that it might remain standing. Demarcating an infrastructure is thus deemed to be a "categorical act" requiring selections and exclusions, assumptions and, sometimes, imaginative leaps.[55] True though all this may be, when it comes to logistics at least, infrastructure also remains a heavy material fact, so much so that without it the aforementioned "*planned movement* of commodities across otherwise fragmented points of production and consumption" would simply not occur.

I am not looking to posit a false opposition here; I take it as sensible why a geographer like Ruth Wilson Gilmore, no stranger to historical materialism, would insist that "feeling" needs to be acknowledged as infrastructure since it derives from and supports definite histories and social relations with profoundly material consequences.[56] Nevertheless, it is the sense of infrastructure as something indelibly material, even physical, that I will largely stick to in the following chapters, not least for the sake of pursuing an argument about the recursive relation between art and logistics that avoids rendering this relation entirely metaphorical. As already noted, there are many ways to study this relation, but the one I have chosen follows the lead set by others engaged in critical logistics research who have shown that "one point of entry" for studying logistics is through "the very banal instruments of the logistical systems themselves."[57] For reasons noted below, the "banal instruments" I foreground in this book include the merchant ship, the oil barrel, the shipping container, and the drone. To clarify, my objects of study are not actually these instruments themselves but rather the ways that artists repurpose them, and also the circumstances under which such instruments belonging to logistical infrastructure become available to be repurposed in the first place.

That infrastructure has a "poetics"[58] and even an "aesthetic life"[59] is, by now, recognized as not only being true but even worthy of study. In recent years, scholars across the humanities and social sciences have embraced critical methods for "reading" infrastructure in terms typically reserved for art, specifically that of semiotics, affect, and embodiment.[60] Though not opposed to such approaches, the method I adopt for examining the interrelation of art and logistics requires going beyond interpreting the "communicative details" in built infrastructure like bridges or airports, be they ancillary or deliberate.[61] I wrote this book aware that attempts at studying culture's entanglement in infrastructure are frequently hampered by various propensities toward physicalism and reductivism. These include the oft-criticized determinism of certain historical materialist frameworks, as well as the contrasting tendency of newer materialisms to reduce infrastructure to "*mere* metaphor" in ways that, as Jennifer Wenzel puts it, "miss the concept-grounding power of the material."[62] Instead of shying away from the infrastructural connection between art and logistics, I try to confront this relation directly, privileging for study artworks made from or using technologies designed to move commodities.

In practice, this principle for selection means that I concentrate on the assemblage of circulation technologies that enables logistics, returning only where necessary to the supply chain management science that commands it.

Dating back to Marx, scholars have long split circulation technologies into two groups: the "transport" tools that physically move stuff from place to place and the "communication" instruments that generate and transmit the information guiding these movements.[63] As a study of how artists make art with instruments such as ships, barrels, containers, and drones, *The Arts of Logistics* primarily deals with the former group (the transport tools), while heeding warnings from scholars of "logistical media" to not assume too clear-cut of a distinction—as if a delivery drone could fly without programming.[64] There is no shortage of scholarly and even popular attention to transport technologies, some might even say there's too much. My decision to privilege transport technologies, however, is purposeful, *because of* and *not despite* all the interest they tend to attract, especially from artists. Each of my chapters profiles a different transport technology: the ship, the oil barrel, the shipping container, and the drone, though other instruments do appear, such as freight trucks, gantry cranes, and pipelines. I settled on these four technologies partly because I needed to write a book of moderate length. However, this particular inventory also allows me to tell the long history of logistics as one of infrastructural violence, which begins with the slave ships of the Atlantic triangular trade and continues today in Silicon Valley's dream of a world without workers.

I am using the word "technology" here deliberately, so as to indicate a particular relation to infrastructure. "What distinguishes infrastructure from technology," Daniel Nemser writes, "is its tendency to become normalized and fade from view, operating just 'beneath' (infra) the surface of the phenomenal world while facilitating the operations on which that world depends."[65] Nevertheless, this suggests that infrastructure, to do its enabling work, is itself reliant on tools, instruments, and other crafted means of production that could in a different context of use be deemed technology. In drawing his distinction between infrastructure and technology, Nemser here also gestures to a common sense that has guided the recent "infrastructural turn" in social theory.[66] This turn holds that infrastructure is "by definition invisible, part of the background for other kinds of work."[67] Typically credited to the anthropologists Geoffrey C. Bowker and Susan Leigh Star, the so-called visibility thesis has licensed the popularity of critical methods like "infrastructural inversion,"[68] in which researchers go "behind the scenes"[69] to investigate what it is that makes society function. Yet the claim that infrastructure becomes visible only when it breaks hardly applies to much of the world for whom infrastructure typically does *not* work, or whose workings often come with adverse effects. As scholars in Black studies and disability studies regularly demonstrate, even when an infrastructure can fade into the background, it never does so for everyone: not for the workers tasked with maintaining it, nor for those it has not been designed to serve. Belief that infrastructures operate offstage is less a reality than it is a privileged "ideal."[70] In this book, I am interested in how and why logistical infrastructure stops working as it supposedly should, how it becomes or remains strange, like when the technological pieces that constitute part of its whole become available for repurposing.

My choice to emphasize the materiality of logistics in this book has also been influenced by other considerations, hinted at above. To speak of logistics in terms of its tools and technologies means troubling the pervasive assumption that logistics only entails a science of supply chain management. Despite the term's well-documented military origins in Napoleonic *logistique*, referring to "the practical art of moving armies,"[71] modern supply chain management textbooks prefer to embrace etymological affinity with the Greek word *logistikos,* meaning "skilled in calculating."[72] The reason is perhaps obvious: even at the level of naming, logistics is removed from the battlefield and promoted instead as belonging to the technical and antipolitical realm of calculation shorn of warfare's violent baggage. Supply chain specialists claim membership in "an application-oriented scientific discipline,"[73] whose scientific standing is bolstered by an arsenal of computing tools, credentialed by master of science degrees, and, as one recent book even insists, backed by the "underlying laws" and "universal truths"[74] of physics. This framing extends into the domain of logistics marketing. For example, in its 2010 "We ♥ Logistics" advertising campaign, UPS boldly declared, "Each day our customers count on us to choreograph a ballet of infinite complexity played across skies, oceans and borders," adopting the frequently repeated comparison of logistics to an artistic discipline synonymous with flawless movement through space and time.[75] Even when companies liken their pursuit to an art form, scientific posturing creeps in to tighten the association of supply chain management with technical precision and control. Critical logistics scholars, too, often accept the industry's narrative, endorsing the notion that logistics is constantly evolving into "a more exact science."[76] However, labeling logistics a science is not the same as stating an objective truth; it means staging or succumbing to a pretense of rationality, rigor, and inevitability.

Within the supposedly scientific field of supply chain management, it is products and not workers that are said to be the objects of command. Such is the premise programmed into the very modularized software that managers use to set production targets and rates of flow, a mechanism for deflecting responsibility over workers' welfare to the demands of someone else issued somewhere else along the chain. In such a system, as Miriam Posner has shown, differential wages and racialized exploitation become incidental to the "algorithmic imperative" for getting the right commodity to the right place at the right time.[77] What Harry Braverman once said of Taylorist scientific management holds true for supply chain management today: "It enters the workplace not as the representative of science, but as the representative of management masquerading in the trappings of science."[78] Framing logistics as a science downplays contingency and dispels politics from the managerial realm of supply chains. Management in the capitalist world-system is fundamentally about controlling labor-power on behalf of capital. What distinguishes contemporary logistics is less the simple fact of managerial command and more the development of an enormous capital-intensive infrastructure through which such commands operate on workers and anyone else caught in its crosshairs.

An astonishing 90 percent of all retail goods are at some point and in some part transported by sea. Without a doubt, logistics underpins much of life as we know it today, yet it does so in ways that imperil and impoverish what we know as life itself. If logistics supports life, it is primarily as a by-product and not as its designed purpose. The means and ends of supply chain capitalism are welded together by seemingly paradoxical impulses. This organization of production promotes social coordination and sustains life, but for the point of furthering capital's pursuit of profit, no matter the actual human and environmental costs. For as much as logistics, through its infrastructure, promises to enable, it also constrains.[79] While often assumed to belong to the apolitical realm of engineers and technocrats, logistics is better characterized as a case study of infrastructural violence. As scholars such as Deborah Cowen, Laleh Khalili, and Rob Nixon have documented, this includes overt forms of violence like war and land dispossession, as well as slower forms such as those that stem from pollution and resource extraction.[80] In addition to these brutal manifestations, logistics also entrenches the "mute compulsion" of capital by restructuring the very material conditions on which social reproduction depends, uprooting and scattering what we need to survive across planetary supply chains.[81]

Besides indicating my focus on artistic production, the plural "arts" in the title of this book is also meant to conjure the idea, mentioned earlier, that "logistics is capital's art of war."[82] This book refrains from attributing to art any special potential for resisting supply chain capitalism. More often than not, my analysis reads as an indictment of art's violent contributions to it, issued in the tone of *j'accuse*. But where there is war, there is possibility for resistance. Several of the artists profiled here—most notably Zina Saro-Wiwa, Allan Sekula, Nida Sinnokrot, and Selina Thompson—recognize the infrastructural violence of logistics and have harnessed their art to seek redress, if not also revenge. Few and far between though they may be, such examples appear throughout this book as reminders that despite logistics being a world-encompassing infrastructure, those most vulnerable to its violent operations are far from powerless.

Art and the Reconfiguration Thesis

What is to be done with logistics? This question points to a recurring theme in the following chapters, interested as I am in contributing to ongoing political conversations over what it would take to repurpose logistical infrastructure for postcapitalist ends. That art should serve as an occasion for engaging what's been called "the reconfiguration thesis" might strike some as odd or incongruous with the stakes of these debates. A part of me is tempted to agree, yet I want to propose that there is something useful to be gleaned from more than half a century of artists adapting transport technologies into art, even if that *something* turns out to be a word of warning.

For the sake of introducing the reconfiguration thesis, I'll begin with where I first encountered it. In a 2011 article for *Mute Magazine*, Alberto Toscano raised the question of whether logistical infrastructure holds postcapitalist revolutionary potential, despite all it has done to entrench capitalist social relations across the planet. He pitched his argument as a counterpoint to what he perceived as a growing preference in socialist and anarchist circles for contending with capitalism's tilt toward supply chains by disrupting its logistical infrastructures and, consequently, the flows they enable. As I discuss further in the Epilogue of this book, Toscano did not dispute the usefulness of tactics like blockades, sabotage, or riots. Instead, his concern was that the allure of disruption should not be allowed to distract workers and social movements from also investigating how logistics could be "potentially reconfigurable."[83] Perhaps to Toscano's chagrin, it has been mostly artists rather than activists or revolutionaries who have so far explored this potential reconfigurability, albeit often toward different political horizons than he had in mind.

Whereas Toscano kept his focus fixed on the use-value of capitalist infrastructure for a revolutionary transition, others insist on the prospect for a broader and more enduring usefulness. These include Nick Srnicek and Alex Williams, who assert that any ecologically sustainable and socially democratic future will require a logistics network that bears resemblance to our current one.[84] Pushing this perspective further, some suggest that socialist planning should even take a page from Walmart's playbook on how to get people what they want and need. First offered as a utopian "thought experiment" by Fredric Jameson, the proposition has since become the subject of an entire book weighing its merits.[85] In *The People's Republic of Walmart*, Leigh Phillips and Michal Rozworski contend that mega-retailers like Walmart offer a blueprint for democratically distributing goods that socialists would do well to adopt: "If only Walmart's operational efficiency, its logistical genius, its architecture of agile economic planning could be captured and transformed by those who aim toward a more egalitarian, liberatory society!"[86] Though issued in a tone more contrarian than utopian, Phillips and Rozworski's stance nonetheless reflects a judicious desire to believe that something must be worth salvaging from the logistical infrastructure in which so much capital and human energy has been sunk.

In stark contrast to such endorsements of reconfiguration, others, like Jasper Bernes, have provided a more bracing assessment, maintaining that any revolutionary struggle must, as "a matter of survival," detach itself "from the planetary factory."[87] Writing in direct response to Toscano, Bernes argues that the longstanding communist faith in the redemptive potential of capitalist technology cannot be extended to logistics. Delinking the productive capacities of a capitalist factory, for example, from the priority of exchange and adapting them to serve noncapitalist ends is, in Bernes's view, a far different endeavor than reconfiguring a global infrastructure built for global labor arbitrage. What makes a Fordist factory potentially useful beyond capitalism is its capacity to enhance worker productivity; however, the same cannot be said for logistical infrastructure, much of which is built to help lower the cost of labor-power by circulating commodities without the additional benefit of producing essential goods. Srnicek and Williams's argument, for instance, blithely assumes that existing logistical infrastructure can be regeared at scale away from "the project of exploiting cheap labour across the world."[88] To Bernes, such hope rings hollow, since "wage differentials are built into the very infrastructure," and without them, "most supply-chains would become both wasteful and unnecessary." The only "use-value which the logistics industry produces" is capital's ability to search the world for the cheapest workers while bending supply chains to avoid class struggle as it arises.[89] Although a factory might feasibly be seized and repurposed to make useful things that sustain life, the logistical infrastructure of supply chain capitalism, according to Bernes, lacks similar redeeming qualities.

Debates over the reconfiguration thesis often approach logistics at a scale that far exceeds the attempts of individuals (like artists) to repurpose its constituent parts. No one necessarily denies that circulation technologies can, in isolated cases, be reused, even for purposes antagonistic to capital accumulation. For example, it should be obvious that a shipping container can be converted into a pop-up gallery, just as it also can be flipped into a barricade. As the Out of the Woods collective puts it, instead of debating whether to seize logistical infrastructure "as a whole" or to let it rot, we might better spend our time asking "how to pull it apart and repurpose its components to new ends."[90] Jameson himself, when posing his initial hypothesis, singled out two circulation technologies for potential repurposing: the shipping container and the Universal Product Code, more commonly known as the barcode. Since Chapter 3 focuses on the former, here I briefly revisit Jameson's thoughts on the barcode so as to give a more rounded sense of what's at stake and what's amiss in the reconfiguration thesis.

Introduced in the early 1970s, the barcode's distinctive black lines now adorn the packaging of nearly every retail commodity in the world, making it, in the words of Jesse LeCavalier, "one of the most ubiquitous features of information and inventory management."[91] Walmart played a pivotal role in spreading the barcode, stipulating early on that suppliers adopt it. Assisted by advances in computing power, barcodes accelerated checkout times, reduced clerical errors, and, most consequentially for Walmart, now provide data that give an increasingly accurate portrait of inventory, which retailers use to anticipate customer demand and cue resupply.

Jameson praises the barcode for having "triumphantly" tamed longstanding distribution challenges by shifting supply decisions from manufacturers to retailers, going so far as to imagine a future when technology like this is used to shape production democratically according to consumer needs rather than corporate profits.[92] In doing so, however, Jameson overlooks the fact that the primary way the barcode altered the balance of power between producers and retailers involved freeing companies like Walmart from direct responsibility for the treatment of workers in their supply pipeline. The data provided by barcodes empower Walmart to impose demands on manufacturers in a manner that cascades discipline onto workers across supply chains, abetting an impersonal system for signaling speedups, reducing wages, and worsening labor conditions.[93] While the barcode is certainly useful in retail and for coordinating distribution, Walmart deploys it most effectively to exploit workers in production. This does not necessarily mean that the barcode cannot be retooled to support the democratic distribution of goods, but what Miriam Posner has said about the possibility for repurposing supply chain management software to improve worker welfare applies equally here: "Technically, it's possible," yet doing so "would be at cross-purposes with almost every other function of the system. On some level, it might even undermine the purpose of having a system in the first place."[94] Imaginable though it may be, technological redemption demands more than rewiring tools or training kinder managers. It would most likely require abolishing entities like Walmart as we know them, and this would include many of the infrastructural systems they built.

When it comes to determining where to place one's faith, the question of reconfiguration is not as straightforward as distinguishing between technologies and the infrastructural contexts they serve. Bernes, for his part, concedes that any revolutionary movement must "make do with what it finds available," though he warns against taking revolutionary uses for granted as unintended "affordances" of these technologies themselves.[95] Despite their differences, Toscano advises similar restraint as Bernes, insisting that any re-functioning be subject to critical scrutiny and struggle. "The test," he writes, "is a practical and political one."[96]

In writing this book, I have found such words of caution to be especially helpful when navigating my way between two seemingly intractable positions on technology. The first asserts that individual technologies are basically neutral, and, as such, can be freely used in contexts other than those for which they were designed, including as art. The second perspective, more pessimistically, contends that technologies can never escape the social relations from which they emerge, meaning that reuse, regardless of the context, will inevitably support said social relations.[97] My central guide in examining attempts to repurpose transport technologies into art has been Bertolt Brecht, specifically his concept of *Umfunktionierung*, or functional transformation.[98] According to the communist writer and director, there is nothing inherent to a capitalist apparatus—whether it is a cultural institution like a theater or a technological network like the radio—that would prevent it from being reused for other purposes. But just because something can be refunctioned does not mean it necessarily should be, nor does such new use guarantee subversion. Writing in 1920s and 1930s Germany with the threat of fascism on his mind, Brecht admonished both artists and revolutionaries against presuming that the tools made available by capitalism are ready-made for any mutinous use someone might devise. Instead, like Toscano and Bernes, he demanded, as a first principle for refunctioning, critical and pragmatic efforts that attacked the social relations governing present use.

That the liberating affordances of any circulation technology plucked from supply chain capitalism's logistical infrastructure must be considered "questionable" is something to which this book attests.[99] Rather than offering a manual for what can be done with logistical infrastructure, *The Arts of Logistics* serves more as a cautionary tale. If nothing else, the art inventoried here demonstrates the many snares that await even the most seemingly minor attempts to repurpose capitalist infrastructure, no matter the degree of aesthetic mediation applied. Whether it is for art or some other context, reconfiguring a circulation technology does not mean severing it from supply chain capitalism and can even entail lending support in new ways. Reconfiguration, as Brecht insisted a century ago, comes with no guarantees.

This holds particularly true in the context of art, irrespective of, and potentially even due to, an artwork's outwardly subversive content. Consider, a final time, the *FedEx* glass works. While by no means built to sabotage or disrupt the courier company, Beshty's sculptures nonetheless carry a critical sheen, displaying the bruising reality shared by the worlds of business logistics and art. Beshty makes no secret of his intent to throw light on the circumstances that bear upon art's circulation, chiefly by inverting the point of shipping for most art: that transport and handling should not alter the object in any way. As Beshty himself notes, his aim is not so much to "reveal the labor and logistics involved in art production" as it is to "not conceal" them.[100] Curators and reviewers have rightly described the *FedEx* glass works as elaborating on the long tradition of artists drawing attention to hidden infrastructures within art institutions, with Beshty pointing specifically to the industry of art transport and its lucrative combination of insurance, security, and transit.[101] Thus his *FedEx* glass works project performs its own kind of infrastructural inversion, though it does so primarily by transforming art world logistics into a new kind of content. In recent years, logistics has become something of a fashionable topic in art, thereby generating a curatorial context wherein growing fascination with this topic actually supports the circulation of Beshty's sculptures from one gallery to the next.

This brings me to a final point regarding art's connection to logistical infrastructure: it is not just artists who need to be aware of their position, but critics as well. Beshty is known for belonging to a generation of theory-savvy artists deeply entrenched in both the gallery system and the critical art discourse that plays a supporting role in legitimizing this system. When Beshty describes the *FedEx* glass works as transforming the courier company into "a tool for aesthetic production as much as it is a system for the movement of goods," I cannot help but think the artist is giving my own definition of the logistical mode of artistic production a run for its money.[102] This raises the question of how a book like the one you are now reading bolsters the logistical mode of artistic production, not least by naming it as such. It will surprise no one to learn that the legitimating function of criticism helps art to circulate through the global market and gallery system.[103] When a prominent curator like Nicolas Bourriaud lauds the *FedEx* glass works series as a cognitive map whose "form is literally produced by its incorporation into a system of distribution (FedEx)," he contributes to the continued circulation of the sculptures.[104] And as James Nisbet observes in relation to Beshty's work in general, this "circulation itself becomes a criterion of valuation."[105] Art criticism, therefore, helps work like Beshty's travel through the art world, integrated as it is into the very logistical infrastructure that undergirds supply chain capitalism.

Here again Beshty has something to say that I find myself eager to hear from an artist working in the logistical mode: specifically, that we should "think of the art world as an analogous industry" to that of FedEx or Amazon or Apple, one "where the network of laborers, cultural managers, and global infrastructure required to shepherd objects from venue to venue is actively obscured in the final reception of art objects within exhibition spaces."[106] The art world, of course, is not merely "analogous" to supply chain capitalism, but is part and parcel of it. This includes criticism and academic research on art. Confronted with this reality, the task of the critic involves avoiding complacency in merely delivering more content to the apparatus, without also actively seeking *other* ways of, to the utmost extent possible, changing or even dismantling it.

Mapping *The Arts of Logistics*

To track how artists have reconfigured circulation technologies since the 1950s, this book privileges forms of live art—performance, installation, and sound art—that lend themselves to literal and material use of such tools. The global spread of the artists I consider follows the geographies of supply chain capitalism itself. My book concentrates on artworks originating in the capitalist core of the North Atlantic and the Asia–Pacific, but it looks as well to artists working elsewhere, most notably in West Africa, the Caribbean, and Palestine. With logistics as a lens, I revisit canonical art by the likes of Christo and Allan Kaprow alongside that of major contemporary figures such as Cai Guo-Qiang and the architect Norman Foster. *The Arts of Logistics* also profiles influential but lesser-known groups like Bow Gamelan

Ensemble and the performance collective Shunt, as well as emerging artists including Lydia Ourahmane, Nida Sinnokrot, and Selina Thompson. In addition to art galleries and museums, the book ventures into more popular venues to examine performances by Trinidadian steel drum bands and Cirque du Soleil.

If the scale and scope of global supply chains dictate the book's geographical and historical range, my focus in individual chapters on specific transport technologies gives this monograph its structure and cohesion. Chapters delve into the history of the merchant ship, the oil barrel, the shipping container, and drone technology to appreciate better the consequences that come from making art out of such tools. Each chapter profiles work by three to five artists and relies on archival research as well as interviews with curators, transport workers, logistics executives, and many of the artists themselves. While covering live art produced since the 1950s, my telling of the story about logistics stretches back centuries and also looks into the future, moving from its origins in the transatlantic slave trade and the postwar revolution in business management, through the expansion of containerization in the 1980s and up to the dream of supply chain automation pursued by capitalist firms today. My argument unfolds across the entire book, but the organization around specific technologies should make it possible for teachers and readers to excerpt as they see fit. Likewise, I have structured individual chapters in such a way that some sections can be read as stand-alone essays on particular artists. In short, please read or share this book in whatever way you find useful.

Chapter 1 tells the long history of logistics through the spectacles that artists and others have created by salvaging wrecked ships. It opens with the dramatic grounding of the ultra-large container ship *Ever Given* in the Suez Canal in March 2021, a spectacle that briefly revived one of the world's oldest pastimes: the spectator sport of salvage. Be it a colonial frigate or a hulking cargo vessel, crowds have long been fascinated to watch salvors rescue wrecked ships. In the first half of the chapter, I situate the *Ever Given* saga within a cultural history of salvage spectacles dating back to the nineteenth century, and I explain how contemporary efforts to prevent maritime loss tethers the slave trade and the period of European colonial expansion to the present. My aim here is to challenge the supply chain management axiom that logistics generates value for capital. Instead, I argue that the capitalist history of salvaging showcases an obsession in logistical calculations with loss prevention.

The latter part of this chapter shifts its focus from the spectacles arising from capitalist salvage operations toward the methods contemporary artists use to create their own spectacles by salvaging the wasted remains of sunken vessels. The distinctive salvage efforts of Bow Gamelan Ensemble, Cai Guo-Qiang, and Selina Thompson provide insights into the historical losses that lie at the core of logistics. Taken together, Bow Gamelan Ensemble's sound art and Cai's installations register the dynamics of empire and racialized dispossession that facilitated the shift in global trade from the Atlantic to the Pacific. Thompson's much-admired performance *salt.*, which draws on her journey aboard a cargo ship along the triangular transatlantic slave trade route, prompts us to revisit chattel slavery as the profound loss that set the wheels of logistics in motion.

If Chapter 1 charts the origins of logistics in European empire and the slave trade, my second chapter digs into the extractive industries that fired the dreams and infrastructure building of the logistics revolution. Chapter 2 explains how early logistics experts fixated on the pipeline as a model for achieving a continuous flow of goods. As the supply chain dream of pipelines flourished in the postwar period, the world of art became saturated with oil barrels. If the pipeline represented a labor-saving infrastructure for moving bulk commodities like oil, the barrel was its antithesis, a physical reminder of the costs required in transportation and storage.

From the steel drums played by Trinidadian musicians to the found objects repurposed by artists in core capitalist countries, oil barrels were everywhere in postwar art, or at least everywhere that oil was extracted and consumed. The first sections of this chapter layer the postwar logistics revolution in business management onto influential live art experiments of the time in North America, western Europe, and Japan that tasked participants with moving objects, most notably oil barrels. Instead of attesting to the increased need for transport labor at the time, the ubiquity of barrels in the art of Allan Kaprow and Christo and Jeanne-Claude, as well as their contemporaries like Group Ongaku, Nam June Paik, and Charlotte Moorman, emphasized the superfluity and meaninglessness of such work, effectively echoing the sentiments of businesses who viewed transport labor as a drag on profits. The chapter finishes in the contemporary oil fields of Algeria, Nigeria, and Indonesia. Recent art by Lydia Ourahmane and Sokari Douglas Camp, both of whom document their difficulties moving empty barrels between Europe and Africa, serve as a reminder that though capital may espouse an ideal of flow, in practice supply chains foster friction when it suits the interests of accumulation. I conclude with site-specific works by Victor Ehikhamenor and Zina Saro-Wiwa that connect the decades-long struggle of the Ogoni people against Shell to expanding forms of militant solidarity across extractive zones the world over.

Chapter 3 moves forward from the logistics revolution in business management to the rise of containerization and considers how shipping containers became the defining infrastructural aesthetic of late capitalist culture. Whereas much critical logistics research focuses on the role of containerization in enhancing capital's ability to exploit workers across the globe, this chapter concentrates on how shipping containers, after dropping out of circulation in supply chains, are frequently redeployed as levers of capitalist dispossession.

The chapter's first case studies, a 1983 site-specific spectacle by Welfare State International and a 2014 immersive performance by Shunt, illustrate how shipping containers have become both symbols and tools of gentrification in the former ports of global cities like London. Huang Yong Ping's 2016 installation *Empires* would seem to address similar issues, yet his attempt to replicate a container yard in the center of Paris, by collaborating with the shipping giant CMA CGM to transport hundreds of empty containers from China, also maps the growing divide between logistical hinterlands and urban cores across the capitalist world-system. Chapter 3 ends in the occupied West Bank, a settler colonial landscape defined by the brutal dispossession of Palestinian territory. In 2014, Nida Sinnokrot made a sculpture, *Jonah's Whale*, from a shipping container that had previously been used both in a settler caravan and as a Palestinian construction site office. Sinnokrot's sculpture captures, in the starkest terms, the infrastructural potential of shipping containers as a lever of dispossession, be it as a tool of gentrification or a weapon in the arsenal of colonial conquest.

Having measured the history of logistics up to the present, my fourth chapter scrutinizes the future of logistics as expressed in the plans of retailers to continue driving down the costs of logistical labor. This chapter focuses on the current efforts of companies like Amazon to promote drone technology as a solution for eliminating the costly so-called last mile of delivery. It opens by examining how Amazon uses advertisements, patents, and warehouse tours to drum up excitement about the possibilities of drone home delivery and warehouse robotics. When viewed in terms of the checkered history of capitalist experiments with labor-saving devices, corporate performances like these make it clear that Amazon's aim is not to replace workers with new technology but to make them increasingly replaceable and thus better subject to managerial control.

From here, Chapter 4 turns from the world of business logistics to that of show business, examining recent drone collaborations between major artists and warehouse automation firms, including Cirque du Soleil's 2016 Broadway production *Paramour*, Anicka Yi's 2021 Tate Modern installation *In Love with the World*, and Flying BeBop's appearances on *Britain's Got Talent*. Drawing on the work of Sianne Ngai, I conclude that drone performances like these are gimmicks that generate an aesthetic experience of wonder while obscuring how businesses are striving to transform the logistical labor process by rendering workers replaceable. This chapter closes by considering one already bungled logistical future—a project to roll out drone delivery in Rwanda designed by Norman Foster. Unveiled at the 2016 Venice Biennale of Architecture, *Droneport* is a reminder of the imperial bias ingrained in the geography of logistics. If Amazon's drone gimmicks showcase the persistence of a capitalist logic of worker fungibility into the future, *Droneport* reminds us that another capitalist logic also endures: that of colonial underdevelopment.

Like this Introduction, my Epilogue links the book's claims about art to broader political debates over what is to be done with logistics. In this final chapter, I move away from art and toward the circulation struggles that are proliferating across the capitalist world-system so as to consider why logistical infrastructures such as ports, pipelines, highways, and railroads have become magnets for social movements like Indigenous water protectors and Black Lives Matter. At first blush, the signal tactics of circulation struggles, like blockades, riots, and sabotage, might seem to run counter to the reconfiguration thesis, especially those projects that promise technological redemption through repurposing. Yet there is a common thread: the underlying assumption that logistical infrastructure is material ready-made for subversion. Inspiring though this prospect may be, it carries the risk of attributing counterlogistical power to materials rather than people. If there is one lesson to be taken from the inventory of art presented in this book, I hope it is the understanding that the potential for a future worth living lies not in the tools that capitalism provides, but in the actions we perform together under circumstances, admittedly, not of our choosing.

1 The Ship
Salvage Spectacles

FOR A WEEK IN LATE March 2021, the grounding of *Ever Given* in the Suez Canal revived one of the world's oldest pastimes: the spectator sport of salvage. While sailing north, the ultra-large container ship veered off course and punched its bow through the bank of the shallow channel, bringing it and some 300 other ships to a halt. The ensuing six-day drama to free *Ever Given* dragged an offstage infrastructure into the limelight. An enormous floating warehouse wedged in the sand might not make for riveting television, but images of a single ship cutting off the primary sea link between Asia and Europe captivated viewers around the world.[1]

The furor generated by *Ever Given* struck many as unprecedented, yet people have long been fascinated by watching salvors recover stranded vessels. Hundreds of years of such salvage spectacles can tell us something about how the capitalist world-system works even when it appears not to be. Loss prevention efforts like the salvaging of *Ever Given* are not an exception to the operations of capitalism; they are one of the logistical bulwarks that keeps this historical system afloat.

In centuries past, salvage spectacles tended to be in-person affairs. Upon hearing word of a shipwreck, crowds would flock to coastlines to witness salvage crews do their work. Sometimes these events involved a degree of audience participation, with spectators stripping beached vessels of parts and cargo. But salvage spectacles are also often highly mediated. Most encounters with *Ever Given*, for example, were shaped by the social media memes and sea shanties the grounded ship inspired (Figure 4). Consider the viral image of an excavator trying in vain to dig out the titanic vessel towering above it. This portrait of cruel optimism served as a canvas upon which

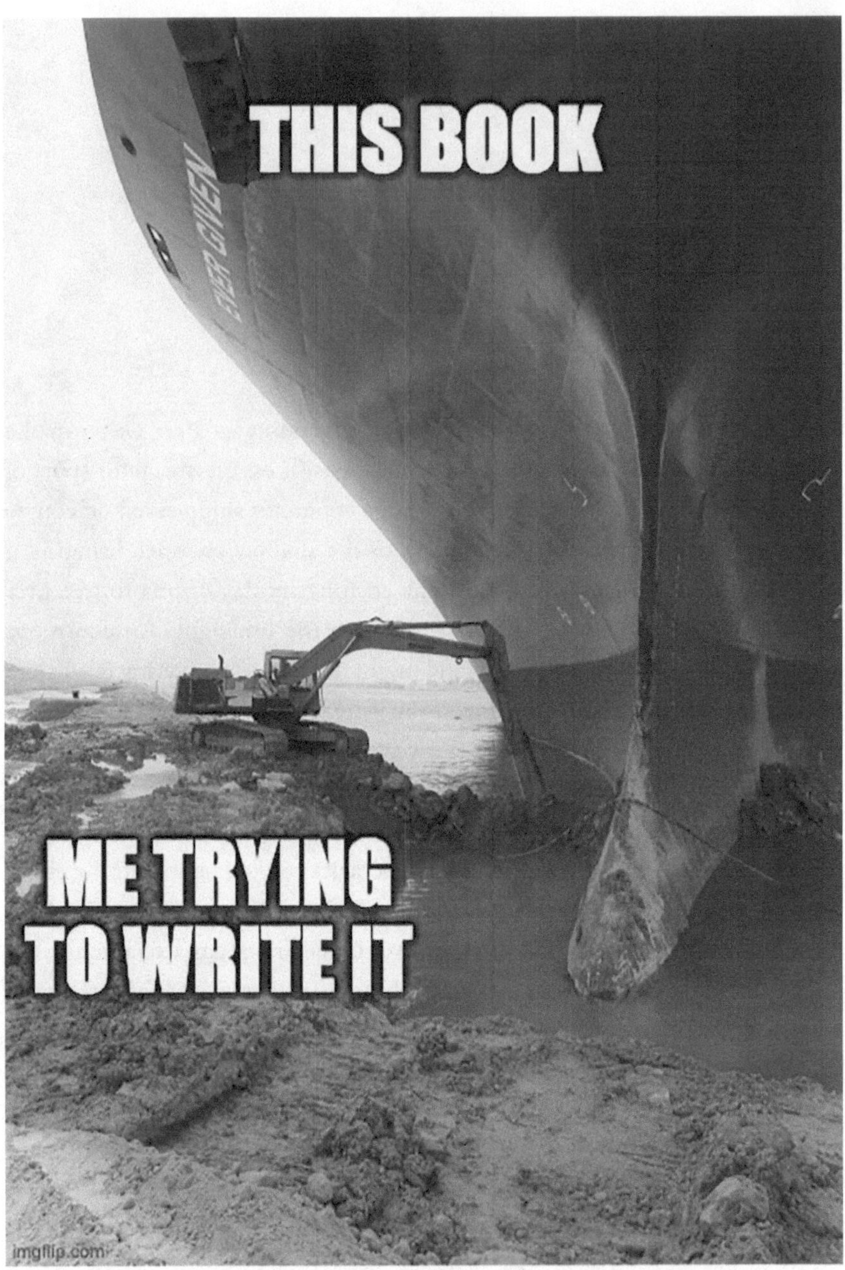

FIGURE 4. Image produced by author with www.imgflip.com, using this template: https://imgflip.com/memetemplate/307885506/Ever-Given

millions of people tweeted their pandemic-induced anxieties and persistent feelings of inadequacy.[2] As we shall see, salvage spectacles typically reach their largest audiences from afar through various forms of representation, including newspapers, books, paintings, and performances. Much of what seemed exceptional about the spectacle surrounding *Ever Given* was, in fact, anything but.

Ever Given is a textbook case of "naval gigantism," an epidemic that afflicts the shipping industry with chronic overcapacity.[3] The world's first dedicated container ship set sail in 1968, and over the next half century, the carrying capacities of such vessels increased by more than 1,200 percent.[4] Despite sluggish growth in the volume of goods needing to go by sea after the 2008 financial crisis, shipowners, in pursuit of market share and spurred by government subsidies, only picked up the pace of the "shipping arms race."[5] In the decade leading up to *Ever Given*'s grounding, the percentage of vessels capable of accommodating more than 10,000 shipping containers soared from 6 percent to 40 percent.[6] The resulting glut of carrying capacity wreaked havoc on the container shipping industry, with ships frequently sailing half empty. As rates plummeted, many firms had no option but to merge or enter alliances with rivals to stave off bankruptcy. *Ever Given* was launched into this fray in 2018, capable of transporting an incredible 20,000 containers, nearly double what the world's largest ships could have handled just a decade earlier. By the time it became lodged in the Suez Canal three years later, seventy ships bigger than *Ever Given* were already afloat. As pandemic lockdowns triggered a surge in global demand for goods, the mismatch between what these colossal ships, now fully laden, could carry and what landside infrastructure was set to handle created bottlenecks that led to widespread shortages and delays.[7] *Ever Given* put this problem on full display when its outsized beam tipped a slight steering correction into an extraordinary blockage of global capital.

Industry insiders tried shrugging off the *Ever Given* affair as just one risk of doing business in maritime shipping. Such reassurances did not deter interlopers from issuing their own less scrupulous diagnoses that *Ever Given* had exposed capitalism's Achilles heel. "The sorry saga underlines the frailty of world trade," proclaimed a columnist in *Wired*, "It took just one gust of wind to bring the whole thing to its knees."[8] Armchair prognoses about the terminal state of capitalism quickly proved to be premature. *Ever Given* was in no position to deliver a definitive break in international trade; the vessel already had 18,000 shipping containers worth of goods on its manifest. After nearly a week parked perpendicularly in the southern end of the Suez Canal, a Dutch salvage team collaborated with an unusually high spring tide to refloat *Ever Given* along with its $700 million worth of cargo. This climax was followed by a hundred-day denouement that relatively few people paid any attention to, but during which the Suez Canal Authority (SCA) held the Japanese-owned ship and its largely Indian crew for a billion-dollar ransom in the appropriately named Great Bitter Lake. Upon its release by the SCA on July 7, 2021, the ship dutifully completed its scheduled run to Rotterdam.[9]

How do we explain the widespread will to misdiagnose a symptom of naval gigantism for the end of capitalism? To hear Charmaine Chua tell it, the pandemic context, then only a year young, offers a clue:

> The workings of global markets, like those of microbes, are typically invisible, dissolved in the abstract, numerical, quasi-magical relations of capital flows. But this? A big boat got stuck. The stuck boat was big. And people had to get it unstuck. . . . For a few days the world seemed a little less inscrutable, brought down to scale by a simpler and more satisfying causality.[10]

Ever Given appeared to many as a beacon in a maelstrom. If the grounded ship supplied anything of use it was the relief that comes with abrupt illumination. But when misjudged, even lighthouses can give false bearings. The message conveyed by *Ever Given* came packaged with a deceptive portrait of how easily global capital can be stopped in its tracks. Analogies comparing the Suez Canal to a blocked artery proliferated, most of which mistakenly equated the circulation of capital with health and overestimated the level of damage a single rogue ship could inflict on the world economy.[11]

There is ample evidence that capital flows can be jammed. Dockworkers frequently refuse to unload ships, water protectors stymie pipelines from crossing dispossessed lands, and anti-police protestors block highways. The list goes on. What deserves scrutiny is the faith that infrastructural faults internal to supply chains (such as giant ships in small channels) triggered by exogenous factors (like "a gust of wind") will be what pushes capitalism over the edge. Logistical infrastructure is engineered to accommodate precisely these sorts of contingencies. Logistics is literally designed to count on loss. "The immobilized ship," Brett Neilson and Ned Rossiter observed a decade before *Ever Given* dug its nose in the sand, "is never equivalent to a systemic-wide failure." More often than not, things grinding to a halt are a chance "to discover new and unforeseen frontiers of capital regeneration."[12] Grounded ships like *Ever Given* present other well-established opportunities for capitalist profit, including salvage. With its want for ruin and wreckage, salvage might seem to contradict the logistical ideals of flow and control. But as the long history of salvaging demonstrates, far from being an anomaly in the logistical workings of capitalism, rescuing ships from total loss is an integral and even rewarded part of it. This chapter, by foregrounding the crucial role of salvage in maritime commerce, seeks to do the clarifying work that *Ever Given* could have done but did not.

Salvaging has a history as old as seafaring itself, yet both the practice of salvage and the spectacles surrounding it have transformed profoundly since the nineteenth century, roughly in line with the evolving political economy of maritime shipping. The history of crowds watching workers rescue wrecked ships from the threat of loss indicates that there is a cultural valence to the economic activity of salvage. Evidence that repurposing ruin suits the cultural logic of capitalism abounds elsewhere too, from the junk bricolages of the *Mad Max* films to the middle-class charm of salvage architecture. For cultural theorists, salvaging also possesses critical potential, such as when it becomes a reading practice for sorting through the capitalist ruins left by wars, slavery, and ecological catastrophes.[13] Yet the prevailing tendency in cultural criticism is to focus on salvage as a technique of representation or interpretation, which often ignores the aesthetic potential of actual salvage operations. Salvage is more than a cultural or critical technique for registering ruin; as an economic activity, it can also be an occasion for collective consumption and a means of repurposing capitalist tools into art.

This chapter underscores the role of loss in logistics by examining the history of salvage spectacles under capitalism. As "the engine of commerce" and the "prototype" of the waged workplace, the ship was essential to both capitalism's development from the seventeenth century and the forms resistance to it would take. The singular importance of the capitalist ship is ingrained in the English language itself, as both "factory" and "strike" have etymological roots in eighteenth-century seafaring.[14] While the role of ships in the rise of capitalism is well known, the significance of salvaging them is frequently overlooked. The first two sections of this chapter combine political-economic and cultural history to explain how efforts to prevent maritime losses tether the period of European colonial expansion to the present. Just as a focus on salvage stretches the history of logistics, the capitalist history of salvaging also highlights an obsession in logistical calculations with loss prevention. *Ever Given*'s place within a lengthy timeline of salvage spectacles exhibits the continuity of our logistical present with the empires of the past.

The second half of the chapter switches focus from the spectacles generated by capitalist salvage operations to contemporary artists who make spectacles of their own by salvaging the wasted remains of boats. After first profiling corporate and activist efforts to salvage ships into art, I turn to the work of Bow Gamelan Ensemble, Cai Guo-Qiang, and Selina Thompson, who each provide distinct perspectives on the historical losses that undergird logistics. Bow Gamelan Ensemble's sound art and Cai's sculptures register the dynamics of empire and racialized dispossession that facilitated the recent shift in global trade from the Atlantic to the Pacific. Thompson's acclaimed performance *salt.*, which is based on her travels aboard a cargo ship along the transatlantic slave trade route, compels us to look back to the slave trade as the source of the profound losses that set logistics in motion.

Logistics as Loss Prevention

Logistics is typically understood as the science of ensuring that the right thing reaches the right place at the right time. If logistics espouses supply chain management ideals of integration and flow, salvage might seem to want the opposite. But salvage is not the wreckage or ruin on which it depends; instead, salvage is the monetary award granted for limiting the losses incurred as a result of such tumult. Salvaging is one way that capitalism transforms loss into reward. In establishing a connection between salvage and the logistical workings of capital, I am following the lead of Stefano Harney and Fred Moten who contend that logistics is not merely "the science of moving property" but also "the science of loss prevention."[15] Here Harney and Moten trouble two tenets of logistics research: the first has to do with the purpose of logistical imperatives in capitalist production, and the second pertains to the historical origins of logistics itself.

Linking logistics to loss prevention implies that the purpose of logistics is not to "add value" to products as they travel around the world but rather to minimize the losses that occur during such movement.[16] Loss prevention is not the avoidance of all loss; it is the ability to count on a certain amount of loss so as to secure a desired yield. Loss prevention involves the practiced skill of distributing losses in the interests of capital, which typically means offloading these losses onto those who are exploited or dispossessed by capital. To think in terms of what is lost rather than what is added by logistics is to recognize how all but a relatively small class of people experience life under supply chain capitalism.

By foregrounding loss prevention, Harney and Moten also shift the origin point of logistical priorities in the capitalist world-system. Scholars typically date the logistics revolution to two postwar transformations in management and technology, when firms restructured their operations to tackle the integrated costs of material handling and, later, when containerization upturned established shipping infrastructures. This tidy historical account has recently come under scrutiny for its "narrowness" and "presentism." Critics, instead, propose tracing the emergence of logistics *avant la lettre*, specifically to the period of British imperial dominance a century earlier when colonial expansion and technological advances like the steam engine combined to revolutionize capitalist planning on a newly global scale.[17] Logistical operations of some kind have played an essential role in industrializing capitalist economies since at the least the nineteenth century. What unites the logistical imperatives of European empire with our own, as Liam Campling and Alejandro Colás put it, is "the *planned movement* of commodities across otherwise fragmented points of production and consumption."[18] Harney and Moten, however, push back the origin date for logistics even further to the sixteenth century. "Modern logistics," they write, "is founded with the first great movement of commodities, the ones that could speak. It was founded in the Atlantic slave trade, founded against the Atlantic slave."[19] While Campling and Colás chart how chattel slavery helped logistics eventually take hold by molding the paths of shipping technologies, laws, financing, and more, they argue that the period encompassing the slave trade was not logistical in itself. In their account, the slave trade, like maritime commerce of the sixteenth and seventeenth centuries more generally, followed the mercantilist logic of commercial capital (buy cheap, sell dear) and was not yet geared to the supremely capitalist objectives of increasing labor productivity and trimming the turnover time of capital. Although logistical planning may have been operational in the slave trade, it was not yet fully subsumed and in service to capitalist shipping.

Harney and Moten pinpoint a more fundamental ambition for logistics: preventing loss, which goes some way to explaining their difference with Campling and Colás. According to Harney and Moten, logistical imperatives are concerned less with moving property than with controlling how, or even whether, said property moves. Logistics designates first and foremost a calculative mode of abstraction, one intertwined with and generative of racism, capable of rendering anything into property to be stored and transported, living human bodies included. From its inception, logistics was obsessed with the prospect of what could be lost, specifically "the potential loss of property that can flee."[20] To prevent such loss, slave trade logistics required restraints like manacles and chains, along with the constant threat and use of violence. But the trade in kidnapped humans also relied on duller tools of loss prevention, such as hedging and efficient stowage. These techniques wickedly turned all kinds of loss—including headroom, fresh air, personhood, even life itself—into profit. Evidence of these seemingly mundane forms of loss prevention stirred much of the outrage that fueled European slave trade reforms and abolition movements in the late eighteenth and early nineteenth centuries. The brutal calculative logic depicted in the diagram of the *Brooks* slave ship and the insurance trial over the *Zong* massacre illustrated in visceral fashion to white Europeans and American settler colonists how the political economy of the slave trade literally counted on the deaths of millions.[21] As Marcus Rediker has argued, the slave trade operated in terms not of loss but of yield, as in "an estimated 14 million people were enslaved to produce a 'yield' of 9 million longer-surviving enslaved Atlantic workers."[22] Instead of adjudicating the debate over how to best periodize logistics, Harney and Moten center the consistent place of loss in the capitalist world-system across its history. Theirs is not so much a historical reframing of logistics as it is a figure-ground reversal that swings what we see logistics as doing, flipping from yield to loss.

Salvage is one mechanism that capital uses to count on loss, but as a concrete activity of rescuing things from the threat of ruin, salvaging predates any historical origins of capitalism. Similarly, traders have long been concerned with the optimal ways to move and store goods. However, it was only in the nineteenth century that activities like salvaging or logistical planning came to be organized along properly capitalist lines. This is not a coincidence. Salvaging is just one way that capital limits losses incurred due to the logistical movement of property. Unlike insurance or the relentless maintenance work that maritime shipping also requires, the types of loss that salvaging prevents tend to be among the most spectacular imaginable: shipwrecks, oil spills, and other headline-grabbing catastrophes. It is all the more surprising, then, that salvage spectacles do not do more to remind us of the losses that the circulation of capital constantly requires. For example, *Ever Given* got stuck in a channel that was originally dug in the 1860s using a forced labor regime that cost hundreds of thousands of lives. For close to ninety years, the Suez Canal was maintained by French and British capital to serve the imperial interests of both nation-states at the grave expense to Egyptians. The week *Ever Given* spent wedged in the sand barely compares to the stretches of time this same artificial waterway was blocked to global trade in 1956–1957 and 1967–1975, years that became high-water marks in decolonial struggle and postcolonial retrenchment respectively.[23] If anything, the spectacle of *Ever Given* planking across the Suez Canal should be viewed as an imperial palimpsest, reflecting the continuity of logistics today with the logistical losses brought into being by European empire.

The Cultural and Political Economies of Salvage

Attempts to salvage wrecked ships have long captivated audiences, the appeal owing less to the shocking fact of a shipwreck and more to the enthralling drama of recovery. As was the case with *Ever Given*, salvage spectacles throughout history have been highly mediated. Consider the example of the French imperial frigate *Méduse*, which seized the cultural imagination after running aground off the coast of present-day Mauritania in 1816. The reduced gunship was on its way to Senegal to restore French control over the colony, following Napoleon Bonaparte's defeat. Reports of murder and cannibalism committed aboard a raft salvaged from the wreckage riveted the European public. Written accounts from survivors circulated widely, prompting further artistic representations such as Théodore Géricault's painting *The Raft of the*

Medusa (1818–19), as well as popular melodramas, operas, and a panorama that toured across the North Atlantic.[24]

Many notable nineteenth-century salvage spectacles were also experienced by crowds who attended shipwrecks in person. In January 1896, when the passenger liner *St. Paul* ran ashore off the coast of New Jersey near the resort town of Long Branch, professional wreckers were joined on-site by tens of thousands of people who journeyed from all over the Eastern Seaboard to witness them work. Long Branch hotels eagerly accommodated this influx of off-season guests, while restaurants catered to them with special menus and rail operators provided direct train services. For those who could not make the trip, photographers and illustrators were present to capture the scene for newspapers and magazines sold across the country. Souvenirs were in plentiful supply, as were skits, poems, and cartoons that added further sensation to the event. The attention given to the *St. Paul* wreckage was "extraordinary," but, as Jamin Wells observes in his chronicle of the affair, the fact that salvage was commodified into a spectacle was "not exceptional."[25] Shipwrecks were relatively common occurrences in late nineteenth-century America and became increasingly easy to consume thanks to the expansion of railroads and the growth of coastal towns equipped to host large crowds.

Salvage spectacles have occurred around the world, but Britain—with its treacherous shorelines, unsettled weather, and abundant trade—is particularly notorious for such things. Writers like Robert Louis Stevenson and Bella Bathurst have recounted the apocryphal history of coastal villagers who, upon learning of wrecks, would gather on nearby cliffs to watch ships die. Some are said to have harbored hopes of failed rescue so that they themselves might take whatever they could from the wreckage. However much we may want to attribute anti-capitalist motives to these "malevolent spectators," most were likely driven by simple necessity or, its opposite, an entrepreneurial spirit.[26] Rumors abound of individuals from Cornwall to Scotland intentionally creating conditions to encourage shipwrecks, such as by not replacing beacons and seamarks or by even more active means. Bathurst tells of "false lights and false foghorns, false harbours, false rescuers, false dawns; even stories of entire coastlines rigged meticulously as stage sets."[27] We need not look too far into the past to discover other examples of opportunistic salvors. In 2007, when dozens of shipping containers belonging to *MSC Napoli* washed onto England's Jurassic Coast, breathless reports of "an army of modern day 'wreckers'" swiping everything from diapers to brand-new BMW motorcycles filled English newspapers.[28] These losses grabbed headlines, but they were relatively minor compared to the £120 million and 924 days it took to clean up the heavily damaged container ship and the oil it had spilled.

Speculations about the enduring appeal of shipwrecks often strip them of historical specificity. In *Shipwreck with Spectator*, for instance, philosopher Hans Blumenberg charts the ruined ships strewn across the history of Western thought, from the Greek academies to the Enlightenment, arguing that shipwrecks have always been an occasion for contemplating the nature of existence.[29] In attempting to explain our fascination with them, Blumenberg treats shipwrecks as if they exist outside of history, as if they have remained unchanged for millennia. However, among the many things that must always be historicized are the catastrophes that the circulation of capital begets. Shipwrecks are no exception.

The maritime wrecks of interest to me, like the salvage spectacles they generate, are inseparable from the shifting political economy of capitalism. The massive growth of maritime trade during the nineteenth century led to larger ships, which, when wrecked, resulted in more impressive sights for spectators. And because expanding trade required more ships, there emerged an uptick in the number and frequency of wrecks that could be watched. Perhaps most important to the changing spectatorial lure of salvage in the 1800s came as a result of a shift in the focus of salvage crews. In earlier salvage operations, the primary goal was to save cargo whose recoverable value tended to be higher than that of the ruined wooden sailboats transporting them. By theatrical standards, this made for a rather poor show since much of the salvage work was performed underwater or otherwise out of sight. As ships grew in size and began using iron hulls and steam engines, they became more expensive. Consequently, the value ratio of what could be saved from a wreck began tilting from cargo to vessel, and the priority of salvors followed suit. Attempts to rescue entire ships made for better entertainment than divers working below the waterline to recover sunk merchant cargo. When combined with the growing significance of spectacle in circum-Atlantic culture of the 1800s, the newly heightened stakes of rescuing entire vessels transformed salvage into an absorbing viewing experience, precisely at the time that holiday infrastructures and visual media made it easier for people to access shipwrecks, either in person or from a distance.[30]

The effort to save stuff from the threat of maritime ruin may be as old as seafaring, but the practice of salvage took on a distinct social form when it became subsumed to capital in the nineteenth century. Until then, salvage operations tended to be ad hoc endeavors performed by decentralized and, frequently, amateur crews.[31] The line separating salvors from scavengers and pirates was perceived as thin, and the composition of the wrecker workforce in the Atlantic was highly racialized and classed.[32] The spread of costly technologies like steam engines, coupled with new forms of business organization, led to a deeper reliance between salvaging and capital investment, transforming wrecking crews into industrial operations. Salvaging entire ships, many of which were larger and heavier than their wooden predecessors, presented more complex challenges than simply saving cargo. This required significantly greater capital outlays to cover the expenses associated with the requisite tools and machinery. The result throughout the nineteenth and early twentieth centuries was a global shift, albeit uneven, from ad hoc wrecking to industrial undertakings that could guarantee the capital, corporate organization, and specialized training needed. If salvors had once been indistinguishable from pirates, by the twentieth century, they were imagined in a rather more respectable light, as "engineers."[33]

The history of SMIT International, the salvage firm credited with refloating *Ever Given*, exemplifies how corporatization, consolidation, and technological innovation joined forces to restructure salvage operations along capitalist lines. The company was founded in the 1840s by Fop Smit, who made his fortune by building the first Dutch wooden steamboats before branching out as a paddlewheel tug operator. His sons expanded the company's towage fleet, and in the 1920s, the SMIT company merged with a Rotterdam competitor to extend operations beyond Europe. SMIT came to international attention in 1957 when it was hired to remove the forty-one ships that Gamal Abdel Nasser had scuttled in the Suez Canal to block invasion by France, Britain, and Israel. In 2010, SMIT was valued at $1.5 billion when it was acquired by the world's largest dredging company.[34] As the history of SMIT suggests, salvage has long been a profitable enterprise. In the mid-1800s, shipwrecks in the Bahamas were so frequent that the salvaged cargo accounted for between one third and one half of the total value of all imports. This figure peaked at 54 percent in 1870, the same year that nearly half of all exports were salvaged goods.[35] Although the frequency of shipwrecks has steadily declined over the past century, salvage remains a lucrative endeavor. Once arbitration finally ends, SMIT is expected to fetch anywhere between $25–$50 million for freeing *Ever Given*.[36]

In legal terms, "salvage" does not refer to the work performed but rather to the reward to which one is entitled for saving a ship or its cargo.[37] Law is essential for distinguishing salvaging from activities that could be mistaken for it, such as plunder or voluntary acts of heroism. Salvors must expect to get something for their rescue efforts, just not the actual stuff they rescue. While salvage law is often presumed to be ancient, this common notion obscures the fact that many of the actors and legal mechanisms involved in salvage today have their origins in European empire. For instance, the international standard contract for arranging salvage, the "Lloyd's Open Form," is administered by Lloyd's of London, which got its start in the seventeenth century as a coffeehouse market specializing in maritime insurance that covered colonial property and cargo, including slaves. Insurance and salvage are just some of the tools that capitalists employ to count on loss, encouraging the risky investments that have helped to expand the capitalist world-system since the eighteenth century.[38]

The very need for salvage would seem to contradict the logistical aspirations of continuous flow, yet the very existence of such ideals depends, in the first place, on the potential of friction and inefficiency, or, to use another word, of loss. Salvaging counts on ruin and wreckage, and so does capital investment. Neither antagonistic nor incidental to the aims of capitalism, salvaging has long been at its service by helping to recover sunk value or even by becoming a capitalist enterprise in its own right. As Anna Lowenhaupt Tsing and Evan Calder Williams have each argued, the fundamental logic of salvaging—"a relentless search for every last scrap of value"—is supremely suited to capital accumulation, if not also to capitalist crisis.[39] The histories of salvage are a reminder that even that which seems incompatible with capitalism is nothing of the sort.

For all that they stand to reveal about capitalism, the spectacles surrounding salvage operations tend more to distract from what such work puts on stark display. Salvage spectacles have been a constant feature of capitalism, but the meanings ascribed to them have shifted over time. *Ever Given*, for example, gave the impression of the system's fragility and fostered a naive sense of the inability for something so enormous to get back on course, be it the vessel or even capitalism itself. In contrast, salvage spectacles of the late nineteenth century signaled a system on the rise. The very existence of such huge ships like *St. Paul* and the capacity of humans and their machines to rescue them from the clutches of nature testified to the technological achievements of capitalism. Despite what salvage spectacles may obscure about capitalism, they can also reflect constant truths about it, provided we view them from the appropriate perspective. Writing in 1956, the same year Nasser nationalized the Suez Canal, the Italian communist Amadeo Bordiga saw in a spate of maritime disasters resulting from shoddy engineering the deadly outcome of an affluent capitalist society that profits from planned obsolescence.[40] Here, during capitalism's so-called Golden Age, Bordiga could plainly perceive in its shipwrecks the brutal evidence of how capitalism counts on loss.

The Salvage Readymade

The aesthetic potential of salvaging is not limited to the collateral spectacles that salvage operations generate. In addition to being a spontaneous occasion for collective spectatorship, salvage can also be a purposeful technique for refunctioning tools of capital into art. Consider the fate that befell a fleet of speedy but modestly sized (4,400 TEU[41]) container ships built by Maersk in the late 2000s. They were designed to make the trip from Shenzhen to Newark in under three weeks, a blistering pace by industry standards. The Danish shipping giant had bet that the swift service promised by these fuel-guzzling vessels would appeal to customers in the fashion and toy industries, who might be willing to pay higher rates to get their goods to market at speed. The gamble proved costly. No sooner had the first five of the $50 million ships launched than the storm of the 2008 financial crisis hit. With trade depressed and fuel prices soaring, Maersk mothballed the entire fleet. But instead of scrapping them, the ships were moored together in a Scottish loch where they became the set for a post-apocalypse-themed children's gameshow broadcasted on the BBC.[42] This particular salvage spectacle was not the by-product of accidental wreckage, but the combined result of industry miscalculation and show business buccaneering. Insofar as the fleet's repurposing into a stage set allowed Maersk to limit some of its losses, this was a salvage act, however extraordinary.

While not unheard of for ships to be repurposed into venues such as museums or clubs, it is exceedingly rare for the types of large vessels (100 gross tons and above) we associate with global maritime trade—including oil tankers, bulk carriers, and container ships—to become available for such cultural reuse. In 2023, 105,493 such ships were registered across the world.[43] When retired, most of these will be sold on to shipbreakers who will cut them into salvageable parts for sale on the secondhand market. The political economy of shipbreaking has transformed markedly in recent decades. A century ago, most breaking took place in countries like the United States and England. Since the 1980s, however, the search for cheap labor and lax regulations has shifted the industry almost entirely to the South Asian subcontinent where beaches in India, Pakistan, and Bangladesh now process more than 86 percent of decommissioned ships. Shipbreaking plays a strategic role in these domestic economies; in Bangladesh, for instance, it yields half of the country's annual steel supply.[44] This, along with the tight budgets of shipping companies, largely prevents withdrawn merchant vessels from becoming available for any purpose other than breaking. Multiple rewards were needed to entice Maersk to salvage its container ships for show business, including positive publicity and the promise of a stopgap that would give the company time to devise ways to sell off or redeploy its uneconomical fleet.

The novelty of Maersk's salvage effort is only matched by one coordinated through the shipping industry's chief antagonist. On March 27, 1998, the International Transport Workers' Federation (ITF) paid a $3 million scrap price for a dry bulk carrier, which they converted into a floating gallery to support their longstanding campaign against flags of convenience (FOC). Founded in 1896, the London–based labor rights organization today represents some 20 million workers from 150 countries, including around half of the world's 1.6 million seafarers.[45] Their aging tween-decker was built in 1979 in England, but at the time of purchase by the ITF, it was flagged to Panama, owned by a Hong Kong company, and operated by a largely Filipino crew.[46] In short, the vessel embodied the FOC system that permits owners to register their ships wherever they choose, typically in countries promising low taxes, loose regulations, and lenient safety standards.

Open registries took off in the early twentieth century when newly decolonized countries like Panama and Liberia used newfound sovereignty to rent out the right to sail under their flags, allowing shipping magnates like Aristotle Onassis to reap enormous profits at massive expense to the welfare and work conditions of seafarers.[47] Since the 1970s, the number of FOC ships has skyrocketed, as has that of designated foreign workers on them, most of whom hail from eastern Europe and Asia, especially the Philippines. The spread of strategic flagging has intensified exploitation aboard merchant ships by squeezing crew sizes and wages, even as cargo capacity grows and turnover time in ports shrinks. While working conditions have deteriorated across the maritime shipping industry in recent decades, conditions are the worst on FOC vessels. Such ships are also the most racially stratified, with officers tending to be white Europeans and ordinary crew members typically recruited from the Global South. The labyrinth of responsibility that results from "flagging out" sets the stage for egregious crimes, like indentured servitude on fishing boats or the abandonment of crews, which became especially widespread during the COVID-19 pandemic.[48] The ITF has led the international fight against FOCs

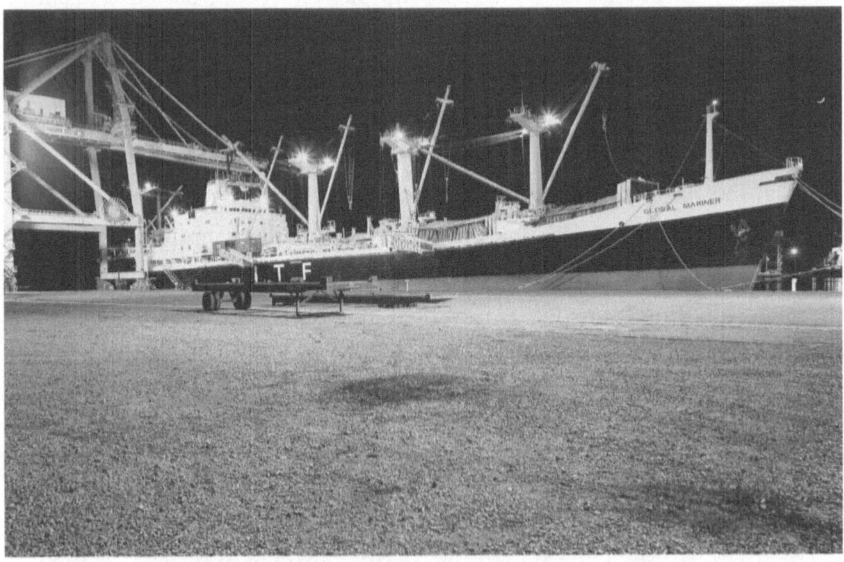

FIGURES 5 AND 6. *Good Ship Bad Ship (Limassol) 1-2*, 1999/2010, from Allan Sekula's series *Ship of Fools*, 2010. © Allan Sekula, courtesy the Allan Sekula Studio.

since 1948 by organizing ship boycotts, running global safety inspections, securing collective agreements on minimum standards, and winning millions in back pay for workers.

The ITF bought their cargo ship to commemorate the fiftieth anniversary of their FOC campaign. After reflagging it to Britain and renaming it *Global Mariner*, they spent $1.8 million to transform the vessel into a nautical exhibition space. The ship's seven holds were adapted into galleries, which a curatorial team filled with photographs, films, and stories detailing the various ills associated with FOC ships. Alongside documentary evidence of injured sailors and cockroach-infested galleys, visitors could watch an animated film about a seafaring mouse and a ship-owning shark or play a video game that put them in the shoes of a stranded sailor. *Global Mariner* opened to the public in London on July 3, 1998, before embarking on a twenty-month voyage around the world. It visited 86 ports in 51 countries and welcomed over 750,000 visitors on board. When in port, the ship played host to a range of events, including political rallies, lectures, concerts, and even a wedding. FOC vessels that crossed its path were shamed with banner drops and by a high-powered projector that plastered hulls with anti-FOC slogans. The crew also lent support to local struggles by engaging in direct actions as they traveled. In Chile, *Global*

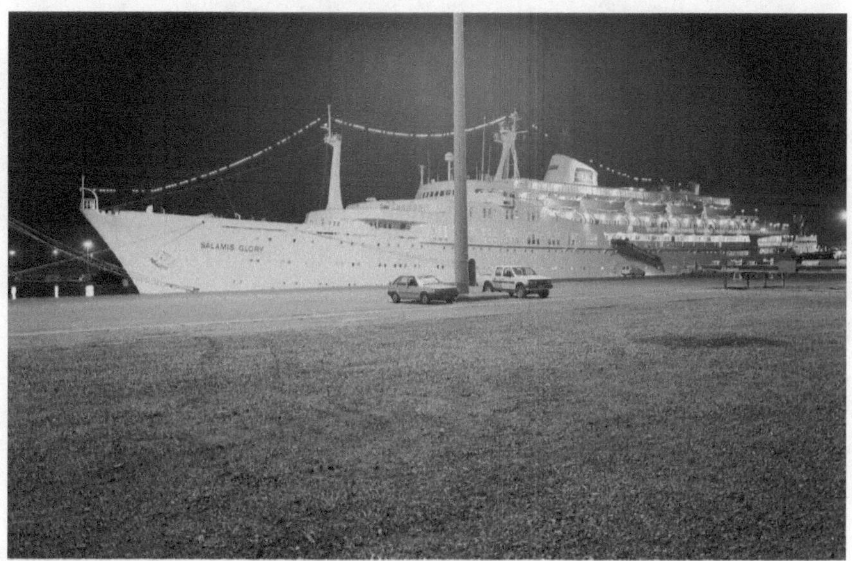

FIGURES 5 AND 6. (Continued).

Mariner delivered food to seafarers abandoned on a FOC ship and even helped blockade another whose owner was refusing to pay their crew.

The *Global Mariner*'s campaign for seafarer rights was impressive, but so was the bill. In total, the project cost the ITF $9 million. Just months after its world tour concluded, *Global Mariner* collided with another ship in Venezuela and sank.[49] While class struggle should not be assessed in terms of value for money, this high price tag indicates the ITF's strategic priority. Despite representing some 700 affiliated labor unions, the ITF operates most like a labor-rights NGO. Many of its advocacy efforts have more in common with corporate campaigning than shop-floor organizing, often unfolding without substantive contributions from the workers represented. Although the ITF is much admired in the global labor movement, its top-down approach remains divisive. Moreover, the stigma from its historic hostility to communist struggles and its postwar collaboration with the CIA lingers.[50] Frustrations boiled over as *Global Mariner* circumnavigated the world. When the ship called at Marseille near the end of its voyage, for instance, French longshoremen, angry with the ITF, refused to help it dock, going so far as to cut its mooring lines. That same year, in 2000, several unions broke from the ITF to form the International Dockworkers Council (IDC), a non-professionalized network run by rank-and-file members through a council model, privileging mutual aid and workplace mobilization over lobbying and symbolic interventions.[51]

For a product of a bureaucratic labor rights organization, *Global Mariner* presented an almost utopian vision of worker control. It was amply staffed by unionized seafarers from fifteen countries around the world. Two different crews rotated in three-month stints and were paid according to a consummate wage scale. When it came to working conditions, *Global Mariner* appeared to practice what it preached. The artist Allan Sekula, who documented three legs of the voyage, celebrated the exhibition and insisted that the ship delivered its most important message through the "exemplary way" it operated. If the holds displayed how bad conditions for seafarers had become, the ship itself proved that things could be different. In both his writing and photographs, Sekula calls *Global Mariner* "the Good Ship" against which all other vessels should be measured (Figures 5 and 6).[52] Representations of life on board approached the quixotic. An ITF-produced documentary of the voyage, for example, juxtaposed the dire plight of seafarers condemned to

FOC ships with the camaraderie enjoyed by the *Global Mariner* crew. Footage of barbecues and playful rites of passage set to Hawaiian slack-key guitar music invited comparisons of the floating workplace to a cruise ship luau.[53] Such scenes might actually have reflected crew experience, but they also run the risk of providing an overly simplistic vision of what it would take to transform the shipping industry from a site of egregious exploitation into one of worker empowerment.

In his travelogue, Sekula himself veers close to romanticization, no less so than when he lauds the ITF for "miraculously" saving the ship from "the *abattoir* of the maritime world," and thereby securing its "rescue and redemption."[54] His 2010 collection of photographs, *Ship of Fools,* taken while aboard *Global Mariner*, knowingly flirts with the genre of utopianism. The title, for instance, alludes to Plato's philosophical sketch in the *Republic* and Sebastian Brant's subsequent 1494 satire of a rowdy crew who, after wresting control of their ship from its captain, proceeds to sail the world feasting and drinking. Intended by Plato as a warning against a society lacking expert governance, Sekula repurposed the allegory to present *Global Mariner* as a dreamland of worker control.[55] Such flourishes are to be excused for the aims of agitation, though they also partly obscure how *Global Mariner* actually operated. For one, hierarchy remained firmly in place on the ship, with jobs largely divided along gender lines; the very few women onboard worked primarily in hospitality.

Sekula applauded the ITF for wrenching the ship free from capital's logistical infrastructure, most notably containerization. Outfitted with its own cranes and a skilled crew, *Global Mariner* had little use for the "larger machine ensemble" required by other ships. This made it, according to Sekula, "a vessel of old-fashioned self-sufficiency." Infrastructural independence conferred "functional autonomy and versatility," leaving it to the crew to chart their own way.[56] Sekula's account painted a picture that showed workers seizing the tools of logistics as a magic bullet for undoing exploitation at sea, albeit without mentioning the resistance that any scaled-up attempt at such logistical seizure would be sure to encounter.

Just as the *Global Mariner's* utopian spectacle presented a stirring image of uncontested worker power, it also issued a fantastical vision of the ease with which logistics, at least in parts, could be redeemed. Sekula certainly held no illusions about what logistical infrastructure is designed to do. Perhaps his optimism can be explained by the fact that he used the world of art, not logistics, to license his prospect, situating *Global Mariner*'s repurposing in the tradition of the Duchampian readymade. In terms of its "ambiguous status as *already existing but transformed* object and context," Sekula writes, the ship was "readymade-like."[57] But what degree of "context" is lost when the object made into art is a cargo ship rather than, say, a urinal? The ease with which a toilet can be ripped from its plumbing and made into art is a far cry from what is required to disconnect a ship from global supply chains. The stakes of such a salvage operation extend beyond the realm of museums and art criticism, influencing the path and horizon of political praxis. None of this is meant to discount the inspiration that Sekula—and us, through his writing and art—rightly found when sailing aboard *Global Mariner.* The problem, though, is one of tactics and strategy: should the meager resources available to capital's antagonists be diverted into a floating museum? This question leads back to the debate over the reconfiguration thesis introduced in the Introduction: would the world not be better off if, instead of salvaging them, we left the instruments of logistics to ruin?

The Instruments of Capital

The bottom lines of shipping firms may limit the availability of large merchant ships to be made into art, but other salvageable vessels and infrastructure abound, many the remains left behind by the logistics revolution. In a pattern repeated across the European and North American littoral, huge portions of the world's maritime infrastructure were rendered idle when containerization and ancillary innovations reshaped how goods were transported and stored. As detailed further in Chapter 3, the docklands of major cities, particularly in overdeveloped capitalist countries, were hit hard in the 1960s when container ships and bulk carriers began redirecting logistical activity to exurban deepwater ports. Even as commercial developers embarked on their own kind of salvage operations by flipping closed warehouses into condos and inactive docks into tourist attractions, a surfeit of ruin remained for others, including artists, to use.[58]

Few would make more artistically from these losses than the sound art collective, Bow Gamelan Ensemble (BGE). Founded in London in 1983 by percussionist Paul Burwell, punk singer and performance artist Anne Bean, and sculptor Richard Wilson, this group spent much of the decade scavenging waterways and brownfield sites for discarded items to repurpose into metallophone instruments, including such varied things as oil barrels, stranded boats, and even entire shipyards. BGE performed around the world, roaming from Norway and Japan to New York and Mexico, but centered most of their salvage efforts on the Thames and its offshoots. The trio's ephemeral spectacles probed the sonic character of maritime ruin and showed 1980s London, with its recently collapsed inner-city docklands, to be an exceptional site for salvors of all kinds. Taking their name from the East London district of Bow they called home and the percussive arrangements of Indonesian gamelan, BGE began by filling indoor music venues with a raucous brand of pyrotechnic-backed percussion before moving outside. On riverbanks and even in rivers themselves, BGE's spectacles jumped scale.[59]

Exemplary of their outdoor work was *Offshore Rig*, which BGE created in July 1987 on a small river island in West London formerly used for building and repairing barges. Tidal boatyards like this had been small but essential players in London's docklands until World War II, after which motorways and then containerization largely displaced commercial traffic from the Thames. By the time BGE moved onto the island, the boatyard had been shuttered for a decade. To create their performance, the trio and their collaborators camped on-site for a fortnight, making instruments out of whatever could be salvaged.[60] They converted the boatyard's three vaulted sheds into theater rigs and fished various tools from the water, including an enormous air hammer and several pontoon boats, which they deployed as floating stages. One reviewer described the location as an "ideal environment" for a group "committed to imbuing the discarded industrial detritus of the past with a bittersweet (literal) resonance for the present."[61] The covered boatyard became a massive, tiered stage, outfitted by BGE with a motley orchestra of horns, sirens, kegs, car springs, bathtubs, barrels, and more. In addition to drumming on these makeshift instruments, the group rang a pair of colossal chimes, one made of a hundred sheets of glass blown by a wind machine and the other constructed from metal lockers they pummeled with a jet of water shot from the hose of a fire brigade boat. The sound of the idling air hammer supplied a background of white noise when it was not being made to bite through metal sheets. At one point, a huge waterfall laced with red dye cascaded from the vaulted roofs. As if this were not spectacular enough, BGE also set off 3,000 pounds of fireworks for good measure. The seventy-minute performance, which ran for three nights, ended in a display of fire as performers pounded the tops of flaming oil barrels with drumsticks covered in paraffin-soaked rags and detonated propane-filled balloons. The audience took in the event while seated on raked risers installed on the foreshore, the water beneath them slowly rising as the tide rolled in.

Throughout *Offshore Rig*, Bean, Burwell, and Wilson traversed catwalks, waded through water, rang bells, lit fireworks, and drummed on, well, everything. Together with their seven-person crew, they performed less like leads than puppeteers, their presence spectral when not actually obscured by steam, shadows, and fire. Shared uniforms of hard hats and safety vests made it difficult to discern who was who, let alone keep track of who was doing what. One attendee rightly described the performance as a "spectacle of impersonality."[62] The effect was deliberate. "We wanted to be anonymous and synonymous," Bean later recalled, "Just operators keeping this entire orchestra going."[63] Their ramshackle tableau of ruin, overshadowing the human labor drawing worth from it, made for an apt metaphor of salvaging, yet this was also a salvage operation. As Bean put it to me: "I thought of the island as an artist's placement, with us working with the phantoms of the old boatyard, renovating their machinery to again pump, splutter and growl."[64]

BGE earned its reputation as "avant-garde East End scrap metal merchants" by scouring dumps, junkyards, and canals for cast-off items.[65] They scavenged with the intent to salvage, typically to retrieve in things the potential to make sound. "There was a palpable sense of *re-activation* in their activities," reported Simon Herbert in his review of *Offshore Rig*, "the sounds and visuals recreated—if not resurrected—the work ethic origins of this site."[66] Salvaging, in its capitalist form, aims to limit the loss of economic value fixed in capital assets like a ship or its cargo. As an aesthetic technique practiced by BGE, however, salvaging meant recovering something of use for making art in found materials. For a 1989 performance called *The Navigators,* the group dug a ruined crane barge out from the mud of Pudding Mill River and refloated it as the central stage in a flotilla that traveled up through the Thames waterways (Figure 7). They cruised for six weeks, staging performances along the

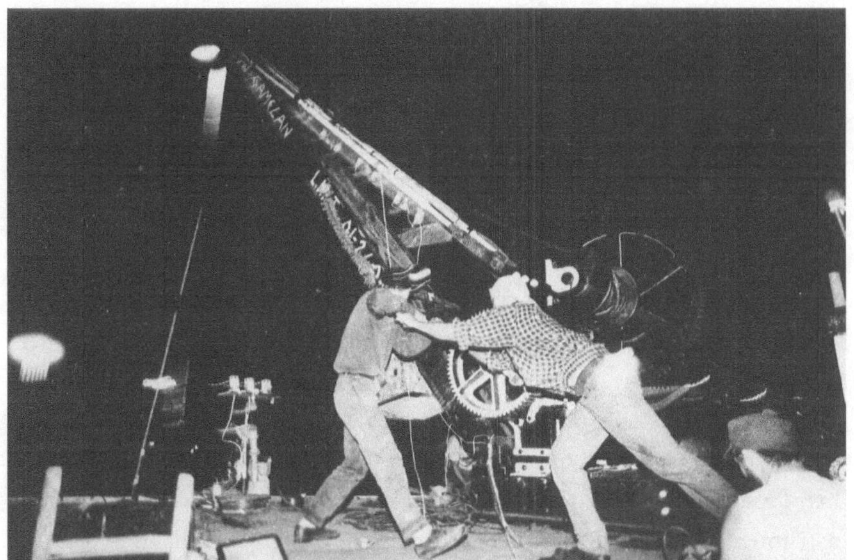

FIGURE 7. Bow Gamelan Ensemble performing *The Navigators,* 1989. *Photo:* Ed Sirrs, courtesy Anne Bean and Richard Wilson.

way, which they dubbed "ports of call." As the assorted vessels and platforms wound their way inland, BGE dredged and dragged from the water all manner of stuff to transform into instruments.[67]

When speaking of the skills that *Offshore Rig* or *The Navigators* required, BGE shied away from words like "composing" or even "performing," preferring instead to speak in terms of work: "welding," "packing," "weightlifting," "labouring."[68] Reviewers too noted a blurring of their art with "industrial activity," likening BGE performances "to watching workers on a building site or stoking the boilers on a ship."[69] In interviews, the group boasted of becoming proficient with tools like arc welders in the way that other musicians might brag about improving at the cello. Their performances were not, however, an imitation of work as art. Instead, they relocated activities from one context to another, making artworks out of dock work. Instead of adorning or stylizing the labor of welding, for example, they embraced the aesthetic potential of the light and sound emitted by a sparking welder. According to Burwell, BGE worked to discover the "aesthetic by-products" of industrial activity.[70] Similar to how gasoline was considered a waste product of kerosene distillation until profitable uses for it were found, BGE squeezed aesthetic worth from the materials they recovered. The light from an arc welder, the sound of a crane dragging rubbish from the river—these were their "aesthetic by-products" from salvaging.

To use the words of Chrissie Iles, BGE performances appealed to spectators because of the "strange fascination" that came with seeing what BGE could do with things not designed as musical instruments.[71] For as much as the junk-strewn structures that BGE crafted bore resemblance to the kinetic sculptures of an artist like Jean Tinguely, their contraptions were always fleeting, built to be performed with and then dismantled.[72] The group neither preserved nor restored what they found. They cut up, took apart, and otherwise altered items as they saw fit. Reviewers and BGE alike described this technique as a kind of refunctioning. That their materials had outlived their "original function" lent them to taking on a new function as musical instruments. A car that has been dumped in the river, Wilson explained, is "released from its function" and made available as "something that your imagination could work on."[73] Salvaging for BGE entailed refunctioning found materials into instruments, which meant finding what was already musical about them.

BGE did not try to conceal the previous uses of the instruments they salvaged. They did not repair or even clean them, allowing the traces of maritime life to infuse their instruments with inadvertent historical depth. Bean, Burwell, and Wilson came together, in part, due to their shared fascination with the Thames and the infrastructures that made it tick: "every bridge . . . every welder . . . every forklift truck . . . every magnetic lifter just absolutely inspired and triggered us."[74] They did not hide the history of their instruments, but nor did their performances say much about this history, at least explicitly. Wilson compared BGE's technique to that of an "old-fashioned" painter who, upon seeing an attractive copse of trees, would "knock out a quick pastoral landscape."[75] The group's own environs happened to be piled high with the ruins left behind by containerization. Whether by intent or happenstance, many of their London performances registered the recent economic collapse of the city's venerable docks. Like the early twentieth-century noise artists Luigi Russolo and Arseny Avraamov, whom BGE claimed as influences, their brand of "musical historicism" derived largely from their choice of instruments rather than any compositional qualities.[76]

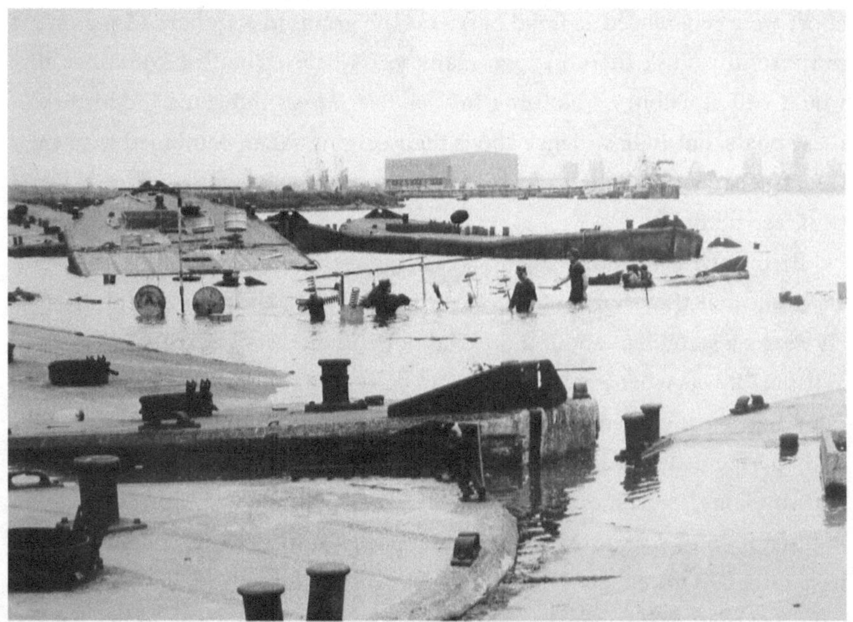

FIGURE 8. Bow Gamelan Ensemble performing *Concrete Barges*, Rainham Marshes, 1987.
Film still courtesy Anne Bean, Richard Wilson, and Alter Image production for Channel 4.

Consider, for example, a 1987 performance in Rainham Marshes, just downriver from London, where BGE performed on and alongside a fleet of beached barges (Figure 8). The ten-hour performance called *Concrete Barges* began at low tide with BGE playing their standard rig of bells, canisters, barrel tops, pipes, and hubcaps on the Thames foreshore.[77] As the day unfolded, the rising water forced the group to retreat to higher ground atop the barges whose metal fastenings and portholes they drummed like xylophones. BGE tapped on the hulls that were slowly filling with water, tracking how sound changes with the tide, all while a documentary crew filmed the performance for public television. Watching at home without knowing any better, it would have been easy to mistake the boats stranded not far from the new deepwater port in Tilbury as a casualty of containerization. However, the fate of these barges had nothing to do with London's dock closures. The boats were originally built to transport petrol during World War II, part of a fleet of 200 concrete vessels the military had ordered on the cheap. Many of those that survived the war effort were redeployed as flood barriers. The group in Rainham Marshes was purposefully sunk there in 1953, many years before the first container ship would call at Tilbury.[78] Nothing in *Concrete Barges* indicated the history of these boats, but BGE's silence about their origins, when combined with their location, could allow these unusual ruins to be mistaken for a vestige of logistical restructuring.

BGE downplayed any historical resonance in their choice of materials, claiming that they turned to scrapyards and the river for practical reasons. "It wasn't a statement about industrial noise, or society's detritus," remarked Wilson. "It was what we could afford to do on the evening."[79] Such insistence did not prevent audiences or the press from reading into the locations where BGE performed. Reviewers categorized their performances as "industrial anthropology,"[80] or, more precisely, "percussive folk music indigenous to an industrial culture entering the terminal phase of its decline."[81] BGE may not have intended to register London's logistical transformation, but they readily admitted their performances were haunted by loss. Bean, for example, has described *Offshore Rig* as "reanimating an industrial part of London. . . . Again, in terms of ghosts—but not ghosts. . . . It's an actual recognition of spaces that had incredible dynamism and energy, an embrace and capturing of that in what we were doing in the present."[82] Instead of trying to restore the past, BGE evoked it as both loss and opportunity.

Haunting became an explicit theme in the trio's collaborations after they stopped performing together as Bow Gamelan Ensemble in 1990, and especially following Burwell's death in 2007. Since then, Bean and Wilson have created performances taking the forms of wakes and séances; at one, they even consumed Burwell's ashes with whiskey.[83] In 2009, the pair collaborated with Miyako Narita aboard a makeshift pontoon raft floating on oil barrels six miles from land. An audience watched from a nearby boat as Bean and Narita carried out a ritual arranged loosely around a Burwell poem, accompanied by Wilson beating a drum and cymbals. This was a lament for Burwell inflected with their surroundings: they floated beside a derelict water fortress built in the Thames Estuary during World War II. Known as the Maunsell Forts, these structures were decommissioned in the 1950s and subsequently housed pirate radio stations. Today, they sit in the middle of a shipping lane where they face the threat of demolition. In a film Wilson made of the performance, a container ship can be seen slowly moving by in the distance.[84] Their remembrance of Burwell was haunted by the specter of logistical loss.

Reviewers and scholars frequently interpret BGE's performances through the lens of mourning, with their corpus described as "a eulogy to the industrial ethic."[85] The affect of mourning became more pronounced in their post-BGE work, such as Wilson's 1999 sculpture *A Slice of Reality.* This artwork, a one-eighth vertical cross-section of a 240-foot oceangoing sand dredger that Wilson acquired from a shipyard in the north of England, was installed on the south foreshore of the Thames in North Greenwich to mark the new millennium. Wilson refers to *Slice of Reality* as a "soundbite," implying that it speaks to something larger—both the entirety of its ship and, more expansively, of maritime history. The sculpture is, he explains, "a lament to the lost industry."[86] Positioned just behind the Richard Rogers designed O2 Arena (originally known as the Millennium Dome) and directly across from the financial district of Canary Wharf that was built atop London's docklands, *Slice of Reality* looks back in time but is also a pointed riposte to the future that has come to be.

One could do worse than apply Wilson's description of *Slice of Reality* to BGE's entire oeuvre. Beyond merely reviving materials associated with London's maritime life, BGE harnessed repertoires of extended sociality, intuitive collaboration, and joyful camaraderie that echoed the spirit of work that once animated these very same waterways. Their performances along the Thames not only salvaged the infrastructure of a bygone era but also rekindled the energy that had fueled it. From my vantage point in 2023, BGE appears to have been lamenting something more specific than a "lost industry." They mourned the loss of labor's power collectively organized but cut short by capital's logistical restructuring. Behind the shadows and through the flames of their salvage spectacles, I glimpse what Ernst Bloch called revolutionary *Ungleichzeitigkeit* (non-contemporaneity): a hauntological lament for the futures canceled by capitalism.[87] As Bloch took care to emphasize, however, attempts to resurrect an unfulfilled utopian spirit can, with some ease, slip into nostalgic longing for a closed past. I admit that, when watching BGE's performances today on video, the line between hauntology and nostalgia seems quite thin, especially because the spectacles, by design, leave little room for nuanced accounting of the histories they evoke. This includes, for instance, the checkered politics of white London dockworkers, some of whom, in the 1960s, infamously blamed immigrants for threats to their jobs, even marching in support of the xenophobic agendas of politicians like Enoch Powell.[88]

I write this some four decades after BGE's performances took place. Having never experienced them in person, I can only speculate, and hope, that memories of such racist displays would have been fresh enough at the time to temper any unchecked nostalgia, and that they would have blended with knowledge of other historical events, such as the London dock strike of 1889, a pivotal moment for the British labor movement. Writing with the Weimar Republic on his mind, Bloch insisted that hauntology and nostalgia often coexist in the same aesthetic experience, creating a brew that is both potent and perilous. That such tension courses through BGE's salvage spectacles is not grounds for dismissal, but constitutes, rather, the ambivalent truth they have to tell.

This truth includes histories not just of labor, but also of capital. Alongside the workers who built and operated Britain's canals, dockyards, and ships, BGE also revered the nineteenth-century engineers, like Thomas Telford and Isambard Brunel, who are credited with designing this early logistical infrastructure.[89] The group embraced the Industrial Revolution as a period when "invention was very romantic," when the aesthetic potential of machines was cherished rather than disavowed.[90] Steam also inspired BGE, who prized its visual and sonic properties, not to mention the machinery it powered.[91] In their performances, steam often vied with the trio themselves in generating noise, making for a cacophonous restaging of England's Luddite history. It was steam, after all, that capital adopted in the early nineteenth century to power its factories and exploit its workers. The respect BGE voiced for icons of industrial architecture and their fascination with steam might appear at odds with their lament for the decline of a particular working-class experience, in such a way that can also ring nostalgic for a history of another sort.

As the steam engine helped entrench capitalist social relations in England, the infrastructures designed by the likes of Telford and Brunel played a pivotal role in expanding British empire.[92] From its maritime application in the 1820s, the steam engine transformed the temporality of moving goods by sea, most importantly by freeing it from seasonal rhythms and weather patterns, which allowed shipping lines to provide more reliable scheduled services. Advances in ship technology combined with the growth of telegraph cables from the

1850s to enable new forms of long-distance industrial planning and coordination, setting the stage for today's supply chains. Steam power also altered the geographies of shipping, since the reliance on coal required installing coaling stations around the world. When the British East India Company and the British Admiralty converted their fleets to steam power in the 1830s and 1840s, a primary order of business was to establish, typically by force, colonial outposts where boats could refuel. This need for coal both supported imperial expansion and depended upon it. As the volume of sea cargo increased sevenfold in the half century between 1840 and 1890, Britain's dominance in steam shipping helped make it the capitalist hegemon and shipbuilder of the world. At the turn of the twentieth century, Britain commanded half of the world's merchant fleet, and as late as 1911, the empire was building 70 percent of oceangoing vessels, all at miserable expense to much of the rest of the world, particularly its colonies.[93] Far from being an unmarked material with which to perform, even steam is entangled in the histories of empire.

BGE exemplifies the astonishing things artists can do by salvaging, and logistical loss was central to their spectacles. Their performances lamented the loss of the collective labor that had powered England's maritime industry, but they also looked fondly on the aestheticized ingenuity that capital used to build the British empire. The central antinomies in the trio's body of work—hauntology and nostalgia, labor and capital—derived from and still speak to the same historical dynamic. Their salvage spectacles rightly presented the logistical restructuring of the capitalist world-system as loss, focusing on the losses experienced in Europe during the logistics revolution of the twentieth century. Logistics, at least as we know it today, was also shaped through other earlier and even greater losses. It is to these that the next two sections turn.

Out of the Wreckage

The late twentieth century's logistical restructuring that haunted Bow Gamelan Ensemble becomes a cause for celebration in the salvage spectacles of Cai Guo-Qiang. Or so it might seem at first glance. Cai is best known internationally for his gunpowder drawings, but since the 1990s, he has also developed a distinct artistic technique of maritime salvaging, the results of which shed light on the flipside to the historical decline of European empire. The wrecked fishing boat he hung in New York's PS1 gallery in 1998 is a case in point. Cai dug the vessel out from the mud of a beach near Quanzhou, a port city on the Taiwan Strait. After shipping it to New York, he pierced the large wooden boat with 3,000 arrows, their tips made of brass and fletching of goose feather. If placed in water, this wasted boat, riddled with holes and missing planks, would surely sink. Yet, hanging in a gallery and buffeted by thousands of quills, it seems to hover (Figure 9). With a small Five-Star Red Flag mounted to the stern and constantly waving in wind generated by an electric fan, this beguiling vessel appears to be a surrogate for China's economy: once stuck in the mud, the enormous ship has been refloated.

When Cai first exhibited the sculpture, titled *Borrowing Your Enemy's Arrows*, Holland Cotter singled it out in an infamous *New York Times* review for its "distinctly nationalistic, implicitly anti-Western bent."[94] Cai's title alluded to the apocryphal tale of Zhuge Liang, a third-century military strategist, who is said to have sailed an empty boat into battle as a ruse to attract enemy arrows, which he planned to reuse. Cotter did not miss the implication.

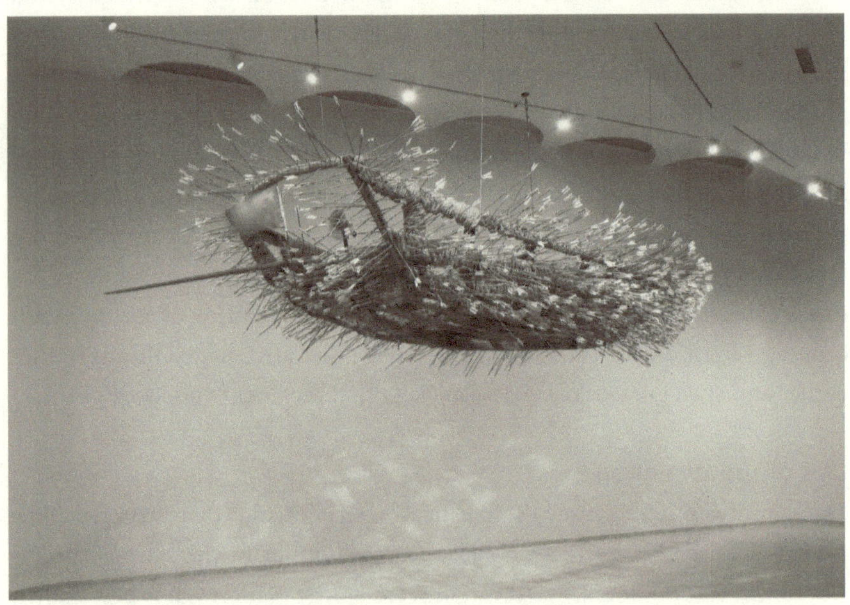

FIGURE 9. Cai Guo-Qiang's *Borrowing Your Enemy's Arrows*, installation view: *Cai Guo-Qiang: I Want to Believe*, February 22–May 28, 2008, Solomon R. Guggenheim Museum, New York. *Photo:* David Heald © Solomon R. Guggenheim Foundation, New York, courtesy Solomon R. Guggenheim Foundation and Cai Studio.

To him, Cai's sculpture exemplified the "opportunistic" approach of contemporary Chinese artists, whom he scorned for being formally derivative and dependent on existing international art markets. Cotter went so far as to hold the long-dead chairman himself responsible. Art like Cai's, he remarked, followed "Mao's famous directive to make foreign things serve China."[95] Although he claimed to be speaking only of the art world, Cotter's comments displayed all the trappings of post–Cold War Sinophobia, from the anxiety that China would leapfrog Western competitors to the older racist trope of China as a parasite. More sober reviews found "irony" in Cai's sculpture, with some suggesting it was a knowing portrait of overconfidence that lampooned nationalist pride.[96] Others preferred to see China depicted not as the upstart antagonist but as the "'passive recipient' of whatever globalisation may stand for."[97] Cai himself disputed any anti-Western bent in the sculpture, emphasizing instead that *Borrowing* exhibits "the trauma of cultural conflicts and the price you pay for opening up."[98] Like much of his work, Cai's salvaged boat became a projection screen for both decolonial sentiments and liberal views on Chinese authoritarianism.[99]

As much as *Borrowing* spoke to its present context, the boat also summoned the past. Today, Quanzhou, the site of Cai's salvage operation (and his hometown), is primarily known as a major global producer of shoes. It also holds an esteemed place in the history of global trade, thanks to Marco Polo's praise of the port city as "one of the two greatest havens in the world for commerce."[100] For Cai to raise a ship from Quanzhou seemed to symbolize China's own return to form. Three years earlier, on the 700th anniversary of Polo's homecoming to Venice, Cai made his own triumphant arrival in the city of bridges aboard a junk boat sourced from Quanzhou as part of the 1995 Venice Biennale. After floating down the Grand Canal, Cai docked at the Palazzo Giustinian Lolin and welcomed visitors on board to peruse the various herbs and medicines his boat carried. On the eve of China's emergence as the workshop of the world, *Bringing to Venice What Marco Polo Forgot* was meant by Cai to "remedy" nascent Western assumptions by reminding the world that China had more to offer than the prospect of inexpensive manufactured goods.[101]

These boats, like others salvaged by Cai, embrace ascent as much as loss, harkening back to China's previous ruinous encounters with Europe. For *The Ninth Wave*, his high-profile 2014 summer exhibition at the Power Station of

Art in Shanghai, Cai once again arrived by water, this time on a barge carrying the exhibition's centerpiece—another battered Quanzhou junk boat (Figure 10). Instead of medicinal herbs, this vessel came loaded with a bestiary of lifeless animals: ninety-nine pandas, leopards, camels, apes, and more, all slumped as if seasick or dead (they were actually made of fur-covered Styrofoam). Cai's voyage to Shanghai took five days, and as Sean Metzger has observed, he followed a merchant route that had played a prominent part in the First Opium War.[102] The performance indexed, among other things, the key event in Europe's underdevelopment of East Asia.

The "great divergence" between Europe and Asia in the nineteenth century is often attributed to the former's privileged access to American colonies, believed to have provided the continent with the necessary resources for industrial development at home and a market abroad to which to sell goods.[103] Disputing this account, others, typically Marxist historians, instead point to the early modern period when an "*already existing* decisive divergence" in

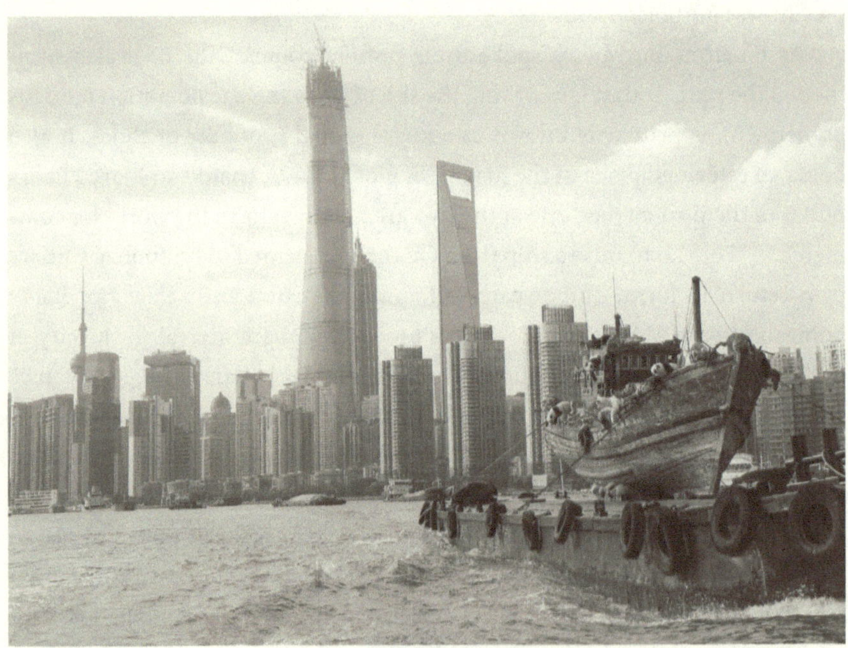

FIGURE 10. Cai Guo-Qiang's *The Ninth Wave*, sailing on the Huangpu River by the Bund, Shanghai, 2014.
Photo: Wen-You Cai, courtesy Cai Studio.

property relations, financial infrastructures, and class divides ignited Europe's imperial engine.[104] Regardless of the differences in these explanations, historians now tend to agree that East Asian development compared favorably with Europe throughout the mercantilist era. From at least the sixteenth century, when commercial capital started integrating the world economy, China boasted a domestic market that was unmatched in size and complexity. But by the early nineteenth century, Europe, led by England, had surpassed East Asia in many economic measures. Struggles between classes and among warring European states fueled both Europe's early industrialization and its imperialist expansion in the nineteenth century. These twin waves converged to flood markets in India and China with cheap goods that devastated local economies. The First Opium War, which took place from 1839 to 1842, marked a turning point as Britain's new steam-powered warships overwhelmed China's tested fleet of wooden junk boats.[105] Like its regional rival Japan, China was subordinated to European empire, then steadily underdeveloped by global capital into one of the world's poorest countries over the next century.

As Cai's barge floated along the Huangpu River into Shanghai, the ruined junk boat created an ambivalent tableau when juxtaposed with the skyscraper-filled waterfront. As with Cai's reply to Marco Polo in Venice, some have interpreted the junk boat's return to the former treaty port in triumphalist terms, for instance, as "capturing China's progression from a 'semicolonial' kingdom to a global power."[106] By repeatedly resurrecting wrecked boats, Cai seems to be registering in aesthetic form what economic historians refer to as the U-shaped "resurgence" of East Asia over the past half century.[107] However, Cai's salvaging also seems distinctly preoccupied with the ruination initiated by European empire and capital. The boats he uses are literal wrecks, the very opposite of Shanghai's gleaming Lujiazui skyline. Salvaging them is both a performance of economic ascent and a commemoration of historical loss.

Critics often associate Cai's work with the Chinese state, partly due to his numerous government secondments and commissions.[108] But his salvaged boats speak to more than China's particular political economy; they also catalogue the disparities of economic transformation across East Asia as a whole. Cai relocated to Japan in 1986, and it was here that he launched his first salvage operation. Collaborating with locals in the coastal city of Iwaki in 1994, Cai excavated a wrecked wooden fishing boat and displayed its ruined keel as *Kaikou—The Keel (Returning Light—The Dragon Bone)* at the Iwaki City Art Museum. The sculpture, with its degraded and jagged wooden planks protruding upwards, resembles a skeletal structure, not unlike a dinosaur fossil. As Cai himself has remarked, the resulting work both symbolizes and evidences Japan's divergence from China, as manifested in the differences between the two nations' maritime fleets at the time.[109]

Europe underdeveloped both Japan and China throughout the nineteenth century, but the Meiji restoration and victory over China in 1895 secured for Japan the resources, territory (including Taiwan and Korea), and Western alliances needed to jumpstart its industrial motor. As Japan pursued its regional ambitions in the early twentieth century, China endured decades of civil war and invasions. For all its ills, the US occupation following World War II helped Japan economically by, among other things, barring domestic military investment and thereby freeing the state to strategically direct resources toward manufacturing and trade. Japan emerged as the biggest winner in the postwar shipbuilding boom that was driven by demand for bulk carriers and oil tankers during European reconstruction and the Korean War.[110] Barely a decade after its defeat in World War II, Japan claimed the title of world's leading shipbuilder in the signal year of 1956. As global maritime capacity expanded and rates plummeted, international shipping experienced unprecedented growth, unmatched since. If Europe, led by England, had benefited the most from the shift from sail to steam power, East Asia, led by Japan, was the most successful in exploiting the advantages of diesel in the twentieth century. The postwar boom continued until the oil shock of the 1970s, by which time Japan was building half of the world's merchant fleet. According to Cai, the wrecked Japanese boat he used in *Kaikou* captured the country's elite economic status by highlighting the obsolescence of wooden vessels in Japan. "In my hometown," Cai commented, "we still had wooden boats."[111] The wreckage in a Japanese coastal city indicated progress, while the continued use of boats made of wood in Quanzhou confirmed the sense that China had been left behind.

To create *Kaikou*, Cai used only the keel of the boat he had recovered, reserving the remaining salvaged wood from the hull to make another work for the same 1994 exhibition. This he named *San Jō Tower*, and it consisted of three separate buildings of increasing size, each with two tiers adorned by sharp corner eaves. While *Kaikou* suggests uneven development, this second sculpture's possible meanings only congealed the following year when Cai revisited the structures for an exhibition at the Museum of Contemporary Art Tokyo. This time, he stacked the three buildings on top of one another to create a pagoda, renaming it *The Orient (San Jō Tower)*. Both the new title and new form invoked a shared, albeit essentialized regional identity. Cai returned a third time to this salvaged wood two years later at the 1997 Venice Biennale. Now called *The Dragon Has Arrived!*, he kept the pagoda intact but hung it at an angle from the ceiling.[112] To the bottom, he attached several Chinese flags, which were blown by a fan to resemble flames. The pagoda had become a rocket taking off, powered by the state itself. *The Dragon Has Arrived!* seemed to wear Chinese nationalism on its sleeve, but the use of Japanese materials and a pan-Asian form tempered the chauvinism. The ascent depicted by Cai was not China's but the region's: here was the much-touted East Asian resurgence.

The 1970s brought Japan's dominance in shipbuilding to a crossroads when the oil crisis capped the growth of supertankers, and regional rivals launched their own shipyards, with South Korean production surpassing Japan's by the end of the century. In 2006, just before the heavily financialized global shipping industry lurched into the world financial crisis, Beijing announced its goal of becoming the world's largest shipbuilder within a decade. China would accomplish this feat by dominating the market for bulk carriers, by far the largest branch of the global merchant fleet. By 2022, China was building nearly half of the world's ships. All combined, the three East Asian shipping giants now produce a remarkable 93 percent of all new vessels annually.[113] Shipbuilding, much like logistics in general, has become a strategic industry in East Asia that signifies the shift of global trade's center to the Pacific.

For an artist committed to exploring economic renaissance as a collective regional project, the timing of a work like *The Dragon Has Arrived!* was inauspicious. In 1997, the Asian financial crisis revealed the risks inherent to the government-backed, export-led growth model that had driven the late twentieth century success of the so-called flying geese formation, comprising Japan, South Korea, Taiwan, Hong Kong, and Singapore.[114] Cai's skyrocketing sculpture could have just as easily been interpreted as a harbinger of decline. To return to his 1998 review of *Borrowing*, Cotter had dismissed contemporary Chinese art as a passing trend. "'Chinese' is hot in the way 'Korean' was a few years ago," he glibly remarked.[115] Like South Korea before it, China was sure to fall back to earth. Whether he intended to or not, Cotter was drawing parallels between artistic trends and economic ones, albeit in a way that tapped into longstanding Euro-American anxieties about the perceived threat of disease and pestilence originating from East Asia. As Iyko Day notes, economic fears about East Asia being a source of "unnatural value" are heavily racialized and tend to overlap with cultural depictions of Chinese people as rats.[116] It was not a coincidence that the 1997–98 financial crisis was dubbed by Western commentators the "Asian Contagion."[117]

Cai is no stranger to such racist discourse and has confronted it directly. In 1996, he installed the massive *Cry Dragon/Cry Wolf: The Ark of Genghis Khan* at New York's Guggenheim, which knowingly prodded Western fears of invasion by creating the impression of a dragon taking flight. To achieve this effect, Cai attached 108 inflated sheepskin bags to a scaffold made of wooden sticks, sloping up from the ground as if the creature was lifting off. At the base, seemingly powering the beast, were three Toyota car engines left running during museum hours. Cai's title used the cultural imaginary around Genghis Khan as a way of combining China's mythical power and Japanese engineering into a monstrous conflation of impending conquest. The sculpture placed the latest fears around East Asia in a long history of bogeymen. Cai took pains to insist he was targeting more than those who were crying wolf about East Asia's economic rise. In his sights was also the presumption shared in East Asia "that its time of world dominance had finally arrived." As Cai himself put it, *Cry Dragon/Cry Wolf* was his way of describing such a belief as "premature, exaggerated and arrogant."[118]

Cai has revisited and thus reinforced this theme of a regional project starring Japan and China in several subsequent boats, all of them requiring collaboration between Chinese and Japanese contributors. For example, on the tenth anniversary of *Kaikou* in 2004, volunteers in Iwaki salvaged another wooden boat for Cai, which he turned into *Reflection—A Gift from Iwaki*. On display, the fifteen-meter wreck looks to be marooned on a white beach, though the sand is actually made of pieces of porcelain, remnants of broken Buddhist statues manufactured near Quanzhou. *Reflection* is both a sculpture and a kind of performance, as Cai stipulates that each time it is exhibited a small team from Iwaki must travel with him to install it.[119] More recently, in

To Build a Ship: Project for Nara Culture City of East Asia (2016), Cai enlisted a crew of Chinese and Japanese shipbuilders to construct a thirteen-meter junk boat on-site at Todai-ji Temple in Nara, Japan. Upon completion, they left the final product floating on the temple's mirror pond. A year later, in August 2017, Cai stranded this same vessel at Nijō Castle in Kyoto atop three large boulders, planting five semimature pine trees in its hull. He named it *Bonsai Ship*. Cai insists that these recent works attest to the centuries-long "mutual inheritance and influence" of "East Asian cultures." According to him, *Bonsai Ship* asks: "Can we continue sailing in this ship together?"[120] The use of a real boat as the occasion to pose this question about furthering a shared project suggests that any answer to it must be cycled through the history and future of shipbuilding. For all that Cai's boats avow collaboration, whether wryly or sincerely, this focus on Japan and China sidelines the rest of the region. Given how uneven the resurgence in East Asia has been, this seems significant but also fitting. As the economies of China and Japan have surged, inequalities among and within nearby countries, especially in Southeast Asia, have intensified.[121]

Cai's salvaged boats, thus, emphasize that losses are not just relics of the past but features of the present. *The Ninth Wave*, his grandest salvage spectacle, signaled exactly this. Tens of thousands of people flocked to see Cai's junk boat when it arrived in Shanghai. Much of the public discussion, especially among Western critics, interpreted it as a bracing reminder of the environmental costs of China's booming economy. The previous year farmers had dumped some 16,000 diseased pigs into the very same Huangpu River that Cai sailed down.[122] The lifeless animals aboard Cai's impoverished ark seemed like a reminder of this event, if not also a portent of even graver things to come, like ecological catastrophes and zoonotic diseases. Adding to the sense of foreboding was the art historical inspiration for the exhibition. *The Ninth Wave* is also the title of a popular shipwreck painting from 1850 by the Russian artist Ivan Aivazovsky, which depicts survivors desperately clinging to the mast of a destroyed clipper. Enormous whitecaps threaten them from all sides, but a ray of hope shines through in the sun rising in the background. The painting promises that rescue, if not actual Christian salvation, will come, but only with considerable loss. China's ascendance as shipbuilder of the world has added fuel to many of the fires already racing through the shipping industry, from gross pollution to its recurring crises of overcapacity.[123] During the 2010s, shipping rates dropped so low that firms controlling three quarters of the container shipping market were forced to merge or ally together to avoid the same fate of bankruptcy that befell one of the world's largest carriers, South Korea's Hanjin, in 2016.[124] While the effects of China's resurgence extend far beyond the world of logistics, Cai's work posits maritime shipping as a starting point for appraising the changes afoot.

The recent history of shipping is exceptional for its growth, but its geographies still largely map onto colonial pasts. The East Asian resurgence, far from marking a break in capitalist history, fits into the historical dynamics of the capitalist world-system. Shipping today is dominated by European and East Asian firms, while much of the Global South remains at the bottom of most value chains, relegated as sites of resource extraction and basic manufacturing, with their domestic markets overwhelmed by imported goods from abroad. Most major supply chains link wealthy economies with just a handful of other countries like Bangladesh, Indonesia, Mexico, Turkey, Vietnam, and a rotating cast in eastern Europe. Despite being home to more than half of the world, Africa, Latin America, South Asia, and Oceania are generally excluded from the core of maritime shipping. No ports from any of these regions figure in the world's top twenty, while East and Southeast Asia dominate the list. European worries that the fulcrum of the global economy has shifted from the Atlantic to the Pacific obscure how the present trade triangle connecting North America, Europe, and East Asia has emerged to allow the capitalist world-system to perpetuate the exclusionary logic of commercial capital. East Asia's gain, in other words, has come at the expense not of European empire but most everyone else.

The Work of Wrecking

With *salt.*, Selina Thompson searches for the losses that set logistics in motion. The widely acclaimed monologue, which had its Bristol premiere in 2016, chronicles Thompson's journey aboard cargo ships and airplanes as she retraced the routes of the transatlantic slave trade. After touring internationally, *salt.* was adapted for television by the BBC in 2021. Thompson was twenty-five years old when she and a filmmaker friend (unnamed in the script) boarded their first ship in Antwerp on February 12, 2016. The voyage to Ghana took three weeks, and after spending ten days in Tema, Thompson flew to Jamaica.

She stayed there to celebrate the Easter holiday and then flew to North Carolina to catch a return ship to Belgium. Two months after setting off, Thompson arrived back home in her parent's kitchen in Birmingham, England. "When I try to remember it," she writes in the script, "it is a dream."[125]

The play's sparse yet redolent set suggests just this. A table, some houseplants, a long piece of blue cloth, and three fluorescent strip lights arranged in the shape of a triangle: nothing tries to recreate where Thompson has been or how she traveled, yet each set piece accumulates meanings over the course of the performance. The triangle of lights mounted to the wall, for example, nods to the shape of Thompson's route, which approximated the triangular one sailed by European slave ships. Instead of probing the mercantilist logic of the slave trade, *salt.* tells "a story of the diaspora / A story of people swept up and scattered across the globe."[126] The play unfolds as a "critical fabulation," Saidiya Hartman's term for the writing practice of giving voice to those, like enslaved Black women, who have been silenced in the official archives of history.[127] *salt.* is a fabulation, but one realized most fully through the labor of performing. The shape of Thompson's journey lends a ritual structure to the performance, which is divided into three "points" (Europe, Africa, Jamaica) and three "sides" (the Hold, the Airport, the Atlantic). The sole performer, who takes on the role referred to in the script as the Woman, recounts the voyage while pummeling a large block of pink salt that she names "the Burden." She begins the hard work by smashing the salt into chunks using a sledgehammer. Later, she switches to a mortar and pestle to grind the smaller pieces into a powder, which she mixes with water to make a salve. The ritual concludes with the Woman holding court near the theater's exit, distributing the remaining chunks of salt to the audience as they leave. She explains that she does this so that "the task of carrying [the Burden] might be communal."[128] In *salt.*, wrecking becomes a visceral spectacle distributed into a collective project of carrying loss.

In creating the performance, Thompson added her name to the growing list of artists who have ventured aboard container ships for the purpose of making art. This practice dates back to at least 1974 when the photographer and sculptor George Levantis, in a trip organized by the Artist Placement Group, set sail on *Tokyo Bay*, which, at its launch was the world's largest container ship, with a capacity of 2,300 TEU.[129] Thompson's script also calls to mind a distinctly contemporary strand of travel writing in which authors tell of their voyages aboard container ships.[130] Thompson arranged her own passage with the help of 200 donors, though several shipping companies now offer artist residencies on their container ships. Most of these programs are intended to generate good publicity, but many of them have backfired. For example, in 2016, Hanjin collaborated with a Canadian gallery to host four artists on ships traveling from Vancouver to Shanghai. When the carrier suddenly declared bankruptcy in late August 2016, its collapse left one of these artists stranded on a Hanjin vessel as ports around the world turned away the line's fleet.[131] Consider as well the "Container Artist Residency," started in 2016 by the embattled Israeli firm ZIM. Over the past decade, ZIM has been targeted by the "Block the Boat" campaign in support of a liberated Palestine, with protestors delaying the unloading of ZIM-operated ships. Following accusations of artwashing, including from one of ZIM's own resident artists, the program has not been renewed.[132] For nearly as long as container ships have been afloat, artists have traveled on them with the intent of making art.

Most art produced aboard container ships varies only slightly in the gloss it puts on logistical infrastructure, settling somewhere between curiosity and sycophantic wonder. Within the expanding field of container ship art, *salt.* is an exception. Thompson's monologue finds a kindred spirit in the photography and film of Allan Sekula, as both artists refuse to be cowed by logistics. Unlike those who surrender to the logistical sublime by crafting exquisite portraits of monstrous things like ultra-large container ships, neither Thompson nor Sekula succumbs to the spectacle. Sekula's art provides ruthless critical context for the logistical infrastructures he meticulously documents, while Thompson is ruthless in another way, refusing to give time, let alone visual form, to such things whatsoever. Her concern in *salt.* lies not with the present shape of supply chains but with making present the irrecoverable past to which they owe their existence. Instead of trying to represent cargo ships, Thompson views them through the lens of the transatlantic slave trade.

Early in the play, when recounting the first leg of her trip to Ghana, the Woman tells of how, before stepping foot on the vessel, she was confronted by the legacy of the slave ship. When boarding, she meets the ship's blonde-haired, blue-eyed captain, whose "infantile, malice-laced bounce" reminds her of Boris Johnson. As a condition for embarking, he orders the Woman and her collaborator to sign a contract agreeing to two terms:

> One: the cargo comes first and takes precedence over everything else,
> And
> Two: at sea, the Master's word is law.
> I sign.
> The Master—[133]

Signing allows the Woman to become a passenger, but it also requires submitting to the Master and becoming comparable to or even less than cargo. This nautical title, "the Master," is a historical holdover, though not necessarily an anachronism. Regarding the slave ship master, Marcus Rediker writes: "He was the monarch of his wooden world. He possessed near-absolute authority, and he used it however he saw fit to maintain social order aboard the ship."[134] The Master on the Woman's vessel wastes no time exerting his power. He forbids the Woman and her collaborator from filming, thereby spoiling one reason for their journey. When warning the pair that "he doesn't want any trouble," he makes clear that he would relish exactly this and the chance it would give him to show who's boss. While he does not admit why he would suspect the pair might give him "any trouble," we get a strong sense of the racist projection at work when he insists, unsolicited, "That his ship is not a slave ship."[135] The shadow of the slave ship is never more evident than when the Master invites the comparison, even and especially if to deny it.

In structural design, European slave ships were largely indistinguishable from other deep-sea sailing vessels of the time. Up until the mid-eighteenth century, most of them were simply adapted for the vile purpose from existing schooners or sloops. However, slave ships did more than convey cargo; they also produced it. By transporting captured people through the Middle Passage, slave ships reduced humans to commodities of unfree labor. As Rediker and many others contend, "In producing workers for the plantation, the ship-factory also produced 'race.'"[136] Racialization, enforced by chains and guns, sheared personhood from those who were transformed into slaves.

The Woman's own legal status as a paying passenger is never in doubt during her voyage, yet anti-Blackness structures her experience throughout.

While dining with the Master and his officers early in the journey, she endures a conversation riddled with racist jokes. Later, the Master seeks her out to share his, once again unsolicited, thoughts on Africa ("he can't help himself"), which he insists is populated by "feral children." He feels it necessary to add that "racism is ancient history." The Woman likens all of this to a beating: "The shock it creates feels like [a] blow to the skull."[137] The crew prohibits her from going on deck while at sea, and when in port, the ship's doors are locked to deter stowaways. The Woman keeps more and more to her windowless cabin, devoid of natural light. She watches *Sankofa* and reads Hartman for company. But even in her cabin she cannot escape the Master, who blasts AC/DC and Led Zeppelin "loud enough to make my room shake" when he is not heard muttering racial slurs outside her door.[138] The morning they arrive in Ghana, the Woman is up at dawn, packed and ready to go, but the Master delays her departure for hours, giving no explanation. This is his last chance to control how she moves. Looking back, the Woman regrets not spitting in his face before disembarking.

Thompson does not equate the racist abuse the Woman withstands with what people captured and made into chattel faced. She is careful to describe the attacks as being "like," but not an actual "blow to the skull." Similarly, she does not conflate the Woman's cargo ship with the slave ship. Instead, *salt.* registers what Colin Dayan and Paul Gilroy have, in their own ways, called the "continuity" of the slaver with the present.[139] The Woman speaks of the past as "a lens" through which to see the present, "distorting everything, and exposing it for what it really is."[140] Rather than collapse the present into past, *salt.* layers the former onto the latter. This is accumulation, not conflation. "Time accumulates" is the refrain the Woman uses to describe her experiences throughout the voyage.[141] Whether in England, Ghana, Jamaica, an airport, or a cabin, the past and the present accumulate. Piling her cargo ship atop the slave ship yields the kind of continuity found in a palimpsest, one that refuses to fully erase what has made the present possible. "I refuse to get over what is not yet over" is the play's other allied refrain.[142]

Thompson names the time she spent on the first ship "the Hold." In seafaring terms, a hold is the generic term for a space in a ship's hull used for stowing cargo. Differently on a slave ship, however, *the hold* rendered those people stowed in it into cargo, requiring restraints like chains and barricades to do so. Just as there is no equating the Woman's ship with a slave ship, there is no mistaking her cabin for the slave ship hold. The Woman herself describes her quarters as being "no worse than the average Travelodge."[143] *salt.* emphasizes such difference not to reject comparison with the past, but to flag a continuity. Instead of rupture and erasure, this is an accumulation. The Woman remains a paying passenger throughout her voyage, but as the three-week trip unfolds, she feels increasingly *like* cargo.

The play presents the hold as a spatial technology that, not isolated to a historically specific or singular place, reduces bodies into things and severs them of personhood. The hold abstracts and subtracts, but it also produces. Christina Sharpe, following the likes of Saidiya Hartman and Édouard Glissant, refers to the hold as the "womb" that births Blackness. Be it a slave ship or a prison cell, the hold produces "blackness as abjection."[144] Writing of the Gold Coast fortresses that held captive Africans due to be transported to New World plantations, Hartman describes the hold as a supremely logistical space built "to warehouse slaves."[145] Thompson's own experience aboard a cargo ship tethers slave trade logistics to today's supply chain capitalism. Like Fred Moten and Stefano Harney, she insists that the continuity has less to do with trade routes or shipping technologies than with the persistent status of "the shipped" and "the containerized," the fact that Black people still are treated as things to be efficiently stowed and kept from escaping.[146] What logistics claims on a balance sheet as gain is experienced by those subjected to it as loss. The hold, Sharpe writes, is a space defined by "the absence of personhood."[147] An exemplary logistical space, it produces loss from the very start. "The cargo comes first, and takes precedence over everything else"—this, again, was the condition for boarding. As suggested throughout *salt.*, Thompson herself might not have become cargo, but, personhood compromised, she experienced the journey as such.

Thompson's performance of stowage places her in a sundry line of artists who have made an art out of shipping people. Many of these performance experiments, which include work by Allan Kaprow and Santiago Sierra, have involved artists conveying others. Thompson, by contrast, transported herself. This aligns her more with the likes of Joseph Beuys or Skip Arnold, the latter who, in a 1993 performance called *Freight*, shipped himself in a crate from Linz to Cologne. The differences with *salt.* are stark, not the least being Arnold's willingness to be treated like an object. Whereas Thompson endured a steady loss of personhood aboard the ship, Arnold made himself into cargo so as to, as Dominic Johnson puts it, "accentuate the personhood associated with the body of the artist."[148] Whiteness and masculinity conditioned *Freight's* particular avowal of personhood, the very opposite of what is registered in *salt.* More comparable, perhaps, is the historic case of Henry Box Brown, who in 1849 shipped himself in a crate from slavery in Virginia into freedom in Pennsylvania. Brown's incredible feat, which he would reenact in his subsequent performance career as a magician, became the way to secure his own personhood in antebellum America. Some have described Brown's deliverance through delivery as "rehears[ing] the magic of logistics," since it relied on technical and organizational advances in the postal service.[149] But Brown's success was an exception to the rule of logistics, which operates to prevent fugitivity, not foster it. When considered alongside the acts of Arnold and Brown, *salt.* provides the more accurate vision of logistics as being founded upon personhood lost.

If Thompson experienced a loss of personhood during her voyage, then both writing and performing *salt.* became her means of redress. *salt.* is a salvage operation, of the sort described by Angela Naimou as being focused on the "wreckage of legal personhood" rather than actual shipwrecks.[150] In this regard, Thompson has less in common with Bow Gamelan Ensemble or Cai Guo-Qiang than with writers Naimou discusses like Hartman and M. NourbeSe Philip who search through the debris of lives lost in the transatlantic slave trade for the purposes of fabulation. "The physicality of the slave ship," Katherine McKittrick argues, conceals and dehumanizes those stowed inside it, and yet "black subjectivity is not swallowed up by the ship itself."[151]

In her introduction to the published play text, Alexandrina Hemsley describes *salt.* as an attempt to "grieve both the documented presences and eroded absences of the slave trade."[152] This retrieval task is daunting since most of those lost remain today only as traces in the documents of slavery, if at all. Ship manifests, captain's logs, merchant ledgers, and bills of sale do not recall human lives trafficked, only humans reduced into property. "To read the archive," Hartman writes, "is to enter a mortuary, it permits one final viewing and allows for a last glimpse of persons about to disappear into the slave hold."[153] The balance sheets of slavers may record profits, but they are foremost records of loss that cannot begin to indicate the extent of what was destroyed. Yet "loss gives rise to longing," Hartman observes, specifically the desire to give an account of the lives lost.[154] The sheer lack of what remains throws up profound questions about the possibility of repair and recovery. To contend with the gaps and the scale of irredeemable loss requires acts of imagination that exceed the catalogues that licensed social death. Imagining beyond the archive is risky—and can slip into the kinds of seductive spectacles of Black suffering that saturate culture and that casually reproduce the violence done. The salvage work Hartman recommends instead seeks to elude pornotroping by admitting from the outset to the very "impossibility" of representation.[155] Hartman herself focuses on the role of writing in fabulation but insists that the "aesthetic mode" adequate to retrieving the lives lost defies genre, form, or discipline. Critical fabulation is defined principally by showing the "laboring" required in the very attempt.[156]

salt. puts such labor on full display, albeit in a more literal way than Hartman might have anticipated. Night after night the Woman smashes her salt. She works on the Burden throughout the play, but the most exhausting wrecking comes during "the Hold." After telling the story of her journey's first leg, the performer lines up eight large chunks of salt, naming each after a different force or figure on the ship. She then proceeds to smash them with a sledgehammer. The first chunk she hits stands in for herself and her collaborator. Then follows, in order, the Crew, the Officers, the Master, the Union, the Company, the States, and—the last piece—"imperialism and racism and capitalism and God knows what else."[157] Each time the Woman introduces a new chunk, she goes back to the start and smashes all that came before. This means that by the end "imperialism . . ." remains largely intact while her surrogate, having been struck eight times, is nearly pulverized. The scene replaces any crystalline vision of value chains with one of logistics as a metonymic chain of domination, each link brutally ground down by those above it. Afterwards the performer is spent, having swung the heavy tool dozens of times. She becomes the very avatar for the labor required to "tell impossible stories."[158]

Throughout *salt.* Thompson works hard to care for her audience, even providing safety goggles for them to wear as she wrecks. Thompson's concern for the eyes of those watching her literalizes a worry for the injury that can come with representations of Black suffering. Thompson has said that the question she kept returning to when devising *salt.* was how to avoid reproducing "that hurt," especially for other Black women in the audience.[159] Thompson's spectacle of wrecking leads to salvage, not rescue. When done smashing, she cleans the space, sweeping up the dust to use in libations and gathering the bits she will give to the audience after the show.

Before closing the ritual, the Woman tells of the final leg of her journey, "the Atlantic." She delivers this dreamlike section as a "eulogy for a woman who has jumped in the sea."[160] One night, unable to sleep, she decides to go up to the deck only to discover her cabin door leaking with water. When she opens it, she finds the corridor replaced by a surging sea. The Woman, we are told, has arrived at the very center of the triangle, and so she leaps into the water, plunging down to meet those who did not survive "the chasm." She descends and drowns, but her body doesn't disappear. Instead, it "becomes a dead living thing / Is reshaped and reformed by the ocean, into chunks of salt, falling like snow in the sea."[161] Salt: a mineral that dissolves but also preserves. In the depths, this woman blurs into Thompson, and both are buoyed by the voice of Thompson's grandmother who died the day she set sail. Her grandmother stands in for still greater losses, a reminder "of all it took to bring me here. Of the need to continue to live. Of how sacred it is to be a descendent of those that were never supposed to survive."[162] The final work that the Woman performs, that of distributing the salt, is one of preservation. This labor is how, as Hemsley writes, Thompson "finds language for the unspeakable."[163]

Thompson's salvage operation makes something of what has been lost without covering over the fact of this loss. Time accumulates. As with any fabulation, the task of *salt.* is not to repair, but to salvage the past and show it to be "inseparable from writing a history of present."[164] The wake of the slave ship can still be felt in *salt.* As Rediker reminds us, the slave ship was both the central "stage" for the slave trade as well as "the historic vessel for the emergence of capitalism" in the late sixteenth century.[165] The slaver was the linchpin in a system that established the capitalist world market by means of dispossession and expropriation. Today's container ship is often singled out as another such technology that revolutionized the global workings of capitalism. But the continuity between the container ship and the slave ship is often ignored. In a critique of Sekula, Sharpe observes how even the most adept critics of logistics today look past or downplay how the shipping containers circling the globe are "connected to the containerization of people" in the slave trade.[166] Thompson, again, is an exception in this regard: *salt.* welds together supply chain capitalism with the transatlantic trade in slaves. She rightly refuses "to get over what is not yet over." While *salt.* delivers a palimpsest made up of the slave ship and the container ship, Thompson does not deny us the satisfaction that comes with watching a spectacle of wrecking. Sledgehammer in hand, she makes no attempt to give new purpose to capital's logistical tools. In another world, *salt.* suggests, such things as our container ships will not be worth saving.

2 The Oil Barrel
Supply Chain Pipedreams

CAPITALIST IDEOLOGY HAS LONG PRIZED an ideal of freely flowing goods, but the reality is more Newtonian. Though touted as ensuring seamless circulation, global supply chains require all manner of blockages to guarantee that capital flows only according to particular interests. Borders, laws, militarization, and policing could all be mistaken as supply chain obstacles, but are, rather, the rubber to the road of international trade. "Friction," Anna Lowenhaupt Tsing writes, "is required to keep global power in motion."[1] Accidents and labor disputes can generate friction, but so can governments and corporations. For instance, oil firms regularly "sabotage" production, stockpile inventory, and reroute tankers to bolster profits.[2] Having long since taken the lead in harnessing friction to its advantage, the oil industry also wrote the book on how to combat barriers to accumulation, especially those that take the form of striking workers or communities protesting polluting pipelines. This chapter explores the many frictions that surround logistical flow by focusing on the history of the oil barrel and its peculiar journey to becoming a ubiquitous object in art.

Welded into sculptures, played as musical instruments, or left to their own ready-made devices, the number of ways that artists have devised to make art from oil barrels is nothing short of astonishing. No one has done more to barrels than Roman Signer. Over four decades, the Swiss artist has rolled them, stacked them, punctured them, worn them, blown them up, and even stood inside them as they were buried in gravel. On why he has devoted so much of his career to such pursuits, Signer has glibly remarked: "I like working with barrels."[3] His technique seems to speak for itself, registering what it also requires: a massive supply of oil barrels. Like all of the pipes, drilling rigs, gasometers, and power plants that artists have repurposed to create and display art, Signer's oeuvre is a testament to the proliferation of fossil fuel infrastructure. But we do not need art to teach us that the consumption of fossil fuels—and with it, the tools for extracting, storing, and moving them—has expanded exponentially over the past century. What else does the accumulation of oil barrels in art since the 1950s have to tell us?

To begin answering this question, let us consider another artwork: Steve McQueen's Turner Prize–winning video installation *Drumroll* (1998), which records the artist rolling an oil barrel through midtown Manhattan for precisely twenty-two minutes and one second. McQueen's oil barrel never makes a visual appearance in *Drumroll.* This is because the filmmaker used it as a camera mount, with two cameras filming through holes in either end and a third through a hole in its side. When exhibited in galleries, the footage is projected onto a triptych of screens, each displaying the barrel's voyage from a different perspective. The resulting installation delivers a relentless visual tumble of skyscrapers, concrete, cars, and feet, accompanied by a cacophonous soundtrack that fuses city noise with the metallic rumbling of the rolling barrel (McQueen has teasingly called the work a "musical").[4] In *Drumroll*, the oil barrel is not an object of representation but rather functions as an instrument for creating and recording friction as a factor of flow. It is, as Michael Newman puts it, "a work that records its own construction."[5] With each revolution of the barrel, McQueen in a bright pink coat briefly flashes up on screen, and throughout the journey, we hear him apologizing to passersby as he pushes his barrel along. These fleeting glimpses of the artist at work could be an allegory for the human labor, often obscured, required to make things flow. But any interpretation of *Drumroll* cannot disregard the context of the film's production, specifically the significance of a Black man publicly performing such an attention-grabbing but seemingly pointless task in Rudy Giuliani's New York during the era of "broken windows" policing.[6] *Drumroll* can be considered a companion piece to Pope.L.'s contemporaneous performance crawls through this very same city, with both artists drawing attention to the fact that the labor of moving is constantly under threat due to racialized projections and their concomitant violence. What might initially seem like a formalist play with found materials in *Drumroll* is also a lived metaphor for the racist regimes that dictate and differentiate the conditions for how freely goods and people can move.

Here, comparing McQueen's singular film to Signer's performance repertoire becomes illuminating, suggesting that the proliferation of art made from oil barrels signifies something specific about the unruly human materiality, call it friction, needed to ensure flow. Oil barrels facilitate the flow of petroleum across the planet, helping to fuel the circuit of capital. However, they can only do so by consolidating a liquid into a cumbersome steel form that must be handled in order to move. Where there is flow in supply chain capitalism, so the oil barrel tells us, friction is not far away.

Global capital is often said to aspire to continuous flow, shunning delays, accidents, negligence, and, above all, sabotage. According to the Organisation for Economic Co-operation and Development (OECD), maritime trade must be kept "as frictionless as possible" or else risk jeopardizing the entire global economy. To this end, the World Bank now maintains a "Logistics Performance Index" that ranks nations based on the reliability of their shipping infrastructures.[7] Fears of disruption are used to justify varied kinds of technocratic and militaristic preemptive measures to ensure infrastructural resilience and enhance supply chain security. Meanwhile, the belief that flow is something "unremittingly positive" extends beyond the realm of trade, permeating political thought and culture. As scholars like Tim Cresswell have chronicled, the fall of the Iron Curtain unleashed a fantasy of frictionless motion as a panacea for social ills.[8] From money and people to ideas and art, everything is assumed to be better off when it can move without encumbrance. Even many of capitalism's professed critics have nurtured the myth that capitalism not only desires continuous flow but has come close to achieving it.[9] I am writing this in the aftermath of disruptions to global trade caused by COVID-19, a time when self-proclaimed supply chain "thought leaders" are preaching that unimpeded flow is a natural logistical state that must be reinstated for life to return to normal.[10]

Today, flow is typically understood as friction's opposite, yet both concepts entered the world of logistics twinned together. For example, in Jay Wright Forrester's influential 1961 book *Industrial Dynamics*, flow served as a framework for comprehending how the discrete domains of production and distribution work together as a unified system, requiring constant adjustments, calibrations, and even deliberate stoppages. Before "continuous flow" gained fame as the central tenet of "just-in-time" manufacturing and its goal of "zero inventory,"[11] Forrester introduced it as a heuristic for judging how a lack of friction, taking form as an unregulated movement of goods, could result in a mismatch between procurement and demand, generating a disruptive bullwhip effect that cascaded blockage disastrously through the "supply pipeline."[12]

As Forrester's terminology suggests, logisticians have long tapped the oil industry for their systems-oriented metaphors of flow. In the 1950s, entities as various as the Office of Naval Research and shipping magnate Aristotle Onassis regarded big oil as a "model" for implementing new transport technologies aimed at reducing circulation costs.[13] The tanker, as Allan Sekula and Laleh Khalili have both critically observed, inspired capitalism's "dream of a fluid world of wealth without workers."[14] But it was the pipeline that ultimately provided the template for automating logistics work. In the 1960s, engineers and management theorists explored myriad ways of adopting pipeline principles to move solids, trialing such things as slurry pipes for conveying wood chips and iron ore.[15] When called upon in 1967 to assess the extent to which shipping containers could make transporting bulkier things like refrigerators or tomatoes less "labour intensive," McKinsey & Company measured the merits of containerization against those of the oil pipeline.[16]

That the pipeline provided the model for a labor-saving circulation technology during the logistics revolution reflects the original purpose behind its invention a century earlier. Modern pipelines were first installed in the oil fields of Pennsylvania in the late 1800s to curb the high labor costs associated with transporting oil in barrels. This early weapon in capital's protracted war on logistics work sought to take advantage of the liquid properties belonging to oil that the solid barrel undid. The barrel has long been an emblem of unwanted friction for capitalism, existing as a surrogate for both human labor and, as described by Timothy Mitchell, "the ability of humans to interrupt the flow of energy."[17] Drawing on the long history of technical fixes that capital has invented to do battle with transport workers, I argue that artworks made from oil barrels are a reminder of the intractable friction that constantly threatens the supply chain pipedream of a world without human labor.

If the last chapter traced the origins of logistics to the losses generated by European empire and the slave trade, this one explores the dynamics of extraction that fueled the imagination and infrastructure building of the logistics revolution. As the logistical dream of pipelines flourished in the postwar period, the art world became inundated with oil barrels, from the found objects repurposed by artists in North America, Europe, and Japan to the steel drums played by Trinidadian musicians. Much of this chapter examines how the barrel's ubiquity among prominent neo-avant-garde artists like Christo, Jeanne-Claude, and Allan Kaprow emphasized the superfluity and meaninglessness of logistics work, which, in effect, seconded the beliefs of transport executives and managers who viewed such labor as a drag on profits. The latter half of the chapter moves to the oil fields of Algeria, Nigeria, and Indonesia to consider several artists whose work with oil barrels divulge how deeply the logistical ideal of flow is tangled up in the friction-filled histories of European empire. By harnessing blockage as an opportunity for producing art, Lydia Ourahmane, Sokari Douglas Camp, Victor Ehikhamenor, and Zina Saro-Wiwa, each in their own way, provide an aesthetic vision of the forms that extractive solidarity might take.

The Logistical Commodity

Oil is the quintessential logistical commodity. No other good requires more attention to its handling, and none is as pivotal to global trade. With some 100 million barrels worth consumed each day, oil is the most trafficked commodity in the world, accounting for one third of all international cargo, 60 percent of which moves by sea.[18] Said to be the "emblem" of capital's "transnational flows," oil also, quite literally, fuels them.[19] Oil is often presumed to be a gift of nature, but there is nothing natural about either its usefulness or its exchangeability. Instead, oil's commodity status owes entirely to the capital investment and social relations that govern its extraction, storage, and transport.[20] As a liquid, its logistical needs are particularly pronounced since oil must be contained immediately after being extracted. And given that many of its biggest consumers (including countries in western Europe and East Asia) lack domestic reserves, oil typically must travel long distances just to be used. The mid-twentieth-century energy transition from coal to oil required huge capital investment in infrastructure like pipelines and tankers to reduce the cost of circulating oil.[21] If any commodity attests to the significance of circulation in global production today, it is oil.

The ease with which oil can be moved is one quality that makes it such a useful commodity. Unlike the flows of wind or water, oil exists as a stock energy form that capital can tap into as and when required. Another hydrocarbon, coal, fueled the Industrial Revolution, though not necessarily because it was cheaper or more powerful than other available energy sources at the start, but because its transportability suited the needs of nascent industrial workplaces. A factory powered by a coal-burning steam engine was not bound to a coal mine in the way a water mill was to a river. As Andreas Malm has shown, this flexibility allowed such factories to be located wherever labor was abundant and pliant, such as in the bustling cities of nineteenth-century England that were teeming with newly proletarianized masses.[22] Coal liberated capitalists from the locational scarcity of labor, and, aided by continued technical innovations, provided a reliable and consistent source of energy.

The qualities that made coal logistically useful to capital only intensified with oil. Yet, from the outset of its extraction in 1860s North America, oil's liquid nature proved to be both "a blessing and curse."[23] Pumping petroleum has always required considerably less work compared to mining coal, but the labor saved during extraction is more than compensated for by what's needed for transportation and storage. As one early observer in Pennsylvania's oil fields lamented, "It was easy enough to produce oil, but far more difficult to convey it to the consumer."[24] Prospectors who struck black gold in Titusville in 1859 resorted to buckets, bathtubs, rags, whiskey barrels, and anything else they could find to collect the oil gushing from the wells. Oil may have been plentiful, but containers for storing it were not. In a pattern that would repeat in early oil fields across the world from Ontario to Baku, demand for barrel-sized containers in Pennsylvania surged. Small cooperages morphed into industrial operations overnight, and barrel recycling became big business. In 1859, new barrels could be bought for fifty cents, but just three years later, their price had skyrocketed to three dollars, making the containers more dear than their contents. Rivaling the expense of the barrels themselves was the cost of transporting them the short distance from the wells to the railroads. Around six thousand teamsters flocked to Pennsylvania in the 1860s to perform this difficult work, and the high rates they charged for moving barrels by horse-drawn carriage along muddy roads ignited the capitalist desire to curtail the power of transport workers.[25]

As capitalist oil producers vied for access to storage and transport infrastructure during the so-called Oil War of the 1860s and 1870s, they were also engaged in an even more consequential campaign against transport workers. In the 1860s, teamsters greeted the arrival of wooden pipelines to Titusville by setting them on fire and tearing them from the ground. Armed patrols and private detectives hired by oil producers cracked down on workers with force, leaving several dead and many more injured. Despite worker militancy, within just a few years, new iron pipelines were connected to most wells in the region. As Christopher F. Jones notes, this early battle taught oilmen a "valuable lesson"—instead of negotiating with transport workers "it was easier to replace them with technology."[26] A decade later in Baku, soaring transport costs combined with a barrel shortage to launch the world's first full-fledged tankers on the Caspian Sea.[27] Businesses would return to this early playbook during the logistics revolution when they were confronted with an uptick in worker revolt in ports, on ships, and along railways. The supply chain pipedream has always aimed, as Charmaine Chua puts it, "to engineer flow out of recalcitrant labor."[28] As we shall see in the next chapter, in the 1950s and 1960s, capital would once again turn to the oil industry for inspiration and material support, as containerization became a pipeline-like method to discipline and replace transport workers through an infrastructure powered by diesel.

The planetary spread of pipelines and the growth of tankers in the twentieth century did not spell the end of the oil barrel. As oil consumption increased globally, the barrel increasingly came into its own. Defined as a watertight container technology that is distinct from and larger than jars or pots, the barrel has a history that spans millennia, but it was only in the early 1900s that the barrel's leaky wooden form was replaced with steel.[29] Although barrel sizes can vary, today's cylindrical drum typically stands a meter tall and can hold a liquid volume of fifty-five gallons, just short of what a pair of workers can feasibly carry or roll.[30] In 2019, the United States manufactured 24 million new barrels while reconditioning an additional 25 million[31]—a century ago, the total number of oil barrels manufactured annually was only 2 million.[32] Over the next decade, the global barrel market is expected to double in value, due largely to increasing oil demand in East Asia.[33] Despite claims that the barrel, now also a unit of financialized exchange, has become "a concept rather than a physical thing," there are more actual barrels in existence today than ever before, used to contain all manner of liquids, from fruit juice to chemicals.[34]

For some, there is no better "evidence" of the oil barrel's "looming obsolescence" than the fact that it has "found new lives in the art world."[35] But artists have been salvaging barrels to make art for at least eighty years. If anything, the prevalence of oil barrels in the art world is proof of what Malm calls the growing "fossil technomass" of capitalism. Fossil fuel consumption leaves behind not only pollution but also a vast outlay of infrastructure: pipelines and tankers, railroads and highways, oil rigs and, yes, barrels. Because this accumulating physical mass of stuff cannot simply be flushed away, much of it gets "incorporated" back into society in new ways.[36] This partly explains why such monstrous things as power plants, gasometers, and drilling platforms are now so often fashionably repurposed into museums and temporary exhibition spaces: they are readily available. Even art that repurposes the fossil technomass to shed light on its adverse effects belongs to this infrastructure's extended lifecycle.[37]

Any confidence one might have that art derived from the fossil fuel infrastructure possesses a special ability to disrupt society's "energy unconscious" must be tempered by the fact that most depictions of our petroculture tend to normalize oil rather than render it strange.[38] Consider the numerous road novels and road films that treat the lifestyle built around the automobile as second nature. Or take Ed Ruscha's influential 1963 book of photographs, *Twentysix Gasoline Stations*, in which avant-garde seriality redounds into positivist realism, transforming the gas station into a natural feature of our social landscape. Even some of the most ardent proponents of "a critical petro-aesthetic"[39] suggest that there is something inherent in oil's biophysics that makes it "difficult to demystify."[40] Concerns regarding the aesthetic challenges of representing oil date back at least a century. In 1929, while struggling to produce a play about an oil company, Bertolt Brecht declared in frustration: "Petroleum balks at the five-act form."[41] Key figures in Energy Studies have cited Brecht's quote to validate claims that "oil resists aesthetic form," while disregarding the fact that the problem Brecht was addressing had nothing to do with the unrepresentability of oil itself. Instead, the communist playwright and director was highlighting the inadequacies of a particular aesthetic form—dialogue-driven bourgeois drama—for capturing the complexities of the oil industry.[42] Remarkable examples of a critical petro-aesthetic abound, from Phel Steinmetz's 1973 reimagining of Ruscha's project to the institutional interventions of activist groups like Liberate Tate. Even contemporary playwrights such as Ella Hickson and Lucy Prebble have embraced Brecht's maxim as a call to devise new dramatic forms suited to the intricacies of big oil.[43] Nevertheless, we remain habituated to a world built by and run on oil, not because of too little representation but rather too much. More often than not, art that engages with oil and its infrastructure reinforces the fetishistic and magical qualities that attach to fossil fuels.[44]

While artists certainly have had a hand in shaping our petroculture, the primary responsibility lies with the oil industry itself. During World War II, huge amounts of capital were invested in expanding the global oil infrastructure, much of which was directed by the US government. Making good on this wartime investment required promoting domestic oil consumption across the capitalist core once hostilities had ended. Oil powered the postwar manufacturing boom, and extraction increased sevenfold by 1973.[45] To illustrate the magnitude of this change, consider that Japan in 1970 imported 99 percent of its energy, with 77 percent of that being oil, up from just 2 percent at the war's end.[46] Meeting the growing demand for oil meant sinking even more capital into extraction and circulation, totaling at least $215 billion between 1955 and 1970.[47] This created a self-reinforcing system where expanded infrastructure prompted expanded use, thus prompting further capital investment. All manner of petroleum-derived products began flooding the capitalist core after the war, ranging from automobiles to plastics. The oil industry, meanwhile, worked tirelessly to advertise its newfound significance to everyday life. Billboards and television specials saturated 1950s America, constantly reminding people of how intricately their lives had become dependent on oil.[48]

One of the most astounding tools in this industry-engineered indoctrination was a ten-minute lecture performance called *The Magic Barrel*, created by DuPont in 1953. In it, a suited host showcased a wide array of products made from petroleum, pulling items such as camera film, latex, and mylar from a fifty-five-gallon barrel, much like a magician would produce a rabbit from a hat. DuPont described the routine in its corporate magazine as an attempt to "familiarize people with the wonder world of petrochemistry," and the company invested heavily in this effort, even training 600 of its employees to deliver the performance.[49] In its first year, 150 magic barrels were used to perform the act for 300,000 people at luncheon clubs, chambers of commerce, and schools (including 230 high schools in New York). Millions more people would encounter *The Magic Barrel* either through live performances or television and radio broadcasts over subsequent years. Domestic success in the United States led to an international tour covering Greece, the Arabian Peninsula, and Japan, supported by the United States Department of Commerce. The show was still on the road in the 1970s when it arrived in Lagos during the Nigerian oil rush.[50] Wherever petroleum-derived commodities flowed in the decades after World War II, advertising followed to help oil secure a foothold in everyday life.

As DuPont's enchanted drum acclimated audiences to oil, other barrels also began circulating in culture, serving as reminders of how deeply intertwined this newly logistical world was with empire. Consider, for example, one of the first steel drum performances in England. On the afternoon of July 26, 1951, a group of eleven musicians from Trinidad arrived at London's South Bank Exhibition Grounds, having been invited to perform at the Festival of Great Britain. As the Trinidad All-Steel Percussion Orchestra (TASPO) set up its rusty assemblage of oil drums, several passersby jeered at the sight. However, they fell silent when the band began playing the melodious "Mambo Jambo." Archival footage reveals the predominately white crowd visibly astonished, with some even going so far as to search for hidden transmitters or instruments, disbelieving that such music could emanate from TASPO's oil barrels.[51]

As the likes of C. L. R. James and Stuart Hall have argued, early steel drum performances like this belong to a long tradition of "ritualised popular resistance" to British empire, dating back to the nineteenth century carnival practice of Afro-Trinidadian drumming, celebrations that white colonial elites frequently tried to suppress by sending in police or banning popular instruments.[52] The steel drum is believed to have emerged in late 1930s Trinidad, replacing horns that had been restricted following the 1937 Butler oil field strikes. Boosted in part by the 1950s calypso craze, the steel drum would become Trinidad's instrument of postcolonial nation building, with its image emblazoned on national coins after independence in 1962.

While inextricably tied to decolonization and postcolonial retrenchment, the steel drum's existence also underscores oil's status as a logistical commodity. Although steel drums today are typically purpose-built from sheet metal, in 1950s Trinidad, they were fashioned from used oil barrels. After a barrel was cleaned over an open fire and trimmed to achieve the desired tessitura, its lid would be meticulously tuned using a hammer and chisel.[53] To quote the Trinidadian novelist Earl Lovelace, the steel drum represents "the part of the oil" that Trinidadians received, not the wealth but the "rubbish."[54] As Paul Gilroy emphasizes, one must remember that the instrument originated "in the oil drums of the Standard Oil Company rather than the mysterious knowledge of ancient African griots."[55] Trinidad's oil reserves were known to the island's earliest colonizers, with Spanish settlers naming the island *Tierra de Brea*, meaning "land of tar." The world's first oil drill was installed on Trinidad in 1859, though the requisite investment for industrial extraction only arrived in the 1920s, following the decline of Trinidad's sugar and cocoa industries and the British Navy's transition to diesel. Within a decade, the island was supplying 40 percent of the British empire's oil. Drilling brought jobs to Trinidad, but the oil fields also became the setting for the 1937 uprising of Afro- and Indo-Trinidadian workers that marked a turning point in anti-colonial struggle throughout the Caribbean.[56] As many believe, it was during these strikes that the first steel drum was forged.

TASPO and other steel drum bands were not the only ones to draw sound from oil barrels during the 1950s. In Japan, for instance, the sound artists Group Ongaku developed a method of collective improvisation using any available objects, including barrels. While Group Ongaku is heralded today for upturning conventional notions of "'legitimate' materials," the same recognition is not extended to Trinidadian steel drum bands, who are typically overlooked in histories of experimental music.[57] One reason for this owes to the instrument's place in popular culture, but, as Nathaniel Mackey argues, it also has to do with the intersection of class with anti-Blackness. "Just think about the Caribbean," he says:

> What are you doing when you take discarded oil barrels and turn them into percussive-melodic instruments, steel band, pan? What are you doing if that's not an experiment? That instrument wasn't there before you started working with it. But you won't see steel band music in any histories of experimental music because the people who carried out that experiment—successfully!—had the wrong paint job and are located in the wrong place.[58]

Group Ongaku's presence in a former imperial hegemon that had transformed into a thriving capitalist ally of the United States facilitated the group's reputation as a sound art pioneer, a path unavailable to Afro-Trinidadian oil field workers.

One noteworthy exception in the steel drum's exclusion from histories of avant-garde experimentation is the time when Marcel Broodthaers incorporated an entire band into an artwork. One day in 1964, while walking through a park in Brussels, the Belgian artist happened upon a busking steel drum band. Recognizing in their instruments an appropriative logic similar to his own, Broodthaers (reportedly with their permission) began arranging various found materials, such as an umbrella and a helmet, around the ensemble. Once finished, he invited friends to come and view the impromptu installation. Broodthaers had appropriated an appropriation, and in doing so, he objectified the performers as found material, with credit for the experimentation going entirely to him. Thus, the steel drum entered the annals of avant-garde art solely through the act of a white Belgian artist who treated the musicians like any other "performance props."[59] I will revisit the connection between the circulation of oil barrels in the art world and histories of imperial extraction later in this chapter. But first, I need to further chart the accumulation of barrels in the art world during the logistics revolution.

Inventory Management

As Trinidadian musicians were forging oil barrels into musical instruments, artists in western Europe, North America, and Japan also began to create art from them, though typically by treating them as found materials open to repurposing. No single artist has used more oil barrels than Christo Javacheff (better known today as Christo). After settling in France in March 1958, the Bulgarian émigré made ends meet by painting portraits for wealthy Parisian women while spending his free time wrapping found objects in fabric. He started with paint cans and glass bottles, before moving onto larger items like chairs, tables, and, eventually, oil barrels. Some have described this early project as a Soviet Bloc exile's systematic study of western European commodity culture, but Christo's technique was largely pragmatic.[60] Unable to afford materials like clay or steel, the aspiring sculptor used whatever he could acquire on the cheap or for free. He covered his objects in resin-soaked canvas, binding them with twine, and then coated it all using a mix of finishes, like varnish, glue, sand, and lacquer. Once dry, the hardened fabric, obscuring the found object, made for something sculptural. While at work on his *Wrapped Objects*, Christo also began binding items in fabric or polyethylene, which he left untreated and tied off with elaborate knots. He called this series *Packages*.

As Christo experimented with making artful packages, the packaging industry was coming into its own. Although the concept of a package, defined as a bundle of things labeled and prepared for sale or transport, is not new, *packaging* only emerged as a distinct industrial process in the late nineteenth century when people became increasingly reliant on manufactured goods produced at considerable distance from where they were consumed. New transport infrastructures, such as railroads and steamships, combined with novel packaging technologies like canning (1810) and folding cartons (1879) to lay the ground for a series of revolutions in packaging.[61] Different from containers of bulk goods that are kept out of sight, industrialized packaging is typically designed with display in mind, often incorporating information or advertising. Initially used to protect finished items as they were brought to market, packaging also increasingly served as a means of generating the trust needed to convince consumers to purchase products made by people they would never meet. As commodity production, fueled by the energy transition to oil, boomed after World War II, packaging assumed unprecedented significance.

Many artists explored this newly packaged world, perhaps none more famously than Andy Warhol, who, before gaining renown for his paintings of Campbell's soup cans and sculptures of Brillo boxes, had worked in advertising. Among the things that distinguished Christo from Warhol was the former's distinct lack of interest in the aesthetics of branding. If Warhol's art could be said to have spotlighted the advertising work of packaging, Christo did the same for the manual labor that packaging demands. This included not only wrapping and tying things but also moving and storing them—work he put on full display when making art with oil barrels. Moving a barrel requires considerable effort. After finding one, typically in a scrap heap, Christo would haul the heavy object all the way up to his seventh-floor studio, where he would clean and bind it with wire and fabric. He would then carry the newly packaged barrel across town some two kilometers to store it in a cellar owned by the parents of his partner and future collaborator, Jeanne-Claude de Guillebon.[62] Over time, Christo began referring to this growing accumulation of wrapped and stowed items as *Inventory* (Figure 11). His project had an extremely small audience, and today, memories of it primarily exist in photographs that show his makeshift installation as nearly indistinguishable from an actual storeroom. In *Inventory*, storage work became art work.

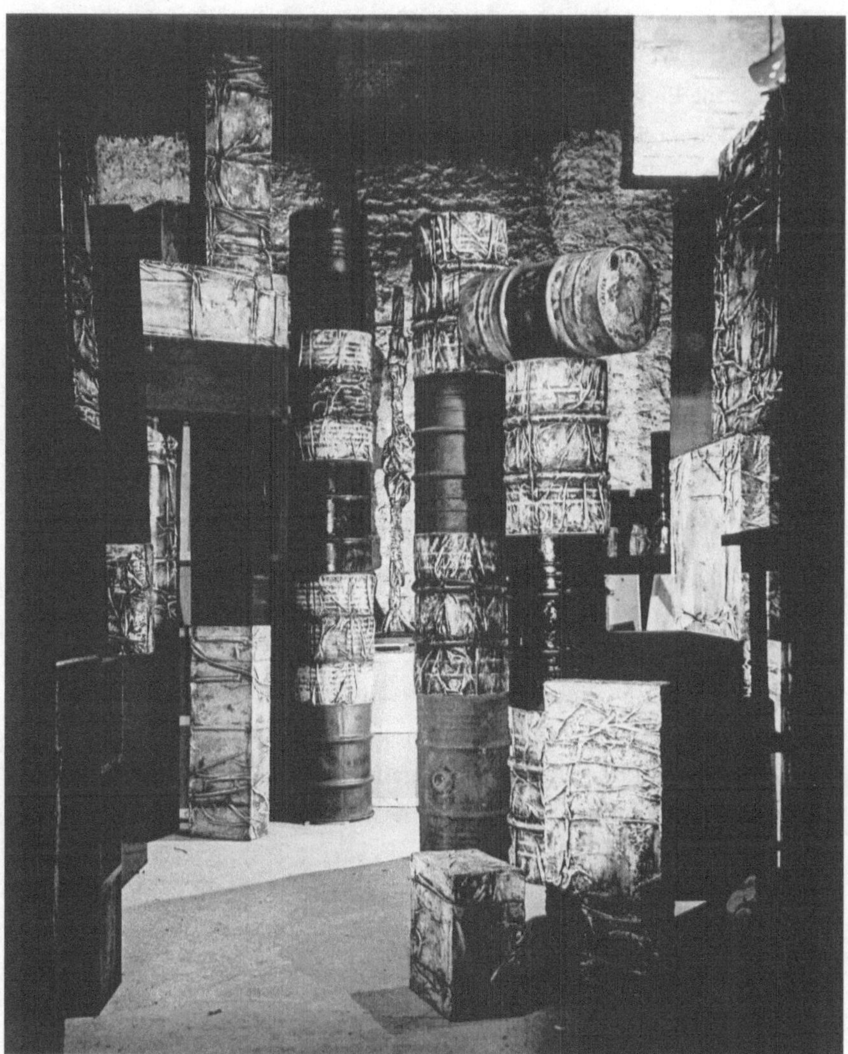

FIGURE 11. Partial view of *Inventory* in Christo's storeroom in the cellar of Jeanne-Claude's mother's apartment at 4, avenue Raymond Poincaré, Paris, 1960. *Photo:* René Bertholo © Christo and Jeanne-Claude Foundation. Reprinted with permission.

Christo began *Inventory* at the same time that capitalist firms were re-evaluating their techniques of inventory management. As Thomas Hine puts it, packaging "links production and consumption," and reforming this process enabled broader shifts in the retail sector that were essential to the logistics revolution.[63] Due in part to early advances in packaging, the concept of self-service retailing rapidly gained traction in core capitalist countries following World War II.[64] As outlined in a 1917 US patent credited to the founder of the Piggly Wiggly retail chain, the layout of the self-service store, with its aisles of open shelving, was derived more from warehouses than traditional grocers. This design placed the responsibility on customers to locate products for themselves. "The self-service model," Jesse LeCavalier explains, "made inventory into display and systematized browsing to ensure that customers would pass by every item that was available. It required customers to absorb new labor roles."[65] By pushing the work of pulling stock onto customers and that of promotion onto advertisers, self-service retail reduced the need for both salesclerks and physical space, suiting the corporate desire to cut handling costs as the postwar economic booms in North America, western Europe, and Japan started to falter.

Self-service retailing revolutionized the shopping experience, but it also contributed to a sea change in inventory management, culminating in the 1970s when barcodes and computing technology further blurred the lines between warehousing and retail. As discussed in the Introduction, mega-retailers like Walmart utilized these information technologies to synchronize production planning with customer demand, thereby streamlining supply pipelines and gaining leverage against manufacturers. New inventory management methods also impacted how factories were organized, no more so than in the just-in-time (JIT) manufacturing system adopted by Japanese carmakers, which promised to abolish fixed stock altogether as a way to reduce costs associated with logistics labor, warehouse space, and unused parts and products.[66] Instead of pushing goods through a supply pipeline, firms shifted to a pull model, where stock was replenished as needed for assembly or demanded by customers. Whether in retail or production, lean inventory management models elevated the ideal of continuous flow into a shibboleth of the logistics revolution. However, the priority given to flow was not necessarily a rupture with past ways of doing things. Toyota, for example, is often erroneously described as "post-Fordist," even though the designer of the Toyota Production System contended that JIT fulfilled the "true intention" of Henry Ford's constantly moving assembly line.[67] Yet, this ideal of inventory flow dates back even further, at least to the nineteenth century when capital investment transformed the storehouse into the modern warehouse, shifting the objective of stowing goods from preservation to exchange.[68] Capitalist warehouses anticipated the modern logistical appetite for continuous flow, acting not merely as depots but as "circulation reservoirs" that were constantly depleted and restocked. Karl Marx likened a warehouse to a busy train station, describing it as "always full, but always full of different travelers."[69] Delays were but drags on profitability.

When interpreted in the context of the logistics revolution, Christo's technique in *Inventory* is revealed to be less about producing readymade art objects and more about inventory management. The act of moving and storing items became even more prominent in his repertoire of artistic production when, in addition to packaging barrels, he started stacking them temporarily for photographs. In the early 1960s, Christo started to use a garage in the southern Paris suburb of Gentilly as a studio, which gave him more space to warehouse his expanding inventory and easier access to outdoor areas for stacking and photographing barrels. This garage also had the added advantage of neighboring an oil barrel yard, bringing Christo's practice even closer to storage work. Photographs from 1961 and 1962 show him stacking barrels one on top of another to build columns several meters high. Scholars often associate these early projects with the readymades of Nouveau Réalisme, a kinship that Christo himself disputed on the grounds of his logistical technique. Instead of creating art by presenting things as they were, Christo, in his own words, was "wrapping" and "arranging too much" to rank among Nouveaux Réalistes like Yves Klein and César: "My work was not ready-made enough."[70] His ephemeral oil barrel sculptures resembled performances more than readymades, characterized as they were by the labor of moving, stacking, flipping, and stowing.

Christo exhibited very little of this art, and he sold even less of it; in fact, most of *Inventory* ended up being discarded by his Gentilly landlord. While the readymade, as John Roberts argues, transforms an existing commodity into an art object "to expose the necessary labour which makes artistic labour possible," Christo's early oil barrel performances, instead, brought attention to the logistical labor required to circulate capitalist commodities.[71] Rather than following the readymade technique of removing a commodity from the sphere of industrial production, Christo made an art out of physically moving things. Although performed during a time when businesses were starting to search for ways to shift the costs of inventory management off their balance sheets, Christo's technique should not be remembered as a heroic avowal of logistics labor, let alone a craftsperson's critique of "streamlined industrial packaging," as some would have it.[72] Instead, *Inventory* put the wastefulness of inventory on full display: the knots on his wrapped packages were always too many; paint cans and bottles, themselves already packages, did not need to be wrapped. Making an art out of inventory management implied that activities like stacking or stowing need not be counted as productive labor as such but could be classified among the most useless of social activities: art. Christo's artistic embrace of logistical labor was, as we shall see, largely a means of devaluing it.

Christo placed logistical work under an even brighter spotlight with his first solo show in August 1961 at Cologne's Haro Lauhus Gallery. He filled the venue to capacity with towering columns of barrels and dozens of wrapped objects that ranged from cans and a typewriter to pianos and even a car. While Christo compared the cluttered venue to "a place where a mover had come," a more apt description came from one reviewer who called it "a warehouse or a junk shop."[73] While showcasing his art of inventory management within the gallery, outside Christo and his partner Jeanne-Claude embarked on a new project, and their first together. The recently opened Haro Lauhus Gallery was situated near the docks on the Rhine River, where the pair stumbled upon a stock of familiar supplies, including oil barrels, rolls of industrial paper, and tarpaulin. After negotiating with the port director, Christo and Jeanne-Claude hired a crew of longshoremen to create sculptures from this found material using cranes and other waterfront tools. The dockworkers covered several mounds of paper rolls with ropes and tarps, fashioning mammoth versions of Christo's wrapped packages. They also built an enormous flat-topped pyramid with dozens of barrels stacked on their sides. Like many of Christo's other sculptures, *Dockside Packages* and *Stacked Oil Barrels* were temporary installations, disassembled two weeks later (Figure 12).[74]

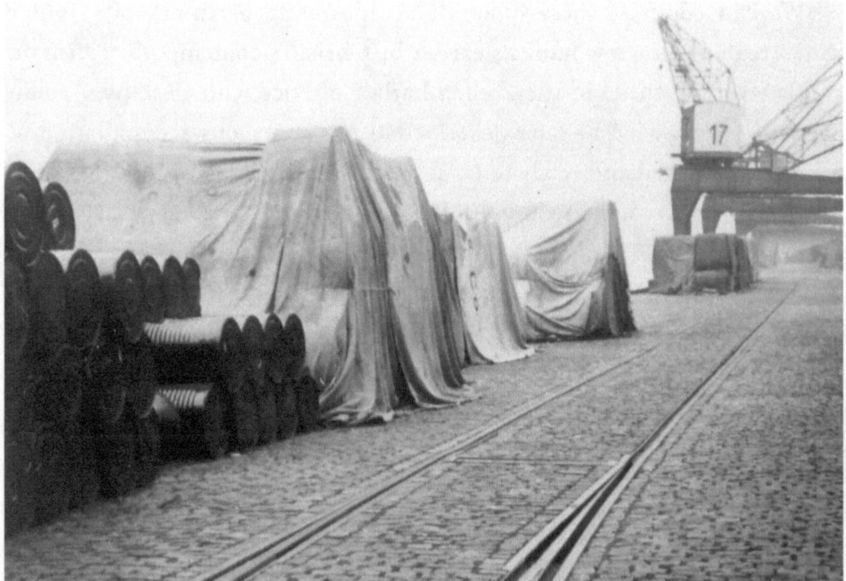

FIGURE 12. Photograph of Christo and Jeanne-Claude's *Dockside Packages* and *Stacked Oil Barrels,* Cologne Harbor, 1961.
Photo: Stefan Wewerka © Christo and Jeanne-Claude Foundation and ADAGP, Paris and DACS, London. Reprinted with permission.

In much the same way that *Inventory* blurred storage work with art work, the Cologne sculptures were also difficult to distinguish from the actual labor of dockworkers. As David Bourdon has observed, "it almost appeared that the artists had merrily photographed 'found' stockpiles."[75] For his earlier sculptures Christo had undertaken much of the manual work himself, but in Cologne he and Jeanne-Claude employed the labor-power of others. In brief essays from the time, the influential curator Pierre Restany celebrated the sculptures for bringing out what was already artful in "the energy of cargo workers."[76] "In ports or warehouses," he wrote, "the cargoes of metal drums are aligned into grandiose but ephemeral architectures." Christo and Jeanne-Claude's aesthetic achievement was to "capture these, alas ephemeral, masterpieces of the handler's energy, and present them in their pure beauty."[77] Nevertheless, it was the managerial commands issued by Christo and Jeanne-Claude that made *Dockside Packages* and *Stacked Oil Barrels* recognizable as art, and not the manual labor of the longshoremen.

We can compare these quayside sculptures to a remarkably similar work created just a few months earlier by Christo's contemporary Arman. While strolling through the French harbor of Nice with Restany, Arman happened upon what he later described as an "enormous accumulation of barrels . . . stacked and ready to be shipped." In the spirit of the Nouveaux Réalistes, Arman signed the found heap and proclaimed it as art to his curator companion. Arman, who reportedly grew envious of the success of *Stacked Oil Barrels*, later insinuated that Christo and Jeanne-Claude had copied him.[78] Although *Stacked Oil Barrels* visually resembled Arman's mound, it relied on a fundamentally different relation between art and labor. Whereas Arman deployed the appropriative logic of the readymade, autographing the results of dockworker labor as art before an art world authority, Christo and Jeanne-Claude hired living labor to create art. Both artworks recognized the aesthetic potential in dock work, but, for Arman, art was a by-product of logistics work. In contrast, Christo and Jeanne-Claude deliberately transformed such labor into art itself, even paying a wage for it to happen.

As Christo and Jeanne-Claude were turning longshore work into art in Cologne, efforts were underway to ready West German ports, most notably those in Hamburg and Bremen, for the containerized trade that would reduce the need for much of this labor.[79] Changes were already afoot in Cologne, where the harbor's commercial functions were being relocated from the inner city to new facilities situated north along the river. The newly opened Haro Lauhus Gallery played an early role in the port's eventual transformation into an entertainment marina and residential district.[80] *Dockside Packages* and *Stacked Oil Barrels*, thus, were part of the logistical shifts then unfolding in the city.

The year 1961 was a pivotal one in the logistics revolution. It witnessed the opening of discussions by the International Organization for Standardization to establish specifications for intermodal shipping containers and marked the first time that Sea-Land Service's trailblazing container shipping business turned a profit.[81] At the start of the year, the "Mechanization and Modernization Agreement" (MMA) between employers and longshoremen came into effect on the West Coast of North America. This agreement helped clear the path for containerization, effectively undoing decades of struggle by dockworkers to implement various work rules that gave them limited control over how and when they worked. These had included, for example, the "four-on, four-off" rule, which had allowed groups of longshoremen to take turns working: as four individuals loaded cargo, another four could rest.[82] Such rules supported the safety and job satisfaction of workers, but employers viewed them as a waste of money that could be eliminated through technology and rationalization. As new labor-saving tools began appearing on the docks during the 1950s, unions representing West Coast dockworkers opened negotiations with employers in an attempt to secure concessions while they still had the opportunity. In exchange for protections related to pay and hiring for veteran longshoremen, the unions agreed to abolish any work rules that mandated "the hiring of unnecessary men."[83]

The consequences for dock work were immediate and profound. The most precarious workers, primarily young or Black, suddenly found themselves out of work. Those who remained were thrust into a radically transformed workplace, with crew sizes reduced and work rules eliminated. Labor productivity, nearly stagnant for decades, soared by 40 percent in the first half of the 1960s, but so did the rates of workplace injury. By 1963, West Coast ports were handling more cargo than ever, using 2.5 million fewer hours of labor to do so. These initial gains for employers were not achieved by introducing new technologies, but rather resulted from squeezing workers with fewer breaks, reduced turnover times, and heavier loads. Work became so intense that unions even began filing grievances that demanded employers invest in labor-saving tools to ease the new burdens.[84] The MMA set precedent for similar negotiations on the East Coast and beyond, paving the way for employers to establish control over ports across the world. Because creating *Dockside Packages* and *Stacked Oil Barrels* had hinged on the autonomy and flexibility of dockworkers that was in the process of being abolished, the very existence of these sculptures reads like evidence supporting the case employers made that "unnecessary men" populated the docks.

Over the course of the following decade, Christo and Jeanne-Claude expanded their experiments with oil barrels to such a scale that they began to work directly with the oil and logistics industries. In October 1968, for instance, the pair filled the foyer of the Institute of Contemporary Art in Philadelphia with 1,240 pristine blue and red barrels, constructing a flat-topped pyramid that reached nearly two stories high.[85] Procuring this number of barrels required persuading the museum's board of directors to reach out to several petroleum corporations on their behalf, including the Gulf Oil Company.[86] That same year, Christo and Jeanne-Claude started collaborating with the Dutch packaging company Janus Vaten to build a three-tiered pyramid of fifty-six barrels for a Dutch collector—a task Janus Vaten replicated a decade later in 1977 when recreating the sculpture for the Kröller-Müller Museum.[87] Janus Vaten's history mirrors that of the packaging industry itself. Starting off as an Amsterdam cooperage in the 1870s, the company transitioned from manufacturing wooden barrels to refurbishing used steel drums after World War II. Today, the company produces some 1.5 million barrels annually for customers that include Russia's Lukoil and offers a range of logistics services, from transportation to warehousing. Its 2018 joint venture with the industry leader Mauser made Janus Vaten partner to one of the world's largest packaging companies, operating in 180 countries and generating $4 billion in annual revenue.[88]

The 256 hours that Janus Vaten invoiced Christo and Jeanne-Claude for the Kröller-Müller Museum sculpture marked just the beginning of the collaboration between these two emerging giants of their respective fields.[89] Between 1967 and 1977, Christo and Jeanne-Claude proposed barrel projects on an increasingly grand scale, most of which were never realized. These plans included projects requiring hundreds of barrels on Lake Michigan, tens of thousands for an endeavor in Otterlo, half a million to be placed on the shoulder of a highway outside Houston, and 10 million to block the Suez Canal.[90] They completed their largest project with Janus Vaten in the summer of 2018, stacking 7,506 barrels on a floating platform in London's Serpentine Lake (Figure 13). For *The London Mastaba*, Janus Vaten committed a team of fifteen workers who needed eight weeks to fabricate and paint the barrels. It took 30 truck deliveries to transport them to London, where a team of divers, builders, marine engineers, and scaffolding specialists spent ten more weeks erecting the enormous sculpture with its 13,000-square-foot base.[91] As with all their projects since the 1960s, Christo financed the $4 million installation entirely through the pair's CVJ Corporation (Jeanne-Claude passed away in 2009), securing lines of credit from banks, using future sales of preparatory sketches, collages, and maquettes as collateral.[92]

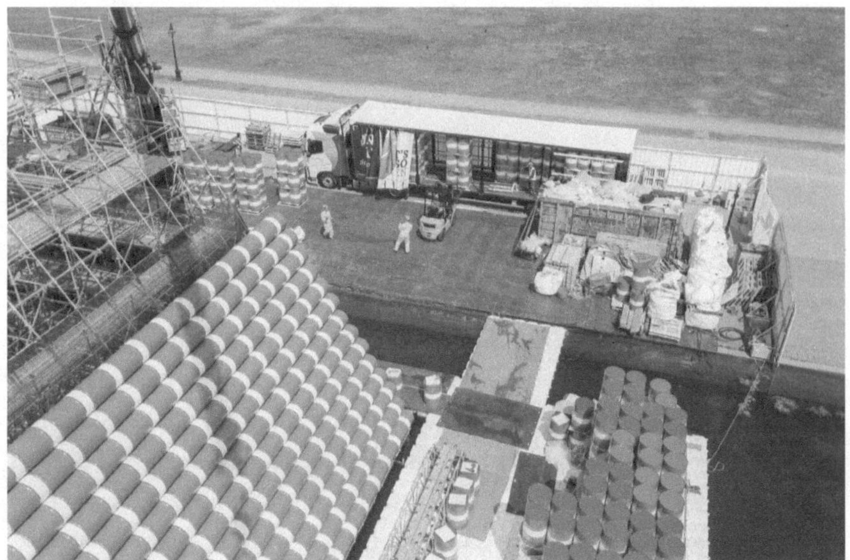

FIGURE 13. Delivery of oil barrels for *The London Mastaba*, Serpentine Lake, London, 2018.
Photo: Janus Vaten, courtesy Janus Vaten.

The London Mastaba is widely seen as a "test"[93] or "a sales pitch"[94] for an even larger pyramid in the Abu Dhabi desert. There Janus Vaten has committed to supplying 410,000 barrels for a towering 49-story sculpture, with intentions of setting up shop in the desert to manufacture them. Planning for this half-billion-dollar project commenced in 1977 and has since included site visits, a full feasibility study in 2007, and extensive negotiations with patrons and government officials. At the time of Christo's death in 2020, *The Mastaba: Project for United Arab Emirates* remained unrealized, but is still in the works.[95] Much has been made of the plans for this orientalist Marfa, especially the symbolic significance of placing so many barrels atop one of the world's largest known oil reserves.[96] Christo, for his part, dismissed critics for overthinking what seems readily apparent about the project: "It is not anything, it is absolutely sculpture. . . . Irrational, totally useless, totally unnecessary."[97] His embrace of artistic autonomy might seem like a dodge for an artwork that will require such enormous capital investment, labor, and coordination. Yet Christo's message of utter uselessness is in keeping with the core idea behind his entire oeuvre of oil barrel art. If completed, the world's largest sculpture, built in a country that has swiftly grown into one of the world's leading logistical economies, will display, like nothing ever before, the wastefulness of oil barrels and the labor required to move them.

Meaningless Transport Work

Christo and Jeanne-Claude's monuments to wasteful logistics labor represent just one of the ways that postwar artists registered the accumulation of oil barrels in the capitalist world-system. In 1961, the same year Christo and Jeanne-Claude supervised *Stacked Oil Barrels* in Cologne, Allan Kaprow created an even more literal display of waste when he tipped truckloads of old tires and oil barrels into the courtyard of Manhattan's Martha Jackson Gallery. Remembered by most as a playground where visitors were free to explore the heap as they pleased, *Yard* has been more aptly described as "a dump."[98] Kaprow chose tires and barrels largely because they were readily available—easy to acquire, but, as it turned out, difficult to throw away. After the exhibition closed, it took gallery staff weeks to clear the courtyard, with much of that time spent figuring out where all the unwanted tires and barrels could go. As Jeff Kelley has observed, *Yard* was more than "a comment on throwaway culture," it was also "part of it."[99] By blurring the boundary between art and trash, Kaprow's installation seemed to be both a complement and a counterpoint to oil industry advertisements of the time like *The Magic Barrel*. *Yard* testified to the new significance of oil but also showed the accumulation of this fossil technomass as waste rather than an achievement.

Even though *Yard* is one of Kaprow's best-known artworks, most descriptions of it recall the tires and forget the barrels.[100] *Yard* was neither the first nor the last time that Kaprow incorporated barrels into his art. Throughout the 1960s, whether at home or abroad, Kaprow's Happenings frequently featured barrels that were, among other actions, hit, thrown, knocked, rolled, and swung into each other.[101] Like many artists who used oil barrels as found material during this period, Kaprow chose them not so much for their symbolic value but because they were easy to obtain. That *Yard*'s oil barrels have been forgotten would hardly have bothered Kaprow, since he himself excluded them from his own later restagings.

When it comes to oil barrels in postwar art, the only thing more striking than their prevalence is the fact that scholars so often overlook them. The legacy of Charlotte Moorman and Nam June Paik's *Variations on a Theme by Saint-Saëns* is another case in point. First performed at the Philadelphia College of Art in February 1965, the routine featured Moorman, an accomplished cellist, playing the opening measures of the mawkish standard, "The Swan," before pausing to dunk herself in a water-filled barrel. With Paik's assistance, she climbed out and returned to her seat to finish the number, dripping from head to toe.[102] For all its notoriety, the performance resembled many others from the time in how it used oil barrels. For example, just a few months earlier in Stockholm, Robert Rauschenberg scaled down a rope hung from the ceiling of the Moderna Museet into an oil barrel full of water as part of the performance *Elgin Tie*.[103] Three years before this, Nobuaki Kojima spent an extended period of the 1961 Yomiuri Indépendent Exhibition in Japan standing inside a barrel while holding a pole draped with a black and white flag.[104] Paik and Moorman kept *Variations* in their repertoire for three decades, performing it more than fifty times around the world, a fact that suggests the pair had reason to assume that barrels would be available wherever they traveled.

Kaprow was among the most logistically minded artists of his generation. His most explicitly transport-related performance was *Transfer—A Happening (For Christo)*, from February 1968. Dedicated to Christo, *Transfer* began with a small group of volunteers gathering at the barrel yard belonging to the Anderson Oil and Chemical Company in Middletown, Connecticut. After loading dozens of empty oil barrels onto two waiting trucks, the group drove to several locations, among them a quarry, a park, a dump, a shopping center, and city hall. At each stop, they unloaded the barrels and stacked them into fleeting sculptures, sometimes wrapping them in paper or spray painting them. They would then pose for a photograph in front of their creation, before disassembling it and moving on.[105] *Transfer* involved considerable work, something the photographs make clear. In the first picture, taken when the group arrived at the Anderson Oil and Chemical Company, the nine participants sit or lean casually among the rusty and dented barrels. As the day progressed, their poses became more intentional, even theatrical. In front of a factory, for example, they stacked the barrels to match the building's smokestack silhouette. For the photograph, each participant raised an arm in the air to mirror the smokestack behind them. Outside city hall, they stood atop a four-barrel-high wall with their backs turned to the camera, saluting the American flag flying atop the building. For their final pose, photographed after returning the barrels, the group sat in the yard with their heads resting emphatically on their hands to signal exhaustion (Figure 14).

By 1968, moving barrels had become such a common element of Kaprow's Happenings that Richard Kostelanetz, in his important critical introduction to Happenings, could imagine the following as a representative score: "Move ten barrels from Spot X to Spot Y by any route that you wish in exactly five minutes."[106] In one of Kaprow's highest profile Happenings, *Gas* (1966), a group of adults and children were given the ridiculous and Sisyphean task of rolling barrels out of a junkyard pit while being sprayed with foam from fire trucks.[107] Happenings like *Gas* and *Transfer* asked participants to perform transport work, albeit for no discernible reason. In this regard, they bring to mind what Kaprow's contemporary, Walter De Maria, called "meaningless work." Far from being an insult, De Maria coined the term to describe actions

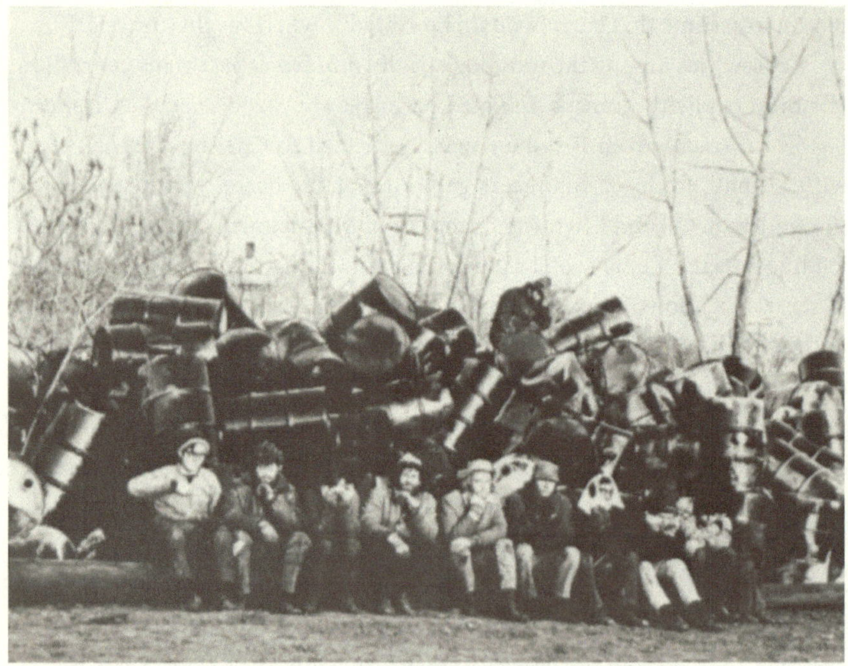

FIGURE 14. Photograph of exhausted volunteers at the final stop of Allan Kaprow's *Transfer*, 1968. *Photo:* Andrew Glantz, courtesy Andrew Glantz, Zenith Design and the Getty Research Institute, Los Angeles (980063).

that, in his view, epitomized art as an autonomous creative action. Any kind of activity could be rendered meaningless, so long as it was carried out not to "make money or accomplish a conventional purpose." Two of the activities cited by De Maria as meaningless work included digging a hole only to fill it and filing papers just to scatter them around.[108] Kaprow embraced the meaningless potential of his Happenings, and even dedicated one of them to De Maria. In *Overtime—A Happening (For Walter De Maria)* (1968), participants spent an entire night in the woods of New Paltz, New York, assembling and moving hundreds of feet of snow fence, over and over again.

Transfer, with all of its loading and unloading, stacking and unstacking, was undeniably an example of meaningless work. The photographs featuring participants striking theatrical poses called attention to the work performed; this set them apart from the considerably more famous images of *Dockside Packages* and *Stacked Oil Barrels*, which are marked by the conspicuous absence of any workers whatsoever. In one of the few attempts to compare these projects, Bourdon suggests that, despite its inspiration from Christo and Jeanne-Claude, *Transfer* "stressed the activity and changes that occurred, making the loading, trucking, and spraying equally important to the periodically stacked barrels."[109] In doing so, Kaprow made transport work seem playful, though also a bit silly. The same cannot be said for *Dockside Packages* and *Stacked Oil Barrels*, which treated the labor involved seriously enough to pay for it. Christo himself emphasized this difference when he classified the work carried out in his art as "real" and the work in Kaprow's art as "make-believe":

> If three hundred people are used, it is not because we want three hundred people to play roles, but because we have work for them. When we go to work, there is a tense feeling, not a relaxed, joyous feeling as in a Kaprow Happening. If we use cranes, it's to do real work, and the crane man must be conscientious or it will not work. My work may look very theatrical, but it is a very professional activity.[110]

Although Christo did not participate in *Transfer*, he met with Kaprow just days after to debrief.[111] Rather than criticize Kaprow's Happenings, Christo acknowledged that a work like *Stacked Oil Barrels*, while useless, was far from meaningless in De Maria's sense, not the least because the dockworkers who made it were paid.

Kaprow, by contrast, believed that, regardless of how closely his performances resembled real activities, they should never "be too much like work." Happenings were meant to "be done with gusto, wit, fun; it's to be play."[112] In keeping with this principle, Kaprow seldom compensated any of his participants. He claimed to prize playfulness as a means through which to extract fresh insights from routine activities, be it brushing one's teeth or laying asphalt. In *Transfer*, he set the task but left it to participants to decide how to accomplish it, issuing only vague directives like, "New site. Barrels stacked. Da-glo red. Triumphal photo."[113] Those who see Kaprow's art as an attempt to critique "instrumental labor" might be tempted to read *Transfer* as a response to how seamlessly Christo and Jeanne-Claude slotted art into industry.[114] By this reasoning, *Transfer* would seem to be a rather conventional 1960s artistic retort to the technocratic managerialism that was then reshaping various logistics professions, such as dock work and truck driving.[115] As chronicled in the writing of Bay Area longshoremen like Reg Theriault and Stan Weir, the waterfront workplace of the 1960s, once characterized by autonomy, creativity, and camaraderie, was fast turning into "a factory job" as rationalization and mechanization took away much of the "fun."[116] In such a context, the playfulness of *Transfer*, which allowed participants to figure out how to best complete the task, could be seen as an expression of worker control that was on the brink of being extinguished by the logistics revolution. Yet Kaprow's intents, as gleaned from his own reading lists and writings, suggest a different interpretation is in order.

At the time Kaprow created *Transfer*, he was drawing inspiration from a similar intellectual well as many logisticians, with Ludwig von Bertalanffy being a key shared influence. Bertalanffy was an Austrian biologist best remembered today as the "founding father" of general systems theory,[117] the interdisciplinary school of thinking that Deborah Cowen credits with causing "the single most important shift" in "logistics thought and practice in the early postwar period."[118] The basics of Bertalanffy's version of systems theory, developed in the 1950s, hold that the universe is composed of numerous interrelated systems, each self-sufficient yet belonging to a larger whole. In the 1960s, his theory gained popularity in academic, industrial, and artistic circles, providing much of the theoretical foundation for the holistic impulse underpinning both "total cost analysis" in businesses logistics and what, in the art world, would be called the "systems esthetic."[119] Art critics and curators like Jack Burnham turned to systems theory to explain the process-based priorities prevalent in much conceptual and performance art in the 1960s and 1970s, and of which Kaprow was a significant player. What Jasper Bernes has said about the appeal of cybernetics for the 1960s neo-avant-garde also describes the influence of systems thinking, as artists endeavored to apply it in ways that explicitly countered "technocratic visions."[120] While logistics textbooks advocated systems theory to attain an "uninterrupted flow of materials,"[121] Kaprow preferred, as he himself put it, a "systems approach that favors openness toward outcome, in contrast to the literal and goal-oriented uses now employed by most systems specialists."[122] *Transfer* defied key logistical principles for achieving continuous flow, most notably the "rule of thumb to avoid the physical handling of materials whenever possible."[123] Not only did Kaprow's Happening feature physical handling, it made a show of it.

For these reasons, it is a surprise that Kaprow's own perspective on the logistical restructuring of capitalist society aligned in key ways with that of the corporate world. Writing in the early 1970s, Kaprow observed, "The issue now is not production but distribution," employing language reminiscent of business logistics literature from that era. While businesses shifted their focus to distribution out of a desire to reduce transport costs, Kaprow did so out of a fascination with automation, which he believed was set to make the "production" of goods a secondary concern to their distribution. Kaprow viewed automation as a cause for celebration, claiming it would release people from jobs in historically labor-intensive sectors like "farming, mining, and manufacturing," thus freeing them to find better ones in "the expanding service industries."[124] Kaprow predicted that a society that had replaced manual work with service work would ultimately succeed in converting the "work ethic into one of play."[125] This vision was optimistic, to the say least. The service jobs Kaprow had in mind mainly encompassed professional services like finance and law. He regarded other types of service employment, especially those that lacked "significant social status" and paid "rather poorly," as "dead ends" that should be either automated out of existence or abandoned by job seekers.[126] While Kaprow was correct in noting the increasing significance of distribution and service work, he was clearly mistaken in attributing this shift primarily to automation. In a country like the United States, the move away from manufacturing, for example, was largely driven by offshoring. Furthermore, the "quality" service jobs that Kaprow anticipated turned out to be more of an exception than the norm within the service sector. Among the "drudgery occupations" that Kaprow proposed be prioritized for automation or elimination were those in transportation.[127] Instead of making logistics work like that performed in *Transfer* more humane or creative, the aim, according to Kaprow, should be to abolish it.

Lest we confuse Kaprow's position with a then-renascent workerism, it is worth noting that the artist asserted that "business" should be entrusted to take the lead in restructuring the world of work. He went so far as to endorse the mantra of workplace modernization that had been previously wielded against workers like longshoremen in the 1960s. Kaprow invited readers to imagine a scenario in which "business wants to automate and scrap expensive payrolls," but then "labor steps in immediately and insists on work crews when one worker or none at all is needed." For Kaprow, the ill effects were obvious: "Management suffers by being prevented from modernizing; labor suffers by doing patently dishonest work."[128] Here, the artist offers a moral defense of capitalist modernization, invoking the very specter of "unnecessary men" that earlier had haunted dockworker negotiations with employers. While *Transfer* may have presented a vision of logistics work made playful, it neither mourned the loss of nor advocated for more gratifying kinds of logistics work. Kaprow critiqued the state of transport labor itself, not to support worker autonomy but because he believed that such jobs should be automated. Similar to *Stacked Oil Barrels* before it, the meaningless work of moving barrels in *Transfer* hinted at a future world where such labor was no longer required.

Administering Blockage

So far in this chapter, I have explored how artists during the logistics revolution made an art out of devaluing transport labor, often in ways that lined up with the supply chain pipedream of a world without workers. In this section and the next, I shift my focus to the present to examine the techniques through which artists working in extractive zones are harnessing friction both to produce art and to display the abrasive underside of global commodity circulation.

I begin with the art of Lydia Ourahmane, who, over the past decade, has created several works by trying, and at times failing, to ship items across international borders. This includes *The Third Choir* from 2014, which, on display, consists of twenty empty and untreated oil barrels, all bearing the distinctive blue and yellow branding of the Algerian petroleum company Naftal. These barrels are arranged as a grid, with four tight rows of five barrels each (Figure 15). *The Third Choir* possesses a sculptural quality reminiscent of art by Christo and Jeanne-Claude, but it also resonates with the long history of artists exploring the sonic potential of barrels, dating back to the Trinidadian steel bands introduced earlier. Resting at the bottom of each of Ourahmane's barrels is a mobile phone. All twenty are synced by a radio transmitter and programmed to play a soundtrack made from ambient recordings Ourahmane collected while gathering the barrels. The phones transform the empty barrels into amplifiers, with the entire assemblage operating together as the artwork's eponymous choir.

Despite its arresting material presence, *The Third Choir* is primarily an exploration of how barrels move, or, more accurately, how they are kept from moving. Exhibited alongside the barrels are binders that contain 934 documents chronicling the arduous process orchestrated by Ourahmane to transport her barrels from the Algerian city of Oran to the Port of Felixstowe in England. This archive includes e-mails, faxes, customs declarations, packing lists, clearance forms, invoices, booking confirmations, and correspondence with government officials. To prevent this paperwork from becoming just a footnote to the display of barrels, Ourahmane has even performed her archive at the openings of exhibitions featuring *The Third Choir.* From behind a desk, she would read aloud six export applications and the rejections she received, making present the loopholes and negotiations that went into making the barrels move. Both the binders and her archival performances, therefore, insist that the coordination and administrative work necessary for shipping are integral and not incidental components of the artwork. Ephemeral labor that would have otherwise been overlooked by the display of barrels becomes the cornerstone of Ourahmane's aesthetic of logistical administration.[129]

Born in Saïda, Ourahmane and her family fled Algeria when she was a child in 2002 to escape the civil war. *The Third Choir* originated as her degree

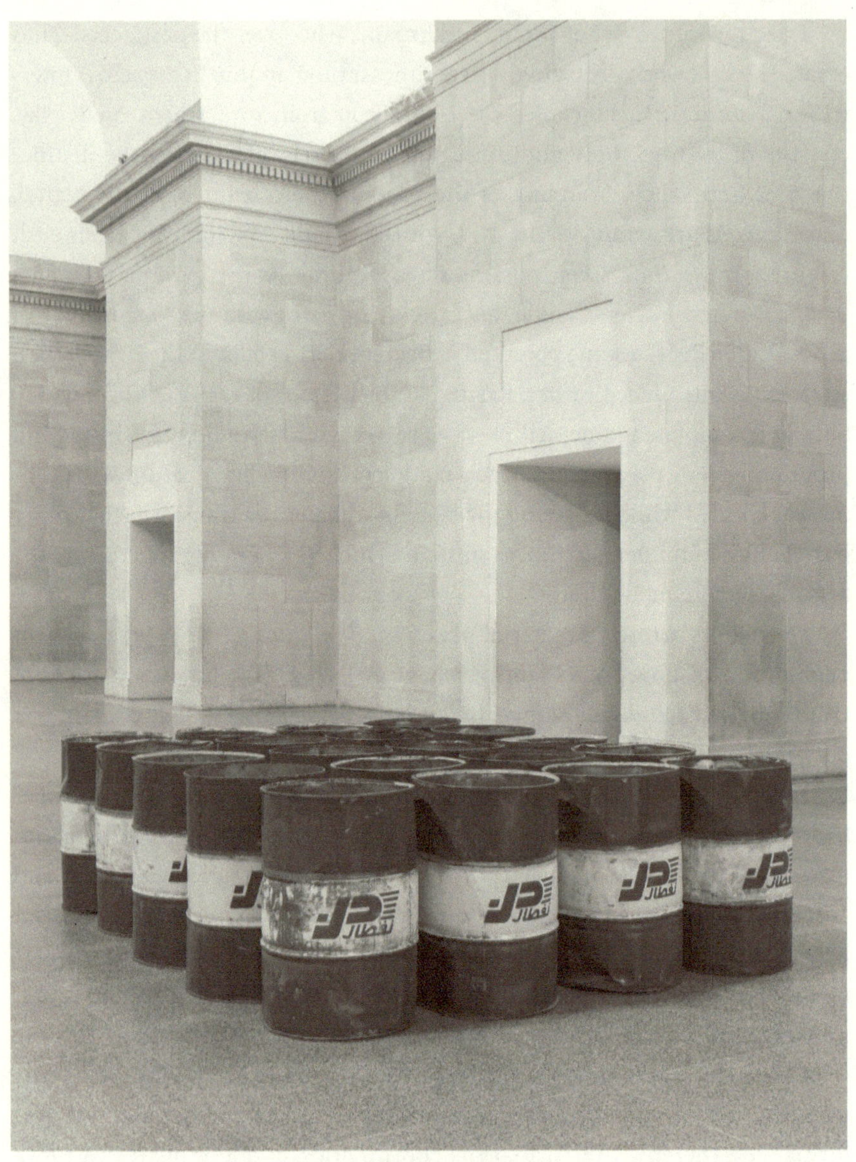

FIGURE 15. Lydia Ourahmane's *The Third Choir,* installation view at Tate Britain, 2023.
Photo: Tate © Lydia Ourahmane and Tate. Reprinted with permission.

project in visual art at Goldsmiths, University of London, based on oral history interviews she conducted with young Algerians who were hoping to migrate to Europe. Her oil barrels were intended to be surrogates for her interviewees, all of whom, like Ourahmane, were the grandchildren of the Algerian revolution, the "third" generation referenced in the artwork's title. Initially, Ourahmane had planned for the oil drums to also represent the driving force behind the desire of those she interviewed to emigrate.

Oil extraction played a pivotal role in Algeria's economic and political development in the decades following independence, but after a quarter century of relative stability, the country's rentier state model faltered due to an economic crisis in the 1980s triggered by a drop in oil prices, which in turn led to the political turmoil and civil war of the 1990s, the so-called Black Decade.[130] While many have attributed this turbulence to the "resource curse" of oil, *The Third Choir* has a different target: the multinational conglomerates whose control over the oil flow has left Algerians to benefit relatively little from the wealth generated through drilling.[131] Ourahmane insisted on using Naftal barrels because, as the subsidiary of Algeria's national petroleum company responsible for selling oil for domestic use, Naftal circulates its barrels extensively within Algeria but never abroad. For her, the barrels symbolize how Algerian oil is repackaged for export by foreign companies like BP. Without absolving the Algerian state of blame, *The Third Choir* stresses the plundering power of foreign oil companies as the root cause of her generation's discontent—or at least this was Ourahmane's intention for the artwork before her shipment of barrels was repeatedly blocked.

After months of planning, Ourahmane traveled to Algeria in April 2014 to scavenge scrapyards, gas stations, mechanics, construction sites, and even private homes for oil barrels, which she had arranged to send to England by shipping container on May 1. As her archive of documents reveals, however, Algerian customs officials rejected Ourahmane's export request. They questioned why she would want to ship items "technically classified as rubbish" instead of just buying new ones in London.[132] Subsequent applications, in which she tried to reclassify the barrels as everything from musical instruments to home décor, were summarily turned down. The trouble, as Ourahmane soon learned, owed to laws dating back to independence that were designed to protect Algeria's cultural heritage and prevent the looting of archaeological sites.

These laws also restricted the movement of art, making it illegal to export movable objects without ministerial authorization. In the end, Ourahmane only obtained permission to ship the barrels after writing directly to Algeria's minister of culture. When her cargo finally departed, it was listed as "Used Barrels for Art Work." By law, her oil barrels could only be considered art once they were in transit.[133]

The Third Choir is a meticulous logistical artwork that underscores the role of friction in circulation. It also brings paperwork, as a form of logistical labor, to the forefront. Ourahmane's display of documents alludes to landmark conceptual art exhibitions from the 1960s and 1970s, which, instead of showcasing art objects, presented drawings, blueprints, invoices, memos, and more that detailed the production processes of minimalist sculptors and conceptual artists. As Sianne Ngai notes, such art of that period was deeply entangled in circulation, with "techniques of dissemination and distribution" being "increasingly folded into the act of production."[134] *The Third Choir* expands on this early "aesthetic of administration" in two significant ways. First, it emphasizes the materiality of the immaterial "post-Fordist knowledge work" often associated with conceptual art by exhibiting the very barrels that were transported.[135] Even more notably, it weaves histories of empire and decolonization into this circulation aesthetic.

As Ourahmane has remarked, by the time the barrels arrived to Goldsmiths on June 7, just days before her degree show was to open, *The Third Choir* had ceased to be "about [the barrels] being there physically" and had become instead centered on the "process" of getting them there.[136] In the end, friction emerged as a fundamental element of *The Third Choir's* production, infusing the artwork with, to use Ourahmane's words, "a momentum and energy that it may not have gathered if the process was straightforward."[137] In this regard, *The Third Choir*'s aesthetic is largely dematerialized, albeit in a way that reveals this term's slipperiness. Objects are central to the installation, but only because the project revolves around the efforts required to transport them, showing how paperwork like invoices are entwined with manual labor and built infrastructure. Even the sounds emitted from the mobile phones inside the barrels evince this; the recordings were collected during long waits Ourahmane spent in customs offices, scrap yards, metal recycling facilities, and the port in Oran.

The administrative work of logistics is nothing new. The business of lifting and moving things has always depended on what Susan Zieger terms "mundane paperwork."[138] This remains as true today as it was at the inception of logistics when documents like bills of lading, correspondence, inventory lists, and captain's logs played a part in shipping millions of people into slavery. Such paperwork functioned as promissory notes of delivery, although the need for such promises indicated the prospect of the opposite panning out. "The nondelivery of goods," Zieger observes, "is the indefinite horizon of logistics."[139] Despite the profoundly different context, similar to these historical records of inhumanity, the documents Ourahmane exhibits are also a record of friction, which she directly links to the legacy of France's colonization of Algeria (a topic she has explored deeply in other artworks). *The Third Choir* creates art out of bureaucratic blockage and the threat of non-delivery. In so doing, Ourahmane makes friction tangible, revealing it to be not an accident but rather an afterlife of empire.

To better gauge the political stakes of *The Third Choir*'s aesthetic of logistical administration, we can draw a comparison with a strand of Christo and Jeanne-Claude's oil barrel projects that also sought to turn blockage into art. Consider, for example, the fourteen-foot-high wall of barrels the pair erected on the evening of June 27, 1962. Spanning the Rue Visconti in the center of Paris, *Wall of Oil Barrels—The Iron Curtain* halted movement on the narrow thoroughfare, disrupting traffic throughout the Left Bank.[140] The intervention evoked the long history of barricades in Paris by both causing a blockage and using barrels to do so. Oil barrels have a deep-seated association with barricades, dating back to at least "the Day of the Barricades" in 1588 when Parisian citizens filled wooden casks with stones and dirt during an uprising against Henry III. Nearly every insurrection in the French capital worthy of the name since has featured similar improvised fortifications built to block flows within the city. While various ingredients, from carts and cars to chains and concrete slabs, have been used to build barricades, barrels have been a staple. The very term "barricade" is derived from the French word *barrique*, meaning a large wooden barrel.[141] Easy to roll and stack, barrels have an insurgent history and ready-made logisticality that imbue them with obstructive symbolic charge. They are reminders that technologies designed to facilitate the flow of goods can be repurposed for opposite ends.

While Christo and Jeanne-Claude's wall spoke in many ways to the history of the barricade, it was by no means hastily constructed for an insurrection. *Wall of Oil Barrels—The Iron Curtain* accompanied the opening of Christo's solo show at the nearby Galerie J, where inside he had installed a matching wall and exhibited ink drawings imagining varied ways that barrels could be used to block entrances to buildings. Invitations to the exhibition opening came with a map showing the half-kilometer route from the gallery to the barrel wall on Rue Visconti, which Christo and Jeanne-Claude illuminated with lights for the benefit of spectators. The invitation also included a brief note from the exhibition's curator, Pierre Restany, who anticipated potential concerns by insisting that the outdoor artwork was "not a barricade improvised in the excitement of a riot." Instead, he described it as a "monumental image of our time," referencing the title's allusion to the Berlin Wall erected the previous summer.[142] For their part, Christo and Jeanne-Claude made every effort to get permission from city officials for their wall. Eight months earlier, they had submitted an application to the Saint-Germain police department, complete with sample images and technical specifications. When they received no response, the pair enlisted Jeanne-Claude's stepfather, a general in the French Army, to petition the prefect of the Paris police, Maurice Papon, on their behalf. This request also went unanswered (though Papon did reply to his "dear friend" later).[143] Having done their due diligence, the pair decided to proceed with their plans. Jeanne-Claude's stepfather was on hand that evening, and when police arrived, the general negotiated with them to allow the work to remain until 1:00 AM. The following day, Christo and Jeanne-Claude obediently appeared at the police station but escaped without so much as a fine.

The fact that the pair bent over backwards to minimize disruption has not prevented scholars from overstating what happened that night, even going so far as to label *Wall of Oil Barrels—The Iron Curtain* "a radical attack on the city's infrastructure."[144] Its form certainly resonated with the recent political turmoil in France stemming from the Algerian struggle for liberation. This includes "the Week of Barricades" that shut down Algiers in January 1960, as well as the campaign of fascist attacks and bombings that turned the Latin Quarter into a hotbed of conflict. In the year leading up to *Wall of Oil Barrels—The Iron Curtain*, Paris police had violently suppressed multiple demonstrations held by Algerians and their supporters, murdering hundreds of people and injuring thousands more.[145] Largely due to its timing, enthusiasts like to paint Christo and Jeanne-Claude's wall as having been built out of anti-fascist and anti-imperialist sympathies with the Algerian cause (France granted Algeria independence just days after *Wall of Oil Barrels—The Iron Curtain*).[146] However, any such portrayal must be tempered by knowledge of how actively the pair tried to collaborate with the very cops who were killing Algerians with impunity and dumping their lifeless bodies into the waterways of Paris. For instance, Papon—the "dear friend" Jeanne-Claude's stepfather appealed to for a favor—helped cover up the now-notorious Paris massacre of Algerian demonstrators on October 17, 1961.

If *Wall of Oil Barrels—The Iron Curtain* commemorated anything related to Algerian decolonization, it was the extractivist imperatives that delayed independence. The discovery of massive oil fields in Algeria in the mid-1950s was one reason why Charles de Gaulle dragged his feet during negotiations, insisting that France be granted priority access to the resource-rich southern region.[147] *Wall of Oil Barrels—The Iron Curtain* serves as the dark reflection of *The Third Choir.* While the latter documented and derived from a desire to resist postimperial plunder, the former indexed the various forces at play, including oil companies and the repressive apparatus of the French state, that colluded to defy decolonization.

Christo and Jeanne-Claude revisited the barricade form in several projects throughout their career together. In June 1968, they proposed installing a wall made of oil barrels outside the Museum of Modern Art (MoMA), which would have blockaded 53rd Street in Manhattan for a day. This idea followed an even grander proposal from a year earlier to barricade the Suez Canal with a wall constructed of 10 million barrels. Neither of these blockades materialized, even though, like *Wall of Oil Barrels—The Iron Curtain*, both were planned to minimize disruption.[148] For example, the daylong barricade outside MoMA was timed to coincide with an exhibition turnover, during which delivery trucks would already be clogging up traffic. Likewise, at the time they imagined the Suez Canal barricade, the vital shipping lane was closed by Egypt as a result of the Six-Day War. Both projects were designed to take artistic advantage of existing obstructions, albeit of staggeringly different types. Christo and Jeanne-Claude's ready-made barricades raised the prospect of something neither was prepared to deliver: the potential of art, produced in the logistical mode, to block the flow of capital.

Dancing on Dead Infrastructure

When Sokari Douglas Camp answered her phone in late August 2015, she expected to receive news that *Grande Lagos* had finally set sail from the Port of Tilbury in England. To her surprise, the caller reported that Camp's shipment, a steel sculpture the shape and form of a bus with eight oil barrels welded to its roof, now rested at the bottom of the River Thames. As it was being hoisted onto the cargo ship, a cable had snapped, causing the sculpture to slip unceremoniously into the water. Traffic at the dock was suspended for four days as scuba divers worked to fish out the enormous thing.[149] Here was proof of art's potential to block the flows of capital.

Disrupting one of England's principal ports had not been Camp's intent when she built the sculpture a decade earlier. Commissioned by the London-based climate justice organization Platform, *Battle Bus* is a memorial to the nine Ogoni activists who were murdered by Nigeria's Abacha military regime in November 1995. Today, the executions are infamous for having been carried out as retribution for the extended struggle of the Ogoni people to force Royal Dutch Shell off their land in the Niger Delta. The commercial discovery of oil in 1956 came with promises that Nigeria, soon to gain independence from Britain in 1960, would transform into a thriving petrostate. But instead of unifying the country, oil divided it along ethnic and regional lines, conforming to the pattern of other rentier states pillaged by fossil capital. During the 1970s oil boom, Ogoniland yielded 15 percent of all Nigerian fossil fuel, yet the Ogoni people received not the wealth from these flows but constant flare-offs, blowouts, and spills that polluted their land and water. Ogoni resistance mounted throughout the 1980s and early 1990s, deploying a mixed repertoire that included everything from peaceful marches to pipeline sabotage. In response, the military unleashed a brutal campaign that came to a head in 1993 with raids on Ogoni villages, which left 2,000 people dead and 30,000 more homeless. When a militant Ogoni group killed four conservative elders, the Nigerian military arrested and executed the acclaimed Ogoni activist and writer Ken Saro-Wiwa, along with eight others. The hangings prompted international condemnation and transformed the Ogoni Nine into martyrs for Indigenous and environmental struggles around the world.[150]

Camp finished her monument to the Ogoni Nine in 2006. A steel banner extending across its windshield bore Saro-Wiwa's name, and his words accusing oil companies of genocide were hammered into the sculpture's sides. On its roof, Camp affixed eight black barrels, one for each of the other slain activists. These barrels, doubling symbolically as urns, held the oil industry responsible for the murders. The sculpture's resemblance to a campaign bus carried the message that the struggle continued. For nearly a decade, the three-ton monument toured cities across Britain, with its interior space functioning as a venue for seminars, workshops, and performances. When it fell into the Thames, *Battle Bus* was bound for the Niger Delta to be permanently installed in Bori City as a gift to the Ogoni on behalf of Camp's Kalabari people. *Grande Lagos* eventually departed England on August 19, 2015, with Camp's sculpture, having been cleaned and repaired, securely on board. However, upon its arrival in Lagos three weeks later, *Battle Bus* was impounded on the orders of Colonel Hameed Ali, Nigeria's comptroller general of customs. Twenty years earlier, Colonel Ali had presided over the tribunal that condemned the Ogoni Nine to death.[151] No official reason for the seizure has ever been provided, and as of 2023, *Battle Bus* remains in custody. Intended to be a galvanizing monument to Indigenous struggle against the flows of global capital, *Battle Bus* fell victim to friction—first in the form of a dockside accident and later at the hands of a petrostate.

In both its materials and underlying motives, *Battle Bus* shares much with an installation by Victor Ehikhamenor, called *Wealth of Nations*. In November 2015, Ehikhamenor stacked 150 battered black oil drums at the entrance to the Jogja National Museum in Yogyakarta, Indonesia, creating an imposing eight-meter-tall wall. He spray-painted the worn and dented surface of each barrel with thick red lines, which, when viewed from a distance, gave the impression of ulcerous wounds or even the grisly work of a firing squad. Born in a small village in Edo State, Ehikhamenor belongs to a generation of artists and intellectuals who left Nigeria during the political turbulence of the 1990s, only returning after civilian rule was restored. Today, he is one of Nigeria's most internationally acclaimed artists, having represented the country at the 2017 Venice Biennale. While *Wealth of Nations* may have resembled a barricade, it was not built to block anything. Instead, the imposing wall pulled visitors into the museum, where *Wealth of Nations* continued. Inside, one could explore a small rectangular room with vibrant yellow walls decorated by a looping black biomorphic pattern, the design inspired by religious motifs from Ehikhamenor's village as if refracted through the eye of Keith Haring. In the center of the room hung three red oil barrels above a filled bathtub. Submerged in the water was a glowing sign that read "Oloibiri," the name of the town where commercial quantities of oil were first found in Nigeria. According to Ehikhamenor, *Wealth of Nations* aimed to connect Nigeria's history of military dictatorship to its oil, with the barrels standing in for the petroviolence that has shaped the uneven flow of national oil wealth.[152]

At the 2016 Ostrale Biennale in Dresden, Ehikhamenor created a sister room to the one in Yogyakarta. Instead of three hanging barrels, this newer work, *Wealth of Nations–Ogoni Nine*, featured nine, one for each of the executed Ogoni. As with *Battle Bus*, the barrels had become surrogates for the hanged. Reviewers have described Ehikhamenor's installations in terms of commemoration, as "monuments . . . made out of the devastation left behind in the misuse of oil wealth."[153] In contrast to the art of Christo and Jeanne-Claude, where oil barrels testified to the presence of "unnecessary" workers, *Wealth of Nations*, like *Battle Bus* before it, memorialized the populations rendered surplus to supply chain capitalism by repurposing the very infrastructure that had brought the violence.

Besides being an allusion to Adam Smith, the title *Wealth of Nations* gestures to how this violence circulates across borders. Ehikhamenor created his oil barrel wall for the thirteenth Jogja Biennale in collaboration with the Indonesian artist Maryanto Beb, who framed Ehikhamenor's barrel wall within an enormous cut-out painting of a flaming oil rig. Like Nigeria, Indonesia has endured a history of extractive violence that dates back to the massacres committed by the Dutch in the late nineteenth century.[154] The Jogja Biennale invoked this shared circumstance by bringing together eleven artists from Nigeria to work alongside twenty-three from Indonesia. Thus, the collaboration between Ehikhamenor and Beb exemplified the festival's purpose, fostering what Christine Okoth calls "an aesthetics of extractive solidarity" among those subject to the infrastructural violence of fossil capital.[155]

I will close this chapter in Ogoniland with the five-channel film *Karikpo Pipeline*, created by Zina Saro-Wiwa on the twentieth anniversary of her father's execution.[156] In it, Ogoni performers wearing antelope masks dance a traditional Karikpo masquerade using the abandoned oil infrastructure left behind by Shell as their stage. Their movements are deliberate and graceful as they dance upon the wellheads, flow stations, and pipelines that once poisoned Ogoniland and now linger like scars. Saro-Wiwa captured much of the performance with a drone, editing the footage in such a way that the dancers appear and vanish atop the shuttered structures as if they were apparitions. Traditionally, a Karikpo masquerade marked the start of the planting season and was performed to ensure fertility. While the film's spectral figures might seem like ghosts of a dying way of life, they signify not decline but the possibility of rebirth. In its site specificity, *Karikpo Pipeline* mourns the damage inflicted on the land and the people, while also repurposing the very tools responsible for the violence into a stage. The performers literally dance upon dead logistical infrastructure, reaching into the well of the past to fashion a future among the ruins.

3 The Shipping Container
Levers of Dispossession

THE CAPITALIST WORLD-SYSTEM IS LITTERED with shipping containers, and so is the world of contemporary art. Today, a shipping container is just as likely to pop up in a photograph or a film as it is to be a pop-up gallery or cinema. Beyond their frequent appearances on television shows and in novels, shipping containers are also increasingly used to make and display art. Sculptors stack them to create public monuments, painters use them as canvases, and choreographers even cast them as dancers.[1] Without a doubt, the shipping container is the consummate logistical infrastructure of contemporary art.

For much of this century, one could purchase a shipping container for under a thousand dollars, making it an affordable shell for various purposes, not limited to art. The advent of container cafés, container hotels, container malls, and luxury container homes has led architects to hype "cargotecture" as "a new important market niche."[2] With migrant detention centers and jails now being built out of them, shipping containers have proven their grimly egalitarian potential: they are as fit to be playgrounds for the rich as they are prisons for the poor.[3] This humble steel box, originally designed for transporting commodities around the world, has evolved into a ubiquitous fixture of everyday life.

The staggering rise of shipping container art is not the fault of artists and architects alone; it is predominantly a consequence of capitalism's logistical restructuring since the 1950s. While containers of some form have always been necessary for transporting cargo, the turn to large, standardized boxes that could be seamlessly swapped across different modes of transportation marked a historic shift.[4] *Ideal-X*, the first commercial vessel stacked with shipping containers, set sail from a New Jersey port in April 1956, and shortly thereafter, containerized trade revolutionized the global shipping industry. Intermodal containers expedited the loading process for ships, trucks, and trains, prompting further innovations that drastically reduced the labor required for circulating commodities worldwide. With the price for moving goods overseas lowered and the ceiling on trade volume lifted, businesses expanded their economies of scale and began relocating manufacturing to regions promising the lowest production costs. The resulting sea change in the division of labor was literally oceanic, as the center of the world economy shifted from the Atlantic to the Pacific. The shipping container is the cornerstone of the logistical infrastructure underpinning supply chain capitalism today. "Without it," as Marc Levinson notes in his sweeping history of the container, "the world would be a very different place."[5]

The history of repurposing shipping containers is nearly as old as the shipping container itself. No sooner had its core specifications been standardized in 1970 than designers began exploring the shipping container's potential uses beyond the transportation of goods. For instance, in their influential 1972 defense of postmodern architecture, Charles Jencks and Nathan Silver celebrated the shipping container as a model for "adhocism," detailing how containers were already being repurposed as military barracks and horse stables.[6] No less than Stewart Brand praised the shipping container's modularity as superior to purpose-built architecture. Silicon Valley's countercultural guru practiced what he preached by penning his 1994 manifesto, which called for an "organic" approach to building design, in an office converted from a shipping container.[7] The fervor continues today as affluent disciples of lifestyle minimalism endorse the "upcycling" of shipping containers into mini-homes as a sustainable remedy for overconsumption.[8] Throughout its short life, the shipping container has suited the desire for design solutions to problems brought about by capitalism, many of which containerization has only exacerbated. While the shipping container's affordances are many, every single one of them fundamentally depends on the dynamics of the logistical infrastructure for which it was invented.

Although shipping containers are vital cogs in time-sensitive supply chains, they also constantly fall out of circulation. On average, a shipping container has a structural life span of ten years, but annually tens of thousands of containers end up stranded in ports around the world for lack of return cargo. Sending a shipping container back to its point of origin empty can be more expensive than manufacturing a new one.[9] The unfilled boxes piling up in the ports of countries that have been deindustrialized are one conspicuous symptom of the trade imbalances and logistical inefficiencies that are baked into supply chain capitalism.

While some companies cut their losses by dispatching shipping containers loaded with trash and hazardous waste to Asia and Latin America, others are increasingly keen to pawn them off to willing buyers. In 2014, the annual number of shipping containers sold or leased for "inland use" surpassed 1 million. That same year, Maersk, the world's largest shipping firm by fleet capacity, launched a new division exclusively devoted to the business of selling on shipping containers, doubling second-hand sales within just two years.[10] Artworks made from retired shipping containers are not weeds that sprout unexpectedly from an otherwise flawless system; they have become part of normal logistical operations, like fruit cultivated in the soil of supply chains. Decommissioned containers can serve practical needs in affordable ways, yet their creative reuse, be it as a pop-up restaurant or a gallery, adds to the fiction that the problem at hand is not an untenable contradiction of the global economy but rather a shortage of curators and architects with the creative acumen to find innovative solutions for supply chain scrap metal.

The shipping container was initially designed as an instrument of global labor arbitrage. By trimming the cost of transportation, it enables capitalism to scour the world for cheap opportunities to produce goods, often far from where they are consumed. For this reason, Allan Sekula aptly dubbed the shipping container "the very coffin of remote labor-power."[11] The role these boxes play in exploiting workers around the world is no secret, but the services they perform for capital when they are no longer transporting commodities has scarcely been explored. Selling on retired containers helps companies manage the costs of expiring fixed capital, and it also opens up the potential for shipping containers to be redeployed as levers of dispossession, such as when they are used as informal housing or enlisted in capital-led projects of gentrification. With its unique potential to facilitate both exploitation and dispossession, the shipping container exemplifies the "dual character" of capital accumulation today.[12] Although not all repurposed shipping containers abet dispossession, the present chapter focuses on those that do, so as to challenge the assumption, shared by no few designers, architects, and artists, that the affordances of retired shipping containers are neutral if not liberating.

When it comes to logistics, the topic of dispossession is often overlooked, not the least by many Marxists whose research on supply chains privileges matters relating to labor regimes and exploitation. In his account of the violent means by which English peasants were stripped of access to land and compelled to secure subsistence by selling their labor-power, Karl Marx described how dispossession worked hand in hand with exploitation to kick-start the process of capital accumulation. While Marx framed this as capitalism's origin story, the intertwined dynamics of exploitation and dispossession remain integral to the workings of capital. Grasping the continued role of dispossession requires considering how it functions as a strategy for controlling land, whether for capitalization through redevelopment or for managing (and containing) surplus populations.[13] As Sandro Mezzadra and Brett Neilson put it, dispossession is not at odds with but rather "inherent" to the "very nature" of exploitation.[14] Likewise, for Glen Sean Coulthard, even in colonial contexts where dispossession seems to take the lead as a strategy of domination against Indigenous communities, exploitation remains co-constitutive for reproducing capitalist social relations.[15] Dispossession and exploitation are, in the words of David Harvey, "dialectically entwined."[16] If nothing else, demonstrating how a tool of exploitation like the shipping container doubles as a lever of dispossession can help underline the dual character of logistics.[17]

This chapter scrutinizes the repurposing of shipping containers into instruments of capitalist dispossession within and through art. Thanks in part to their frequent appearances as set pieces in blockbuster movies, shipping containers have become a symbol of global capitalism. However, the connection between art and the capitalist use of shipping containers does not end here. The repurposing of shipping containers for making and displaying art provides the most concrete and widespread example of the recursive relationship between artistic production and logistics. After outlining my method for examining the shipping container as an infrastructural aesthetic, I turn attention to a 1983 site-specific spectacle by Welfare State International and a 2014 immersive performance by Shunt, both of which were staged in London at different moments in the history of containerization. Together, these performances illustrate how the shipping container evolved into a symbol and a tool of eviction in deindustrializing cities.

My third case study is Huang Yong Ping's 2016 installation *Empires*, an astonishing example of the partnerships that have emerged between artists and logistics companies in recent years. A collaboration between Huang and the shipping giant CMA CGM, *Empires* involved the transport of hundreds of shipping containers from China to the Grand Palais in Paris, where they were used to construct a redolent landscape taking the form of a container yard. For CMA CGM, the temporary installation showcased the firm's delivery prowess, but when read against the grain, it also offers a chance to map the growing divide between logistical hinterlands and urban cores, as well the role of population management therein. The chapter concludes in the settler colonial landscape of Palestine, where, in 2014, Nida Sinnokrot created the sculpture *Jonah's Whale* from a single shipping container that had previously been used as both an Israeli settler caravan and a Palestinian construction site office. With singular force and clarity, Sinnokrot's sculpture exhibits the range of ways that shipping containers are used as levers of dispossession, including as weapons of territorial conquest.

Unremarkable Infrastructure

Aesthetically speaking, the shipping container may possess "all the romance of a tin can," but it has been a cornerstone of the global capitalist production process for half a century.[18] As I detailed in Chapter 2, the consultants and engineers who were first tasked with restructuring businesses according to the ideal of continuous flow during the logistics revolution looked to the pipeline as a model for treating goods passing through it as much like liquids as possible. Turning this supply chain pipedream into reality, however, required millions of huge metal boxes, not to mention enormous ships, towering cranes, vast ports, extensive road and rail networks, among much else.

The shipping container's success owes primarily to its purpose-built ability to connect different modes of transport. Containerization is, fundamentally, a form of intermodalism that makes it possible to easily transfer large containers across ships, trucks, and trains. However mundane this achievement might seem, it satisfies the deep-seated capitalist desire to reduce the human labor necessary for moving commodities. While the tankers and slurry pipelines of the mid-twentieth century demonstrated that even bulk commodities like wheat or iron ore could be moved and stored like liquids, the challenge of break-bulk freight persisted. Even with tools like conveyer belts and forklifts, every single refrigerator, crate of beer, or sack of potatoes still had to be handled several times before reaching consumers. In the 1950s, a ship traveling across the North Atlantic might carry some 200,000 different items that required weeks of stowage work performed by human hands at either end. Transport costs made up between 10 and 20 percent of a commodity's price, with half of that attributed to just the labor needed for loading and unloading.[19] After World War II, truck, rail, and ship firms fiercely competed with one another for business, but the prospect of intermodalism united them against a common enemy: their workers. Why pay a crew of dockworkers to move cargo from a truck to a ship, risking damage and pilferage, when a single crane could pluck a large container full of goods from a trailer and place it on deck? The postwar gains won by unionized dockworkers in ports across the world only intensified the determination of capitalists to limit the power of logistics labor. Containerization was, and remains, class war disguised as technological innovation.

Instructive here is the story, often repeated, of the shipping container's invention, one that gives credit almost entirely to the American trucking magnate Malcom McLean. Frustrated by traffic on US roads in the 1950s, McLean set out on a mission to swap the jammed highways of the Atlantic Coast with the open waters of the Atlantic Ocean. He ordered engineers to devise a system that would let his trucks deposit their trailers on ships to be collected by other trucks at a different port. In April 1956, before an audience of politicians and corporate executives, McLean's company showed a proof of concept by transporting fifty-eight specially designed metal boxes aboard the converted World War II oil tanker *Ideal-X* from Newark to Houston. What would have cost $5.83 per ton to load as loose cargo had dropped, so McLean claimed, to just ¢15.8. In a nod to his dream of stitching together terrestrial and oceanic transport, McLean christened his new venture Sea-Land Service.[20]

Publicly demonstrating the shipping container's intermodal potential was one thing, but building the infrastructure that containerization required to function at a planetary scale was quite another matter. Standardization was critical in guaranteeing interchangeability throughout the system. As early as the 1950s, the US Navy had insisted on setting domestic standards for shipping containers to ensure compatibility between commercial and military vessels. For shipping containers to serve the capitalist world-system, however, global standards were needed. It was not until 1970, after a decade of negotiations, that member nations of the International Organization for Standardization finally agreed on the shipping container's core specifications, which included its standard length—the twenty-foot equivalent unit (TEU). In addition to intense government intervention, intermodalism also demanded extensive deregulation, particularly in the United States, where truck and rail laws were relaxed to open domestic transport to international players.[21]

If standardization and deregulation provided the legal guarantee of integration, various Cold War conflicts created the circumstances for the global expansion of containerized trade. Containerization was not born in a corporate boardroom but was forged on the battlefield, the product of protracted class and colonial wars.[22] For example, the closure of the Suez Canal for eight years following the Six-Day War in 1967 altered the geography of global shipping in the container's favor. Meanwhile, the American war in Vietnam brought shipping containers to the Pacific when the Pentagon recruited Sea-Land Service to help rationalize its supply chains. With military containers emptied in Vietnam, Japanese firms were invited to fill them with consumer goods for export to the United States at rock-bottom rates. The first commercial shipping container service between the United States and Japan launched in 1967, followed soon after by connections to Hong Kong, Taiwan, the Philippines, and Australia. With the rise of just-in-time (JIT) manufacturing in the 1980s, shipping containers became newly prized as warehouse substitutes.[23] Today, some nine out of every ten items purchased in a country like England have, at some point and in some part, traveled in a shipping container. Without the approximately 44.2 million shipping containers circulating around the planet, the capitalist world as we know it would come to a standstill.[24]

Today, shipping containers are not only found floating on the high seas and clogging up our highways; through their cameos in films and television shows, they also occupy a prominent place in the cultural imagination. For many, the shipping container has transcended its status as "the single most important technological innovation underpinning the globalization of trade" to become the very emblem of globalization itself.[25] As both a tool and a symbol of supply chain capitalism, it might seem reasonable to assume that artworks featuring the shipping container would have particular potential for orienting people to the dizzying space of a world spun by logistics.

Alberto Toscano and Jeff Kinkle have tested this very hypothesis and identified several useful examples, most notably the films and photographs of Allan Sekula. They have also outlined the risk that shipping container art may exacerbate rather than alleviate disorientation, typically by nurturing a false sense of bearing or comfort. One of the biggest potential offenders, according to Toscano and Kinkle, is the fashion in film and television to adopt the shipping container as a "narrative emblem and device," as exemplified in the second season of *The Wire*, which opens with Baltimore dockworkers discovering thirteen trafficked women dead in a shipping container.[26] The revelation confirms general intuition that whatever mystery the container hides is a dangerous one, but the misery narratively loaded into *The Wire*'s container is too literal. The gruesome revelation cannot encompass the extent of "the structures of power that subtend the circulation of commodities."[27] By focusing on the grisly contents of a single shipping container, the television series suggests that the menace begins and ends with this one box, redirecting our gaze from the exploitative world-system of capitalism to a criminal cartel.

This narrative-driven fetish finds a visual art complement in the landscape port photography of shipping containers by artists such as Frank Breuer and Edward Burtynsky. Unlike *The Wire,* images like these actually attest to the enormity of containerization, but they do so by replicating a pleasingly minimalist geometry that succumbs to both the modernist allure of "seriality, repetition and modularity" and the sublime.[28] The sprawling spectacle of order in such photographs conveys a heartening sense of permanence and rationality, reassuring viewers that they are in good hands. Beautiful images like these offer opportunities to relish being bewildered and unwind any desire to scrutinize the systems in which shipping containers circulate.

For all that Toscano and Kinkle chart the political potential and pitfalls of representing shipping containers in culture, their method of interpretation does not account for the real-world logistical arrangements that many representations of shipping containers require. Nor do they consider the growing trend of using shipping containers to create and display art. Take, for example, Clare Bayley's 2007 play *The Container,* which tells of a group of asylum seekers making a desperate journey to England inside a shipping container. The drama offers a poignant depiction of the hardships faced by refugees, but its realist dramaturgy yields the kind of narrative that sidelines imagination of the complex systems within which containers function. And yet, a critical method of interpretation that pays attention only to plot and visuality cannot account for the full dynamics of Bayley's play as it was actually staged. When *The Container* premiered at the Edinburgh Fringe Festival in 2007, it was performed in an actual shipping container, with the twenty-eight-person audience crammed inside along with the cast. This infrastructural fact of performance did not free *The Container* of a story-generated container fetish. On the contrary, the intimacy of shared space heightened it by leaving audiences with even less room to contemplate the shipping container beyond what the narrative provided.

The repurposing of shipping containers into physical infrastructure for art is widespread, found in venerable institutions and small venues alike. In addition to realist plays like *The Container*, which employ shipping containers as narrative devices, there are also theatrical productions that replicate the logistical sublime identified by Toscano and Kinkle in landscape port photography. For example, Es Devlin's set for a 2015 production of *Rise and Fall of the City of Mahagonny* at London's Royal Opera House used shipping containers as the building blocks for Kurt Weill and Bertolt Brecht's dystopian metropolis. As the city of Mahagonny grew over the course of the opera, so did the number of containers onstage. This culminated after intermission in the astonishing reveal of a mountain of shipping containers—some real, some *trompe l'oeil* set pieces—stacked to the ceiling of the lavish theater.

With a similar effect but in a different locale and disciplinary context, Anselm Kiefer has built a 200-acre studio compound nestled in the French Cévennes, much of it constructed of shipping containers and concrete container casts. The renowned German painter has described his teetering container towers that dot the mountainous landscape as "reverse architecture," intended to implant the fluid forms of contemporary society into nature.[29] When experienced in person or through Kiefer's mammoth paintings of them, the boundary dividing the shipping container from the natural world strives to dissolve. Both Devlin and Kiefer, by transforming shipping containers into sublime landscapes, avow containerization as a second nature.

Most artists who repurpose shipping containers do so to take advantage of their ready-made infrastructural qualities. Touring performances, such as the situational game *3rd Ring Out* by Metis (2010) and numerous traveling exhibitions, for example, use shipping containers primarily for their portability.[30] Some artists have even embraced the box's cramped internal dimensions, like the theater company Darkfield, which finds the confined space ideal for crafting immersive audio environments.[31] Art venues made from shipping containers are popping up around the world; these include permanent spaces like Seoul's Platoon Kunsthalle and Wellington's Performance Arcade, as well as the temporary outdoor container stages that proliferated during the COVID-19 pandemic.[32] Plans are even underway to build the Container Globe, a mobile performance venue inspired by the design of Shakespeare's Elizabethan theater and assembled from stacked shipping containers.[33] None of these examples, however, hold a candle to the full-sized shipping container stadium built in Doha that hosted half a dozen soccer matches during the 2022 Qatar World Cup. The innovative design of Stadium 974 (named for the number of containers it used) garnered praise from journalists for its sustainability while distracting from the tournament's body count.[34]

Many of the most well-known examples of art made with shipping containers, however, have attracted little attention to their physical infrastructure. Take, for example, Christoph Schlingensief's notorious 2000 provocation *Bitte Liebt Österreich!* (*Please Love Austria!*), a fake reality show that gave the Austrian public the chance to watch a group of asylum seekers live for a week inside a complex of containers built in the center of Vienna. Each day spectators could go online and vote for which contestant they wanted to see expelled from the country. Scholars have scrutinized Schlingensief's xenophobic travesty and the minor riots it incited but have paid only cursory attention to the fact that the performance was housed in shipping containers.[35] Such indifference seems understandable, given that the scandal triggered by *Bitte Liebt Österreich* had little to do with the shipping containers themselves. This also speaks to the very infrastructural effectiveness of shipping containers: after all, reliable infrastructure typically does not draw interest in why or how it persists.

A quarter century ago, Sekula observed that "containerization obscures more than the heterogeneity of cargoes."[36] New deepwater facilities built to accommodate container ships, he argued, had pushed ports out of major cities and out of the minds of many. "Logistical life," as Charmaine Chua notes, "has become peripheral to the imagination of the metropolis."[37] Yet reminders and remainders of logistics can be found all around us today, thanks in large part to the proliferation of shipping container art and architecture. In a city like London, which exemplifies the type of logistical transformation that Sekula described, shipping containers have become part of daily life, housing everything from shops and hotels to schools and COVID-19 vaccination centers. However, the growth of shipping container art does not necessarily restore infrastructural awareness of the sort that Sekula believed containerization had compromised. Instead, such art brings people into close, even intimate relation with the instruments of capital, only to risk further mystifying supply chain capitalism by transforming the shipping container into either something mundane or a passing fad. Worse yet, as we will see, much shipping container art serves capitalist dispossession.

The Logistics of Dislocation

By cutting the costs of transporting goods around the world, containerization brought about a historic "delocalization" of industry, in which sites of production became untethered geographically from their consumer markets.[38] While the resulting transformation is typically understood as deindustrialization, this terminology emphasizes the loss of manufacturing jobs in the capitalist core while overlooking how local markets in regions historically underdeveloped by capital have been flooded with commodities produced elsewhere. Partial as it is to manufacturing work, the framework of deindustrialization can also obscure the effects that delocalizing industry has had on linked sectors like logistics. Containerization altered not only where goods are made but also how they are transported and handled. This change was most conspicuous in the docks, where the longshore jobs that survived containerization were largely relocated to the new deepwater facilities that replaced urban ports. For containerization to enhance capital's capacity for exploiting workers in manufacturing, extreme acts of dispossession were required. Containerized trade displaced maritime life throughout the capitalist world-system, but, as Levinson writes, "Nowhere was the transformation more tumultuous than in Britain."[39]

For a time in the nineteenth century, London was the beating heart of the British empire and home to the world's busiest port. Trade was processed through a sprawling system of enclosed docks and purpose-built waterways that covered an area of eight square miles east of Tower Bridge. Despite heavy bombing during World War II, London's docklands continued to handle a quarter of British trade on the eve of containerization. In part due to postwar labor activism, London dockworkers enjoyed wages that were 30 percent higher than those in factories. However, when the first shipping containers arrived in London from New York in March 1966, port productivity growth was lagging far behind wage gains, and management structures were bogged down by inefficiencies. The British government's efforts in the late 1960s to modernize its major waterfronts came too late to prevent collapse, as ports in Rotterdam and Bremen had already beat London and Liverpool out of the blocks in the race to attract container ships by lengthening docks, installing new cranes, and deepening channels. When Sea-Land Service completed its first transatlantic voyage with an all-container ship in April 1966, Malcom McLean's company chose to skip London entirely.[40]

The writing was on the wall: in 1967, a report from McKinsey & Company commissioned by the British Transport Docks Board (BTDB) predicted the impending demise of London's port.[41] Containerization was expected to halve British shipping costs, but achieving these savings required, among other things, the consolidation of numerous local ports scattered along the British coast. Only those capable of accommodating the infrastructure needed to welcome container ships and transport containerized goods inland by truck or rail would survive. The natural bends and shallow beds of the Thames, coupled with London's off-river dock system, made the inner-city port unfit for containerized trade. Recognizing this, in the late 1960s, the BTDB began building five deepwater berths and twenty acres of container storage twenty miles downriver from London in Tilbury. Despite resistance from trade unions, including two years of industrial action by Tilbury dockworkers, shipping containers quickly proved their value by boosting hourly productivity and cutting turnaround time for ships from ten days to thirty-six hours. National container throughput tripled during the 1970s, and a backwater port in Felixstowe, located ninety miles northeast of London, rose to handle 40 percent of this volume.[42] The metropole's logistical life was well on its way to being dislocated.

From the moment Sea-Land Service first called at Felixstowe in 1967, London's once-thriving docklands started collapsing, beginning with the closure of the East India Docks that same year. By 1971, London had already lost half of its wharves, and a decade later, the demise of the Royal Docks, which had tried but failed to adapt to containerized trade, marked the end of London proper as a port of any significance. Some 2,000 acres of land went derelict, and almost all of the 31,448 dockworker jobs registered in 1955 disappeared, taking with them tens of thousands more in nearby factories, ship-repair depots, and warehouses. These closures uprooted entire communities that had grown around the docks, and between 1961 and 1981, the unemployment rate for men rose to 21.4 percent, even as the population declined by 28 percent.[43] The shipping container had been designed to facilitate exploitation, but rolling it out resulted in immense dislocation. What occurred in London would not be unique. Historic ports in major cities around the world were emptied of the logistical life and labor that had sustained them for generations, leaving their waterfronts and piers to decay before being demolished or repurposed into commercial districts and tourist attractions.[44]

London's logistical dislocation was registered culturally in many ways. In addition to popular representations like the 1980 gangster film *The Long Good Friday*, which used the abandoned docks as its backdrop, artists also engaged with the upheaval more directly. One of the most prominent local interventions was *Raising the Titanic*, an outdoor spectacle staged by Welfare State International in August 1983 on Dock B of Limehouse Basin.[45] The four-hour performance, which ran for two weeks, used the sinking of the *Titanic* as an allegory for dispossession in the area. Each night, 325 spectators arrived at the dock to find it transformed into an open-air market. Local residents and community groups sold food and crafts from stalls designed to look like lifeboats, their purveyors cast as survivors of catastrophe. Meanwhile, a string quartet played and roving bands of actors performed short skits introducing the themes and protagonists of the show to come. The lively marketplace was abruptly closed when an enormous crane truck appeared on the scene, pushing its way through the crowd to the end of the dock. There, it fished out a seventy-foot metal frame from the water, announced by one actor to be the stern of the sunken *Titanic*. After being ushered to their seats in a raked grandstand, the audience watched as a forklift stacked two pairs of shipping containers on top of each other. The sides of the containers facing the audience had been removed to create a dollhouse-like set. The musical that followed purported to show the final hours of the *Titanic* through a dozen rough-and-ready vignettes. These comical episodes were linked as much by plot as by the use of props made from found rubbish. In one scene, for example, the ship's captain dined with a wealthy passenger on a banquet of bicycle tires, and another featured two cleaners sweeping the deck of the ship using a pair of broken vacuums like brooms. Amidst such a salvaged theatrical landscape, the corroded shipping container set seemed entirely at home.[46] *Raising the Titanic* concluded when the forklift returned to remove the shipping containers, once again revealing the *Titanic*'s skeletal stern, now ablaze. Nearby, a large iceberg floated into view on a pontoon boat outfitted with exploding fireworks. As the spectacle ended in fire, the audience joined the cast for a party on the docks that lasted well into the night.

Raising the Titanic was a culmination of Welfare State International's work up to that time and is remembered today as a landmark production.[47] Founded in 1968, the group first made its name by staging plays, parades, and pyrotechnic events. Its work, both in England and abroad, blended nomadic wandering with community-sited engagement and vaudevillian spectacle with Beckettian dramaturgy. Welfare State International chose the *Titanic* story as a parable for Thatcher's Britain, depicting a stratified society in which many are condemned to drown so that a few can thrive. According to director John Fox, it was intended to be "a kind of ritual exorcism of capitalism."[48] But the performance addressed its present through more than its plot or polemical themes. The shipping container set, for instance, literalized the *Titanic*'s stark class divides. In a late scene, the stokers attempted to climb up from the depths of the engine room, only to be beaten down by wealthy passengers dancing in death masks atop the containers. The shipping containers also anchored the production in the former docklands. As Fox described it, the shipping containers injected a sense of "irony" because they "represented the very reason the economic life of the dock had come to an end."[49] Welfare State International's target was not so much containerization as the capital-led redevelopment of the area. While shipping containers today are emblems of remotely globalized exploitation, in *Raising the Titanic* they symbolized brute local dispossession.

Limehouse Basin was one of London's first docks to close, doing so in 1969. Located on the north bank of the Thames, the marshy area around Limehouse Basin had been an important site of shipbuilding for centuries. After 1820, the area's commercial significance picked up with the opening of Regent's Canal Dock, which became a key spot for transshipping cargo, especially coal. The depopulation, unemployment, and deprivation that hit the district in the 1970s set a pattern that would be repeated across the rest of the former docklands. Early efforts to address the port's collapse by supporting the needs of local residents stalled with Thatcher's election in 1979. No sooner had the last of the docks closed than the Tory government launched the London Docklands Development Corporation (LDDC) in 1981 to oversee redevelopment of the area, which was rebranded as the London Docklands.[50] Financed primarily by the state with major property developers at the helm, the unelected quango held full planning authority over the area, which it exercised to seize civic plots, buy public-sector property (most belonging to the Port of London), and push out existing tenants by issuing compulsory purchase orders. Before the collapse, 95 percent of residents in the area had lived in social housing, but instead of bolstering this stock, the LDDC either sold it off to private capital or let it rot. Most of the 6,000 homes built under the LDDC in the first half of the 1980s were bought by private owners, causing land prices to soar.[51] Of the thousands of jobs created in the early years of the LDDC, most were in finance or hospitality and filled by commuters, leading local unemployment to rise to 32 percent by 1986.[52] The LDDC, meanwhile, offered tax breaks, below-market rents, and other incentives to lure banks and media companies into the skyscrapers newly erected atop the heart of the former docks in Canary Wharf, and serviced by a rapidly constructed airport and light railway system. The LDDC rebuilt the London Docklands—just not for the communities who had called the area home for generations.

Limehouse was among the first districts targeted by the LDDC for redevelopment.[53] Welfare State International staged *Raising the Titanic* on a dock that was slated to become part of a private marina, with many of the warehouses surrounding the basin already undergoing conversion into waterfront condos. Nearby, private developers were emptying housing that had been built for dockworker families half a century earlier and renovating them into upscale flats.[54] No single scheme better encapsulated the class war underway than the Limehouse Link, a mile-long tunnel bored beneath Limehouse to connect London's existing financial district to the new one in Canary Wharf. Instead of improving Limehouse for existing residents, the LDDC spent £300 million so that investment bankers could drive under it.[55]

The London Docklands has become a case study of the Lockean rationale used to justify neoliberal gentrification. From the early modern enclosures of the English countryside to the colonization of Indigenous territory, dispossession has long been defended by pledges to improve land that is said to be going to waste.[56] Such rhetoric saturated the London Docklands, with Michael Heseltine, the main political force behind the LDDC, infamously describing the area as "6,000 acres of forgotten wasteland."[57] During the 1980s, the LDDC spent £31.3 million on advertising to woo prospective residents to the area with promises that the new Docklands "will feel like Venice and work like New York."[58] As two activists involved in campaigns to resist the LDDC recalled, "It was not enough that [existing residents] were dispossessed and politically disenfranchised but they had to be rendered *invisible* too."[59]

Raising the Titanic contributed to the broad social movement that emerged to challenge the LDDC's projection of the London Docklands as *terra nullius*. The struggle in the 1980s relied on a range of tactics, from occupations and sit-ins to tenant organizing and the so-called People's Armadas, when thousands of people took to the Thames in boats to protest outside the Houses of Parliament.[60] Artistic interventions also played a significant role. To create *Raising the Titanic*, Welfare State International's team of sixty performers, designers, technicians, and engineers set up camp on the docks, with most of them living in tents. Since few in the ensemble had connections to Limehouse, they spent the summer on-site collaborating with local arts organizations and working with some 150 residents to develop the production. Community members contributed by selling food at the pre-show market, crafting paper lanterns and puppets, and even performing. Welfare State International made no secret of its political sympathies. For example, the program for *Raising the Titanic* provided space to activist organizations like the Limehouse Development Group, whose insert avowed opposition to "all speculative development plans" and featured an image from the film *Jaws* with a caption that read "Keep the sharks out of Limehouse Basin."[61] One community organizer positioned the production as part of a larger struggle "to show there were ways of using the area other than building luxury flats."[62]

Despite its political commitments and its advertised claims that *Raising the Titanic* was created "for and with the residents of Limehouse," Welfare State International's engagement with locals was fraught.[63] The project was funded by the Arts Council and commissioned for a major arts festival, the London International Festival of Theatre (LIFT). This meant that working-class Limehouse residents with access to subsidized tickets were ultimately outnumbered by LIFT's typical creative class audience. In some respects, Welfare State International's attempt to resist dispossession seemed to herald it. The group effectively took over the dock for the summer, spending half of its £30,000 budget on fencing and security to protect its materials. Some of those involved offered perfunctory self-criticism, stating, "The community had to be kept out in order to be included."[64] When asked whether audiences picked up on the link between the production's use of shipping containers and their own dispossession, Fox noted to me: "To be honest I don't imagine that they made any connection. Maybe the arty ones did, but the locals were just pissed off with our fireworks waking them up."[65] For all its sins, what distinguishes this early example of shipping container art from many that would follow was Welfare State International's commitment to making visible the people who were being dispossessed. The use of shipping containers in *Raising the Titanic* articulated a local common sense that containerization was predicated on dispossession.

Containerized Gentrification

Raising the Titanic was one of the earliest significant examples of art using shipping containers as a physical infrastructure. In the decades since, the London Docklands has become ground zero for artistic and architectural experiments with shipping containers. The tipping point came in 2001 with the construction of Container City, a three-story complex of red shipping containers assembled in Trinity Buoy Wharf and designed as artist studios and workspaces. A year later, this boxy structure was connected by bridges to a newer and larger sibling, Container City 2. Hailed as "probably the most recognizable container building in the world," this multicolored five-story ziggurat-style monstrosity is today home to an array of designers, artists, and arts organizations.[66] According to Urban Space Management (USM), the firm responsible for overseeing the site, Container City confirms the "off the shelf" potential of shipping containers as building blocks for urban areas undergoing regeneration.[67] But these buildings also demonstrate something else about the repurposing of shipping containers into art and architecture. From the nineteenth century until its closure in the 1980s, Trinity Buoy Wharf was home to a lighthouse and beacon workshops. The wharf was sold to the LDDC in 1988, and then it was leased to USM for redevelopment into a creative and entertainment compound. USM's landmark experiment in "container urbanism" was only made possible by London's logistical dislocation, underscoring the connection between containerization and dispossession.[68]

Being the very model of shipping container architecture, Container City paved the way for numerous similar projects both in London and beyond.[69] This includes *The Boy Who Climbed Out of His Face,* an immersive performance created by Shunt that ran for six weeks in August and September 2014. When viewed from the outside, the dozen shipping containers that Shunt stacked on a disused coaling jetty in North Greenwich appeared as though they were waiting to be loaded onto the deck of a ship. But instead of filling them with cargo, the London performance collective transformed its forty-foot elongated boxes into thickly crafted theatrical environments. Audiences toured these shipping containers in small groups, immersing themselves in a succession of worlds that ranged from a jungle safari to something resembling a nightmarish dinner party. Shunt installed its containers just downriver from the dock where Welfare State International had set up camp three decades earlier. While *The Boy* had little in common thematically with *Raising the Titanic*, its location and shared infrastructural aesthetic placed it on the same timeline of dispossession. Whereas Welfare State International's use of shipping containers indexed how containerization worked with Thatcherism to displace entire communities in the London Docklands, *The Boy* exhibits the process of gentrification that has unfolded since.

Shunt's performance had little to say about containerization explicitly, but its shipping containers were impossible to ignore. They appeared prominently in advertising for *The Boy*, and the names of shipping companies like Hanjin and Hamburg Süd remained emblazoned on their corrugated steel sides throughout the performance run. Yet Shunt provided no clue as to what to make of its shipping containers. When I arrived outside the container complex for my tour, an attendant instructed me to remove my shoes and socks and place them in a white shoebox, which I then carried during the performance. With sand and water to trek through, this seemed a sensible measure. It resonated loosely in other ways too—shipping containers and shoes, both emblems of globalization.

With our shoeboxes in hand, my group entered the first shipping container, although once inside, it looked nothing of the sort. The walls were made of pristine paneling instead of weathered metal, and the narrow space was bathed in yellow light. The container was devoid of fittings, save for a slender table that spanned its length. An erratic performer wearing lavish pearls and an unnerving latex mask was waiting for us. Her white pantsuit matched her white wig. She directed us to place our shoeboxes on the table, alongside several others that were already there. Perusing the boxes, she discovered a surprise in one of them—a small trove of jewelry. But before anyone could lay claim to the contents, it was time to move on.

Our host pulled back curtains revealing another room that, as it turned out, was an extension of the container we were in. This new space seemed to extend far into the distance, but this was only an optical illusion; the room's dimensions subtly narrowed, distorting perspective and making the room appear longer than it actually was. After passing through a door at the opposite end, we found ourselves in a cramped club with poster-covered walls, blaring house music, and a crowded dance floor. Some of the people there were dancing, while the rest swayed awkwardly. Soon, the music ceased, replaced by a voice from a loudspeaker telling those who had been informed they were "winners" to move along. My group hadn't received any such news, but apparently the others had. As they departed, the music resumed, and we took their place dancing.

The structure of *The Boy* as a tour offered little opportunity for audiences to orient themselves to the worlds that Shunt had fashioned inside its shipping containers. Nor was there a chance for a coherent plot or story to develop. Publicity for *The Boy* on Shunt's website featured evocative quotes from books like Charles Kingsley's 1863 children's novel *The Water-Babies* and Joseph Conrad's *Heart of Darkness*, yet audiences were hard-pressed to establish meaningful connections between these texts and what awaited them on the tour. The literary clues were less signposts indicating clear destinations than they were breadcrumbs sprinkled by Shunt in the containers. While not misleading, where they led was largely open to interpretation by those who found them.

The performance ended, for example, by playfully alluding to Kingsley's novel. My group exited the final room by climbing up a rickety set of metal stairs to an outdoor walkway built on the roofs of the shipping containers we had just wandered through. From this new vantage point, I could see that the shipping containers were arranged in the shape of a rectangle. The middle of this complex was filled with water, within which a single container was partially submerged, one end angled up into the chilly night air. A bearded performer stood naked on this sinking container, sometimes playing an ethereal swan song on an electric guitar or trying on a red sequined gown (Figure 16). Floating in the water around him were dozens of dolls, both the stranded shipping container's cargo and, it seemed, the water-babies of Kingsley's title. Striking as it was, this final tableau was more visually arresting than symbolically meaningful. The subtlety of the allusion to Kingsley's novel made it an incidental task for spectators to decipher why Shunt chose to materialize *The Water-Babies* in such a wryly literal manner.

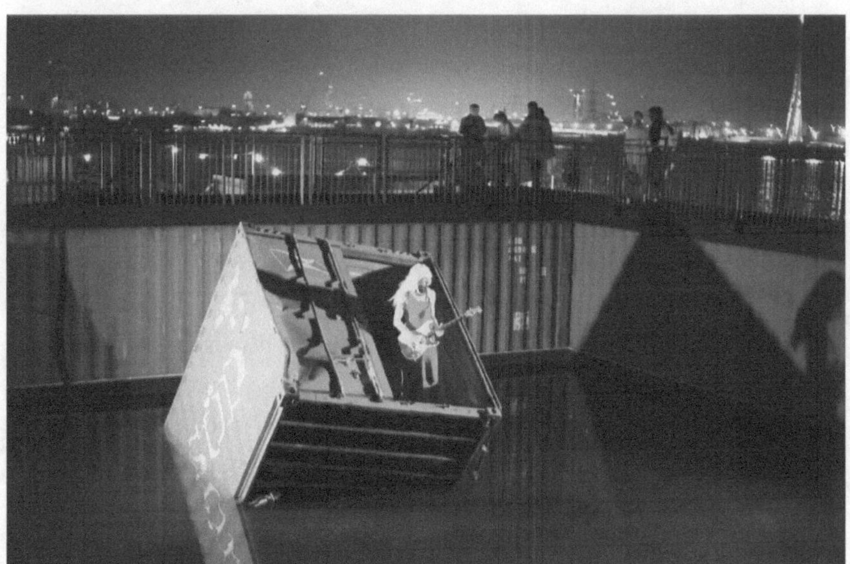

FIGURE 16. Tom Lyall in Shunt's *The Boy Who Climbed Out of His Face*, 2014. *Photo:* Susanne Dietz. Reprinted with permission.

Inside an earlier shipping container, we explored a sandy jungle environment, but whether this was a nod to *Heart of Darkness* remains unclear. The lonely performers I came across throughout the tour could have been embodiments of Mr. Kurtz, although this interpretation is likely more my own attempt at untangling the performance's scattered references than it is an understanding shared by others. We can take a cue here from Shunt itself, who described *Heart of Darkness* in its permit application to the local authority as "starting material." Rather than stage the novel, Shunt explained that the performance would offer "a more experiential and lyrical play with the content of Conrad's most famous book."[70] Literature used in *The Boy* were prompts and not organizing principles for performance—not to mention a convenient way for Shunt to make its plans legible to city bureaucrats and prospective audiences.

While *The Boy* may not have relied on a narrative to escort audiences through the performance, Shunt did not leave its visitors entirely at sea. Just as the shipping containers, with their physical resemblance to tunnels, led progressive movement during the forty-five-minute performance tour, they also kept contained what was otherwise a fragmented experience. The closest I came to a guide in *The Boy* was its shipping container infrastructure. When the doors locked and lights suddenly cut out in one unadorned container, my awareness of where I was shaped my reaction to the noises generated by a powerful speaker system. The din of whirring and slamming metal suggested that the shipping container, with us inside, was being hoisted onto a ship. Soon, the sound of splashing water washed through the pitch-black space. Our vessel had set sail. There was no guarantee where a spectator's mind would wander during *The Boy*, but it was to shipping containers that thoughts likely returned. At that moment, I could not help but be reminded of the distressing news from that very day about thirty-five Afghan refugees discovered in a shipping container in the Port of Tilbury, just downriver from London. One person had died during the desperate passage to England. No sooner had the lights switched back on in the shipping container than my group was ushered into an entirely different world. The constant cognitive adjustments required when moving from one environment to the next during *The Boy* only made it more challenging for thoughts to cohere. Although audiences could not take the shipping containers for granted, Shunt never indicated what should be made of them. Adding to the disorientation, Shunt played with the senses in various ways throughout the tour. Aromas and visual ruses filled the containers, and I was constantly aware of the changing textures beneath my bare feet. In one container I felt sand; in another water. Reminders of logistical infrastructure were ever-present, yet there was no mistaking *The Boy* for a cognitive map.

Four decades ago, when he first introduced his influential theory of cognitive mapping, Fredric Jameson could confidently state that late capitalism felt like a newly discomfiting place.[71] By now, much of this novelty has surely worn off. The very fact that one can grab a coffee from a shipping container café without a second thought is evidence enough of this. We have grown accustomed to not understanding exactly where we sit within the totality of supply chain capitalism. If one does not feel adrift, can one desire a cognitive map? Here was the political potential, however tenuous, of Shunt's shipping containers: *The Boy* proposed that capitalism can still be disorienting. Whether this was intentional or not, Shunt's shipping containers made logistics seem strange again. In this regard, *The Boy* departed from much shipping container art and architecture, especially those container houses where one can actually feel at a home. Although there was no way of becoming lost inside Shunt's container complex, *The Boy* made logistical disorientation palpable nonetheless. What any given audience member went on to do with this feeling, however, was another matter. The confusion elicited by the performance likely left many visitors simply feeling perplexed, supply chains or not. Whatever the political usefulness of such an aesthetic of cognitive *unmapping* might be, in Shunt's case, as we will see, it came at a price of collaborating with a local project of dispossession.

Shunt is no stranger to working outside the conventional infrastructures of London theater. Since forming in 1998, the ten-person collective has staged and curated performances in an array of unconventional spaces across London, including long-term residencies in railway arches and one-off productions in a tobacco warehouse and a biscuit factory.[72] To create *The Boy*, Shunt partnered with Managing Mayhem, a marketing and event services firm whose corporate clients have included the Olivier Awards, Louis Vuitton, and Mini. When it came to modifying the shipping containers, they turned to Adaptainer, one of England's oldest container-conversion specialists.[73] Shunt received top billing for *The Boy*, but the performance was only made possible with support from the property investment company Knight Dragon, which provided the disused coaling jetty in North Greenwich and the permits necessary to refit it as a performance space. Knight Dragon's owner is the Hong Kong jewelry magnate Henry Cheng, who was worth an estimated $20 billion in 2014, making him the world's second-richest property investor with holdings in the UK. At the time of the performance, Knight Dragon was busy redeveloping North Greenwich.[74]

Once a significant industrial site for manufacturing, shipbuilding, and electrical production in London, North Greenwich was left derelict by the closure of London's docks. By the 1980s, all of its factories and power plants had shuttered. The peninsula is situated directly on the Thames, just a stone's throw from central London, but toxic soil from a former gasworks and the absence of passenger rail service left the area largely idle for decades.[75] Since 2000, capital investment has poured into the 200-acre site, now remarketed as "Greenwich Peninsula." Already touted as one of Europe's largest regeneration projects in 2004, Knight Dragon expanded the initial development plans after buying full control of the $9.5 billion endeavor from its partners in 2013. Their revised 2015 scheme promised to transform Greenwich Peninsula into a "digital creative arts district" with 15,000 homes and 325,000 square feet of commercial space.[76]

The Boy's role in this real estate landscape is difficult to ignore. The redevelopment of North Greenwich made the performance possible, and, in turn, *The Boy* supported Knight Dragon's pursuits. As Michael McKinnie has argued, the arrival of a theater to a former industrial district can announce that an area once "devoted to manufacturing goods" has opened for the business of "offering services."[77] Establishing a theater in a disused factory or warehouse can be comforting; amid profound social and urban transformation, a repurposed industrial building provides a "nostalgic invocation of a stable past."[78] To the extent that Shunt's performance helped spread word of Greenwich Peninsula's makeover into London's newest hub of entertainment and luxury living, *The Boy* resembled McKinnie's model of theater as a tool for "civic self-fashioning."[79] However, Shunt's shipping containers could not offer the same sort of reassuring sentiment that McKinnie attributes to theaters that repurpose a postindustrial city's existing industrial edifice. This is because shipping containers differ from industrial buildings in both their form and function. Most notably, shipping containers are designed to be mobile, which lends them the transient temporality that has led to their widespread use as structures for pop-up cafés and stores, especially common in London. Shipping container architecture is performative architecture. It announces what it enacts: impermanence, flexibility, and interchangeability.

Along with their distinctive temporality, shipping containers also lack the historicity of industrial buildings. Closed factories are deindustrial leftovers, while shipping containers are supply chain linchpins. A repurposed container provides no continuity with a fondly recalled Fordist past and its mythologized promise of stability. Containerization, after all, made it cost-effective to deindustrialize metropoles like London. In such cities today, shipping container architecture often accompanies redevelopment projects that involve demolishing existing built environments instead of reusing them. Over the past decade, shipping containers have popped up as restaurants, galleries, and shops at construction sites across London, serving as affordable stopgaps that obliterate the past to usher in a dicey future.

Long a prime site for investment by the global capitalist class, London real estate prices soared in the years following the 2008 financial crisis as cheap money fueled speculative investment in brick-and-mortar assets. Greenwich Peninsula exemplifies the staggering development-by-demolition projects that emerged to take advantage of this booming property market.[80] Construction cranes, manicured pathways, and amenities like the O2 Arena and a corporate-sponsored cable car service have all but supplanted the district's industrial infrastructure. The defunct coaling jetty used for *The Boy* was one exception. Shunt's performance inaugurated the jetty's new identity as "The Jetty," which Knight Dragon marketed as a "temporary platform for immersive performance" and "home to a pop-up cocktail bar and a street food venue."[81] During *The Boy*'s run, shipping containers housed more than just Shunt's performance. Everything on The Jetty—its bar, kitchen, lounge area, and concert stage—was put inside shipping containers. The transience expressed by these shipping containers paralleled the construction underway right across from the box office (also made from a shipping container). Visitors picking up tickets for *The Boy* could not miss hoarding panels advertising new luxury towers that promised prospective buyers "a unique opportunity for riverside living in a new district for London."

The Jetty's function in this enormous redevelopment project explains why a global property development firm would support an experimental immersive performance like *The Boy*. Knight Dragon promoted Shunt's performance as the first in "a dynamic programme of pop-ups celebrating Greenwich Peninsula."[82] According to journalist Dan Hancox, pop-ups in London are typically "a lunge to inject coolness and spontaneity" into areas lacking such status.[83] Neither convenience nor cost alone made shipping containers the infrastructure of choice for The Jetty's pop-ups: the crown jewel of Shoreditch, one of London's most dramatically gentrified neighborhoods, is a pop-up mall built from matte-black shipping containers where shoppers can drink craft beer and eat Korean–Mexican fusion tacos before attending a taxidermy workshop. The Jetty's shipping containers were more than a provisional infrastructural necessity as the area underwent construction; they were also a pitch to investors, suggesting that Greenwich Peninsula could become the next Shoreditch.

The same year that Shunt built its container complex, over 3,000 mostly working-class and Black residents were pushed out of their homes in the Heygate housing estate in Elephant and Castle to make room for a new private development called "Elephant Park." In the years that spanned the estate's demolition and Elephant Park's opening, a trendy shopping center made from shipping containers called The Artworks was installed on the site, as if heralding the transition underway. London's most egregious case of dispossession in recent memory was buoyed by shipping container architecture.[84]

As part of Knight Dragon's permit application to transform North Greenwich's coaling jetty into a pop-up arts venue, Shunt submitted a performance treatment that framed *The Boy* as a chance to explore "the connection that Conrad makes in *Heart of Darkness* with London and the Thames and a mysterious and unexplored land (which was The Congo)."[85] Knight Dragon certainly shared Shunt's enthusiasm for taking audiences on an expedition of sorts. However, the "mysterious and unexplored land" they hoped visitors would discover was Greenwich Peninsula. Soon after *The Boy* closed, the *Evening Standard* ran a feature on the district that hailed its future as a "hi-tech village for arty, foodie, design-savvy Londoners." As evidence, London's most-read newspaper pointed to the crowds that filled The Jetty's shipping containers during Shunt's brief stay.[86]

A Logistics Empire

Containerized trade severed historic maritime cities from their ports, but the dispossession that hit places like London was just the beginning. Over the past half century, the spread of containerization has demanded near constant infrastructural expansion, especially into the hinterlands where much of the capitalist world-system's storage, sorting, and transshipment activities are now concentrated. Logistical dispossession was not a singular or original sin confined to overdeveloped countries; it has since spread, most notably in the Global South. The infrastructure of containerization, being horizontal rather than vertical, has a ravenous appetite for surface space and devours entire landscapes to make way for the railroads, highways, terminals, and low-rise distribution centers needed for the movement and sorting of shipping containers. The Port of Shanghai, for example, is the world's busiest for container throughput (47.4 million TEU in 2022) and has a geographic footprint nearly a quarter the size of Northern Ireland.[87] Acquiring the space that containerization demands has entailed upturning both human and nonhuman life the world over. Shanghai's deepwater berths were created *ex nihilo* some thirty kilometers from the shore on an expanse of reclaimed land connected by the world's longest sea bridge.[88] In earlier periods of capitalist history, hinterlands were considered the rural opposite to urban industrial metropoles. However, today, as Phil Neel observes, hinterlands are the apogee of industrial activity, home to power plants, factory farms, refineries, and expansive logistics complexes. Logistical labor, like so much of the work performed in the hinterlands, is integral to the global capitalist production process but remains largely "disavowed."[89] As the saying goes: out of sight, out of mind.

Containerization has played a major role in pushing logistical life out of cities. For its part, the spread of shipping container art has done little to restore consciousness of the supply chains that underpin modern life. Instead, the repurposing of shipping containers, whether for art or for other ends, is more likely to acclimatize us to supply chain capitalism, rendering its logistical infrastructure into either an unremarkable fixture of everyday life or a passing trend.

In 2016, Huang Yong Ping created *Empires*, a colossal installation that seemed to defy the habituating function of shipping container art by putting the container terminal on full display. For the Monumenta art show, Huang collaborated with CMA CGM, the world's third-largest container shipping company, to have 305 containers delivered to the Grand Palais in the center of Paris. Strolling through the grandiose building's cavernous nave, surrounded by stacks of multicolored shipping containers, was not unlike the experience, or so one might imagine, of moving through a modern port. Adding to the sense of uncanny was the imposing presence of an aquamarine gantry crane stationed in the center aisle. While building a shipping container yard might seem a surprising way for Huang to have fulfilled such a prestigious art commission, the aesthetic qualities of the modern port are well remarked upon; Laleh Khalili, for example, writes of how "the balletic movement of the cranes" and "the polychromatic angularity of stacked containers" combine to create an "awesome spectacle of technology."[90] What Toscano and Kinkle call the "collateral aesthetic effect" of container ports is, for most of us, all the more enticing since such spaces are today typically off-limits to visitors.[91]

For as much as *Empires* resembled a container yard, there was no mistaking the ornate Beaux-Arts building that housed it for a twenty-first century port (Figure 17). However, instead of detracting from the aesthetic experience, the Grand Palais, which opened in 1900 to host the World's Fair, intensified

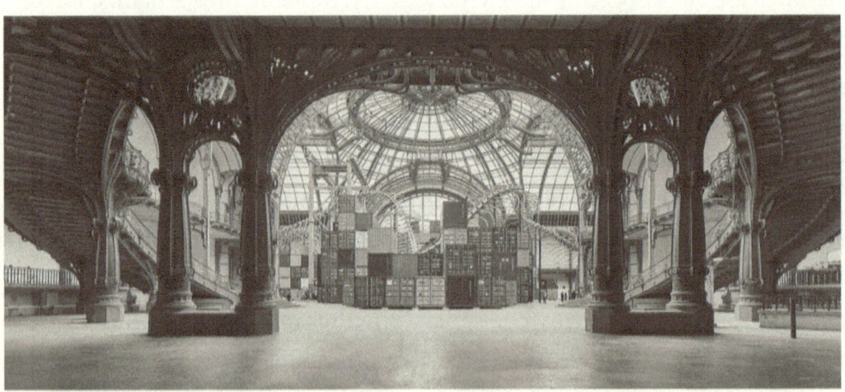

FIGURE 17. Huang Yong Ping's *Empires,* Grand Palais, Paris, 2016. *Photo:* Daniel Schäfer © Huang Yong Ping and ADAGP, Paris, 2023. Courtesy archives Huang Yong Ping and Mennour, Paris.

it by framing Huang's stacked shipping containers as art. When viewed from the building's curving balconies, *Empires* appeared akin to the logistical landscapes found in a Frank Breuer or Edward Burtynsky photograph. Curators and reviewers alike categorized *Empires* as a landscape, describing the topography of the stacked shipping containers as giving the impression of hills and a valley.[92] The installation granted access to and even heightened the latent aesthetic potential of a shipping container port, tipping the balance from the mundanely logistical toward the logistical sublime.

But *Empires* was meant to be more than an immersive environment for spectators to experience. Positioned throughout the landscape, Huang installed other things that begged for interpretation. For example, winding its way up, over, and around the shipping container stacks was the skeleton of an enormous aluminum serpent suspended from the ceiling. Weighing 133 tons and stretching 254 meters, the snake demanded attention while also making itself at home in the lofty environs. Its exposed metal vertebrae complemented the iron ribs of the Grand Palais's barrel-vaulted glass roof, its body moving in lockstep with the architectural rhythm of the spiraling staircases and balustrades. Resting on the ground near the exit, its huge skull grinned with 120 menacing teeth. Outsized skeletal snakes loom large in Huang's oeuvre, though what they mean is rarely self-evident or even consistent. The serpentine form in *Empires* said something about global trade, but exactly what was impossible to say. This did not keep critics from competing to read it as everything from "a surrogate for the multinational corporation" to a symbol of "Paris's particular fears and divisions over immigrants."[93]

The urge to interpret only intensified as one moved toward the center of Huang's container yard. Waiting to be discovered there was a five-meter black bicorn hat made of bitumen, balanced atop two small stacks of containers to create an arch that vied with the larger crane stationed behind it. The gigantic hat was modeled on the one worn by Napoleon Bonaparte in an Antoine-Jean Gros painting from 1808 commemorating French victory over the Russians at the Battle of Eylau. Whether this was some kind of joking reference to the Napoleon complex remains unclear, but one thing seems certain: the towering container stacks, the giant snake, and the huge hat were all meant to make one feel small. The curator Jean de Loisy rightly noted the many "layers" of meaning that *Empires* possessed.[94] To help parse them, the accompanying gallery text provided a convenient key:

> The containers evoke globalization, as vehicles for the circulation of wealth. The bicorn evokes the endless power struggles that drive the world and all the industrialists, politicians, military men and tyrants who long to wear that famous hat. The snake slithering over the work, mouth wide open, appears to jeopardize the ambition of these powers, while the loop that it forms symbolizes the infinite nature of this cycle of glory and destruction.[95]

So much for the task of the critic. Whether or not one finds this official interpretation convincing, it insists that *Empires* was designed to be deciphered and not just experienced. *Empires* presented in a single work the two aforementioned representational problems that Toscano and Kinkle associate with shipping container art. When not astonishing visitors with its spectacle of the logistical sublime, the installation stoked a desire to decode the meaning of global trade through surface appearances.

In many ways, *Empires* epitomizes the infrastructural overlap between art and logistics that this book studies. At first glance, *Empires* might appear to be yet another addition to the growing list of shipping container art fashionably mounted in cities across the Global North, akin to Shunt's *The Boy Who Climbed Out of His Face*. What set *Empires* apart is the fact that it was not just a collection of shipping containers but, for all intents and purposes, a functioning shipping container yard. While most shipping container art uses boxes that are no longer in circulation, *Empires* broke with convention by employing containers that were still actively involved in shipping. Huang's containers were transported from China to Paris, and after the exhibition closed, they went back to work. With *Empires*, Huang blurred the boundary between art and logistics, putting CMA CGM's shipping containers on display while simultaneously stowing them away.

Although the 305 shipping containers used in *Empires* pale in comparison to the 15.6 million that CMA CGM's 453 ships moved in 2016, getting them to the Grand Palais was far from straightforward.[96] The project required six months of planning and several weeks of installation. The first shipping containers were offloaded in the Port of Le Havre on March 28,

2016, having traveled from Qingdao and Shanghai aboard *CMA CGM Bougainville* (formerly the world's largest container ship). They were then taken inland by barge and stored in Gennevilliers until trucks began transporting them on the final leg to Paris on April 25. With trucks arriving at fifteen-minute intervals, causing traffic jams along the Champs-Élysées, it took a fortnight to deliver all the shipping containers to the Grand Palais. Meanwhile, hundreds of people worked day and night to assemble the installation.[97]

Empires was a logistical undertaking through and through, a fact that most reviewers completely ignored. While much was made of what *Empires* had to say about global supply chains, very few commentators acknowledged how deeply it was entangled in them. Reviews almost seemed to assume that *Empires* had been magically delivered to the Grand Palais by Huang himself, all but erasing any trace of the actual living logistical labor that went into making it. The fact that *Empires* was so thoroughly enmeshed in the world of logistics did not prevent it from fostering a logistical myopia.

CMA CGM, on the other hand, made sure to highlight the logistical work that went into *Empires*, proudly advertising its participation in one of France's cultural events of the year. Their press release announcing the installation proclaimed CMA CGM as being "at the heart of the creation of the masterpiece, by providing its containerships, containers and its technical and logistical expertise."[98] For the Marseille-based company, 2016 was a banner year, and, even so, in its annual report, CMA CGM touted *Empires* with as much fanfare as it did its $2.4 billion acquisition of the Neptune Orient Lines, which expanded the firm's market share to 12 percent.[99] CMA CGM may have diverged from art critics who disavowed the logistical work behind *Empires*, but the company was nonetheless reticent about what the installation actually had to say about logistics. Nowhere did CMA CGM, which was founded with state backing in the 1850s to service French colonies, even mention that the installation was called *Empires*. For their part, Huang's team downplayed possible tension between any critical messages that could be read into *Empires* and CMA CGM's contributions to it. Monumenta's president, speaking on behalf of the famously taciturn Huang, confirmed the artist's interest in "the mechanisms of globalization" while insisting "he does not take a position for or against it."[100] Likewise, the exhibition guide compared Huang to an Impressionist painter who "describes a present-day economic landscape" albeit "from a non-judgmental perspective."[101]

Such rhetorical gymnastics seemed designed to tame any critical impulse in *Empires*. Just as importantly, these efforts at framing also conveyed a particular vision of logistics as something beyond judgment, as if criticism should be reserved solely for matters of technocratic inefficiency and not social, geopolitical, or climatological consequence. CMA CGM paraded their expertise in logistical coordination and resource command but made no reference to the actual labor its workers performed. "CMA CGM is a privileged observer of global economic exchanges," remarked its CEO, claiming that *Empires* "expresses" the company's formidable managerial vision.[102] Here we have the idyllic view of logistics as a management science promoted by a shipping company, in which supply chains exist as an orderly spectacle free of politics and human workers. For CMA CGM, *Empires* presented a chance to leave visitors in awe of all that a shipping giant could do.

Such were the official takes that surrounded Huang's Grand Palais installation, all of which, in differing ways, denied the role of living logistical labor in producing it. We can, however, approach *Empires* against the grain of licensed interpretation. Instead of focusing on what *Empires* had to say about logistics, we can examine the installation's role in logistics itself. The shipping container is often described as a metaphor for globalization, yet it has also been more discerningly spoken of as a synecdoche that indexes the infrastructure that exceeds it. Something similar has been said of the container port, which, despite being fenced off by razor wire, is "only one slice" of a world-encompassing infrastructure.[103] The container yard that Huang and CMA CGM built in Paris may have seemed like a totality, but it was part of a broader logistical infrastructure that stretches from Le Havre and Gennevilliers to Qingdao and Shanghai. *Empires* did more than call attention to logistical life; it effectively brought a piece of the logistical hinterlands into the metropole. Together with the traffic jams CMA CGM's delivery trucks caused along the Champs-Élysées, *Empires* insisted that logistics operates even in those places, like the centers of global cities, where logistical life tends to be disavowed and devalued.

Huang has noted that *Empires* was partly inspired by the transformation of his hometown of Xiamen.[104] When Huang moved to France in 1989,

Xiamen was just emerging as a significant locale for global trade. In 1980, a year before the London Docklands Development Corporation launched, Xiamen was designated one of China's first four special economic zones. The coastal city quickly attracted huge sums of foreign direct investment, becoming a model for other developing urban areas.[105] Today, Xiamen is a metropolis of 7 million people and home to the fourteenth busiest port in the world for container throughput. The port is the largest in Southeast China, making Xiamen a major supply chain hub and the economic capital of the Taiwan Straits.[106]

Xiamen's logistical rise tracks with that of China itself, whose emergence as the workshop of the world has coincided with it becoming the world's logistics powerhouse. Today, China produces almost all of the world's shipping containers (more than 95 percent) and a leading portion of the ships and ancillary equipment, like cranes, used to move them.[107] The country dominates the list of the world's largest ports, and since the 2008 financial crisis, the state and Chinese companies have invested heavily in maritime, rail, and road infrastructure beyond its borders. This includes buying up foreign container terminals around the world, loaning a half-trillion dollars to countries across the Global South, and, most notably, pushing the Belt and Road initiative to, among other things, connect China with Europe through a transport system that wraps around South Asia, East Africa, and the Mediterranean.[108] "Rather than world factory," Deborah Cowen suggests, "China might be better conceptualized as a logistics empire."[109]

Building China's logistical infrastructure has helped fuel boom times for urban elites in cities like Xiamen, but it has also deepened deprivation in rural areas already subject to state land grabs and forced removals. Even within Chinese cities, immiseration is growing. "Accumulation by dispossession is not just a rural phenomenon," observes Eli Friedman; "the urban subaltern has also come under the threat of the bulldozer."[110] Huge numbers of proletarianized migrants with no choice but to abandon the countryside do so at the risk of running afoul of a state regime armed with varied instruments for controlling the flow of labor in the interests of capital. This includes the notorious *hukou* household registration system as well as even more coercive means like mass evictions and compulsory relocation orders, often implemented along ethnic and racialized lines.

To profit off the dire housing crisis facing migrant workers in cities like Shanghai, entrepreneurial landlords have even taken to renting out shipping containers as improvised apartments, packing in five tenants per TEU.[111] As a work of art that doubled as a container yard, *Empires* said nothing about this state of affairs in China, let alone how such dispossession abets and even reinforces exploitation. Yet, as a synecdoche for logistics, Huang's installation was already tangled up in it.

Landscaping Dispossession in Palestine

Containerization is, first and foremost, an infrastructure for global labor arbitrage. Though geared to facilitate exploitation, establishing the conditions necessary for containerized trade to function at a planetary scale has required profound acts of dispossession. If, as Deborah Cowen puts it, "Logistics maps the form of contemporary imperialism," we need look no further for evidence of this than the history of the shipping container, forged as it was through wars and colonial occupations.[112] An imperialist drive is hardwired into the shipping container's modular logic, which, Charmaine Chua notes, entails "an encompassing logistical vision, one that was and continues to be global in its ambition."[113] But a shipping container's role in empire does not end when the box stops moving goods. It extends as well into the many ways that shipping containers are repurposed. Be it as a leisure infrastructure for the global elite or as the improvised architecture of our planet of slums, shipping containers have become default levers for dispossessive projects the world over. By way of conclusion then I end this chapter in the occupied West Bank, a settler colonial landscape defined by the dispossession of Palestinian territory, in which shipping containers have also played a part.

In 2014, Nida Sinnokrot cut a shipping container into eleven even cross sections and named it *Jonah's Whale* (Figure 18). When exhibited, the Palestinian American artist spaces the segments accordion-style, such that visitors can walk between them should they wish. If viewed end-on through the doors splayed open, the shipping container looks to be intact, but, seen from the side, the gaps give the impression of a cucumber swiftly sliced. *Jonah's Whale* invokes a history of sculptural surgery, splicing together Gordon Matta-Clark's brick-and-mortar carvings with Damien Hirst's clinical displays of fauna in formaldehyde. Sinnokrot inverts the shipping container's

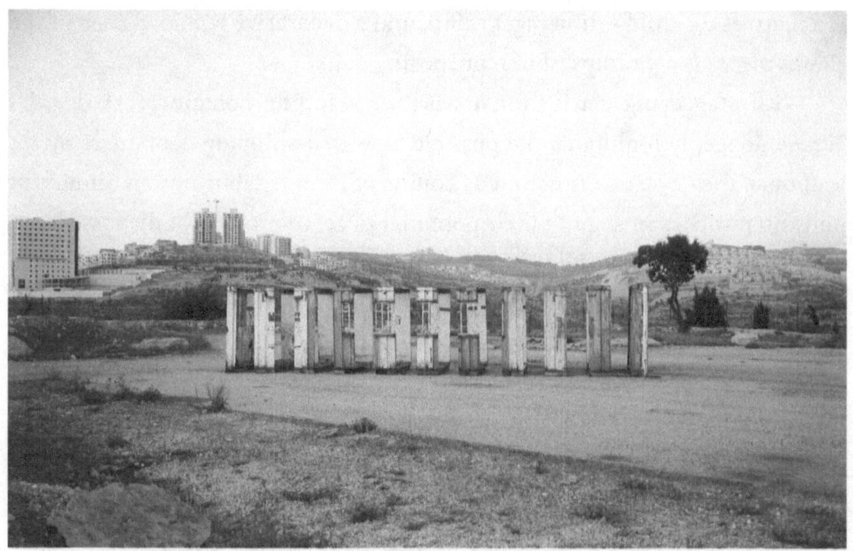

FIGURE 18. Nida Sinnokrot's *Jonah's Whale*, installed in the West Bank, 2014. *Photo:* Nida Sinnokrot © Nida Sinnokrot, courtesy the artist.

aesthetic function by rerouting attention from its surface appearance to the inside, thus spoiling the mystery of its contents before interest is even aroused. The slicing lampoons a liberal desire for transparency, dismissing the notion that we can understand a world transformed by containerized trade through isolated acts of revelation, as if learning what any single box has inside it could tell us something meaningful about the capitalist world-system now spun by supply chains. With its biblical allusion to the story of Jonah, the sculpture's title further obscures the shipping container by inviting comparison to the ribcage of a beached whale. Sinnokrot undermines the shipping container's ready-made aesthetic as well as its designed purpose, his cuts leaving it useless for intermodal transport. And yet, even before going under the knife, the shipping container's life of moving goods was long behind it. In an accompanying essay, Sinnokrot explains that his shipping container, which the artist found in a junkyard, had previously been deployed as a makeshift outpost for an Israeli settler caravan in the West Bank and later became a Palestinian construction site office in East Jerusalem.[114] *Jonah's Whale* literally dissects this specific container's histories of use. One slice, for example, shows a cross section layered with slivers of steel, wire, insulation, drywall, brown carpet, a red mattress, a child's drawing, graffiti, and a decorative window. Each of the eleven pieces is a palimpsest of repurposing.

With staggering clarity for a work of shipping container art, *Jonah's Whale* doggedly highlights the possible lives that shipping containers might lead once they cease to function as coffins of remote labor-power. Sinnokrot pulls no punches in staging their potential to serve projects of dispossession. Most significantly, *Jonah's Whale* flags how shipping containers have become one of many "mundane" technologies used to build what Eyal Weizman calls "Israel's architecture of occupation."[115] For decades the Israeli state has tolerated, if not openly encouraged, settlers in the West Bank to push against the borders of occupied territory. When settlements came under enhanced international scrutiny with the 1993 Oslo Accords, Israel, in a show of nominal compliance, started cracking down on the most egregious acts of vigilante dispossession. But instead of discouraging settlers outright, the Israeli state and military handed them a new rulebook to follow. Impermanence and mobility became essential features of settlements, and prefab houses, whose homely accoutrements declared settler intent, gave way to structures like mini-homes made from shipping containers. Being affordable and transportable, the shipping container suits a settler's need to up and move when told to do so by Israeli soldiers.

Shipping containers are most commonly found in so-called outposts, the illegal settlements notorious for testing territorial limits. In addition to providing shelter, shipping containers also perform a symbolic function for settlers who leave them on hilltops in full view of Palestinian villages and farms: the shipping container as threat and way to lay claim. "The aim is to grab maximum territory in minimum time," a monitor for Peace Now has remarked. "It starts with a shipping container, then perimeter lighting, then an approach road, then more containers and mobile homes—and you have a new settlement."[116]

Shipping containers are useful for settlers, but they also suit the "elastic geographies" of the occupation as promoted by the Israeli state.[117] Each new conflict and betrayal brings with it a change to the occupation's boundaries, with the shipping container being just one movable border technology that gives shape to this erratic frontier, working in cooperation with separation walls, roadblocks, checkpoints, and more. Although unpredictability and fluidity might seem to run against the interests of Israeli state dominion, as Weizman argues, chaos serves it in several ways, such as by extending a strategy of "obfuscation" that helps "naturalize the facts of domination" or, more straightforwardly, by upturning Palestinian lives.[118] Chaos projects a sense that circumstances are too complicated for a territorial solution, implying instead that only those with a view on the ground, like the Israeli state, have the competence to resolve what they themselves created. The symbolic temporality of tools like shipping containers buttresses the occupation's founding myth that the "unregulated process of violent dispossession" is merely temporary, a state of exception many decades long and counting.[119] To prevent anyone encountering *Jonah's Whale* from thinking that this shipping container is an isolated crime, Sinnokrot created *Caravans* (2013–14), a portrait series profiling dozens of other such settler shelters scattered across the West Bank. The tessellated effect in *Caravans* echoes the work of Hilla and Bernd Becher, but instead of using patterns of industrial architecture to evoke a feeling of the industrial sublime, Sinnokrot brings the shipping container crashing down to earth, spotlighting it as a lever of dispossession.

Jonah's Whale is more than just documentary evidence of dispossession; it is also an instrument through which to see dispossession differently. The sculpture requires viewers to move around and even through it. Its eleven segments and the spaces between them are frames through which to observe one's environs. Sinnokrot has installed the work just three times to date, including in a white cube gallery in Berlin and a church in Cologne. The first time was outside on a former Israeli military base near Ramallah, where it fractured and obstructed the view of the West Bank hills surrounding it, dimly mirroring the shipping containers left by settlers on similar hillsides.

Trained as a filmmaker, Sinnokrot understands the designed function of a shipping container as being analogous to that of a camera—both are apparatuses geared to standardizing time and space through capture and containment. The defiant gesture of cutting up a container, then, finds companions in Sinnokrot's filmic work, which has entailed such violations as nailing a camera shutter to a wall and scraping away the frame lines of celluloid film. His slicing can also be compared to the technique of editing a film, especially since the visual experience of moving slowly around the shipping container resembles the animated staccato of a flipbook. Sinnokrot associates *Jonah's*

Whale with the genre of landscape. Following the likes of Denis Cosgrove, he recognizes landscape not as something given or even representable but rather as a standardizing perspective or a way of seeing. According to W. J. T. Mitchell, landscape painting, especially in its European tradition, has served as the "'dreamwork' of imperialism," a way of presenting lands as wasted or uninhabited, and therefore ripe for the taking.[120] For Iyko Day, landscape art has long been used to foster a settler colonial perspective, emptying the land in imagination to legitimate its clearing in reality.[121] *Jonah's Whale* is not an example of landscape art as such, but it points to how this shipping container and others like it are used for the purpose of landscaping dispossession.

The settler colonial landscape of the West Bank has been shaped using various tools. While *Jonah's Whale* employs one of these, Sinnokrot is perhaps best-known for showcasing another. *Ka (Oslo)* is made of two standing backhoe arms, both drilled into the ground and arranged so that they stretch out into the sky, like the sculpture is pleading with God.[122] The title refers to the Oslo Accords, and the parts used are all taken from the 1993 JCB backhoe model, which Sinnokrot collected from junkyards across the West Bank. In 2018, he installed *Ka (Oslo)* in the courtyard of the Palestinian Museum in Birzeit for its inaugural exhibition. Like *Jonah's Whale*, *Ka (Oslo)* foregrounded a tool of dispossession but also seemed to subvert it. Set on a hill with a grand vista of the West Bank spreading out before it, *Ka (Oslo)* appeared as proof that the leveling instruments of settler colonialism can be repurposed as gestures of defiance. *Jonah's Whale* would seem to make a similar point, especially in how it foregrounds the shipping container's subsequent life as a Palestinian construction site office. Both works, at first glance, imply a resolve to build on the land despite the constant threat of eviction or invasion, using the very tools of dispossession to do so. Yet the resistant affordances in *Ka (Oslo)* and *Jonah's Whale* are far more ambivalent than this.

What seems like a bold statement against bulldozer demolition in *Ka (Oslo)* also critically alludes to the very instruments being used for Palestinian property development in the West Bank. Sinnokrot describes the upturned shovels in *Ka (Oslo)* as "a refusal to dig, a refusal to comply, a refusal to keep one's head down."[123] The object of refusal here is twofold: the settler state and capital-led development. With its traces of a Palestinian construction site, *Jonah's Whale* pushes back against visions of urban development as resistance, suggesting instead complicity with settler colonialism. Since the Oslo Accords and especially over the past fifteen years, urban development has become a strategy of both capital accumulation and state building in the West Bank. The Palestinian National Authority (PA) pitches private infrastructural investment, especially in housing, as a national priority—one step toward establishing state power with or without territorial sovereignty. For critics, the push to build and to "modernize" normalizes the occupation by seeking to secure capital accumulation and state legitimacy under conditions of continued political subordination. As Kareem Rabie puts it, state building in this context has come to mean "replac[ing] liberation and moral claims with modernization so as to stabilize local jurisdiction over a territory within Israel."[124] For Sinnokrot, like Rabie, excavators and shipping containers are tools of Israeli state violence as well as a particular kind of capital-led Palestinian state building. As the misery of the former is distributed across the occupied territories, the latter gets concentrated into pockets of affluence at the city level. This is the state as an accumulation strategy, in which political agency is predicated on global market integration and pitted against liberation. The free movement of capital comes at the expense of the free movement of people, with the interests of an aspiring bourgeois class prioritized over those of most everyone else living and dying under occupation, particularly in Gaza.

Sinnokrot has displayed *Jonah's Whale* together with *Rawabi* (2013–14), a sculpture made of a camel's jaw bearing a set of gold-capped teeth. *Rawabi* takes its name from the controversial West Bank property development launched in 2008 by the Palestinian real estate magnate Bashar Masri, backed financially by the Qatari government's sovereign wealth fund, and promoted politically by former PA Prime Minister Salam Fayyad. Envisioned as a "high-tech" city with jobs provided by internet giants like Google and purposefully designed to suit the tastes of 40,000 upper-middle-class residents, the $1.5 billion development has been decried by critics for normalizing the occupation.[125] Even as Rawabi remains under construction, it has become emblematic of the belief that problems posed by settler colonialism can be resolved by jumpstarting global capital investment at a local level and deepening capitalist social relations. Sinnokrot gives acerbic aesthetic form to such faith by depicting Rawabi as gold teeth artificially implanted in a decaying jaw.

Returning to *Jonah's Whale*, Sinnokrot interprets the biblical story that serves as the sculpture's namesake in terms of indebtedness: the prophet Jonah was swallowed by a whale "for defaulting on a promise made to God." For Sinnokrot, *Jonah's Whale* is a meditation on "the pathological debts that hold claim on our lives": this includes housing debt.[126] Cities across the West Bank have long been plagued by a severe shortage of affordable housing, a result largely of land theft. The crisis has only intensified in recent years with the rise of a mortgage market backed by the same international capital that enables developments like Rawabi and the gentrification of neighborhoods in Ramallah. "Precarity is nothing new to Palestinians," Sinnokrot writes, "But bubble economics, consumer debt and real estate speculation are the contemporary ingredients of that experience in the West Bank."[127] Sinnokrot disputes that capital-driven property development resists occupation, and *Jonah's Whale* instead recontextualizes it as a project that saddles communities with debt and marginalizes extant modes of living, all under a banner of modernization and improvement. State violence, in the form of the settler outpost, and state building, in the form of the gentrifying Palestinian city, are shown to be sutured together by global capital, taking the fitting form of a shipping container.

Jonah's Whale is unique for how it dissects one shipping container's histories of use, and even more so for highlighting how these uses are geared toward dispossession. But for Sinnokrot, there is nothing inherent to the shipping container that makes it special as a lever of dispossession. The shipping container suits dispossession because of its ubiquity and not its design. Settler colonialism, like capitalism more generally, makes do with what's at hand. As I have shown in this chapter, the global proliferation of shipping containers makes this technology singularly useful for tracking the dual character of capitalism today and the role of logistics therein. For all that *Jonah's Whale* registers about dispossession in Palestine, it has little to say about containerization itself. But through its use of a shipping container, *Jonah's Whale* divulges that exploitation and dispossession are two sides of the same coin.

4 The Drone
Last-Mile Gimmicks

"FROM THE STEAM ENGINE TO the forklift to today's robotic pickers and packers"—so opens a recent report by McKinsey & Company—"the history of logistics is also a history of automation."[1] To hear the world's oldest and largest management consultancy firm tell it, as the past has gone with logistics so will the future, traveling along an inexorable curve upwards to ever-greater investment in the technological infrastructure for moving goods. Proof for McKinsey & Company's prediction seems to be in plenty. Just consider the world's ports where automated stacking cranes and straddle carriers are laying the foundation for a paradigm shift in dockside management. Or take a look inside the warehouses sprouting up across the planet's hinterlands and staffed by a growing corps of palletizing robots. Soon there will be fleets of driverless freight trucks, or so the Elon Musks of the world promise us, that will further streamline the landside shipping routes over which more than two thirds of all goods in the United States travel. And what about all of the drones already showing off their delivery chops by hauling life-saving supplies through disaster zones? Is it not just a matter of time before they are redeployed to bring me lunch from my favorite taqueria? Ports, warehouses, highways, even that costly last mile of delivery: robots seem all but set to storm the sphere of circulation, delivering savings for businesses and stealing away huge swaths of logistics jobs. "As automation proceeds," so McKinsey & Company predicts, "logistics costs might fall by up to 40 percent."[2]

Having so far chronicled the history of logistical infrastructure, this final chapter pivots its view to peer into the future. But rather than trying to read tea leaves, my aim here is to scrutinize the buoyant tales that the logistics industry tells about its future self. Such stories, often overflowing with robots, are crafted to elicit wonder and astonishment. Consider, as an example, the thousands of patents that Amazon files each year. These range from the fantastic (like airborne distribution centers hitched to dirigibles and serviced by flying drones) to the terrifying (see my discussion of Amazon's worker cage below). As Alessandro Delfanti writes, a patent "is an investment in a desired future," and, judged by money for research and development alone, no company has invested as much to secure a favorable future for itself as Amazon ($22 billion spent as of 2018).[3] Though most of the plans outlined in their patents will never come to pass, this mountain of prophetic paperwork nevertheless indicates a clear direction of intended travel as the company pursues its mission to "reimagine now."[4] During the five years preceding the COVID-19 pandemic, Amazon filed over a thousand patents targeting inventory management alone. These included ideas for new technologies that ranged from augmented reality visors and haptic wristbands to floor sensors designed to track both goods and workers. Yet, as we shall see, for all the talk of disruptive innovation in logistics, Amazon's machinic ambition is largely consistent with the aspiration that has long guided the expansion and development of capital's logistical infrastructure: for a workplace where workers are not so much made unnecessary as they are rendered disposable.

No single logistics technology has generated more publicity for Amazon than its drones. Across hundreds of patents, the company has pitched all manner of systems for drone delivery, like docking stations on lampposts and shipping containers equipped with fully automated stocking, charging, and repair stations. While stalwarts like Walmart and startups such as Zipline are ahead of Amazon in the race to roll out delivery drones, no other company has matched the sheer scope of its imagination. "Technological futures are always publicly performed," argues Delfanti in his account of how Amazon uses patents to communicate its ambitions to investors and consumers.[5] In this chapter, I consider other ways that logistics companies like Amazon are performing the future, from elaborate advertisements to actual performances created in collaboration with artists. Drones are my primary focus, a technology with logistical potential that is as celebrated as it is dubious.

Like most sectors of capitalist industry, logistics is full of technological gimmickry. For every innovation that has taken hold to transform how goods are moved and stored, countless more have captured the imagination only to be unceremoniously tossed aside. To take but one example from history, when reporting on the merits of containerization in 1967, McKinsey & Company dangled before its readers the tantalizing prospect of a different means for seamlessly transporting goods between sea and land: the hovercraft.[6] Today, myriad logistical technologies, even more unproven than drones, arouse, like catnip, the fascination of futurists, perhaps none more so than the Hyperloop—a hypothetical low-pressure sealed tube that uses magnets to propel large pods filled with commodities (or even people) at very high speeds.[7] I will be the first to admit that I am unfit to judge the technical viability of drones, hovercrafts, or Hyperloops. Of more concern to me is the desire that gimmicks like these express for ridding the world of unruly impediments to circulation.

The drone is the exemplary logistical gimmick, evoking amazement at all it can do, while raising eyebrows about what exactly it does. In *Theory of the Gimmick*, Sianne Ngai argues that the misgivings generated by gimmicks typically relate to concerns about human labor. Gimmicks are essentially labor-saving devices; they promise to save time and reduce work; yet, in so doing, they constantly foreground the necessity of work itself. The gimmick is "capitalism's most successful aesthetic category but also its biggest embarrassment and structural problem." Ngai continues:

> With its dubious yet attractive promises about the saving of time, the reduction of labor, and the expansion of value, [a gimmick] gives us tantalizing glimpses of a world in which social life will no longer be organized by labor, while indexing one that continuously regenerates the conditions keeping labor's social necessity in place.[8]

The gimmick promises to reduce human labor all the while drawing too much attention to the work it performs. With a long history, capitalist gimmicks are not limited to the entertaining realms of magic tricks or Rube Goldberg drawings; they also can be found throughout capitalist industry, taking the form of engineer sketches and patents that hint at capitalism's pipedream of doing away with workers.

Today, drones operate as gimmicks, not because they lack real-world applications, but because they produce an aesthetic experience of wonder that both obscures and makes visible what they so often propose to replace: human labor. As Ngai asserts, when one is captivated by a gimmick, the "shadow" of its promise is never far away, that is, "the becoming 'superfluous' of value-productive labor and rise of more uncertainly productive kinds."[9] Amazon's varied performances with drones exhibit key features of the gimmick form, showing the company's desired future to be one wherein machines do not so much replace human workers but instead help make such workers replaceable.

As performed by companies like Amazon, the future of logistics will, much like its history, be shaped by automation. While often understood as following an exponential curve shooting up into the future, automation, as I understand it, is more a process that conforms to a longstanding political-economic logic, what Karl Marx called, "The General Law of Capitalist Accumulation."[10] Capitalism depends on human labor as the source of surplus value while also striving to render workers superfluous to its production process. Systemically, the aim and endgame of accumulation is not to abolish human labor, as doing so would deprive capital of its very lifeblood. Instead, capitalist firms constantly try to make their workers disposable, though not always by replacing them with robots. As Jason Smith and Aaron Benanav have each recently argued, machines can assist capital in reducing labor costs, but they are often pricey additions to the labor process, demanding large upfront outlays that lock them into the workplace until investment can be recouped. There is no more powerful "disincentive" for automating a production line than the prospect of finding a cheaper pool of labor. "When workers will take jobs that are poorly paid because nothing else is available," Smith writes, "there is little reason for business owners to invest in expensive and soon obsolete machinery to do their work."[11] Making human workers replaceable, whether with machines or other humans, confers the flexibility cherished by capitalists to swell or shrink their workforces as accumulation requires. Instead of a future without human workers, drone gimmicks put on display the capitalist aspiration to make workers fungible.

In turning to the future, this chapter risks entering the realm of conjecture. Inevitably, anything I say about the feasibility (or not) of particular technologies like the drone is likely bound not to come true. But I have no interest in speculating when or whether drones will start delivering pizzas or picking warehouse stock. Instead, I am more concerned to understand what drone gimmicks reveal about the proposed future for logistics work presently being pursued by companies like Amazon. In line with the rest of this book, I foreground the role that art is being made to play in these performances of the future. And as it turns out, drone gimmicks bind the art world to supply chains more tightly than anything we have encountered so far in *The Arts of Logistics*.

The first part of this chapter considers the diverse means, including commercials and fulfillment center tours, that companies like Amazon currently use to showcase the future of drone home delivery. Such corporate performances comprise just one way that major logistics players benefit from the gimmickry of drones. Far grander are the frequent collaborations between startups and artists in contexts that range from Broadway to television talent shows. In addition to offering companies easy opportunities for advertising, such performances also come with practical benefits, like the chance to take risks in new settings without investor pressure to succeed. In surveying the continued entanglement of art in logistics, I aim to temper the ebullient belief, sometimes voiced on the Left, that "Amazon offers techniques of production and distribution that are just waiting to be seized and repurposed."[12] I end the chapter by moving away from the Global North markets that Amazon has its sights set on to examine the proliferation of drone gimmicks in regions historically underdeveloped by capital. The final section focuses on the architect Norman Foster's bungled plan to bring "civic"-minded drone delivery to East Africa. If Amazon's drone gimmicks exude a timeworn capitalist desire for worker fungibility, Foster's *Droneport* signals the persistence of another political-economic logic endemic to capitalism: colonial underdevelopment.

Showcasing Automation at Amazon

Once belonging solely to the realm of science fiction, uncrewed aerial vehicles (UAVs) have become the stuff of living nightmares, armed as they now are with explosives and God's Eye surveillance systems. But drones, the common name for UAVs, are also fast emerging as a fixture of everyday life, and for reasons other than evening news reports of overseas military strikes. Over the past decade, drones have become *civilianized*, used for routine tasks by farmers, building surveyors, camera crews, hobbyists, and more. This industry term, "civilianization," while intended to describe the repurposing of

UAVs for a rapidly expanding consumer market, also implies a kind of retargeting, as drones are being increasingly deployed by police to surveil and even kill suspects.[13]

The mounting visibility of UAV technology and its proliferating uses combine to make the drone, as Adam Rothstein puts it, "a singular inflection point of fear, of paranoia, of wonder, of technological wizardry, and of future possibility."[14] Arguably no single entity has invested more money to shape hearts and minds about drone technology than Amazon. The company kicked off its public offensive in December 2013 when then-CEO Jeff Bezos unveiled Amazon's plans for drone home delivery during a high-profile interview with the now-disgraced journalist Charlie Rose on *60 Minutes*. "I know this looks like science fiction," Bezos insisted as he ushered Rose into a secret room at Amazon headquarters, "but it's not." There on display was a collection of Amazon's latest generation of octocopters. "Oh, man . . . Oh, my god!" was all that a stunned Rose could muster in reply.[15] What is it about an encounter with drones that elicits astonishment and wonder? And how does a company like Amazon benefit from cultivating such feelings?

On *60 Minutes*, Bezos played the role of a backroom tinkerer, casually showing off what he had been working on in his spare time: "Let me show you something," he coolly says to Rose before the big reveal. Yet this was no improvised pulling back of the curtains; it was, of course, a carefully coordinated stunt timed to coincide with the start of the holiday shopping season. To accompany the interview, Amazon unveiled the first in a series of commercials introducing the world to Prime Air, the name of their promised drone delivery service. Each of these advertisements follows the same narrative arc and features similar *dramatis personae*: a young white child, belonging to an apparently affluent family, is urgently in need of a crucial piece of wholesome sports apparel. Coming to the rescue is a nonplussed parent ready with Prime Air's pizza-like guarantee of thirty-minute delivery. After the mother or father clicks "Buy," the commercials cut to an Amazon fulfillment center, largely devoid of humans, where the desired product is magically loaded onto a waiting drone that then duly takes flight, soaring above verdant fields before gently landing in a generous garden. As the drone embarks on its journey home, the family gathers outside to wave goodbye, grateful for the service it has so admirably performed.[16]

Amazon released its last and sleekest iteration of the commercial series on Cyber Monday in 2015, starring Jeremy Clarkson, freshly hired by the online retailer after being let go from the BBC for allegedly punching a producer in the face. A brash English celebrity famous for hawking fast cars on *Top Gear*, Clarkson seemed well qualified to endorse the viability of Amazon's new toy. In this final advert, he plays the role of narrator, turning Prime Air's plot into a kind of fairy tale.[17] "This is a story from the not-too-distant future," he declares while sauntering into the family's open-plan kitchen. As the drone takes off from its fulfillment center, which Clarkson reassures us is "not too far away," he begins recounting facts about Amazon's "miracle of modern technology." For example, it can fly for 15 miles, reach an altitude of 400 feet, and travel at a speed of 56 mph. It is fully automated and equipped with "sense and avoid technology" that helps it steer clear of obstacles, demonstrated in the commercial when the drone elegantly dodges a hot air balloon. After the "amazing innovation" completes its mission, Clarkson grandly announces: "Balance is restored to the universe!"

The polish of this final Prime Air commercial implied that Amazon, in 2015, was making good progress on its drone delivery service. Not only was the original octocopter now replaced by an "amazing hybrid design" that switched from helicopter to airplane mode, but the fulfillment center had been entirely redesigned around the drones, with bespoke landing pads and retractable roof portals. Even the commercial's higher production values, such as the additions of bouncy music and Clarkson as spokesperson, suggested a leap forward. Two holiday seasons since first being introduced to the world, Prime Air seemed well on track, even though it was not.

Bezos had promised Rose that Amazon customers could expect delivery by drone as soon as 2018, but today, a decade later, Prime Air remains in trial, beset by technical and regulatory problems. For years, Amazon led the charge in lobbying the Federal Aviation Administration (FAA) and equivalent bodies in Europe to open up airspace for commercial drones. Yet policy changes have been slow, not helped by highly publicized disruptions caused by hobbyist drones like those that shut down London's Gatwick airport in December 2018.[18] As a result, Amazon has confined most of its tests to the English countryside while watching from the sidelines as competitors launched services in other markets: the e-commerce giant JD.com has rolled out limited commercial delivery in China, and the startup Zipline now boasts the world's largest network in Rwanda. Despite receiving FAA clearance for tests in 2020, Amazon's drone program continues to be hampered by managerial ineptness, layoffs, and frequent crashes, including one that sparked a twenty-acre brush fire. I am in no position to predict what the future holds for Prime Air; as of 2023, however, Amazon is still vowing to deliver half a billion packages via drone by decade's end.[19] Time will tell.

In the race to make drone home delivery a reality in the United States, Amazon faces stiff competition from rivals like Walmart and Google. As Astro Teller, former head of Google's Wing program (official job title: Captain of Moonshots) explained in a 2014 advertisement, drone delivery "aspires to take another big chunk of the remaining friction out of moving things around in the world."[20] To clarify, the "remaining friction" Teller and other executives have in mind is the so-called last mile, when a parcel, having been funneled through a pipeline of distribution centers and sortation hubs, is handed off to the courier tasked with getting it to your doorstep.

For a company like Amazon, last-mile costs are nothing to sneeze at. In 2013, the year Bezos announced Prime Air, Amazon spent a staggering $6.4 billion on shipping. As its customer base rapidly grew, that number increased tenfold, hitting $61 billion by the end of the decade—this despite the company's many successes in trimming per unit cost of shipping. With demand for home delivery soaring during the COVID-19 pandemic, total shipping costs for Amazon leapt up to $76 billion in 2021 and are continuing to climb.[21] The last mile is, by far, the most cost-intensive leg of a package's journey. To rein in expenses, the Everything Store has put all options on the table, adopting a seemingly contradictory program of buying its own cargo jets and vans to bring shipping in-house while continuing to outsource delivery to major couriers and an expanding ensemble of gig economy freelancers. All the while Amazon has maintained its pledge to continue reducing the time of "free shipping."[22] Over the past decade, Amazon has patented all manner of technological solutions to lower delivery costs, from crewless container ships to driverless lorries equipped with 3D printers for making products on demand. Nevertheless, its quest to clear the last mile by flying over it has garnered, by far, the most attention.

Unnamed Amazon executives, who were reportedly taken aback by Bezos's appearance on *60 Minutes*, described his promise of drone home delivery as a case example of "cookie licking," a tech industry term for when a company claims to have done something before actually doing it so as to generate publicity and discourage potential competitors.[23] From the start, Prime Air was engineered to surprise and impress. Clarkson's fairytale language of miracles and amazing innovations, for instance, seemed designed to replace public fears and paranoia about drones with feelings of wonder and wizardry. Clarkson's narration steers clear of military terms, referring to Amazon's drones as a "family" rather than a fleet or a squadron. Amazement and the quotidian are two sentiments that rarely sit together easily. Amazon, however, seeks to cultivate awe and comfort to encourage the public (and regulators) to keep an open mind as to what else a drone might deliver besides targeted assassinations. These early corporate drone performances, thus, were less proof of concept and more a means of stoking curiosity about the affordances built into drone technology.

Enchanted language saturates Amazon's research and development strategy. As CEO, Bezos was known to insist that employees dream up ideas for a "magical product," even bestowing projects with charmed names. Amazon's grocery delivery service, for example, was initially called "Amazon Magic" and subsidiary services were introduced as "Houdini," "Presto," and "Rabbit."[24] The company has also developed a reputation for showing off new technologies in highly public ways. In 2019, Amazon began trialing a small six-wheeled cooler-like robot called Scout for package delivery in North American suburban neighborhoods. Given its need for human accompaniment (workers had to remove and hand over said packages), Scout struck many as a publicity stunt, with TechCrunch calling the robot "as much of a brand ambassador as it is an experiment in the future of last-mile delivery."[25] Amazon is by no means alone in showcasing its technology in such ways, as competitors regularly aim to create their own media spectacles, such as by introducing delivery robots to college campuses or testing how fast their drones can deliver pizza.

Amazon's drones, thus, were clearly designed to call attention to themselves. Instead of operating as backstage infrastructure, they were made for the spotlight. In other words, Amazon's drones are gimmicks. To label them as such is not to discount their possible future infrastructural usefulness but to recognize the specific role they perform at present for Amazon. The contemporary meaning of "gimmick" dates back to the 1920s, when it was used to describe tricky gadgets of varying sorts: gambling cheats and literary gags are said to be gimmicks, but so too are technological novelties. In her magisterial account of gimmicks, Sianne Ngai lists in passing airborne drones as the most contemporary of examples, though her exemplar is the Rube Goldberg machine that proposes to accomplish a simple task in an unnecessarily elaborate way.[26] Gimmicks inspire awe, but they also arouse suspicion. When we call something gimmicky, Ngai writes, "we mean we see through it—that there is an uninvited transparency about how it is producing what we take to be its intended effect."[27] As noted earlier, the gimmick often takes form as a labor-saving device. The labor that a delivery drone is designed to save is evident enough: work performed by humans along the last mile.

In addition to patents, commercials, and real-world trials, Amazon also exhibits its cutting-edge logistics technology through its popular fulfillment center tours. When Bezos first announced to shareholders his plan to start in-person tours in 2014, he noted that he himself was "amazed" every time he visited a fulfillment center, and assured that others would likewise "be impressed."[28] On the booking website for tours, the company entices prospective visitors with similar promises of enchantment: "Come witness the magic that happens after you click 'buy' on Amazon."[29] So what is so amazing and magical about a fulfillment center? Judging strictly by the messaging of the hour-long tour, in which workers enlisted as corporate ambassadors whisk visitors through the sorting process, the machines are the thing, specifically Amazon's orange Roomba-like robots who spend their days carting yellow shelving units to waiting workers. Fulfillment center visitors are meant to marvel at these Kiva bots, named for the startup that invented them, which Amazon bought in 2012 for $775 million (more on this later).

On the fulfillment center tours I have taken, the sheer number of times my guides said the word "amazing" led me to wonder whether they had a quota to hit. Even the online booking page tries to prime this kind of feeling:

> If you are imagining a warehouse filled with handcarts and all the books in one place and apparel in another, picture this: orange robots balancing towers of goods twirling in what looks like a choreographed dance across shiny concrete floors, miles of conveyor belts and ramps carrying inventory across the building, and shipping labels practically flying onto boxes, blown by puffs of air.[30]

Amazon's Kiva bots are unquestionably impressive. Strong and smart, each of them can lift 1,500 pounds, and their movements are coordinated by one of the world's most efficient inventory management computer systems.[31] But, after a few moments of watching the robots do their work, they become, well, boring. Promised the thrill of the logistical sublime, Amazon's tours ultimately deliver an experience that is the supply chain equivalent of a disappointing zoo. This resemblance is only compounded by fact that, for reasons of workplace safety, the Kiva bots do their work inside a large cage (the so-called robot field). Nonetheless, demand for tours of fulfillment centers has long been high. When first announced, bookings for the year were filled within weeks, calling to mind the public fascination that met the River Rouge Factory when Henry Ford welcomed tour groups inside a century earlier. There is a symmetry here that expresses the shift to supply chain capitalism: if Ford once gave customers a chance to see how commodities are manufactured, Bezos now exhibits how they get moved.[32]

Amazon's tours seem crafted to do more than simply satisfy curiosity about the workings of the world's largest logistics company. As the journalist Sarah Miller puts it in her review of one tour, Amazon has opened "its doors to the world so that, Wonka-like, they might see 'the magic' of high-tech item distribution up close and hopefully ignore the bodycount."[33] And by putting them on display, Amazon also appears intent on countering the growing notoriety of its robots. With cameos on television shows and mentions in rap songs, Kiva bots now figure in popular culture as harbingers of automation and destroyers of jobs—there's even a video game with them cast as the villain.[34] They make a brief appearance at the end of Heike Geissler's acclaimed autofictional account of working at a fulfillment center in Leipzig, Germany, when the narrator, speaking in the second person, reads in the news that Amazon has purchased Kiva Systems: "Although you're not a futurologist," she writes, "you can predict with almost 100 percent certainty what the company will do in the future. It's all clearly recognizable."[35]

More spectacular is artist Simon Denny's *Amazon Worker Cage* (2019), a life-sized 3D-printed rendition of an infamous 2016 Amazon patent for a large cage mounted on top of a Kiva-like bot that can move employees through warehouses to pick items using a large robotic arm. Ostensibly designed to protect workers as fulfillment centers become increasingly crowded with moving hardware, critics have seized on the carceral symbolism of the worker cage as evidence of Amazon's plans to literally yoke humans to machines. Others, like André Spicer, have referenced this patent to make an even more bracing observation: "The company doesn't need a robotic cage for workers, it already has one of the most all-pervasive control systems in history."[36] From the handheld scanners that dictate and monitor all facets of an employee's working day to the meshed camera systems that ensure they stay on track, the future heralded by the worker cage is, in fact, present. It is no wonder that Geissler's narrator seems strangely at ease to learn that the robots are coming: "You knew all that long ago, and you don't have any objection."[37]

Geissler might be disappointed to know that Amazon insists its robots are *not* actually gunning for anyone's jobs, so much so that this message is one of the "5 facts" about them the company lists on the web page for Amazon Robotics.[38] But just because robots are not coming to take anyone's place at Amazon does not mean they are not already transforming the workplace. Amazon's tours are performances that claim its robots are not meant to enslave but to collaborate with human workers. This is a point that the company shouts at anyone who will listen. Topping the list of the facts to know about Amazon's robots is this: "man and machine are already working hand in hand at Amazon." Kiva bots, for example, are said by Amazon to cut in half the distance that a fulfillment center worker walks each day, and effectively "make work easier for our employees."[39] This harmonious language emphasizing synergistic partnership between workers and technology saturates the retailer's public-facing statements on its robots. In addition to stressing how "amazing" the Kiva bots are, the guides on my tours repeatedly stressed the value of "cooperation" with them.

Before simply dismissing Amazon's messaging as a disingenuous attempt to dispel fears that automation spells the end of work as we know it, it is worth noting that the company's tours make no secret of the fact that Amazon needs more workers for its fulfillment centers. In fact, the tours themselves are scripted like recruiting events. After suspending tours at the start of the first COVID-19 lockdown, the company resumed them a year later, pivoting from in-person visits to "virtual tours" sited in locations around the world. Despite the change in medium, the content has remained remarkably the same, especially when it comes to the rosy gloss on what working at Amazon is like.

In the live virtual tours I took in 2021 and the recordings of others I have watched, guides stressed how easy it is to apply for a job and detailed the benefits and bonuses we could earn. Our future employer was even willing to help pay our tuition should we want to go back to school and upskill.

At the time of relaunching its tours online, Amazon had become ravenous for workers. Pandemic lockdowns triggered soaring demand for home delivery, and the company responded with an unprecedented international hiring spree, the scale of which analysts have compared to the US industrial war effort of the 1940s.[40] In 2020, Amazon added a half-million new jobs internationally, most of them in fulfillment centers—bringing its total number of employees to 1.3 million. This is double what Walmart, the world's largest corporate employer, hoovered up during the same period. Even more astonishing, this number does not account for employee turnover or the 200,000 seasonal workers brought on only for the holidays, nor even the roughly 500,000 delivery drivers under Amazon contracts but not formally employed by the company. The 50 percent increase in its workforce accompanied a massive infrastructural expansion; in the United States, for example, Amazon tripled the number of warehouses and hubs it uses for last-mile delivery. To support its recruitment drive, Amazon unleashed an advertising blitz of commercials, billboards, and mailers and offered signing bonuses as high as $3,000. As one of few employers with job openings during lockdowns, candidates were not in short supply: 384,000 people applied to work at Amazon in the United States and Canada in a single week in September 2020.[41] Robots may be coming to Amazon in droves, but so too are human workers. As of late 2023, Amazon claims to have 520,000 Kiva bots working in its fulfillment centers internationally, bringing the total number of robots currently "working collaboratively" with employees to 750,000.[42] This makes for approximately one robot for every two humans.

As far as the labor process goes, what Kiva bots do—bring shelves to workers—is nothing entirely new. The idea of moving work to workers was a principle of the Fordist assembly line and was already operative in nineteenth-century slaughterhouses. Kiva bots simplify and speed up the task at hand, so the work that Amazon calls "easier" could just as well be described as "deskilled." As a long line of labor-process theorists like Harry Braverman have argued, with deskilling typically comes workplace intensification.[43]

Amazon might indeed value collaboration between robots and humans, even if it neglects to mention that the arrival of Kiva bots to a warehouse can bring a fourfold increase in quotas and a 50 percent spike in the injury rate.[44] Nor does the company mention how teaming workers up with robots limits sociality with other humans, and, as a result, blocks opportunities to share grievances and plot what to do about them.

Amazon's Kiva bots do more than intensify work and boost productivity. By simplifying the labor process, they also help make workers replaceable, reducing the knowledge and training necessary for the job. A worker need not even learn the layout of a fulfillment center if a robot is just going to bring the aisle to them. This makes it easier for Amazon to slot workers in where and when they are needed—a managerial approach that suits a company with extraordinary employee churn and a need to be able to swell its ranks during the holidays and then shrink down afterward.[45] The recent rapid expansion of online retailing during the COVID-19 pandemic brings considerable uncertainty regarding the future pace and scope of growth. Thus, it makes economic sense for a company like Amazon to hire cheap workers who are more easily disposable than expensive robots.

The tendency toward replacing workers with machines is often said to be inevitably checked by the general cheapening of labor-power that occurs as increasing numbers of workers find themselves without a job.[46] This may be true, but it does not fully account for the fact that the priority of many companies is not to replace workers with machines but to make workers replaceable. This is especially true in logistics, an industry populated with stockers and truckers who self-identify as "throwaway people."[47] Despite the "spectre of automation" that haunts its workers, as Delfanti writes, Amazon is "actually much more pragmatic about the continued need for human labor. Workers will remain because they are cheaper and easier to control and discard than robots."[48] Much of what warehouse workers do, like picking items, still cannot be done at cost by robots. This certainly could change, but it would not undo the principal motive that guides Amazon's investment in robots. One of its patents, for instance, laments automation as "expensive and time-consuming to implement, unlike a human workforce, which can be allocated according to need."[49] For all the public fixation on its robots, what Amazon actually counts on most when it comes to its bottom line is the fungibility of its workers.

Despite having a high human-to-robot ratio, only a small minority of Amazon's fulfillment centers globally uses its roboticized shelving method. New fulfillment centers and other logistics hubs continue to be built without this system, especially in places where labor-power, often racialized, runs cheap.[50] Yet even workers who are not collaborating with shelf- and attention-grabbing robots remain subject to the company's data-driven and algorithm-assisted managerial regime. Much like Amazon's delivery drivers, most fulfillment center employees are equipped with tracking tools like computer scanners, meaning they are already monitored and controlled by technology other than robots. In fact, it is only through this technology that workers can navigate Amazon's system of "random stow," in which products are stored not in a rational order but on the most convenient shelf available to save space and time. Only the computer can keep track of where everything is.[51] Amazon's control over its workers hinges, in other words, on its command over its inventory. "Patents for drone delivery get all the media attention," write Leigh Phillips and Michal Rozworski, but "the true wonders at the heart of its operations are actually the esoteric mathematical techniques that help it to manage and simplify its optimization problems."[52] Here, we can glimpse one purpose that unites all the varied technological gimmickry at Amazon. Whether they are functional tools like Kiva bots or speculative ones like delivery drones, Amazon's logistics technology diverts attention away from the techniques of managerial control the company already relies on to make the growing number of workers it employs replaceable.

The Show Business of Business Logistics

When Amazon launched Prime Air in 2013, so-called civilian drones were only just taking root in everyday life. They have since become an increasingly normal part of many workplaces, used for tasks that range from farming and land surveys to surveillance and policing. Their presence is felt most keenly in entertainment, however, where drones are not just a hot topic in art but also an actual tool for making it. For example, drones have become a ubiquitous camera mount in film and photography, with the top-down "soda straw" perspective being a definitive aesthetic of 2010s cultural production, found in *James Bond* films and nature documentaries alike.[53] Less ubiquitous, though no less notable, is the trend for drones to be cast as performers in their own right, a phenomenon that first emerged in the world of experimental dance but which has long since gone mainstream.[54] Over the past decade, drones have competed in the NBA Slam Dunk Contest, carried handbags down a Prada runway, and wrestled in a WWE match. If that were not enough, there is now a Drone Racing League with a broadcasting deal through ESPN.[55] Most significant, however, is the niche that drones have carved for themselves in the world of pyrotechnics. Today, no concert, gala, or global sporting event seems complete without an illuminated swarm of drones. They were even on hand in November 2020 to help Joe Biden celebrate his election victory.

While representations of drones on television and film often lean toward a "pessimistic, dystopian" tone, performances by drones tend to evoke feelings of wonder and astonishment.[56] We have already seen how Amazon cultivates emotions like these through its own drone gimmicks. Though originating in the logistics industry, Amazon's drones should also be understood as playing a prominent part on the cultural stage of drone performance. The link between the logistical uses of drones, such as delivering parcels or checking inventory, and their entertaining work as performers is not happenstance and extends far beyond Amazon. Moreover, it signals a new revolving door between show business and the business of logistics automation.

A case example of logistics partnering with art was Cirque du Soleil's *Paramour*, a musical romp through the Golden Age of Hollywood that combined the company's well-known acrobatics with a cheap love triangle plot. The production premiered on Broadway at the 1,900-seat Lyric Theater in May 2016 with a cast of 38 performers and a $25 million budget that outdid even its competitors.[57] Despite receiving mixed reviews, *Paramour* fared well at the box office, raking in over a million dollars each week. The run closed after just a year when the producers of *Harry Potter and the Cursed Child* reportedly offered Cirque $23 million to vacate the Lyric early so that the blockbuster J. K. Rowling vehicle could move in.[58] *Paramour* was a groundbreaking production for Broadway, being the first resident performance on the Great White Way to feature drones. Near intermission, as two of the leads performed an amorous *pas de deux*, eight drones costumed as lampshades floated into the air, encircling the couple before dipping and diving in a bid to add charm to the romantic scene. The drones flew autonomously, following a rough choreographic plan while making real-time adjustments using a distributed intelligence system of algorithmic programming and sense-and-avoid technology. At an estimated cost of $500,000 to develop, the drone performance ranks among the most expensive two-minute dance numbers in Broadway history.

Despite their humdrum role as lighting fixtures, Cirque's drones were designed to enchant. "A lampshade is an everyday object," noted their lead engineer. "To see them fly, it's like magic."[59] In terms of plot, the appearance of the flying lampshades was inexplicable, but no less diegetically so than the dozens of other performers who contorted, juggled, tumbled, trampolined, teeter-boarded, or trapezed their way through the two-hour show. Circus has long been defined, since at least the eighteenth century, by humans wowing audiences by performing with nonhuman entities, be they animals or technological novelties. This makes Cirque, with its reputation for blending virtuoso human performers and sophisticated technology, less of an exception than a fitting standard-bearer for circus today. Cirque's most famous experiment with technology was also its most expensive: the enormous rotating video screen stage for *KÀ*, a $200-million Las Vegas show that was described as, at the time of its premiere in 2005, if not "the most lavish production in the history of Western theatre," then "surely the most technologically advanced."[60] Collaborating with drone technology in *Paramour* helped set Cirque apart in the competitive performance landscape of Broadway. In the words of one Cirque executive: "For the three minutes they're watching those lampshades, the audience is witnessing a $500,000 moment. They may love it or they may hate it, but they can't see it anywhere else on Broadway."[61] *Paramour*'s drones attracted attention, but they did not upstage Cirque's human performers. The flying lampshades added to the theatrical spectacle without becoming a spectacle unto themselves. What distinguished *Paramour* from a trade fair exhibit for UAV technology was Cirque's ability to embed its drone display in a larger theatrical world. The production, a sympathetic spectator might say, showcased the aesthetic possibilities for collaboration between drones and human performers.

Drones may not have competed with or even replaced humans in *Paramour*, but the Montreal-based company's entire business model is built on the principle that their performers be replaceable. The very design of Cirque's shows, down to its impersonal costumes and reliance on stock gymnastic and acrobatic techniques, emphasizes the skilled acts of its ensemble over any unique or distinguishing traits of individual performers. By detaching skill from human workers in this way, Cirque leverages the existence of a reserve army of performers across the world with the requisite athletic abilities but without many workplaces in which to apply them. High rates of injury (and even death) combine with Cirque's relentless model of year-round touring to make the company dependent on what Erin Hurley has called "a replaceable body."[62] All of this is made possible by Cirque's aesthetic of anonymity as a "circus without stars" and the fixed-term contracts it offers employees.[63]

Replaceable workers collaborating with advanced technology: Cirque seems to be operating by the same managerial philosophy as Amazon, despite the differing level of skill that working for a circus entails. But skilled labor is an artificial category that primarily indexes the high costs of training and accreditation rather than the social usefulness of a particular skill. "Automation replaces tasks, not jobs," writes Jason Smith.[64] Whether a worker can be replaced by a machine or another human has little to do with the level of skill said task demands. Insofar as they are trained to perform tasks that most of us cannot, Cirque's acrobats are extraordinarily skilled. However, this does not mean they are not replaceable with other performers possessing similar skill sets. As work at both Cirque and Amazon suggests, the more a job is broken down into identifiable tasks, the easier it becomes to swap out workers, regardless of how much or how little skill a task requires. Whether it's stuffing a book into a box or jumping rope while standing on stilts, managers overseeing task-oriented workplaces simply want someone to get the job done as cheaply and with as little protest as possible. Much like Prime Air, *Paramour*'s drones were meant to draw attention to themselves and, in doing so, produce a sense of wonder at what technology can do. As we shall see, they also generated ambivalent feelings about the relationship between drone technology and human labor by providing a reminder, however obscured, of the potential for workers to be replaced. Thus, the world's largest theater company shares more with the world's largest logistics company than a simple fondness for showcasing technology.

The connection between Cirque and Amazon runs deeper still, down to the very drones used in *Paramour*. They were developed by Verity Studios in Zurich, which was founded in 2014 by the Canadian-born roboticist Raffaello D'Andrea. Known for his dazzling TED Talks that feature drones playing paddleball and stacking bricks, D'Andrea was also the co-founder of Kiva Systems, where he oversaw the invention of the very robots now used in Amazon fulfillment centers.[65] Verity Studios, with its motto "The Magic Is Real," has become a major player in drone performance. The affiliated Flying Machine Arena, located at the Swiss Federal Institute of Technology (where several core members of Verity Studios, including D'Andrea, worked as researchers), served as an early testing ground for its drones, made to perform a variety of gimmicky tasks, such as building bridges and playing catch.[66] Online videos of these performances, some of which went viral, helped Verity Studios land spots on stadium tours by major musicians like Drake, Céline Dion, and Metallica. In 2018, the company raised $18 million in Series A venture capital financing, making it the best-funded company in the growing commercial indoor drone market.[67]

D'Andrea left Kiva Systems (now Amazon Robotics) before starting Verity Studios, but the logistics industry has never been far from his work with UAVs. While building drones for the likes of Cirque, he and his team were pulling double duty developing a proprietary "warehouse automation solution" that used their drone technology.[68] In 2020, Verity Studios branched out into Verity AG, a logistics technology firm that specializes in providing businesses with indoor drone systems for inventory management. "Like bees collecting pollen to make honey at the hive," so Verity AG's website reads, its drones fly day and night assessing stock, thus "free[ing] up warehouse personnel to focus on more value-added tasks."[69] In just its first two years, Verity AG successfully transitioned from a drone entertainment company to an industry leader in cutting-edge warehouse management systems, serving clients in twenty countries, including Maersk and IKEA.

Verity AG proudly wears its show business credentials, presenting its partnership with Cirque as a testament to the quality of its product. "Born in the lab, bred on Broadway," declares one corporate profile of the company.[70] Clients, in turn, make much of Verity's background as a way to emphasize their own commitments to innovation. IKEA, for example, boasts of using "tech incubated in show-business" to "transform [its] supply chain."[71] Verity's initial years as a drone entertainment studio were useful for attracting investor interest, while their early performances in the Flying Machine Arena offered opportunities to accumulate flight time, trial software, ensure system resilience, test battery life, and more. Creating gimmicks, in essence, gave the company chances to innovate and excuses to fail. What's more, they also provided a clue as to the possible future uses of drone technology beyond scanning stock. As D'Andrea's TED Talks clearly demonstrate, Verity's drones can already carry and stack blocks, dodge obstacles, and recover on the fly—all skills that are essential for picking inventory and delivering it.[72]

Verity is not alone in using drones to bridge the worlds of show business and business logistics. For years, Intel operated the world's largest drone entertainment division, creating spectacular light shows for high profile events like the 2018 Olympic Games opening ceremony in Pyeongchang and the 2017 Super Bowl Halftime Show starring Lady Gaga.[73] In 2016, a group by the name of Flying BeBop reached the semifinals of *Britain's Got Talent* with a series of saccharine routines set to pop songs performed by human dancers alongside a swarm of drones.[74] Flying BeBop was a marketing vehicle created by the consumer drone company Parrot and BeTomorrow, a Bordeaux-based software consultancy. This initial partnership later morphed into a full-fledged business called Dronisos, specializing in commercial drone performances. Like Verity, it too has its own bewitching slogan: "Experience the Magic." Dronisos has produced large-scale displays around the world, from Dubai to Orlando, providing advertising for Parrot and spreading awareness of its swarm software.[75] In 2020, Dronisos announced it was expanding operations to explore "the future of drone automation" and how its technology could be applied "to solve new challenges for inspections, surveying and mapping, security, and defense industries."[76]

Not limited to popular entertainment, drone collaborations also extend into more rarefied corners of the art world. Take, for example, Anicka Yi's admired 2021 installation, *In Love with the World*, which transformed the Turbine Hall in London's Tate Modern into an enormous terrarium inhabited by large floating robots resembling octopuses and puffer fish. Yi's "aerobes" drifted through the space, guided by an AI system that responded in real time to the body heat and location of onlookers. Pitched by the South Korean artist as an attempt to reset how humans relate to machines, reviewers described the installation as "mesmerising."[77] To create *In Love with the World*, Yi collaborated with dozens of partners, including microbiologists, engineers, anthropologists, and even perfumers. A startup called Pozyx provided Yi with the real-time location system (RTLS) that guided the aerobes' movements. Applying their ultra-wide broadband technology to a museum was a change of pace for the Ghent-based company whose primary business involves selling RTLS kits to warehouses to track inventory and workers.[78] Pozyx was founded in 2015 and, like Verity, is one of many players in the increasingly crowded sector of warehouse automation. The Tate Modern collaboration brought good publicity and garnered a useful client testimonial from Yi: "Pozyx's accurate positioning technology is truly amazing in making this concept a reality."[79]

As the examples of Verity, Dronisos, and Pozyx suggest, drone performances contribute to the expansion of logistics automation in various ways. However, as we observed with Amazon, for all that automation might seem oriented toward a future without workers, chasing this horizon has quite different effects in the present. The recent proliferation of industry-backed drone gimmicks in art and entertainment highlights an abiding capitalist logic for rendering logistics workers replaceable as profitability and capital accumulation demand. To appreciate the impact of automation aspirations on logistics in the here and now, look no further than Cirque du Soleil and Amazon.

Two years after closing on Broadway, *Paramour* relocated to Hamburg's Neue Flora Theater in 2019. That summer, I traveled to Germany expecting to experience firsthand the drones I had read so much about. Yet, when the big moment in the performance arrived, instead of UAVs lifting off from the stage, there were humans in harnesses hoisted into the air by ropes. Cirque had replaced its flying lampshades with acrobats, having decided that the cost of adapting the drones to German safety standards outweighed their contributions to the show. What might seem like a minor setback in the inexorable "rise of the robots" is better understood as a capitalist parable about the fungibility of human labor-power.[80] Half a century ago, economists William Baumol and William Bowen argued that the live quality of performance, the fact that it is consumed at the time of being produced, makes it exceptionally difficult to augment a performer's hourly output with new technology. The lessons learned from show business would inform Baumol's influential theory of the "cost disease," which addresses the limits of automating care and other kinds of service work.[81] As Cirque's replacement of drones with humans suggests, robots are not always worth the investment, especially when an employer has a flexible reserve army of workers who can be swapped in and out as needed.

Less than a year after my disappointment in Hamburg, the performers who put *Paramour*'s drones out of work were themselves without jobs. Early in the COVID-19 pandemic, Cirque cut nearly their entire global workforce, letting go of some 3,500 employees in June 2020. The layoffs came as Cirque filed for bankruptcy protection in Canada and the United States, three months after lockdowns forced it to drop the curtain on forty-four shows around the world from Hangzhou to Las Vegas—this included Hamburg, where *Paramour* closed on March 12. Cirque performed in miniature the dramatic downturn that COVID-19 triggered in many sectors of the global economy, especially in hospitality and personal services.[82] At the start of 2020, essays and books like Daniel Susskind's *A World Without Work* had been stoking fears that robots, having already pushed workers out of factories, were now marching on service jobs.[83] By March, however, the swift spread of a deadly zoonotic virus had become the force disrupting such workplaces, not machines.

If Cirque's bankruptcy laid bare the dire circumstances that much of the service sector faced during lockdowns, the pandemic proved to be "the ultimate perfect crisis" for online retailers like Amazon.[84] Instead of closing their gates to employees, firms in the business of getting goods to consumers became starved for labor-power, and logistics workers, duly recognized as *essential*, saw their ranks swell. To borrow a phrase from Gabriel Winant's account describing the treatment of healthcare workers during the pandemic, those laboring in logistics were revealed to be, in the estimation of capital at least, "collectively indispensable yet individually disposable."[85] As demand for delivery and web hosting skyrocketed, Amazon's revenue followed suit, increasing by $100 billion. The share of wealth belonging to the billionaire class in the United States exploded by 20 percent in the first months of the pandemic. Jeff Bezos came out the biggest winner, reaping a cool $34.6 billion. That summer, the economic historian Robert Brenner dubbed this a moment of "escalating plunder." The virus only accelerated what had been already in the works.[86]

The gimmick, as Sianne Ngai puts it, is "a miniature model of capital itself," since it exemplifies several features of what Marx called "the moving contradiction."[87] Capitalism relies on labor-power provided by human workers for surplus value, but also constantly tries to either replace these workers with technology or enhance their productivity through it, thereby undermining the very conditions of capital accumulation. "Overperforming and underperforming, encoding either too much or not enough time, and fundamentally gratuitous yet strangely essential," the gimmick, Ngai writes, exudes the countervailing pressures under which capitalism puts itself, and whose crisis tendencies it staves off by trying to render workers replaceable. Capitalist gimmicks place this ambition on full display, while simultaneously obscuring and distracting from it by "focusing exclusively" on the role of technology.[88] Drone gimmicks, as choreographed by companies like Amazon and Cirque, give a sense of the moving contradiction that hampers the future of logistics automation: namely that capitalism cannot do without human labor.

McKinsey & Company expect the market for warehouse automation to expand at a 23 percent annual clip this decade, exceeding $50 billion by 2030.[89] Even if such predictions prove true and investment in machines continues to grow, the endgame is not to eliminate all human labor from warehouses, but rather to render it fungible by transforming logistics work into ever-more definable tasks that enhance capital's control over the labor process. Instead of a future that is novel when compared to the past, drone gimmicks suggest the persistence of capital's ambition to make those tasked with performing the work of logistics eminently replaceable.

"All Roads and Railways Led Down to the Sea"

So far this chapter has focused on the future of logistics automation in the capitalist core of North America and Europe, but drone gimmicks are also proliferating across the Global South. There they carry a different promise of how the future will rhyme with the past, this one imbued with the logics of empire. If Amazon's gimmickry augurs a future of replaceable logistics workers, the neocolonial drone gimmick foretells entire populations made surplus to the capitalist production process while still tethered to its markets.

Without a doubt, the consummate neocolonial drone gimmick is Norman Foster's *Droneport*, an ostensibly humanitarian endeavor aimed at developing a UAV network across the African continent for delivering essential medical supplies. What distinguishes the esteemed British architect's plan from those of the many startups scrambling to bring drones to Africa is his emphasis on building a delivery network around stylishly designed mini-hangars. Foster and his team unveiled their first droneport prototype in May 2016 at the Venice Biennale of Architecture (Figure 19).

Far less grand than the Beijing and London airports for which Foster is renowned, his blueprint for the "world's smallest airport" nevertheless made for an elegant thing: a door-less arching chamber within which drones could be loaded, serviced, and even manufactured.[90] Eventually, construction is to follow the "kit-of-parts" model Foster initially dreamed up for colonizing the moon, in which only the machines needed for construction would be delivered to the site, leaving all raw materials to be sourced locally. The Venice droneport was built with 18,000 bricks made of compressed earth and cement, naturally cured, its vaulted ceiling lined inside by tile (future droneports are to feature inlays decorated with local cultural motifs). Bricks for the prototype were provided by the LafargeHolcim Foundation for Sustainable Construction, the greenwashing arm of the Holcim Group—one of the world's

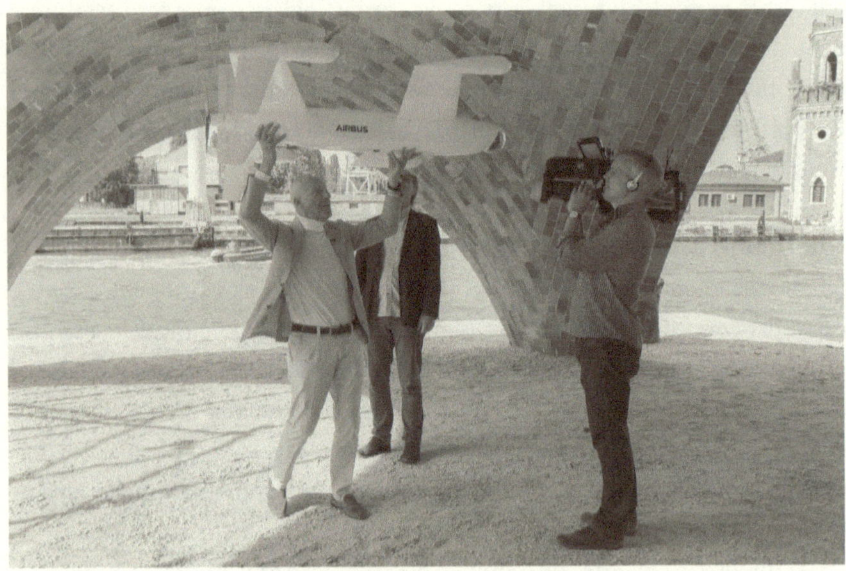

FIGURE 19. Norman Foster unveiling the prototype of *Droneport* at the Venice Biennale of Architecture, 2016.
Photo: Nigel Young © Nigel Young/ The Norman Foster Foundation. Reprinted with permission.

largest cement producers—though Foster expected that future ones would be 3D-printed on-site and incorporate solar cells designed by his fellow art-world luminary Olafur Eliasson. It took four weeks for a core team of four university students led by a Master Mason to construct the droneport. Their work was filmed with the intent of making a how-to guide for future local teams in East Africa and beyond.[91]

The Venice prototype was a proof of concept, but it also came loaded with promises that would never be kept. According to the Norman Foster Foundation (NFF)—the philanthropic organization that spearheaded the project—the first droneport was to be built in Rwanda within six months of the Venice unveiling, with drones starting to transport life-saving blood soon after. By 2020, the droneport network was to blanket 44 percent of the country's mountainous terrain, and the NFF anticipated that "every small town in Africa and in other emerging economies" could have their very own droneport by 2030. More than just a landing pad for UAVs, droneports were to be job creators and providers of varied services, including health clinics, post offices, 3D-printing shops, and "e-commerce trading" hubs. Computer animations that the NFF circulated to the press depicted droneports nestled in forests and on hillsides, each seamlessly integrated into village life with drone runways running parallel to soccer fields. Droneports would start off by saving lives, then pivot to being, as the NFF insisted, the center of "community life."[92] A media blitz of press releases, Gates Foundation–sponsored content, and interviews with Foster himself all eagerly looked forward to 2017 when the first of many droneports would land in Rwanda. I am writing this in 2023, and not a single droneport outside Venice has ever been built.

Droneport has been criticized for embodying many of the worst features of "humanitarian architecture," a loosely defined movement of accomplished architects who propose design solutions for ecological disasters and capitalist underdevelopment, with little intention of realizing them.[93] Foster's project gave newly literal meaning to the oft-disparaged penchant of privileged artists and activists parachuting in and out of the Global South, making it a fitting centerpiece to an architecture festival with the title "Reporting from the Front." When asked whether he had received "positive feedback from the ground in Africa" about *Droneport*, Lord Foster answered in the affirmative, albeit evasively: "Positive feedback from Jonathan, yes."[94] "Jonathan" here refers to Jonathan Ledgard, a Shetland-born, Lausanne-based novelist, self-described futurist, and former East Africa correspondent for *The Economist*. Ledgard was the one who first introduced the idea of a droneport to Foster, after writing a hagiographic portrait of the architect in *The Economist*. Without knowing any better, a visitor to Venice might have mistaken *Droneport* as a parody of the tragic nineteenth-century scramble for Africa. One critic acerbically described it the following way: "A British lord uses Swiss digital technology to 'optimize' mud tile vaults, a humanitarian window dressing as Western companies literally remap the African continent."[95]

As the white leader of organizations with names like Afrotech and the Future Africa Initiative, Ledgard had been peddling the idea of bringing drone delivery to the African continent for years when he persuaded Foster to make *Droneport* the flagship project of his new philanthropy. Before teaming up with Foster, Ledgard had tried to build a humanitarian drone company for transporting blood to places inaccessible by road, with the aim of paving the way for a commercial delivery service. "This future will be radical," Ledgard prophesized in a 2014 manifesto published in *Wired*: "yes, cargo drones will be useful in wealthy countries with dispersed populations. But the biggest opportunity is in Africa. Many people are going to save a lot of lives and make a lot of money putting the donkey [Ledgard's idiosyncratic term for drones] there first."[96] As Amazon and Walmart focused on "instant gratification and last mile delivery" in the Global North, Ledgard, by contrast, wanted to lay claim to "the middle mile in poorer countries."[97] He set his sights first on Kenya, until the country banned commercial drones citing threats from al-Shabaab. By the time Foster came on board, Ledgard was busy wooing Rwanda's President Paul Kagame (also known to Ledgard from his days at *The Economist*) to front one-third of his delivery company's set-up costs, or about $2.2 million. When Ledgard ran into difficulties raising the remaining funds, Kagame turned to the Silicon Valley startup Zipline, which not only had venture capital backing but also possessed its own drone technology—another crucial ingredient that Ledgard lacked. Subsequent attempts to make inroads in Tanzania by staging a drone competition on Lake Victoria with the World Bank in 2018 garnered Ledgard a glowing profile in *The New Yorker* but similarly fizzled out.[98]

Zipline would go on to achieve almost everything Ledgard had proposed, not surprising given how much Ledgard's business plan resembled Zipline's own. But whereas Ledgard and Foster set themselves apart through their droneports, Zipline has never pretended to be building civic infrastructure. Their drones are launched like slingshots and drop packages instead of landing. Founded in 2011, Zipline now operates the world's largest drone delivery network, valued at $4.2 billion as of 2023. In 2022, the company made a quarter of a million deliveries in Rwanda and Ghana.[99] Ledgard was correct in predicting that someone would make "a lot of money" with drones in Africa; it just wouldn't be him. He has since turned his attention, perhaps predictably, to the humanitarian potential of artificial intelligence and blockchain.

Zipline's success in Rwanda has demonstrated the viability of delivery drones, lending support to claims made by Ledgard that UAVs could help bridge the gap between Africa's lack of roads and its growing population. When promoting *Droneport*, the NFF promised that drones would provide a continent lacking investment in built transportation systems with an "infrastructural leap."[100] Why waste money on roads and rail when you could just move cargo by drone? Here the NFF took a page directly from Ledgard, who had long advocated for delivery drones in just such terms, likening their potential in Africa to the mobile phone, which he called the "Kalashnikov of communication." Much in the same way that cellular telephone networks had allowed the continent to skip laying extensive landlines, Ledgard contended that rolling out drones could help Africa avoid having to construct roads, a good thing too, since, as he also averred, "There will never be enough cash for Africa to build out its roads."[101] Ledgard rightly pointed the finger at European empires for having privileged infrastructure for exporting raw materials and resources overseas instead of constructing transport networks within Africa. But in advising that an entire continent should leapfrog building infrastructure that people could use to get around, his proposal replicated a colonial logic of underdevelopment that prioritizes moving commodities over the well-being of humans.

The way that drone delivery in Africa is now unfolding resembles the history of underdevelopment even more egregiously than Ledgard's speculative plans. Companies primarily from Europe and North America, backed by international organizations like the Gates Foundation and the World Bank, are rushing to gain a foothold in Africa's potentially huge e-commerce market, often sidling up to political regimes with despotic tendencies to do so. Once again, countries like Rwanda are being treated as laboratories for technological experiments, incurring misfires and accidents so that richer countries do not have to. To date, corporate trials of drone delivery have been held disproportionately in the Global South, frequently in disaster zones to exploit relaxed regulations, like Haiti after the 2012 earthquake.[102] Capitalism is always loath to let a good catastrophe go to waste. For all its neocolonial ills, *Droneport*, with its emphasis on establishing a "civic presence," nonetheless held to a vision of infrastructure as having the possibility to serve communities and not just the flow of commodities.[103] In the end, however, the proposal to build meaningful infrastructure turned out to be little more than a marketing ploy that distinguished one huckster's plan from those of a slew of Silicon Valley startups. *Droneport's* promise of civic infrastructure was, in other words, a gimmick easily tossed aside.

"All roads and railways led down to the sea," observed Walter Rodney in *How Europe Underdeveloped Africa*: "They were built to extract gold or manganese or coffee or cotton. They were built to make business possible for the timber companies, trading companies, and agricultural concession firms, and for white settlers."[104] The failure of *Droneport* to take off suggests that the operating logic behind infrastructure building in the colonial period will—should current conditions hold—remain true into the future: "Any catering to African interests was purely coincidental."[105]

EPILOGUE
The Blockade

EXPLOITATION AND DISPOSSESSION ARE NOTHING new in the history of capitalism. The difference today is that these twinned dynamics of capital accumulation have been bolstered by a world-enveloping infrastructure built to scatter the production of the things we need to live across planetary supply chains, all for the purpose of keeping profit rates afloat and without regard to the swelling costs for human and nonhuman life. Thanks to this system's delivery prowess, the bill is rapidly coming due. And under current conditions at least, the lion's share will not be paid by those responsible for having made the charges.

What, then, is to be done with the logistical infrastructure of supply chain capitalism? According to some, the priority should be to embark on a long march of harm mitigation in sync with a degrowth agenda. Armed with progressive antitrust policy, logistics workers and social movements would first constrain, then shrink, and ultimately dismantle enormous players like Amazon and Maersk, dissecting them to identify what can be repurposed to serve social needs.[1] Others, sometimes in tension with such degrowth perspectives, though still touting left-wing credentials, offer a ruddier view of the path ahead: instead of reduction and disassembly, logistics is to be seized by techno-savvy socialists ready to accelerate its inbuilt potential for democratizing human satisfaction and establishing communal luxury.[2] Options for humbler detours dot the horizon as well, including improvised rag-picking projects in which people make do with things as they find them—for example, flipping shipping containers into flood barriers or scuttling oil rigs so coral reefs can grow around them.[3] Many also insist that the worst offending components, like coal-fired power plants and private jets, must be urgently taken offline by any means necessary.[4]

The prospects for reconfiguring logistical infrastructure seem to be as vast as our imagination and the built environment itself, yet projects of repurposing can cut both ways. Police, for instance, have long since proven themselves skilled in the art of deploying supply chain tools to quell unrest—to give just one example, in 2001 Swedish riot cops built makeshift barricades from a hundred shipping containers to defend a meeting of the EU Summit in Gothenberg against militant protests.[5] As the dismal yield from nearly two centuries of communist faith in capitalist fettering suggests, the path ahead is less likely to be a gentle downhill stroll toward a dawn of democratic flourishing than a steepening slog through a rugged terrain scarred by forest fires and teeming with ethnonationalist militias armed with killer drones. Any serious consideration of the "transitional horizon" for logistics must acknowledge the reality that much of this infrastructure is, in the words of Alberto Toscano, "unthinkable outside of capital's irrational rationalities."[6]

Art rarely figures into debates over the postcapitalist use-value of logistics, despite the long history of artistic experiments with repurposing this infrastructure's component parts, a sample of which I have studied in this book. There are good reasons why art seldom enters such discussions, with the most obvious being that much of what artists do would appear incidental to a project of securing from fixed capital something useful beyond that of capturing profits. True though this may be, as I have shown in the preceding chapters, art has a thing or two to contribute to the reconfiguration thesis. For one, art produced in the logistical mode (i.e., using capitalist transportation technologies or techniques) can offer chances to view infrastructure otherwise, be it to glimpse from a situated perspective the violence that the circuit of capital requires or to map the scale and scope of its engineered failures. The idea that art might shed light on the workings of supply chain capitalism likely needs no further elaboration here. Less evident, however, remain the practical lessons art can provide projects of reconfiguration. If anything, the inventory I have collected amounts to more of a series of cautionary tales than it does a handbook filled with useful ideas from artists about what can be done with logistical infrastructure. If art repurposed from transportation technologies could be said to contribute anything practical to debates about reconfiguration, it is as further proof that the liberating affordances of capitalist infrastructure cannot be assumed but must always be tested in the course of struggle, which likely means in a realm beyond art.

And yet, in writing this book I have also come across artists whose practices point to *what can be done to* logistical infrastructure besides repurposing it. This includes the Ogoni performers in *Karikpo Pipeline,* who extended their community's blockade by dancing atop mothballed Shell wellheads and flow stations, or the crew of *Global Mariner,* who moored their floating museum in the paths of merchant ships to keep them at bay. However rare such artistic interventions may be, they display a stirring resolve to treat logistics as a target to strike rather than as material waiting to be reconfigured. To these examples, we can add others that reveal infrastructure as a terrain of counterlogistical struggle. Consider, for instance, the performance tours and field trips that Rozalinda Borcilă has organized across Chicago over the last decade, charting how oil pipelines, distribution centers, and police stations have supplanted sacred Indigenous sites.[7] Operating along similar lines is Dread Scott's 2019 *Slave Rebellion Reenactment*, in which hundreds of performers spent two days traversing the twenty-four-mile path of the 1811 German Coast uprising outside New Orleans; their combined movement becoming a means for mapping a contemporary landscape of petroleum refineries, grain elevators, warehouses, and railways onto the remnants of slave labor camps and plantations.[8] Such collective performances double as introductions to logistical terrain, planting in the minds of participants the thought that one day they might return to such places for reasons other than making art. It is to this horizon, one defined by something different than reconfiguration, that I now turn as I conclude this book.

The years I have spent writing *The Arts of Logistics* have been filled with stark reminders of the friction that plagues capital circulation. A partial list would include shipwrecks, hurricanes, shipping line bankruptcies, and COVID-19, not to mention the staggering uptick in the number of struggles targeting logistical infrastructure. Although ports and pipelines may not be necessarily new terrains of contestation, as Deborah Cowen puts it, orientation toward "infrastructures of oppression" has become "a hallmark of activism in an era of global circulation."[9] Given all that capitalism has invested in logistics, it makes sense for its antagonists to have followed suit.

Be it the spectacular rage of a riot or a clandestine act of sabotage, there are many ways to disrupt circulation. Yet scholars and activists widely agree that it is the blockade that has emerged today as the leading counterlogistical tactic, from European dockworkers hindering arms shipments bound for Yemen to the water protectors who held their ground at Standing Rock.[10] What remains to be shown in this book is how logistical infrastructure exists as something to obstruct rather than repurpose. The recent resurgence of the blockade in both theory and practice has rekindled debates about its tactical function. For some, the blockade appears as a shrewd means for leveraging the demands of workers and social movements at chokepoints, while others proclaim blockading to be an insurrectionary end in itself.[11] These perspectives are tempered by those who caution against viewing the blockade as a "magic bullet solution," emphasizing instead the need for a more sober analysis of the tactic's limitations within a broader repertoire of circulation struggles.[12] In turning my attention toward efforts at blockading, I look to extend the central claim of this book that the possibilities for a future worth living are not built into logistical infrastructure but lie elsewhere, namely in what we can do together.

This book opened with a blockade—and will end with many. When tens of thousands of us shut down the Port of Oakland on November 2, 2011, our action became evidence of both the tactic's "contemporary resurgence" and also, as some have since claimed, its limitations.[13] The history of blockading long predates the logistics revolution, but its proliferation today suits our political-economic terrain in which circulation has taken the lead in capitalist production. For all that logistical restructuring has expanded and entrenched capitalist social relations across the world, it has also introduced new vulnerabilities. The need to avoid bottlenecks while reducing labor costs in manufacturing requires tightening chokepoints elsewhere, such as in seaports, at transit warehouses, and on highways. Though located around the world, the sites essential for moving raw materials, parts, and final products are not evenly sprinkled about but instead consolidated into dense clusters and seams, a bit like tightly packed sawdust. Making this landscape only more explosive are the "just-in-time" priorities of supply chains that leave local economies with only the inventory they need in the short term, without the productive forces necessary to replenish them. In this regard, the logistics revolution is said to have inaugurated new opportunities in the struggle against capitalism. However true this may be, it should not be mistaken for a relative weakening of capitalism. Logistical vulnerability, as Søren Mau reminds us, signals "only *potential* weakness" and not its actuality.[14] Counterlogistical power resides not within capitalist infrastructure itself but rather in the actions of those engaged in transforming this vulnerability into actual weakness.

Workers at ports and inside logistics companies have been, arguably, the most effective at taking advantage of this new terrain so far, leveraging their strategic position within chokepoints to secure contract gains and intervene in issues outside the workplace. As examples of the latter, consider the dockworkers around the world who, to protest Israeli bombings in Gaza, have refused to handle vessels transporting military equipment, or recall the wildcat strikes that swept the Suez Canal in February 2011 and helped topple the Egyptian president, Hosni Mubarak.[15] Logistical landscapes have also become sites of struggle for those not employed in them, no less than when such infrastructures constitute a threat in and of themselves, as exemplified by the oil and gas pipelines dug into Indigenous lands across North and South America. Today, social movements are also increasingly turning toward logistics even when its infrastructure seems to have little directly to do with the struggle at hand. In the case of the Oakland blockade, the motley concerns of Occupy seemed distant from the port, regardless of subsequent reflections emphasizing the action's solidarity with longshoremen. A similar point could be made about the many highway blockades that have been mounted in defense of Black lives in recent years. To hear some tell it, social movements turn to logistical chokepoints chiefly as a kind of force multiplier for protest: "Beyond merely attracting media and government attention," explains Martin Danyluk, "the immobilisation of commodity flows offers a source of leverage that can compel officials to negotiate on terms they might not otherwise entertain."[16] Valid as this claim is, premeditated calculation of this sort only partially explains why struggles are gravitating toward logistical infrastructure and adopting fitting tactical forms. What's more, such criteria can slip with startling ease from being a means of explanation and avowal to a cause for dismissal, especially of struggles that muster in a moment's heat.

Counterlogistical struggle is more than a game of hide and seek. Social movements target sites of circulation not only because this is where capital now directs so much of its efforts, but also because this is where partisans find themselves prepared to act. As Joshua Clover points out, it is not like "anyone wakes up in the morning and thinks to themselves, 'today is a good day for a circulation struggle!'"[17] Many people, shunted into atomizing service jobs or excluded, often along racialized lines, from waged work altogether, now find that the opportunities for collective action have shifted, together with conventional forms of class belonging, away from workplaces as such to spaces of circulation: highways, marketplaces, city squares, ports, and the like. This shift has even led some to correlate "a proliferation of the blockade and a waning of the strike as such."[18] Whatever the specifics of the current field of class antagonism may be, there is little reason to doubt that tactics like blockades, riots, and occupations, oriented as they typically are to the sphere of circulation, are well suited to the political-economic terrain of supply chain capitalism.

Blockades both require and create stillness. This makes the tactic palatable to a broad spectrum of political principles: the liberal ethic of nonviolence, the libertarian belligerence to disrupt the status quo, the insurrectionist desire to make everything stop, and the decolonizing resolve of Indigenous peoples to remain. This suggests that the blockade's current resurgence owes something to how its formal qualities, like stillness, align with our historical conjuncture.

Consider, then, a blockade that expressly invited attention to its form. On a chilly February evening in 2009, an unidentified person, dressed against the cold in a winter coat and knit cap, stepped onto an access road in the Port of Stockholm and blocked the path of a truck convoy that had just disembarked a ferry. Horns blaring, the lead vehicle pulled right in an attempt to snake around the solitary blockader, who sidled left to keep obstructing the way. A halting dance ensued as the freight truck inched this way and that, its partner responding in lockstep. Ten meters and ten minutes later, the blockader walked away without even glancing back. The column of six trucks drove on, seemingly unruffled by what had just transpired.

With its limited duration and scale, this blockade reads like a rehearsal for grander ones to come, of the sort that shut down the Port of Oakland two years later. However, the disruption in Stockholm was actually a performance choreographed by Santiago Sierra, with the freight trucks cast as his unwitting ensemble. It was staged for the opening of a retrospective on the Spanish

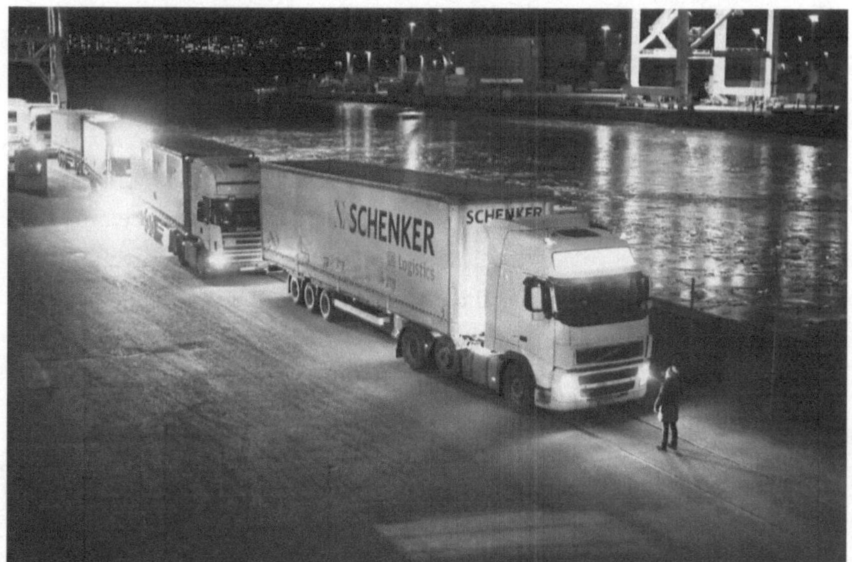

FIGURE 20. Santiago Sierra's *Person Obstructing a Line of Containers*, 2009. Film still © 2023 Artists Rights Society (ARS), New York / VEGAP, Madrid. Reprinted with permission.

artist's career at Magasin III, a contemporary art museum located in the port. Captured on film by a camera mounted high on the venue, the resulting black-and-white video, titled *Person Obstructing a Line of Containers*, was then shown as part of the exhibition (Figure 20).[19] Sierra's blockade slotted neatly into his notorious repertoire of performances that seem engineered to antagonize, which has included hiring undocumented migrants to stand inside boxes for hours, paying sex workers to be tattooed, and pumping car exhaust into a former synagogue in Germany.[20] The unannounced obstruction in the Port of Stockholm saw Sierra employ one of his favorite techniques of provocation: the blockade. Over the past three decades, he has closed a footbridge in Mexico City using rolls of tape, replaced the entrance to a London gallery with sheets of corrugated metal, and bisected a park in Wiesbaden with ten-foot-high military barricades. Sierra created his most infamous blockade in 1998 when he hired a driver to jackknife a big rig across a Mexico City freeway, filming the event from an overpass. *Obstruction of a Freeway with a Truck's Trailer* brought traffic to a standstill for four minutes, at which point the truck simply straightened out and drove off.[21]

Sierra's blockades are designed to disrupt, although the artist prefers to discuss them in terms of their aesthetic form. For instance, he has likened his Mexico City highway blockade to a "minimalist"[22] sculpture, stating: "This piece consisted of positioning a white prism perpendicular to the road, generating a traffic jam."[23] Similarly, *Person Obstructing a Line of Containers* fits within a lineage of performance art, with its reliance on endurance, surprise, and bodily vulnerability evoking iconic experiments by artists such as Chris Burden and Marina Abramović. These art-world precedents notwithstanding, Sierra himself has framed his Stockholm port blockade as an homage to the 1989 standoff between a column of tanks and a solitary protestor in Tiananmen Square on its twentieth anniversary.[24] At the time of its performance, *Obstruction of a Freeway with a Truck's Trailer* in Mexico likewise resonated with the proliferation of road blockades being erected across Latin America by peasant and unemployed worker movements, including the piqueteros in Argentina, the regantes in Bolivia, and the Zapatistas in Chiapas. Nevertheless, despite Sierra's declared interest in "interrupting the fluids of the capitalist system," the politics of his blockades remain challenging to pin down.[25] Instead of making demands or expressing political sympathies, Sierra privileges aesthetic qualities of composition, interruption, and spectacle. By stripping them of overt political content, he renders his blockades as experiments in form, both tactical and aesthetic.

Sierra is not the only artist to have repurposed the blockade to create art. Alongside representations of blockades in visual art and popular culture, examples also abound of artists who have made actual blockades, mining the tactic for its formal features. This includes the oil barrel barricades that Christo and Jeanne-Claude set up during the early years of the logistics revolution (discussed in Chapter 2), as well as more recent road blockades by Lin Yilin in Guangzhou and Heather Peak and Ivan Morison in Wellington. While such performances might warrant criticism for transforming political action into spectacle, they also convey certain truths about the blockade as a tactical form. By repurposing the tactic into material for a gallery opening, Sierra's *Person Obstructing a Line of Containers* serves as a reminder, albeit obliquely, that the blockade is not tied to specific contexts or situations, let alone particular motives or objectives. The blockade is a form fit for many occasions.

As I was first drafting this Epilogue, another blockade reminiscent of Sierra's kicked off in the Port of Oakland. In July 2022, hundreds of truck drivers parked their container trailers across the port's terminal access gates, causing operations to grind to a halt at a time when supply chains were still grappling with the lingering effects of COVID-19. Their blockade took aim at a new California state law written to enhance protections and benefits for gig economy workers. Commercial trucker organizations, however, claimed the legislation undermined the self-identity of drivers as small business owners, and would burden them with new costs.[26] The year 2022 witnessed a slew of blockades resembling this one, as truckers around the world repurposed their vehicles to disrupt capital flows, often in support of Far Right political projects. The most infamous were those that bookended the year: the vaccine-skeptical Ottawa "Freedom Convoy" and the Bolsonarist roadblocks, which swept across Brazil following the election of Luiz Inácio Lula da Silva.[27] These truck blockades confirm that the Left does not have a monopoly on the tactic. However, other recent examples, like the Yellow Vests (*gilets jaunes*) highway disruptions and wildcat strikes by Palestinian truckers in Gaza, offer a more accurate portrait of the tactic's ideological flexibility.[28]

This is as true historically as it is today. The blockade, as both a tactic and term, has military origins, with the overlap dating back at least to seventeenth-century naval cordons.[29] Today, governments and corporations regularly block flows of goods, money, and people to secure their own interests, reminding us that blockages are often integral to the circulation of capital. Viewed in this light, Sierra hiring a truck driver to obstruct a highway is less an artistic misuse of the tactic than it is confirmation of the blockade's plasticity. The performance owed largely to the fact that the blockade, as a tactical form, is already untethered from any specific political content. For this reason, a lesson can be drawn from Sierra's many blockades, one that calls to mind words from Clover once again: "We are not on the side of the riot but of the George Floyd Uprising; not in solidarity with blockades but with the history of Indigenous land and water protection."[30] Even more than art, a blockade should not be judged on the grounds of form alone.

Sierra's blockades also underscore the ambivalence of interruption. At first glance, his interventions seem like proof that disrupting robust infrastructures can be as easy as an individual choosing to step into the path of a slow-moving convoy. The allure is akin to that of other spectacular blockages, such as the grounding of the *Ever Given,* which, as discussed in Chapter 1, generated a counterlogistical spectacle highlighting the fragility of global circulation. Sierra's blockades evoke a similar prospect that flow can be cut off at any time. But whereas *Ever Given* pointed to causes like infrastructural faults and natural accidents, Sierra, by hiring people to do this work, insists on the capacity of people to shut down a system often assumed to be beyond human comprehension and control. Regardless of the empowering or sobering truths contained in such counterlogistical spectacles, they can also be deceiving. The *Ever Given* meme froze blockage in time, suggesting permanence in what was inevitably just a temporary six-day disturbance. Created as performances and films, Sierra's blockades appear to embrace ephemerality, yet their actual dramaturgy emphasizes the ease of obstruction and release. This presents a deceptive vision of what it takes to shut infrastructure down, implying that circulation can be turned on and off by individuals as simply as a faucet. What's more, they overlook the likelihood of the state to respond to such interruptions with force, or that of capital to absorb or offload any losses incurred. Nowhere is the reality of securitization to be seen, whether in the guise of cops or financialization.

Sierra's blockades, therefore, fixate on the moment of interruption. Both *Person Obstructing a Line of Containers* and *Obstruction of a Freeway with a Truck's Trailer* exemplify what it means to make "a fetish out of rupture," a political hazard that Alberto Toscano attaches to the blockade.[31] While not denying the potential power of blockading, Toscano warns against elevating this "tactic" into a "strategy" and consequently conflating a form of intervention with a political horizon.[32] His words of caution, first issued in 2011 and elaborated subsequently, directly responded to the insurrectionist manifestoes of groups like the Invisible Committee, which were filled with aphorisms like "Power is logistic. Block everything!"[33] Writing again in 2013, Toscano observed a similar temptation to mistake temporary interruptions for revolutionary confrontations in the narrative that developed around the 2011 Port of Oakland blockade.[34] For Toscano, evaluating this, or any, blockade requires considering it within a longer *durée* than the moment of blockage allows. In the case of Oakland, doing so would seem to lay bare the tactic's limit: just hours after shutting the port down, we left of our own accord and business resumed, almost as if we had never been there. Such a fact would seem to be evidence enough to temper any claims that our blockade amounted to an "unmediated confrontation with or negation of the social form of value."[35] Yet, if the window of time for evaluation were to be extended still further, one would see that many of us returned to the port the very next month in an attempt to repeat and spread the blockade across the entire West Coast. Rhythm and not rupture is the temporal register that best describes the proliferation of blockades today, appearing as they do "less as revolutionary captures of capital flows than as episodic struggles," to borrow words from Charmaine Chua.[36] This is no reason to dismiss the tactic's effectiveness but is rather proof of its expansion in both space and time.

I am not one to deny the attraction and mobilizing power of images drawn from moments of rupture. Yet, time is clearly out of joint in Sierra's blockades, insofar as they display the dangers that come with reducing the tactic's temporality to a singular moment. Purposefully circumscribed in duration, there is no before or after in his blockades, no history or follow-on effects with which to reckon and learn. The sheer number of blockades that Sierra has created speaks to the tactic's proliferation, but none of them exists in sequence with the others. Designed with clear beginnings and decisive ends, none has potential for elaboration. In this regard, each recommends that such an action should never go too far, that one should know when to walk off or drive away, lest the symbolic blockage becomes too real. As much as he fetishizes rupture, Sierra also infantilizes it. The casualness with which his blockades are both initiated and resolved evince a pointlessness in the very act. The blockade, typically performed solo in Sierra's oeuvre, becomes a lark severed from commitments to collective action. It is no wonder, then, that his disruptions cater, however knowingly, to critiques of the tactic as an adventurist thrill. As Toscano might put it, Sierra's blockades fixate on "subtraction and interruption," when the point should be to embrace tactics like this for how they open onto opportunities for "attack and expansion."[37]

Just a decade ago, scholars could confidently describe the logistics revolution as "the most underinvestigated revolution of the twentieth century."[38] Surely, this is no longer the case, given all of the attention now being paid to it by researchers, activists, and, of course, artists. While there is still more to be learned, we now know much about how restructuring capitalist production according to the demands of circulation has transformed social life the world over. But putting such a strong spotlight on logistics has also had unintended consequences. The most notable of these, in my opinion, is the growing temptation to pin the ills befalling our planet to the *present* organization of capitalist production around supply chains, instead of to capitalism as a historical world-system. Logistics is only one of capital's arts of war, and not the enemy in its entirety. Just as the riddle before us exceeds the question of what is to be done with infrastructural tools like shipping containers and pipelines, so too do the potential solutions.

Blockades seem to indicate a political horizon different from, or even antithetical to, that of reconfiguration. It was, in fact, his concern over "the centrality of a theory and practice of *interruption*, targeted at logistical apparatuses" that prompted Toscano to consider the possibilities for "emancipatory refunctioning" in the first place.[39] I have spent much of this book scrutinizing the prospect that logistical infrastructure, in its materiality, is brimming with hidden affordances, pointing instead to the social relations that inevitably restrict any attempt at repurposing. Logistics outstrips the technologies, built environments, and other materials that typically represent it in the cultural imaginary. Just as the "potency" of logistics cannot be assumed to exist "on material grounds alone," the same applies to efforts at subverting it.[40]

Although the blockade seems to provide an alternative answer to the question of what is to be done with logistics, many who would advocate rendering infrastructure "useless"—such as through obstruction or sabotage—risk reducing logistics to its physical forms.[41] If the reconfiguration thesis emphasizes the materiality of technologies and fixed capital, its supposed obverse, the blockade, can be said to focus on the flow of material goods. In both cases, logistical infrastructure is presumed to be ready-made for subversion. Consider, for example, a reflection on the Port of Oakland blockade, which insisted that the "mere materiality" of supply chains makes "the sphere of circulation . . . the preeminent site of contestation," since disrupting the physical flow of goods would have cascading consequences for social reproduction.[42] Though I share the underlying desire expressed here, this particular line of thinking threatens to conflate the physical movement of things with capital circulation, as if interrupting the former would necessarily short-circuit the latter. As Toscano puts it, we must understand "circulation less literally."[43]

At the beginning of this book, I noted that circulation includes all manner of activities required to realize value in exchange, encompassing more than the transportation and distribution of physical goods. This is one reason why capitalism can weather episodic blockages, as it can defray the costs of delay and nondelivery through hedging or insurance, and why capitalist firms deliberately generate friction of their own to keep profit rates up. A *less literal* understanding of circulation should encourage us to think of struggle as directed "not simply against material flows but against the social forms that channel them."[44] Although the logistics revolution has introduced new opportunities for political struggle, it would be a mistake to think of the resulting infrastructure and their chokepoints as ready-made sites of confrontation. It is not the "brute materiality of chokepoints . . . that interrupt[s] capital flows," so Chua asserts with Kai Bosworth, "but people."[45] Counterlogistical power resides not in capitalist infrastructures as an unintended affordance, but in the social forces arrayed against them. In addition to the physical forms that logistics assumes, we must contend with the capitalist relations that precede and underlie it, that set the constraints and enabling conditions for producing the very materials specific to supply chain capitalism. To this end, Cowen, Chua, and others have written of the need for "queering logistics"[46] as a means to grasp the necro and biopolitical character of capitalist circulation today and to recognize that any struggle "against supply-chain capitalism requires much more than episodically interrupting its material flows."[47] It is not enough for movements to be *against* extant infrastructures of life; they also need to be *for* new ones.

None of this is meant to dismiss the usefulness of a tactic like the blockade. Although typically seen as a means of negation, blockades often serve as modes of "counter-reproduction," requiring care and sociality while also fostering conditions for further struggle.[48] There's no better evidence of this than the proliferation of efforts by Indigenous-led movements in North America to obstruct pipelines, highways, and railroads that cut through dispossessed lands. Writing about the Grassy Narrows road blockade by the Anishinaabe people that has persisted in northwestern Ontario since 2002, Glen Sean Coulthard challenges the notion of blockades as fleeting or "reactive" actions.

Instead he reframes them as an "affirmative *enactment* of another modality of being, a different way of relating to and with the world."[49] Likewise, Nick Estes describes the struggle against the Dakota Access Pipeline in defense of the Standing Rock Sioux Tribe as both a "fight *against* settler colonialism" and one "*for* Indigenous life and just relations with human and nonhuman relatives, and with the earth."[50] According to Leanne Betasamosake Simpson, blockades like those of the Wet'suwet'en and their allies that swept through Canada in early 2020 should be seen as a "generative refusal"[51] that performs a dual function: "Blockades are both a refusal and an affirmation. An affirmation of a different political economy. A world built upon a different set of relationships and ethics. An affirmation of life."[52] Vital to Simpson's account is the "ethic of care" needed for maintaining and reproducing blockades.[53] If it is to be *for* anything, a blockade requires reproduction.

November 10, 2023. Blockaders have returned to Oakland. On November 3, dozens of people took to the port to stop *Cape Orlando*, an American military cargo vessel, from departing with supplies to Israel. Some even locked themselves onto the ship in a desperate effort to keep it at bay.[54] For weeks now, Gaza has been under siege, with Israeli forces bent on waging a scorched-earth campaign through the world's largest open-air prison.

Just days later, on November 6, when *Cape Orlando* arrived up the coast in Tacoma, Washington, hundreds of people were ready and waiting to block it from being loaded. To these blockades, we can add many others—in Barcelona and Bristol, St. Charles and Santa Barbara, Melbourne and Sydney. I'm beginning to lose track.

I woke up this morning—the day I am to submit the final draft of this book—to messages from friends who were on their way from London to Kent to join a blockade, soon to be 500-people strong, of a factory belonging to the weapons manufacturer BAE Systems. It's early still. Too early to tell how far these blockades will spread.

Notes

Epigraph

1. George C. Thorpe, *Pure Logistics: The Science of War Preparation* [1917] (Washington, DC: National Defense University Press, 1986).

Prologue

1. On the history of containerization in Oakland, see Marc Levinson, *The Box: How the Shipping Container Made the World Smaller and the World Economy Bigger* (Princeton, NJ: Princeton University Press, 2006), 191–197; Peter Cole, *Dockworker Power: Race and Activism in Durban and the San Francisco Bay Area* (Urbana: University of Illinois Press, 2018), 117–147.

Introduction

1. I draw the term "supply chain capitalism" from Anna Lowenhaupt Tsing to describe the prevailing organizational "form" that governs capitalist production today, namely planetary supply chains. Anna Lowenhaupt Tsing, "Supply Chains and the Human Condition," *Rethinking Marxism* 21, no. 2 (2009): 148–176.

2. On the "long downturn" thesis, see Robert Brenner, *The Economics of Global Turbulence: The Advanced Capitalist Economies from Long Boom to Long Downturn, 1945–2005* (London: Verso, 2006).

3. For an introduction to critical logistics research, see Charmaine Chua, Martin Danyluk, Deborah Cowen, and Laleh Khalili, "Turbulent Circulation: Building a Critical Engagement with Logistics," *Environment and Planning D: Society and Space* 36, no. 4 (2018): 617–629. Additional key contributions are referenced throughout this book.

4. See, for example, Kelly M. Rich, Nicole M. Rizzuto, and Susan Zieger, "Reading Infrastructure," in *The Aesthetic Life of Infrastructure: Race, Affect, Environment*, ed. Kelly M. Rich, Nicole Rizzuto, and Susan Zieger (Evanston, IL: Northwestern

University Press, 2023), 1–19; Alberto Toscano and Jeff Kinkle, *Cartographies of the Absolute* (Winchester, UK: Zero Books, 2015).

5. On these topics, see David Joselit, *Heritage and Debt: Art in Globalization* (Cambridge, MA: MIT Press, 2020); Fernando Domínguez Rubio, *Still Life: Ecologies of the Modern Imagination at the Art Museum* (Chicago: University of Chicago Press, 2020); Nizan Shaked, *Museums and Wealth: The Politics of Contemporary Art Collections* (New York: Bloomsbury Academic, 2022); Hito Steyerl, *Duty Free Art: Art in the Age of Civil War* (London: Verso, 2019).

6. Charmaine Chua, "Logistical Violence, Logistical Vulnerabilities," *Historical Materialism* 25, no. 4 (February 2017): 167–182, quote at 169.

7. Søren Mau, *Mute Compulsion: A Marxist Theory of the Economic Power of Capital* (London: Verso, 2023), 289.

8. See Andrew Dickson, "How to Move a Masterpiece: The Secret Business of Shipping Priceless Artworks," *The Guardian*, March 21, 2019, https://www.theguardian.com/artanddesign/2019/mar/21/how-to-move-a-masterpiece-secret-business-shipping-priceless-artworks-art-handling; Jeremy Harding, "Nautical Dramas," *London Review of Books* 43, no. 14 (July 15, 2021), https://www.lrb.co.uk/the-paper/v43/n14/jeremy-harding/short-cuts

9. Robert J. Keith, "The Marketing Revolution," *Journal of Marketing*, no. 3 (1960): 35–38, quote at 35. On the logistics revolution, see W. Bruce Allen, "The Logistics Revolution and Transportation," *Annals of the American Academy of Political and Social Science*, no. 553 (1997): 106–116; Ronald H. Ballou, "The Evolution and Future of Logistics and Supply Chain Management," *European Business Review* 19, no. 4 (July 2007): 332–348; Richard F. Poist, "Evolution of Conceptual Approaches to Designing Business Logistics Systems," *Transportation Journal* 26, no. 1 (1986): 55–64. For critical histories, see Edna Bonacich and Jake B. Wilson, *Getting the Goods: Ports, Labor, and the Logistics Revolution* (Ithaca, NY: Cornell University Press, 2008), 3–22; Deborah Cowen, *The Deadly Life of Logistics: Mapping Violence in Global Trade* (Minneapolis: University of Minnesota Press, 2014), 23–52.

10. Allen, "The Logistics Revolution and Transportation," 107.

11. Brenner, *The Economics of Global Turbulence*, 55–61.

12. Donald J. Bowersox, Edward W. Smykay, and Bernard J. La Londe, *Physical Distribution Management: The Logistics Problems of the Firm* (London: Macmillan, 1968), 12.

13. Peter Drucker, "Physical Distribution: The Frontier of Modern Management," in *Readings in Physical Distribution Management: The Logistics of Marketing*, ed. Donald J. Bowersox, Bernard J. La Londe, and Edward W. Smykay (New York: Macmillan, 1969), 3–8, quote at 4. See also Peter Drucker, "The Economy's Dark Continent," *Fortune* 65, no. 4 (April 1962): 103, 265–270.

14. Cowen, *Deadly Life of Logistics*, 38; Taiichi Ohno, *Toyota Production System: Beyond Large-Scale Production* (Boca Raton, FL: CRC Press, 1988).

15. See especially Brenner, *The Economics of Global Turbulence*. See also Giovanni Arrighi, *The Long Twentieth Century: Money, Power, and the Origins of Our Times*, 2nd ed. (London: Verso, 2010).

16. Annie McClanahan, *Dead Pledges: Debt, Crisis, and Twenty-First-Century Culture* (Stanford, CA: Stanford University Press, 2017), 12–13. On the spatial fix, see also David Harvey, "Globalization and the 'Spatial Fix,'" *Geographische Revue*, no. 2 (2001): 23–30.

17. On the military inheritance of logistical infrastructure, see Alejandro Colás, "Infrastructures of the Global Economy: The Shipping Container as a Political Artefact," in *Technology and World Politics: An Introduction*, ed. Daniel R. McCarthy (New York: Routledge, 2018), 146–164; Cowen, *Deadly Life of Logistics*; Laleh Khalili, *Sinews of War and Trade: Shipping and Capitalism in the Arabian Peninsula* (London: Verso, 2020); Marc Levinson, *The Box: How the Shipping Container Made the World Smaller and the World Economy Bigger* (Princeton, NJ: Princeton University Press, 2006), 178; Thomas Reifer, "Labor, Race, and Empire: Transport Workers and Transnational Empires of Trade, Production, and Finance," in *Labor Versus Empire: Race, Gender, and Migration*, ed. Gilbert G. Gonzalez, Raul A. Fernandez, Vivian Price, David Smith, and Linda Trinh Võ (New York: Routledge, 2004), 15–32, at 20–25.

18. Cowen, *Deadly Life of Logistics*, 51.

19. Jasper Bernes, "Logistics, Counterlogistics and the Communist Prospect," *Endnotes* 3, 2013, https://endnotes.org.uk/articles/logistics-counterlogistics-and-the-communist-prospect

20. Stefano Harney and Fred Moten, *The Undercommons: Fugitive Planning & Black Study* (Wivenhoe, NY: Minor Compositions, 2013), 92.

21. Karl Marx, *Grundrisse: Foundations of the Critique of Political Economy*, trans. Martin Nicolaus (London: Penguin Classics, 1993), 524–525, quote at 525.

22. Mau, *Mute Compulsion*, 276.

23. Intan Suwandi, *Value Chains: The New Economic Imperialism* (New York: Monthly Review Press, 2019).

24. For an overview of this, see Cowen, *Deadly Life of Logistics*, 10–11. For an influential example of what is described here, see Manuel Castells, *The Rise of the Network Society*, 2nd ed. (Chichester, UK: Wiley, 2011).

25. Karl Marx, *Capital: A Critique of Political Economy, Volume 1*, trans. Ben Fowkes (London: Penguin Classics, 1990), 279. Marx's discussion of circulation can be found across his critique of political economy; see especially Karl Marx, *Capital: A Critique of Political Economy, Volume 2*, trans. David Fernbach (London: Penguin Classics, 1992), 207–229; Marx, *Grundrisse*, 516–549.

26. Whether in production or circulation, transportation and distribution outlays are typically considered an incidental expense. Such outlays expended in circulation may be essential for ensuring that exchange happens but, because they occur beyond production, they contribute little or nothing to the actual usefulness of a

finished product. Instead of being a productive investment, these costs, regardless of how necessary they are for ensuring that ownership of a commodity literally changes hands, drag on surplus value. Like the labor of a cashier, this work also tends to count as a "*faux frais*" (Marx, *Capital,* 2, 226)—another incidental cost of exchange. There is as well the related matter of transport costs incurred before exchange and within a production process, and which involve transport workers in production who, for example, move parts from storage to an assembly line. Whether such transport work belongs to production or not has caused all manner of disagreement among readers of Marx, this despite the fact that in *Capital* and related writings Marx was adamant that transport of this kind—that which is required to make things—"belongs to the production process itself" (Marx, *Grundrisse,* 534). To suggest that identical transport activities like pulling stock or delivering goods can belong to both production and circulation might seem an error, but it is entirely consistent with the logic of Marx's value theory of labor, applicable as much to transport work as it is to domestic work: whether an activity belongs to "production" depends less on the concrete activity performed than on the economic context and social relations that engulf it.

For useful contributions to this debate, see Liam Campling and Alejandro Colás, *Capitalism and the Sea: The Maritime Factor in the Making of the Modern World* (London: Verso, 2021), 55–63; Charmaine Chua, "Containing the Ship of State: Managing Mobility in an Age of Logistics" (PhD dissertation, Minneapolis, University of Minnesota, 2018), 124–140; Joshua Clover, *Riot. Strike. Riot: The New Era of Uprisings* (London: Verso, 2016), 17–31, 129–152; Ian Gough, "Marx's Theory of Productive and Unproductive Labour," *New Left Review,* no. 76 (December 1972): 47–72; David Harvey, "The Geography of Capitalist Accumulation: A Reconstruction of the Marxian Theory," in *Spaces of Capital: Towards a Critical Geography* (New York: Routledge, 2001), 237–266; Isaak Il'ich Rubin, *Essays on Marx's Theory of Value,* trans. Miloš Samardžija and Fredy Perlman (Delhi: Aakar Books, 2008), 196–209.

27. The reason has to do largely with the fact that transport labor, like that performed by a dockworker or a truck driver, more resembles a service than it does manufacturing, insofar as an act of transport is produced in the same moment as it is consumed and typically does not generate a physical product. This temporal and tangible hitch makes it especially difficult to squeeze value from a transport worker's labor-time without the help of machines or managerial discipline, the costs of both always counting against surplus value. For a comparison of transport work to service, see Michael Heinrich, *An Introduction to the Three Volumes of Karl Marx's "Capital,"* trans. Alexander Locascio (New York: Monthly Review Press, 2012), 134. For an overview of Marx's perspective on the costs of machines and managers against surplus value, see Jason E. Smith, *Smart Machines and Service Work: Automation in an Age of Stagnation* (London: Reaktion Books, 2020), 92–113.

28. Suwandi, *Value Chains,* 42–67, quote at 45.

29. Clover, *Riot. Strike. Riot,* 142.

30. Marx, *Grundrisse*, 524. David Harvey and Joshua Clover provide two of the clearest explanations for why the expansion of the logistics infrastructure has intensified capitalist crisis. According to Harvey, sinking such huge amounts of capital into transport infrastructures increases both the relative and absolute costs of circulation, which over time, as the organic composition of capital increases, eats into the rate of profit such efforts seek to bolster. Harvey, "The Geography of Capitalist Accumulation," 248. Clover, meanwhile, emphasizes how the pursuit of profitability by individual firms through means of circulation imperils the overall health of the capitalist world-system by undermining capacity to create value, signaling "the contradiction between capital as a whole and individual capital." The turn to logistics indicates not a renewal of value production for the capitalist world-system, but "the collapse of value production at the core of the world-system." Clover, *Riot. Strike. Riot*, 25, 23.

31. See, for example, Rubio, *Still Life*, especially 182–211.

32. The term "unnecessary men," was a key principle behind "The Mechanization and Modernization Agreement," discussed further in Chapter 2.

33. See Max Haiven, *Art After Money, Money After Art: Creative Strategies Against Financialization* (London: Pluto Press, 2018); McClanahan, *Dead Pledges*.

34. Jasper Bernes, *The Work of Art in the Age of Deindustrialization* (Stanford, CA: Stanford University Press, 2017); Judith Hamera, *Unfinished Business: Michael Jackson, Detroit, and the Figural Economy of American Deindustrialization* (Oxford: Oxford University Press, 2017).

35. Petrus Liu, *The Specter of Materialism: Queer Theory and Marxism in the Age of the Beijing Consensus* (Durham, NC: Duke University Press, 2023); Jisha Menon, *Brutal Beauty: Aesthetics and Aspiration in Urban India* (Evanston, IL: Northwestern University Press, 2022). For an account that foregrounds the role of global circuits of trade in contemporary art albeit without addressing the topic of logistics specifically, see Sean Metzger, *The Chinese Atlantic: Seascapes and the Theatricality of Globalization* (Bloomington: Indiana University Press, 2020).

36. Bernes, *The Work of Art in the Age of Deindustrialization*, 24. See also Jack Burnham, "Systems Esthetics," *Artforum* 7, no. 1 (September 1968): 30–35; Helen Anne Molesworth, *Work Ethic* (University Park: Pennsylvania State University Press, 2003), 172–173. For the "dematerialization of the art object" thesis, see Lucy R. Lippard, *Six Years: The Dematerialization of the Art Object from 1966 to 1972* (Berkeley: University of California Press, 1997). Despite being largely absent from Bernes's book, he has, elsewhere, authored several of the most trenchant critiques of logistics. See, for example, Bernes, "Logistics, Counterlogistics, and the Communist Prospect."

37. Bernes, *The Work of Art in the Age of Deindustrialization*, 24."

38. On the history of ice and logistics, see On Barak, *Powering Empire: How Coal Made the Middle East and Sparked Global Carbonization* (Berkeley: University of California Press, 2020), 53–82; Hiʻilei Julia Hobart, *Cooling the Tropics: Ice, Indigeneity, and Hawaiian Refreshment* (Durham, NC: Duke University Press, 2022); George Reynolds, "Super Cubes: Inside the (Surprisingly) Big Business of Packaged Ice," *The*

Guardian, December 10, 2020, https://www.theguardian.com/news/2020/dec/10/super-cubes-inside-the-surprisingly-big-business-of-packaged-ice

39. See the documents on *Fluids* collected in Boxes 12 (folders 9 and 10) and 13 (folders 1, 2, and 3) available in "Series III. Project Files, 19461999" of the Allan Kaprow Papers, the Getty Research Institute, Los Angeles. See also Jeff Kelley, *Childsplay: The Art of Allan Kaprow* (Berkeley: University of California Press, 2004), 120–127; Philip Ursprung, *Allan Kaprow, Robert Smithson, and the Limits to Art*, trans. Fionna Elliot (Berkeley: University of California Press, 2013), 108–113.

40. For important examples of this, see Sam McBean, "Circulating Desire: Queer Logistical Aesthetics," *Feminist Media Studies*, August 11, 2022, 1–15, https://doi.org/10.1080/14680777.2022.2110606; Alberto Toscano, "The Mirror of Circulation: Allan Sekula and the Logistical Image," *Society and Space*, July 31, 2018, https://www.societyandspace.org/articles/the-mirror-of-circulation-allan-sekula-and-the-logistical-image; for examples of scholars who consider the embeddedness of film and literary production in logistical infrastructure, see Kay Dickinson, *Supply Chain Cinema: Producing Global Film Workers* (London: Bloomsbury Academic/British Film Institute, 2024); Mark McGurl, *Everything and Less: The Novel in the Age of Amazon* (London: Verso, 2021).

41. Matthew Hockenberry, Nicole Starosielski, and Susan Zieger, "Introduction: The Logistics of Media," in *Assembly Codes: The Logistics of Media, ed. Matthew Hockenberry, Nicole Starosielski, and Susan Zieger* (Durham, NC: Duke University Press, 2021), 1–20, quote at 5.

42. Toscano and Kinkle, *Cartographies of the Absolute*, 195–207.

43. Walead Beshty, "*FedEx* Works 2007– . . . Federal Express and the Corporate Modular," n.d., https://www.actionstakenunderthefictitiousnamewaleadbeshtystudiosinc.com/fedex-works-2007

44. Toscano and Kinkle, *Cartographies of the Absolute.*

45. Beshty in Steve Miller, "Walead Beshty: The End Game (Interview)," *Musée*, October 15, 2018, https://museemagazine.com/features/2018/10/15/walead-beshty-the-end-game

46. Dave Hirschman, "'Cast Away' Delivers Goods for FedEx," *Chicago Tribune*, January 8, 2001, https://www.chicagotribune.com/news/ct-xpm-2001-01-08-0101080173-story.html

47. In a second series, *FedEx* copper works (2011), Beshty ships mirror-polished copper boxes cut and shaped into the dimensions of FedEx boxes, which literally record the fingers that handled it, as well as any shifts in acidity, humidity, and temperature.

48. Fredric Jameson, *Postmodernism; or, The Cultural Logic of Late Capitalism* (Durham, NC: Duke University Press, 1991), 51–52.

49. Larne Abse Gogarty, "Inert Universalism and the Info-Optimism of Legibly Political Art," *Selva*, no. 4 (2022): 53–68, quote at 57; italics in the original.

50. I draw this litany from Chua, "Logistical Violence, Logistical Vulnerabilities," 169–170.

51. Campling and Colás, *Capitalism and the Sea*, 263; italics in the original.

52. Marx, *Grundrisse*, 524–525.

53. Paul N. Edwards, "Infrastructure and Modernity: Force, Time and Social Organization in the History of Sociotechnical Systems," in *Modernity and Technology*, ed. Thomas J. Misa, Philip Brey, and Andrew Feenberg (Cambridge, MA: MIT Press, 2003), 185–225, quote at 186.

54. Stephen Graham and Nigel Thrift, "Out of Order: Understanding Repair and Maintenance," *Theory, Culture & Society* 24, no. 3 (May 2007): 1–25, https://doi.org/10.1177/0263276407075954; Daniel Nemser, *Infrastructures of Race: Concentration and Biopolitics in Colonial Mexico* (Austin: University of Texas Press, 2017); AbdouMaliq Simone, "People as Infrastructure: Intersecting Fragments in Johannesburg," *Public Culture* 16, no. 3 (September 1, 2004): 407–429. On the history of infrastructure as a term, see Ashley Carse, "Keyword: Infrastructure: How a Humble French Engineering Term Shaped the Modern World," in *Infrastructures and Social Complexity: A Companion*, ed. Penelope Harvey, Casper Bruun Jensen, and Atsuro Morita (London: Routledge, 2017), 27–39.

55. Brian Larkin, "The Politics and Poetics of Infrastructure," *Annual Review of Anthropology* 42 (2013): 327–343, quote at 330.

56. Ruth Wilson Gilmore, "Abolition Geography and the Problem of Innocence," in *Futures of Black Radicalism*, ed. Gaye Theresa Johnson and Alex Lubin (London: Verso, 2017), 225–240, at 236–240.

57. Jesse LeCavalier, *The Rule of Logistics: Walmart and the Architecture of Fulfillment* (Minneapolis: University of Minnesota Press, 2016), 8. See also On Barak, *On Time: Technology and Temporality in Modern Egypt* (Berkeley: University of California Press, 2013).

58. Larkin, "The Politics and Poetics of Infrastructure."

59. Rich, Rizzuto, and Zieger, "Reading Infrastructure."

60. Adriana Michele Campos Johnson and Daniel Nemser, "Introduction: Reading for Infrastructure," *Social Text* 40, no. 4 (December 1, 2022): 1–16. On affect, see especially Kai Bosworth, *Pipeline Populism: Grassroots Environmentalism in the Twenty-First Century* (Minneapolis: University of Minnesota Press, 2022), 38.

61. Rich, Rizzuto, and Zieger, "Reading Infrastructure," 3.

62. Jennifer Wenzel, "Rediscoveries of the Ordinary; or, All That Is Solid . . .," in *The Aesthetic Life of Infrastructure: Race, Affect, Environment*, 203–212, quote at 210; italics in the original. Wenzel holds to account fellow travelers of new materialism, specifically Caroline Levine, *Forms: Whole, Rhythm, Hierarchy, Network* (Princeton, NJ: Princeton University Press, 2015). For the pivotal critique of the base-superstructure model of materialism as it relates to culture, see Raymond Williams, "Base and Superstructure in Marxist Cultural Theory," *New Left Review*, no. 82 (December 1973): 3–16.

63. See Marx, *Grundrisse*, 524–525. See also Peter Dicken, *Global Shift: Mapping the Changing Contours of the World Economy*, 6th ed. (New York: Guilford Press, 2011), 81.

64. Hockenberry, Starosielski, and Zieger, "The Logistics of Media," 3. On logistical media, see also John Durham Peters, *The Marvelous Clouds: Toward a Philosophy of Elemental Media* (Chicago: University of Chicago Press, 2015); Ned Rossiter, *Software, Infrastructure, Labor: A Media Theory of Logistical Nightmares* (New York: Routledge, 2016); Nicole Starosielski, *The Undersea Network* (Durham, NC: Duke University Press, 2015).

65. Nemser, *Infrastructures of Race*, 17.

66. On the "infrastructural turn," see Johnson and Nemser, "Introduction: Reading for Infrastructure."

67. Susan Leigh Star, "The Ethnography of Infrastructure," *American Behavioral Scientist* 43, no. 3 (November 1999): 377–391, quote at 380.

68. Geoffrey C. Bowker, *Science on the Run: Information Management and Industrial Geophysics at Schlumberger, 1920–1940* (Cambridge, MA: MIT Press, 1994), 10.

69. Geoffrey C. Bowker and Susan Leigh Star, *Sorting Things Out: Classification and Its Consequences* (Cambridge, MA: MIT Press, 1999), 38. For a critique of this "visibility thesis," see Rich, Rizzuto, and Zieger, "Reading Infrastructure," 3.

70. Kathryn Furlong, "STS Beyond the 'Modern Infrastructure Ideal': Extending Theory by Engaging with Infrastructure Challenges in the South," *Technology in Society* 38 (August 2014): 139–147. See also Lauren Berlant, "The Commons: Infrastructures for Troubling Times," *Environment and Planning D: Society and Space* 34, no. 3 (2016): 393–419; Jasbir K. Puar, *The Right to Maim: Debility, Capacity, Disability* (Durham, NC: Duke University Press, 2017); Samantha Dawn Schalk, *Black Disability Politics* (Durham, NC: Duke University Press, 2022).

71. Antoine-Henri Jomini, *The Art of War*, trans. G. H. Mendell and W. P. Craighill (Philadelphia: J. B. Lippincott, 1862 [1838]), 252.

72. Cowen, *Deadly Life of Logistics*, 26. For an example of the preference for *logistikos* in logistics textbooks, see Sten A. O. Thore, *Economic Logistics: The Optimization of Spatial and Sectoral Resource, Production, and Distribution Systems* (New York: Quorum Books, 1991), 1. On the military origins of logistics, see also Manuel De Landa, *War in the Age of Intelligent Machines* (New York: Zone Books, 1991), 105–114; Martin van Creveld, *Supplying War: Logistics from Wallenstein to Patton* (Cambridge, UK: Cambridge University Press, 1977).

73. Wilhelm Dangelmaier, Willibald Günthner, Peter Klaus, Ludger Overmeyer, Werner Rothengatter, and Jürgen Weber, "Towards a Science of Logistics: Cornerstones of a Framework of Understanding of Logistics as an Academic Discipline," *Logistics Research* 2, no. 2 (2010): 57–63, quote at 58.

74. Robert B. Handfield and Tom Linton, *Flow: How the Best Supply Chains Thrive* (Toronto: University of Toronto Press, 2022), 1. For an account of logistics as a Kuhnian "scientific community," see Peter Klaus, "Logistics Research: A 50 Years' March of Ideas," *Logistics Research* 1 (2009): 53–65, at 53.

75. On the UPS campaign, see Cowen, *Deadly Life of Logistics*, 197–231, quote at 204; Jesse LeCavalier, "The Restlessness of Objects: Choreographing Fulfillment," *Cabinet*, no. 47 (2012): 90–97.

76. Sandro Mezzadra and Brett Neilson, *The Politics of Operations: Excavating Contemporary Capitalism* (Durham, NC: Duke University Press, 2019), 149.

77. Miriam Posner, "Breakpoints and Black Boxes: Information in Global Supply Chains," *Postmodern Culture* 31, no. 3, 2021, https://doi.org/10.1353/pmc.2021.0002

78. Harry Braverman, *Labor and Monopoly Capital: The Degradation of Work in the Twentieth Century* (New York: Monthly Review Press, 1974), 86.

79. On this, see Hannah Appel, Nikhil Anand, and Akhil Gupta, "Introduction: Temporality, Politics, and the Promise of Infrastructure," in *The Promise of Infrastructure*, ed. Nikhil Anand, Akhil Gupta, and Hannah Appel (Durham, NC: Duke University Press, 2018), 1–38.

80. Cowen, *Deadly Life of Logistics*; Khalili, *Sinews of War and Trade;* Rob Nixon, *Slow Violence and the Environmentalism of the Poor* (Cambridge, MA: Harvard University Press, 2011). See also Keller Easterling, *Extrastatecraft: The Power of Infrastructure Space* (New York: Verso, 2016); Stephen Graham, "When Infrastructures Fail," in *Disrupted Cities: When Infrastructure Fails*, ed. Stephen Graham (New York: Routledge, 2010), 1–26; Dennis Rodgers and Bruce O'Neill, "Infrastructural Violence: Introduction to the Special Issue," *Ethnography* 13, no. 4 (December 2012): 401–412.

81. Mau, *Mute Compulsion*, 282–289.

82. Bernes, "Logistics, Counterlogistics, and the Communist Prospect."

83. Alberto Toscano, "Logistics and Opposition," *Mute Magazine* 3, no. 2, August 9, 2011, http://www.metamute.org/editorial/articles/logistics-and-opposition; Toscano's essay responded to points raised by the Invisible Committee. See The Invisible Committee, *The Coming Insurrection* (Cambridge, MA: Semiotext(e), 2009). Bernes coined the term "the reconfiguration thesis" in "Logistics, Counterlogistics, and the Communist Prospect," his response to Toscano.

84. Nick Srnicek and Alex Williams, *Inventing the Future: Postcapitalism and a World Without Work* (London: Verso, 2015), 150–152.

85. Fredric Jameson, *Valences of the Dialectic* (London: Verso, 2010), 423.

86. Leigh Phillips and Michal Rozworski, *The People's Republic of Walmart: How the World's Biggest Corporations Are Laying the Foundation for Socialism* (London: Verso, 2019), 3.

87. Bernes, "Logistics, Counterlogistics, and the Communist Prospect."

88. Srnicek and Williams, *Inventing the Future*, 150.

89. Bernes, "Logistics, Counterlogistics, and the Communist Prospect."

90. Out of the Woods, "Disaster Communism Part 3–Logistics, Repurposing, Bricolage," *Libcom*, May 22, 2014, http://libcom.org/blog/disaster-communism-part-3-logistics-repurposing-bricolage-22052014

91. LeCavalier, *The Rule of Logistics*, 63. See also Jordan Frith, *Barcode* (New York: Bloomsbury Academic, 2023).

92. Jameson, *Valences of the Dialectic*, 422.

93. See Ashok Kumar, *Monopsony Capitalism: Power and Production in the Twilight of the Sweatshop Age* (Cambridge, UK: Cambridge University Press, 2020); Suwandi,

Value Chains. For a critique of Jameson on this, see Robert Faivre, "Jameson's Spiritual Reawakening: Labor Theory in the Time of Wal-Mart," *The Minnesota Review*, no. 87 (2016): 149–159.

94. Miriam Posner, "The Software That Shapes Workers' Lives," *New Yorker*, March 12, 2019, https://www.newyorker.com/science/elements/the-software-that-shapes-workers-lives

95. Bernes, "Logistics, Counterlogistics, and the Communist Prospect."

96. Alberto Toscano, "Lineaments of the Logistical State," *Viewpoint Magazine*, no. 4, September 28, 2014, http://viewpointmag.com/2014/09/28/lineaments-of-the-logistical-state

97. On these debates generally, see David F. Noble, *Forces of Production: A Social History of Industrial Automation* (New Brunswick, NJ: Transaction, 2011 [1984]).

98. On Brecht's theory of *Umfunktionierung*, see Bertolt Brecht, "Notes on the Opera 'Rise and Fall of the City of Mahogany,'" in *Brecht on Theatre: The Development of an Aesthetic*, ed. Marc Silberman, Steve Giles, and Tom Kuhn, trans. Steve Giles (London: Bloomsbury Methuen, 2019), 61–70; Bertolt Brecht, "The Radio as a Communications Apparatus," in *Brecht on Film and Radio*, ed. Marc Silberman (London: Methuen, 2000), 41–46; Bertolt Brecht, "The Threepenny Lawsuit," in *Brecht on Film and Radio*, 147–199. See also Walter Benjamin, "The Author as Producer," in *The Work of Art in the Age of Its Technological Reproducibility, and Other Writings on Media*, ed. Michael W. Jennings, trans. Brigid Doherty, Thomas Y. Levin, and Edmund Jephcott (Cambridge, MA: Harvard University Press, 2008), 79–95.

99. Bernes, "Logistics, Counterlogistics, and the Communist Prospect."

100. Beshty quoted in Natalie Hegert, "Walead Beshty: In Conversation," *The Seen*, November 28, 2018, https://theseenjournal.org/walead-beshty-in-conversation/

101. Stacy Boldrick, "Transience: Curating Ephemeral Art," in *The Contemporary Museum: Shaping Museums for the Global Now*, ed. Simon J. Knell (London: Routledge, 2019), 105–127.

102. Miller, "Walead Beshty."

103. See Isabelle Graw, *High Price: Art Between the Market and Celebrity Culture*, trans. Nicholas Grindell (New York: Sternberg Press, 2009), especially 229–232.

104. Bourriaud quoted in Boldrick, "Transience," 112.

105. James Nisbet, "Walead Beshty: PROCESSCOLORFIELD," *X-TRA* 14, no. 2, 2011, https://www.x-traonline.org/article/walead-beshty-processcolorfield

106. Walead Beshty, "*FedEx* Works 2007– . . . Black Boxes," 2007, https://www.actionstakenunderthefictitiousnamewaleadbeshtystudiosinc.com/fedex-works-2007

Chapter One

1. For a detailed account of how *Ever Given* got stuck in the Suez Canal, see Brendan Greeley, "The Bank Effect and the Big Boat Blocking the Suez," *Financial Times*, March 25, 2021, https://www.ft.com/content/171c92ec-0a44-4dc5-acab-81ee2620d3c1

2. For an overview of *Ever Given* memes, see Anna Schaverien, "Why the Internet Loves the Suez Canal Stuck Ship Saga," *New York Times*, March 27, 2021, https://www.nytimes.com/2021/03/27/world/suez-canal-stuck-ship-memes.html

3. Michele Acciaro, "Naval Gigantism: Rationale and Limits," quoted in Marc Levinson, *Outside the Box: How Globalization Changed from Moving Stuff to Spreading Ideas* (Princeton, NJ: Princeton University Press, 2021), 188.

4. Charmaine Chua, "Containing the Ship of State: Managing Mobility in an Age of Logistics" (PhD dissertation, Minneapolis, University of Minnesota, 2018), 215.

5. Levinson, *Outside the Box*, 143–151, 185–195, quote at 149.

6. UNCTAD (United Nations Conference on Trade and Development), *Review of Maritime Transport 2021* (Geneva: UNCTAD, 2021), 33, https://unctad.org/system/files/official-document/rmt2021_en_0.pdf

7. Harry Dempsey, Philip Georgiadis, and Sylvia Pfeifer, "Too Big to Sail? The Debate over Huge Container Ships," *Financial Times*, March 28, 2021, https://www.ft.com/content/3dc797d0-7268-49a4-b0b5-3d11479cbe7f

8. Alex Christian, "The Untold Story of the Big Boat That Broke the World," *Wired*, July 22, 2021, https://www.wired.co.uk/article/ever-given-global-supply-chain; for other examples, see Salvatore Mercolgliona, "The Suez Logjam Shows How Fragile Our Global Trade System Is," *Washington Post*, March 26, 2021, https://www.washingtonpost.com/outlook/2021/03/26/suez-canal-ship-logistics/; Amanda Mull, "The Big, Stuck Boat Is Glorious," *The Atlantic*, March 25, 2021, https://www.theatlantic.com/technology/archive/2021/03/were-going-to-need-a-smaller-boat/618414/

9. See Harry Dempsey, "Ever Given Owners Reach Deal with Egypt over Suez Canal Blockage," *Financial Times*, June 23, 2021, https://www.ft.com/content/49eef695-55e2-4f19-8648-a97c774c250f

10. Charmaine Chua, "The Ever Given and the Monstrosity of Maritime Capitalism," *Boston Review*, May 4, 2021, https://bostonreview.net/class-inequality-politics/charmaine-chua-ever-given-and-monstrosity-maritime-capitalism

11. On this, see Aaron Jakes, "The World the Suez Canal Made," *Public Seminar*, April 2, 2021, http://publicseminar.org/essays/the-world-the-suez-canal-made/

12. Brett Neilson and Ned Rossiter, "Still Waiting, Still Moving: On Labour, Logistics and Maritime Industries," in *Stillness in a Mobile World*, ed. David Bissell and Gillian Fuller (London: Routledge, 2011), 51–68, quote at 58.

13. Angela Naimou, *Salvage Work: U.S. and Caribbean Literatures amid the Debris of Legal Personhood* (New York: Fordham University Press, 2015); Evan Calder Williams, *Combined and Uneven Apocalypse* (Winchester, UK: Zero Books, 2010), 14–71; Evan Calder Williams, "Salvage," *Journal of American Studies* 49, no. 4 (2015): 845–859.

14. Peter Linebaugh and Marcus Rediker, *The Many-Headed Hydra: Sailors, Slaves, Commoners, and the Hidden History of the Revolutionary Atlantic* (London: Verso, 2007), 150, 219–221.

15. Stefano Harney and Fred Moten, *All Incomplete* (New York: Minor Compositions, 2021), 17.

16. Levinson, *Outside the Box*, 133. I have in mind the "value chain" framework in supply chain research that describes how businesses or countries contribute different parts and services to a given product, the combined costs of which are then reflected in the product's final market price. Value chain analysis examines how firms and countries compete with one another to contribute parts and services that make up a higher portion of this final price. "Moving up the value chain" typically means being in the position to contribute relatively more specialized or technologically sophisticated components to a product. This is the difference between providing, for example, the plastic shell to a smart phone and the sophisticated cameras or user-interface software. The value chain framework traces its origins, however now distorted, to the Marxist-oriented approach of world-systems analysis and has become a widely accepted analytical tool in business logistics and supply chain management. The value chain framework is also used by many Marxist historians, sociologists, and geographers, this despite the fact that what Karl Marx meant by "value" (indicating a social form) is a far cry from how supply chain researchers typically understand the term and its relation to price. On the history and variations of the value chain framework, including its origins in world-systems analysis, see Jennifer Bair, "Global Capitalism and Commodity Chains: Looking Back, Going Forward," *Competition & Change* 9, no. 2 (2005): 153–180; Wilma A. Dunaway, "Introduction," in *Gendered Commodity Chains: Seeing Women's Work and Households in Global Production*, ed. Wilma A. Dunaway (Stanford, CA: Stanford University Press, 2014), 1–26. For uses of the value chain framework in a Marxist account of supply chains, see Ashok Kumar, *Monopsony Capitalism: Power and Production in the Twilight of the Sweatshop Age* (Cambridge, UK: Cambridge University Press, 2020); Intan Suwandi, *Value Chains: The New Economic Imperialism* (New York: Monthly Review Press, 2019).

17. Liam Campling and Alejandro Colás, *Capitalism and the Sea: The Maritime Factor in the Making of the Modern World* (London: Verso, 2021), 213–266, quote at 219.

18. Campling and Colás, *Capitalism and the Sea*, 263; italics in the original.

19. Stefano Harney and Fred Moten, *The Undercommons: Fugitive Planning & Black Study* (Wivenhoe, NY: Minor Compositions, 2013), 92.

20. Stefano Harney and Fred Moten, *All Incomplete* (New York: Minor Compositions, 2021), 17.

21. The *Brooks* diagram was a schematic illustration of the slave ship *Brooks* (also sometimes referred to as *Brookes*) depicting the brutal and inhumane circumstances that enslaved African people were forced to endure during the Middle Passage. Beginning in the late 1780s, abolitionists in England and the Americas used the drawing to raise awareness of the moral reprehensibility of the slave trade and to agitate for reform. See Simone Browne, *Dark Matters: On the Surveillance of Blackness* (Durham, NC: Duke University Press, 2015), 45–50; Marcus Rediker, *The Slave Ship: A Human History* (London: J. Murray, 2007), 308–342. The massacre aboard the slave ship *Zong* took place in late 1781 when crew members murdered more than 130 enslaved African

people by throwing them overboard. The ensuing insurance trial, in which the *Zong*'s owners sued their insurers to cover a claim for loss of property, brought increased public attention to the cruelty and horrors of the slave trade. See Ian Baucom, *Specters of the Atlantic: Finance Capital, Slavery, and the Philosophy of History* (Durham, NC: Duke University Press, 2005). On the legacy of loss in both the *Brooks* diagram and the *Zong* massacre, see Christina Sharpe, *In the Wake: On Blackness and Being* (Durham, NC: Duke University Press, 2016), 26–67.

22. Rediker, *The Slave Ship*, 5.

23. On the history and connection of the Suez Canal to empire and its afterlives, see Aaron Jakes, *Egypt's Occupation: Colonial Economism and the Crises of Capitalism* (Stanford, CA: Stanford University Press, 2020).

24. See Jonathan Crary, "Géricault, the Panorama, and Sites of Reality in the Early Nineteenth Century," *Grey Room* 9 (2002): 5–25; Christine Riding, "Staging the Raft of the Medusa," *Visual Culture in Britain* 5, no. 2 (2004): 1–26.

25. Jamin Wells, "The Lure of the Shore: Authenticity, Spectacle, and the Wreck of the St. Paul," *New Jersey History* 126, no. 2 (2011): 58–83, quote at 59.

26. Bella Bathurst, *The Wreckers: A Story of Killing Seas, False Lights, and Plundered Ships* (London: HarperCollins, 2006), xiv.

27. Bathurst, *The Wreckers*, xv.

28. Julian Wardlaw, "Tenth Anniversary of the MSC Napoli Shipwreck Disaster," Environment Agency, January 18, 2017, https://www.gov.uk/government/news/tenth-anniversary-of-the-msc-napoli-shipwreck-disaster; see also Bella Bathurst, "Whatever Happened to the BMW Booty?," *The Guardian*, January 13, 2008, https://www.theguardian.com/uk/2008/jan/13/bellabathurst.theobserver; Steven Morris, "If You Go Down to the Beach Today . . . You're Bound to Find Something to Steal," *The Guardian*, January 23, 2007, https://www.theguardian.com/environment/2007/jan/23/pollution.uknews

29. Hans Blumenberg, *Shipwreck with Spectator: Paradigm of a Metaphor for Existence*, trans. Steven Rendall (Cambridge, MA: MIT Press, 1997).

30. On the history of salvage during this period, see David Cressy, *Shipwrecks and the Bounty of the Sea* (Oxford: Oxford University Press, 2022); Cathryn J. Pearce, *Cornish Wrecking, 1700–1860: Reality and Popular Myth* (Woodbridge, UK: Boydell & Brewer, 2010); Jamin Wells, *Shipwrecked: Coastal Disasters and the Making of the American Beach* (Chapel Hill: University of North Carolina Press, 2020). On the history of spectacle in circum-Atlantic culture at the time, see Joseph R. Roach, *Cities of the Dead: Circum-Atlantic Performance* (New York: Columbia University Press, 1996).

31. On how salvage was reorganized starting in the mid-nineteenth century, see Jamin Wells, "Professionalization and Cultural Perceptions of Marine Salvage, 1850–1950," *Northern Mariner* 17, no. 2 (2007): 1–22; Wells, *Shipwrecked*, 107–36.

32. See Kevin Dawson, "History Below the Waterline: Enslaved Salvage Divers Harvesting Seaports' Hinter-Seas in the Early Modern Atlantic," *International Review of Social History* 64, no. S27 (April 2019): 43–70.

33. See Wells, "Professionalization and Cultural Perceptions of Marine Salvage, 1850–1950," 1.

34. On the history of SMIT, see the company's website: https://web.archive.org/web/20120208180641/http://www.smit.com/sitefactor/page.asp?pageID=560; for details on the takeover by Boskalis, see Staff, "Boskalis Clears Smit Takeover Milestone," *Reuters*, March 27, 2010, https://www.reuters.com/article/idUSTRE62QoVU20100327

35. James M. Wright, "The Wrecking System of the Bahama Islands," *Political Science Quarterly* 30, no. 4 (1915): 618–644, at 636.

36. David Sheppard and Harry Dempsey, "Boskalis: The Go-To Company When You Ground Your Ship in the Suez Canal," *Financial Times*, April 1, 2021, https://www.ft.com/content/44b08a32-1192-4b6d-9005-9751856a22b2

37. On the legal definition of salvaging, see Pearce, *Cornish Wrecking, 1700–1860*, 41–60. On the modernization of salvage law, see Wells, *Shipwrecked*, 48–53, 118–119.

38. Campling and Colás, *Capitalism and the Sea*, 31–47; Khalili, *Sinews of War and Trade*, 163–171; Anita Rupprecht, "Excessive Memories: Slavery, Insurance and Resistance," *History Workshop Journal* 64, no. 1 (January 1, 2007): 6–28.

39. Williams, "Salvage," 845. See also Anna Lowenhaupt Tsing, *The Mushroom at the End of the World: On the Possibility of Life in Capitalist Ruins* (Princeton, NJ: Princeton University Press, 2015).

40. Amadeo Bordiga, "Weird and Wonderful Tales of Modern Social Decadence," trans. David Brown, 2003 [1956], https://www.marxists.org/archive/bordiga/works/1956/weird.htm

41. The TEU, or twenty-foot equivalent unit, is the standard but imprecise measurement for judging the cargo capacity of container ships. One TEU generally refers to one twenty-foot-long intermodal shipping container, though the forty-foot-long container is more common and counts as two TEU.

42. Levinson, *Outside the Box*, 144–145; Robert Wright, "World's Fastest Container Ships Mothballed," February 22, 2010, https://www.ft.com/content/65e522dc-1fce-11df-8deb-00144feab49a; to give the makeshift stage added stability, another container ship was lashed to the fleet; this vessel's name was, appropriately, *Sealand Performance*.

43. UNCTAD (United Nations Conference on Trade and Development, *Review of Maritime Transport 2023* (Geneva: UNCTAD, 2023), 29, https://unctad.org/system/files/official-document/rmt2023_en.pdf

44. UNCTAD, *Review of Maritime Transport 2023*, 37. For an overview of the shipbreaking industry, see Camelia Dewan, "Living with Toxic Development: Shipbreaking in the Industrializing Zone of Sitakunda, Bangladesh," *Anthropology Today* 36, no. 6 (2020): 9–12; Andrew Herod, Graham Pickren, Al Rainnie, and Susan McGrath Champ, "Global Destruction Networks, Labour and Waste," *Journal of Economic Geography* 14, no. 2 (2014): 421–441; OECD, "Ship Recycling: An Overview," OECD Directorate for Science, Technology and Innovation, 2019, https://www.oecd-ilibrary.org/science-and-technology/ship-recycling_397de00c-en; Maria Sarraf, Frank Stuer-Lauridsen, Milen Dyoulgerov, Robin Bloch, Susan Wingfield, and Roy

Watkinson, "Ship Breaking and Recycling Industry in Bangladesh and Pakistan," World Bank, 2010, https://documents1.worldbank.org/curated/en/872281468114238957/pdf/582750ESW0Whit1LIC10110987911web10pt.pdf; Martin Stopford, *Maritime Economics* (London: Routledge, 2010), 648–652.

45. On the history of the ITF, see International Transport Workers' Federation, *Solidarity: The First 100 Years of the International Transport Workers' Federation* (London: Pluto Press, 1996).

46. Unless otherwise noted, details on the *Global Mariner* campaign are taken from its archive available online here: https://web.archive.org/web/20000524141627/http:/www.itf-ship.org/ship/s1page.htm; see also Allan Sekula, "Between the Net and the Deep Blue Sea (Rethinking the Traffic in Photographs)," *October* 102 (2002): 3–34.

47. On the history and current practice of open registries, see Campling and Colás, *Capitalism and the Sea*, 142–163; Leon Fink, *Sweatshops at Sea: Merchant Seamen in the World's First Globalized Industry, from 1812 to the Present* (Chapel Hill: University of North Carolina Press, 2011), 178–190; Naimou, *Salvage Work*, 47–91; Stopford, *Maritime Economics*, 666–675. For global seafarer numbers, see UNCTAD, "Seafarer Supply, Quinquennial, 2015 and 2021," *UNCTAD Stat*, 2021, http://stats.unctad.org/seafarersupply

48. Drew Hinshaw and Joe Parkinson, "Crews Are Abandoned on Ships in Record Numbers Without Pay, Food or a Way Home," *Wall Street Journal*, October 8, 2021, https://www.wsj.com/articles/crews-are-abandoned-on-ships-in-record-numbers-without-pay-food-or-a-way-home-11633699978

49. For the 2002 UK government report on the accident investigation, see https://www.gov.uk/maib-reports/collision-between-dry-cargo-vessel-global-mariner-and-container-vessel-atlantic-crusader-on-the-orinoco-river-venzuela-resulting-in-global-mariner-sinking; after the tour, an interactive documentary DVD and model of the *Global Mariner* was hosted at Expo 2000 in Hanover, Germany.

50. On the ITF, see Katy Fox-Hodess, "Building Labour Internationalism 'From Below': Lessons from the International Dockworkers Council's European Working Group," *Work, Employment and Society* 34, no. 1 (February 2020): 91–108; Antonina Gentile, "World-System Hegemony and How the Mechanism of Certification Skews Intra-European Labor Solidarity," *Mobilization: An International Quarterly* 21, no. 1 (March 1, 2016): 105–127.

51. On the IDC and its differences with the ITF, see Fox-Hodess, "Building Labour Internationalism 'From Below'."

52. Sekula, "Between the Net and the Deep Blue Sea," 31.

53. See *Global Mariner: Life at Sea*, available online at https://www.youtube.com/user/holger500/videos

54. Sekula, "Between the Net and the Deep Blue Sea," 30.

55. For similar interpretations, see Gail Day, "Allan Sekula's Transitive Poetics: Metonymy and Metaphor in Lottery of the Sea, Ship of Fools and the Dockers' Museum," in *Allan Sekula: Ship of Fools / The Dockers' Museum*, ed. Hilde van Gelder (Leuven:

Leuven University Press, 2015), 57–70; Jeroen Verbeeck, "The Residual Poetics of Mutiny in Allan Sekula's *Ship of Fools / The Dockers' Museum* (2010–2013)," *Image & Narrative* 18, no. 2 (2017): 12–32.

56. Sekula, "Between the Net and the Deep Blue Sea," 31.

57. Sekula, "Between the Net and the Deep Blue Sea," 29; italics in the original.

58. On the history of port city redevelopment, see Alice Mah, *Port Cities and Global Legacies: Urban Identity, Waterfront Work, and Radicalism* (Basingstoke, UK: Palgrave Macmillan, 2014).

59. Many of the details in this section draw from author e-mails with Anne Bean and Richard Wilson in 2021 and 2023. On the origins of BGE, see Rob La Frenais, "Disbelief Systems: Interview with Bow Gamelan Ensemble," in *Anne Bean: Self Etc*, ed. Rob La Frenais, (Bristol: Intellect, 2018), 254–276. BGE maintains a website with detailed descriptions, photographs, posters, videos, and other archival materials of their major performances: http://bowgamelan.com/

60. BGE worked with locals who had knowledge of the island, as well as the Thames Steam Launch Company and the American percussionist Z'EV. *Offshore Rig* was produced by the nearby Watermans Arts Centre in Brentford for the 1987 LIFT festival and ran July 16–18. Details and materials are archived at http://bowgamelan.com/bge-offshore-rig-1987.html; a documentary was made for the UK television program *Alter Image* (dir. Jane Thorburn, 1988), archived online by BGE at https://vimeo.com/484891492

61. Simon Herbert, "A Smokey Watershed," *Performance Magazine* 49 (September–October 1987): 39.

62. Review in *Melody Maker*, quoted at http://bowgamelan.com/bge-damned-near-run-thing-1988.html

63. Julian Cowley, "Great Noises That Fill the Air," *Random Spectacular*, no. 2 (2014): https://issuu.com/stjudes/docs/great_noises_that_fill_the_air

64. Bean e-mail with author October 23, 2023.

65. Chrissie Iles, "Spark Fly," *Performance Magazine* 35 (June–July 1985): 20–23, quote at 20.

66. Herbert, "A Smokey Watershed," 39; italics in the original.

67. Details about *The Navigators* and materials are archived at http://bowgamelan.com/bge-the-navigators-1989.html

68. Rob La Frenais, "Industrial Revolution: Artist Bow Gamelan on Life Behind the Welding Torch," *Performance Magazine 40* (March–April 1986): 29–30, quote at 30.

69. Iles, "Spark Fly," 22.

70. La Frenais, "Industrial Revolution," 30.

71. Iles, "Spark Fly," 22.

72. Tinguely's influence on BGE came largely through the sculptor Stephen Cripps, with whom Bean and Burwell had collaborated before his death in 1982. See Sandra Reimann, ed., *Stephen Cripps: Performance Machines* (Vienna: Verlag für Moderne Kunst, 2017); Jeni Walwin, "Volatile Materials in Image Making: The Appeal of Fire

and Explosives in the 20th and 21st Century, Using the Work of Stephen Cripps as a Point of Articulation," *Performance Research* 18, no. 1 (2013): 149–157.

73. Wilson interviewed in La Frenais, "Industrial Revolution," 30.

74. Bean interviewed in La Frenais, "Disbelief Systems," 267. Before forming BGE, the three had spent time as friends exploring the river and its backwaters by boat and even collaborating on scattered performance interventions, some of which involved boats and bridges. These earlier performances included *Sunken Boat* (1978), in which Bean and Burwell sounded out the hull of a sunken boat moored near Butler's Wharf where they lived. See Dominic Johnson, "Hiding in Plain Sight: An Interview with Anne Bean," in *The Art of Living: An Oral History of Performance Art* (Basingstoke, UK: Palgrave Macmillan, 2015), 41–64, at 60–61.

75. Wilson interviewed in La Frenais, "Industrial Revolution," 30.

76. Fredric Jameson, "Foreword," in *Noise: The Political Economy of Music, Theory and History of Literature* (Minneapolis: University of Minnesota Press, 1985), vii–xiv, quote at xi.

77. For details relating to *Concrete Barges,* see http://bowgamelan.com/bge-concrete-barges-1987.html; a documentary of the performance was made called *51° 29.9' N, 0° 11' E* (dir. Jane Thorburn, 1987) for the UK television program *Alter Image.* The video is archived online by BGE at https://vimeo.com/484866531

78. On the history of the concrete barges, see www.concretebarge.co.uk

79. Wilson interviewed in Cowley, "Great Noises That Fill the Air," n.p.

80. Rob La Frenais, "In Sea," *Performance Magazine* 43 (September–October 1986): 35.

81. Husband, "Bow Gamelan Ensemble," *Performance Magazine* 30 (June–July 1984): 5.

82. Bean interviewed in La Frenais, "Disbelief Systems," 263.

83. Details of these performances are available here: http://bowgamelan.com/wob.html

84. The film, *A Crumbling Fort That No One Visits* (dir. Richard Wilson 2009) is available at http://www.richardwilsonsculptor.com/performance/a-crumbling-fort-that-no-one-visits-2009.html; this performance was part of a project involving dozens of artists creating work to remember Burwell called *TAPS.* For details, see http://bowgamelan.com/post-bge-taps-2010.html; on the current state of the Maunsell Forts, see Hugh Morris, "Second World War Sea Forts Could Become Luxury Hotel," *Telegraph*, December 30, 2015, https://www.telegraph.co.uk/travel/news/Second-World-War-sea-forts-could-become-luxury-hotel/

85. Husband, "Bow Gamelan Ensemble," 5.

86. Wilson, quoted in the documentary *Slice of Reality* (dir. Ryan Burnham, Luke Robson and Aymen Fahmi, 2015), available at https://vimeo.com/484891492; for details on *Slice of Reality,* see https://www.richardwilsonsculptor.com/sculpture/slice-of-reality-2000.html

87. Ernst Bloch, *Heritage of Our Times*, trans. Neville Plaice and Stephen Plaice (Cambridge, UK: Polity Press, 1991). On hauntology, see Mark Fisher, *Ghosts of My*

Life: Writings on Depression, Hauntology and Lost Futures (Winchester, UK: Zero Books, 2014).

88. See Peter Fryer, *Staying Power: The History of Black People in Britain* (London: Pluto Press, 2018), 390–393.

89. Brian Catling, "Paul Burwell: Experimental Performance Artist," *Independent*, February 9, 2007, https://www.independent.co.uk/news/obituaries/paul-burwell-435617.html

90. Wilson interviewed in La Frenais, "Industrial Revolution," 30.

91. See Burwell interviewed in La Frenais, "Industrial Revolution," 29. Their collective fascination with the Industrial Revolution extended into later work that used restored steam ships and railroad stations to commemorate England's industrial history. See Wilson's *1513: A Ship's Opera* (2013) and Wilson and Bean's collaboration on *Blast* (2007). Details on both are available here: http://bowgamelan.com/post-bge.html

92. On this history, see On Barak, *Powering Empire: How Coal Made the Middle East and Sparked Global Carbonization* (Berkeley: University of California Press, 2020); Campling and Colás, *Capitalism and the Sea*, 219–26; Laleh Khalili, *Sinews of War and Trade: Shipping and Capitalism in the Arabian Peninsula* (London: Verso, 2020), 22–24; Andreas Malm, "The Walls of the Tank: On Palestinian Resistance," *Salvage*, no. 4, 2017, https://salvage.zone/in-print/the-walls-of-the-tank-on-palestinian-resistance/; Vaclav Smil, *Two Prime Movers of Globalization: The History and Impact of Diesel Engines and Gas Turbines* (Cambridge, MA: MIT Press, 2010), 12–19.

93. Campling and Colás, *Capitalism and the Sea*, 230–231.

94. Holland Cotter, "Art That's a Dragon with Two Heads," *New York Times*, December 13, 1998, https://www.nytimes.com/1998/12/13/arts/art-that-s-a-dragon-with-two-heads.html

95. Cotter, "Art That's a Dragon with Two Heads."

96. Sheldon H. Lu, *Chinese Modernity and Global Biopolitics: Studies in Literature and Visual Culture* (Honolulu: University of Hawai'i Press, 2007), 102. See also Dana Friis-Hansen, Octavio Zaya, and Takashi Serizawa, *Cai Guo-Qiang* (London: Phaidon Press, 2002), 26; Anne Wedell-Wedellsborg, "Contextualizing Cai Guo-Qiang," *Kontur*, no. 20 (2010): 9–18, at 10–11.

97. Xiaoping Lin, "Globalism or Nationalism?: Cai Guoqiang, Zhang Huan, and Xu Bing in New York," *Third Text* 18, no. 4 (2004): 279–295, quote at 284.

98. Cai quoted in Friis-Hansen, Zaya, and Serizawa, *Cai Guo-Qiang*, 26.

99. For a similar reading of ambiguity and ambivalence in Cai's oeuvre, focusing on his *Venice's Rent Collection Courtyard* (1999), see Hentyle Yapp, *Minor China: Method, Materialisms, and the Aesthetic* (Durham, NC: Duke University Press, 2021), 65–69.

100. Marco Polo, *The Travels of Marco Polo*, ed. Henri Cordier, trans. Henry Yule (New York: Dover, 1993), https://www.gutenberg.org/files/10636/10636-h/10636-h.htm

101. Elena Cué, "Interview with Cai Guo-Qiang," *Alejandra de Argos*, September 15, 2014, https://www.alejandradeargos.com/index.php/en/all-articles/21-guests-with-art/329-interview-cai-guo-qiang#; see also Aihwa Ong, "'What Marco Polo Forgot': Contemporary Chinese Art Reconfigures the Global," *Current Anthropology* 53, no. 4 (August 2012): 471–494.

102. Sean Metzger, *The Chinese Atlantic: Seascapes and the Theatricality of Globalization* (Bloomington: Indiana University Press, 2020), 239.

103. Kenneth Pomeranz, *The Great Divergence: China, Europe, and the Making of the Modern World Economy* (Princeton, NJ: Princeton University Press, 2000).

104. Robert Brenner and Christopher Isett, "England's Divergence from China's Yangzi Delta: Property Relations, Microeconomics, and Patterns of Development," *Journal of Asian Studies* 61, no. 2 (May 2002): 609–662, quote at 613; italics in the original. See also Giovanni Arrighi, Po-Keung Hui, Ho-fung Hung, and Mark Selden, "Historical Capitalism, East and West," in *The Resurgence of East Asia: 500, 150 and 50 Year Perspectives*, ed. Giovanni Arrighi, Takeshi Hamashita, and Mark Selden (London: Routledge, 2003), 259–333; Ho-fung Hung, *The China Boom: Why China Will Not Rule the World* (New York: Columbia University Press, 2016), 19–33.

105. On the history of the junk boat and its supersession by the steam-powered ship, see Arrighi et al., "Historical Capitalism, East and West," 270; Jennifer Wayne Cushman, *Fields from the Sea: Chinese Junk Trade with Siam during the Late Eighteenth and Early Nineteenth Centuries* (Ithaca, NY: Cornell University Press: 1993).

106. Metzger, *The Chinese Atlantic*, 239. As representatives from Cai's studio have noted to me in e-mails, this interpretation is more in keeping with the artist's intention for the performance.

107. See, for example, Giovanni Arrighi, Takeshi Hamashita, and Mark Selden Arrighi, eds., *The Resurgence of East Asia: 500, 150 and 50 Year Perspectives* (London: Routledge, 2003).

108. On this, see Wedell-Wedellsborg, "Contextualizing Cai Guo-Qiang," 16.

109. "Reflection," Art21, 2011, https://art21.org/read/cai-guo-qiang-reflection/

110. On this history, see Arrighi et al., "Historical Capitalism, East and West," 294–308; Hung, *The China Boom*, 34–51. Between 1950 and 1975, shipping grew at an annual rate of 5.7 percent. In the period spanning 1850 to 2000, by contrast, it expanded an average of 2.8 percent. On the postwar shipping boom and Japan's role therein, see Campling and Colás, *Capitalism and the Sea*, 240–250; Stopford, *Maritime Economics*, 38–41, 119–131, 621–623. On the emergence of the diesel engine in shipping, see Smil, *Two Prime Movers of Globalization*.

111. "Reflection," 21.

112. For an account of the naming and renaming of this work, see Michelle Yun and Reiko Tomii, "Catalogue," in *Cai Guo-Qiang: I Want to Believe* (New York: Guggenheim Museum, 2008), 194. For Cai on the process behind the work, see Artspace Editors, "Detonating Cultural Borders: An Interview with Cai Guo-Qiang," *Artspace*,

January 26, 2018, https://www.artspace.com/magazine/interviews_features/book_report/detonating-cultural-borders-an-interview-with-cai-guo-qiang-55234

113. The total for China is 46.6 percent, South Korea is 29.2 percent, and Japan is 17.2 percent. UNCTAD, *Review of Maritime Transport 2023*, 31. On this history, see Campling and Colás, *Capitalism and the Sea*, 145–149; Levinson, *Outside the Box*, 100–103; Stopford, *Maritime Economics*, 621–625.

114. Hung, *The China Boom*, 76–83.

115. Cotter, "Art That's a Dragon with Two Heads."

116. Iyko Day, *Alien Capital: Asian Racialization and the Logic of Settler Colonial Capitalism* (Durham, NC: Duke University Press, 2016), 130.

117. See Karl Jackson, ed., *Asian Contagion: The Causes and Consequences of a Financial Crisis* (Boulder, CO: Westview Press, 1999).

118. Cai quoted in Artspace Editors, "Detonating Cultural Borders."

119. For Cai's overview of the requirements, see "Reflection," 21.

120. Cai Studio, "Cai Guo-Qiang Unveils Large-Scale Installation in Kyoto: A Tongue-in-Cheek Examination of East Asian Relations Today," *Cai Guo-Qiang Studio Blog*, August 21, 2017, https://caiguoqiang.wordpress.com/2017/08/

121. On these disparities, see Hung, *The China Boom*, 52–86.

122. For an example of these interpretations, see Frank Langfitt, "China's Pollution Crisis Inspires An Unsettling Art Exhibit," *NPR*, August 23, 2014, https://www.npr.org/sections/parallels/2014/08/21/342189261/chinas-pollution-crisis-inspires-an-unsettling-art-exhibit?t=1634225634622

123. Peter Orszag, "Huge Container Ships' Biggest Problem Is Emissions," *Bloomberg*, March 30, 2021, https://www.bloomberg.com/opinion/articles/2021-03-30/huge-container-ships-biggest-problem-is-emissions

124. Campling and Colás, *Capitalism and the Sea*, 258.

125. Selina Thompson, *salt.* (London: Faber & Faber, 2018), 15.

126. Thompson, *salt.*, 15.

127. Saidiya Hartman, "Venus in Two Acts," *Small Axe: A Caribbean Journal of Criticism* 12, no. 2 (2008): 11.

128. Thompson, *salt.*, 52.

129. This placement had precedent in the Seafarers Education Service, which arranged classes for seafarers on Ocean Fleets ships. See Naomi Hennig and Ulrike Jordan, "George Levantis: Ocean Fleets Ltd. 1974/75," *Context Is Half the Work: A Partial History of the Artist Placement Group*, 2015, https://en.contextishalfthework.net/exhibition-archive/ocean-fleets-ltd-197475/; Simon Rycroft, "The Artist Placement Group: An Archaeology of Impact," *Cultural Geographies* 26, no. 3 (2019): 297.

130. For popular examples, see Horatio Clare, *Down to the Sea in Ships: Of Ageless Oceans and Modern Men* (London: Vintage, 2015); Rose George, *Ninety Percent of Everything: Inside Shipping, the Invisible Industry That Puts Clothes on Your Back, Gas in Your Car, and Food on Your Plate* (New York: Metropolitan Books, 2013).

131. "Twenty-Three Days at Sea Residency" was launched in 2015 by Access Gallery. See Access Gallery, "Twenty-Three Days at Sea, Chapter One," press release, 2015, https://accessgallery.ca/programming/twenty-three-days-sea-chapter-one; Kevin Griffin, "Access Gallery Chooses Artists for Inaugural 23 Days at Sea," *Vancouver Sun*, March 16, 2015, https://vancouversun.com/news/staff-blogs/access-gallery-chooses-artists-for-inaugural-23-days-at-sea; the story of the stranded artist, Rebecca Moss, was covered internationally. See Ashifa Kassam, "'Bobbing Aimlessly': Container Shipper's Collapse Leaves British Artist All at Sea," *The Guardian*, September 14, 2016, https://www.theguardian.com/artanddesign/2016/sep/14/artist-stranded-container-ship-rebecca-moss-hanjin; a film by Moss about her experience called *International Waters* premiered at the 2017 Venice Biennale.

132. See Brian Boucher, "Explore the High Seas in an Artist Residency on a Container Ship," *ArtNet*, September 30, 2015, https://news.artnet.com/market/artist-residency-container-ship-335979; for a critique of ZIM written by one of the artists involved, see Mari Bastashevski, "The Perfect Con," *e-flux Journal*, no. 75, September 2016, https://www.e-flux.com/journal/75/67148/the-perfect-con/; the residency website is http://www.containerartistresidency01.org/; on Block the Boat, see https://blocktheboat.org

133. Thompson, *salt.*, 24.

134. Rediker, *The Slave Ship*, 58.

135. Thompson, *salt.*, 24.

136. Rediker, *The Slave Ship*, 10. See also Emma Christopher, *Slave Ship Sailors and Their Captive Cargoes, 1730–1807* (Cambridge, UK: Cambridge University Press, 2006).

137. Thompson, *salt.*, 26–27.

138. Thompson, *salt.*, 28.

139. Joan Dayan, "Paul Gilroy's Slaves, Ships, and Routes: The Middle Passage as Metaphor," *Research in African Literatures* 27, no. 4 (1996): 7–14, quote at 7; Paul Gilroy, *The Black Atlantic: Modernity and Double Consciousness* (Cambridge, MA: Harvard University Press, 2003), 4–19.

140. Thompson, *salt.*, 22.

141. Thompson, *salt.*, 25.

142. Thompson, *salt.*, 22.

143. Thompson, *salt.*, 28.

144. Sharpe, *In the Wake*, 74.

145. Saidiya Hartman, *Lose Your Mother: A Journey Along the Atlantic Slave Route* (London: Serpent's Tail, 2021), 110.

146. Harney and Moten, *The Undercommons*, 93.

147. Sharpe, *In the Wake*, 94.

148. Dominic Johnson, "Rudimentary Things: Becoming an Object in the Performances of Skip Arnold," *Art History* 43, no. 3 (June 2020): 540.

149. Matthew Hockenberry, Nicole Starosielski, and Susan Zieger, "Logistical Magic," in *Assembly Codes: The Logistics of Media*, ed. Matthew Hockenberry, Nicole

Starosielski, and Susan Zieger (Durham, NC: Duke University Press, 2021), 52. On Henry Box Brown, see Daphne A. Brooks, *Bodies in Dissent: Spectacular Performances of Race and Freedom, 1850–1910* (Durham, NC: Duke University Press, 2006), 66–130; Hollis Robbins, "Fugitive Mail: The Deliverance of Henry 'Box' Brown and Antebellum Postal Politics," *American Studies* 50, no. 1 (2009): 5–25.

150. Naimou, *Salvage Work*, 10.

151. Katherine McKittrick, *Demonic Grounds: Black Women and the Cartographies of Struggle* (Minneapolis: University of Minnesota Press, 2006), xii.

152. Alexandrina Hemsley, "Introduction," in Selina Thompson's *salt.* (London: Faber & Faber, 2018), 7–8, quote at 7.

153. Hartman, *Lose Your Mother*, 17.

154. Hartman, "Venus in Two Acts," 4.

155. Hartman, 11. On pornotroping, see also Saidiya Hartman, *Scenes of Subjection: Terror, Slavery, and Self-Making in Nineteenth-Century America* (New York: Oxford University Press, 1997); Hortense J. Spillers, "Mama's Baby, Papa's Maybe: An American Grammar Book," *Diacritics* 17, no. 2 (1987): 64–81; Alexander G. Weheliye, "Pornotropes," *Journal of Visual Culture* 7, no. 1 (April 2008): 65–81.

156. Hartman, "Venus in Two Acts," 9; 11. On fabulation in relation to performance, see Tavia Nyong'o, *Afro-Fabulations: The Queer Drama of Black Life* (New York: New York University Press, 2019).

157. Thompson, *salt.*, 31.

158. Hartman, "Venus in Two Acts," 10.

159. Jen Harvie, "Interview with Selina Thompson," *Stage Left*, 2018, https://soundcloud.com/stage_left

160. Thompson, *salt.*, 49.

161. Thompson, *salt.*, 50.

162. Thompson, *salt.*, 51.

163. Hemsley, "Introduction," 8.

164. Hartman, "Venus in Two Acts," 4.

165. Rediker, *The Slave Ship*, 41.

166. Sharpe, *In the Wake*, 29.

Chapter Two

1. Anna Lowenhaupt Tsing, *Friction: An Ethnography of Global Connection* (Princeton, NJ: Princeton University Press, 2005), 7.

2. Timothy Mitchell, *Carbon Democracy: Political Power in the Age of Oil* (London: Verso, 2011), 145. See also Christopher F. Jones, "How Pipelines Constrict Oil Flows," *Limn*, April 2018, https://limn.it/articles/how-pipelines-constrict-oil-flows-2/

3. Roman Signer, "Barrel," trans. Nicholas Grindell, *Frieze*, no. 10, May 13, 2013, https://www.frieze.com/article/roman-signer-fass

4. David Gritten, "Shame: Steve McQueen Interview," *Telegraph*, January 14, 2012, https://www.telegraph.co.uk/culture/film/filmmakersonfilm/8994878/Shame-Steve-McQueen-interview.html

5. Michael Newman, "McQueen's Materialism," in *Steve McQueen* (London: Institute of Contemporary Arts, 1999), 21–35, quote at 30.

6. See Alessandra Raengo, "Blackness and the Image of Motility: A Suspenseful Critique," *Black Camera* 8, no. 1 (2016): 191–206, at 199–200.

7. Quoted in Deborah Cowen, *The Deadly Life of Logistics: Mapping Violence in Global Trade* (Minneapolis: University of Minnesota Press, 2014), 56, see also 59–61.

8. Tim Cresswell, *On the Move: Mobility in the Modern Western World* (New York: Routledge, 2006), 25.

9. For example, see Zygmunt Bauman, *Liquid Modernity* (Cambridge, UK: Polity Press, 2012).

10. Robert B. Handfield and Tom Linton, *Flow: How the Best Supply Chains Thrive* (Toronto: University of Toronto Press, 2022).

11. Taiichi Ohno, *Toyota Production System: Beyond Large-Scale Production* (Boca Raton, FL: CRC Press, 1988), 4.

12. Jay Wright Forrester, *Industrial Dynamics* (Mansfield Centre, CT: Martino Fine Books, 2013), 65.

13. Peter Cole, *Dockworker Power: Race and Activism in Durban and the San Francisco Bay Area* (Urbana: University of Illinois Press, 2018), 135; Laleh Khalili, *Sinews of War and Trade: Shipping and Capitalism in the Arabian Peninsula* (London: Verso, 2020), 235. On the significance of the "systems approach," see Cowen, *Deadly Life of Logistics*, 33–34; Michael C. Jackson, *Systems Approaches to Management* (New York: Kluwer Academic, 2000), 62–66.

14. Allan Sekula, *Fish Story*, 2nd ed. (Düsseldorf: Richter, 2002 [1995]), 134. See also Khalili, *Sinews of War and Trade*, 234–236.

15. See, for example, Grant Miller Davis and Stephen Walter Brown, *Logistics Management* (Lexington, MA: Lexington Books, 1974), 258–262.

16. McKinsey & Company, *Containerization: The Key to Low-Cost Transport* (London: Report for British Transport Docks Board, 1967), 5.

17. Mitchell, *Carbon Democracy*, 36. See also Anthony N. Penna, *A History of Energy Flows: From Human Labor to Renewable Power* (London: Routledge, 2020), 90–92.

18. Khalili, *Sinews of War and Trade*, 1.

19. Michael Watts, "Oil, Development, and the Politics of the Bottom Billion," *Macalester International* 24 (2009): 79–130, quote at 79. See also Satya Savitzky and John Urry, "Oil on the Move," in *Cargomobilities: Moving Materials in a Global Age*, ed. Thomas Birtchnell, Satya Savitzky, and John Urry (New York: Routledge, 2015), 180–198, at 180.

20. See George Caffentzis, "The Oil Paradox and the Labor Theory of Value," *Minnesota Review*, no. 87 (2016): 160–170, at 162–164, https://doi.org/10.1215/00265667-3630916; John Bellamy Foster, *Marx's Ecology: Materialism and Nature* (New York: Monthly Review Press, 2000), 167.

21. On the energy transition from coal to oil, see Bruce Podobnik, *Global Energy Shifts: Fostering Sustainability in a Turbulent Age* (Philadelphia: Temple University Press, 2006), 92–100.

22. Andreas Malm, *Fossil Capital: The Rise of Steam-Power and the Roots of Global Warming* (London: Verso, 2016).

23. Christopher F. Jones, *Routes of Power: Energy and Modern America* (Cambridge, MA: Harvard University Press, 2014), 91.

24. Quoted in Jones, *Routes of Power*, 97.

25. On this history, see Keith Fisher, *A Pipeline Runs Through It: The Story of Oil from Ancient Times to the First World War* (London: Allen Lane, 2022), 108–138; Jones, *Routes of Power*, 89–121; Penna, *A History of Energy Flows*, 89–92; Daniel Yergin, *The Prize: The Epic Quest for Oil, Money, and Power* (New York: Simon & Schuster, 1991), 19–34.

26. Jones, *Routes of Power*, 108.

27. See Fisher, *A Pipeline Runs Through It*, 208–211; Vaclav Smil, *Oil: A Beginner's Guide* (Oxford: Oneworld, 2013), 111; Yergin, *The Prize*, 59.

28. Charmaine Chua, "Containing the Ship of State: Managing Mobility in an Age of Logistics" (PhD dissertation, Minneapolis, University of Minnesota, 2018), 15.

29. On the history of the barrel, see Robert Hardwicke, *The Oilman's Barrel* (Norman: University of Oklahoma Press, 2012); Richard Norment, "Drums/Pails, Steel," in *The Wiley Encyclopedia of Packaging Technology*, ed. Kit L. Yam (Hoboken, NJ: John Wiley, 2009), 375–381.

30. The capacity of physical barrels tends to break from the barrel as a unit of measurement, which equate to 42 US gallons (159 liters). While the origins for the forty-two-gallon measure are up for debate, the standard was codified in Pennsylvania oil fields, first in practice among producers in the 1860s then in federal law in 1882. See Hardwicke, *The Oilman's Barrel*.

31. "Industry Statistics: Steel Drums; Plastic Drums; Intermediate Bulk Containers," RIPA, 2019, https://www.reusablepackaging.org/wp-content/uploads/Industry-Production-Statistics-2019-Final-5.pdf

32. Norment, "Drums/Pails, Steel," 376.

33. See "Steel Drum Market Outlook (2022–2031)," *Future Market Insights*, 2022, https://www.futuremarketinsights.com/reports/steel-drums-market

34. Brian Jacobson, "Oil Barrels Aren't Real Anymore," *The Atlantic*, September 8, 2017, https://www.theatlantic.com/technology/archive/2017/09/oil-barrels/539238/

35. Jacobson, "Oil Barrels Aren't Real Anymore."

36. Andreas Malm, "Long Waves of Fossil Development: Periodizing Energy and Capital," in *Materialism and the Critique of Energy*, ed. Brent Ryan Bellamy and Jeff Diamanti (Chicago: MCM', 2018), 161–196, quote at 165. See also Alf Hornborg, *The Power of the Machine: Global Inequalities of Economy, Technology, and Environment* (Walnut Creek, CA: AltaMira Press, 2001).

37. For an exemplary treatment of this context for culture and art, see Jeff Diamanti, *Climate and Capital in the Age of Petroleum: Locating Terminal Landscapes* (New York: Bloomsbury Academic, 2021).

38. Patricia Yaeger, "Editor's Column: Literature in the Ages of Wood, Tallow, Coal, Whale Oil, Gasoline, Atomic Power, and Other Energy Sources," *PMLA* 126, no. 2 (March 2011): 305–326, quote at 309.

39. Sheena Wilson, Adam Carlson, and Imre Szeman, "On Petrocultures: Or, Why We Need to Understand Oil to Understand Everything Else," in *Petrocultures: Oil, Politics, Culture*, ed. Sheena Wilson, Adam Carlson, and Imre Szeman (Montreal: McGill-Queen's University Press, 2017), 3–20, quote at 6.

40. Stephanie LeMenager, *Living Oil: Petroleum Culture in the American Century* (Oxford: Oxford University Press, 2014), 92.

41. Bertolt Brecht, "On Subject Matter and Form," in *Brecht on Theatre*, ed. Marc Silberman, Steve Giles, and Tom Kuhn, trans. Romy Fursland and John Willett (London: Bloomsbury Academic, 2019), 48–50, quote at 49.

42. Imre Szeman, *On Petrocultures: Globalization, Culture, and Energy* (Morgantown: West Virginia University Press, 2019), 186.

43. Ella Hickson, *Oil* (London: Nick Hern Books, 2016); Lucy Prebble, *Enron* (London: Methuen Drama, 2009).

44. See Fernando Coronil, *The Magical State: Nature, Money, and Modernity in Venezuela* (Chicago: University of Chicago Press, 1997); Robert Vitalis, *Oilcraft: The Haunting of U.S. Grand Strategy in the Gulf* (Stanford, CA: Stanford University Press, 2020). See also Christopher F. Jones, "Petromyopia: Oil and the Energy Humanities," *Humanities* 5, no. 2 (2016): 36.

45. Podobnik, *Global Energy Shifts*, 92–100; Vaclav Smil, *Energy Transitions: History, Requirements, Prospects* (Santa Barbara: Praeger, 2010), 75–104.

46. Smil, *Energy Transitions*, 92–94.

47. Podobnik, *Global Energy Shifts*, 99.

48. On this, see Matthew T. Huber, *Lifeblood: Oil, Freedom, and the Forces of Capital* (Minneapolis: University of Minnesota Press, 2013), 61–96.

49. "The Magic Barrel," *Du Pont Magazine* (November 1954): 20. On *The Magic Barrel*, see Kevin Martin, "A Dupont Lesson in Petrochemistry, 1957," *Hagley Library*, May 21, 2018, https://www.hagley.org/librarynews/video-dupont-lesson-petrochemistry-1957; a 1957 film of *The Magic Barrel* featuring Harold Thompson as host is archived at https://digital.hagley.org/VID_1995300_B07_ID02_02; the film is available at https://www.youtube.com/watch?v=FAuKQJ-ZdBI

50. Andrew H. Apter, *The Pan-African Nation: Oil and the Spectacle of Culture in Nigeria* (Chicago: University of Chicago Press, 2005), 24–25.

51. On TASPO, see Shannon Dudley, *Music from Behind the Bridge: Steelband Spirit and Politics in Trinidad and Tobago* (Oxford: Oxford University Press, 2008), 55–57, 95–102; Kim Johnson, *From Tin Pan to TASPO: Steelband in Trinidad, 1939–1951* (Kingston, Jamaica: University of the West Indies Press, 2011). Footage of TASPO's performance from the BBC documentary *The 1951 Festival of Britain: A Brave New World* (2011) is available at https://www.youtube.com/watch?v=-Y3jgxz-mYA

52. Stuart Hall, "Calypso Kings," *The Guardian*, June 28, 2002, https://www.theguardian.com/culture/2002/jun/28/nottinghillcarnival2002.nottinghillcarnival; on the anticolonial history of the steel drum, see C. L. R. James, "Presence of Blacks in the Caribbean and Its Impact on Culture," in *At the Rendezvous of Victory: Selected Writings* (London: Allison & Busby, 1984), 218–235. On the history of the steel drum generally, see John Cowley, *Carnival, Canboulay and Calypso: Traditions in the Making* (Cambridge, UK: Cambridge University Press, 2003); Dudley, *Music from Behind the Bridge*; Shannon Dudley, "Steel Band/Pan," in *Encyclopedia of Percussion*, ed. John Beck (New York: Routledge, 2007), 363–388; Jocelyne Guilbault, *Governing Sound: The Cultural Politics of Trinidad's Carnival Musics* (Chicago: University of Chicago Press, 2007); Stephen Stuempfle, *The Steelband Movement: The Forging of a National Art in Trinidad and Tobago* (Philadelphia: University of Pennsylvania Press, 1995).

53. The process for making a steelpan is recorded in Pete Seeger's 1956 documentary *Music for Oil Drums* and an accompanying book. See Peter Seeger, "The Steel Drum: A New Folk Instrument," *Journal of American Folklore* 71, no. 279 (1958): 52–57. See also Andrew R. Martin, "A Voice of Steel Through the Iron Curtain: Pete Seeger's Contributions to the Development of Steel Band in the United States," *American Music* 29, no. 3 (2011): 353–380.

54. Lovelace quoted in Jacob Campbell, "The Nature of Hydrocarbons: Industrial Ecology, Resource Depletion, and Politics of Renewability in Trinidad and Tobago" (PhD Dissertation, Tucson, University of Arizona, 2014), 52.

55. Paul Gilroy, "The End of Anti-Racism," *Journal of Ethnic and Migration Studies* 17, no. 1 (October 1990): 80.

56. On the strikes, see Campbell, "The Nature of Hydrocarbons," 37–43; Fisher, *A Pipeline Runs Through It*, 480–488; Kevin A. Yelvington, *Producing Power: Ethnicity, Gender, and Class in a Caribbean Workplace* (Philadelphia: Temple University Press, 1995), 49–54.

57. David Toop, *Into the Maelstrom: Music, Improvisation and the Dream of Freedom: Before 1970* (New York: Bloomsbury Academic, 2016), 144. On Group Ongaku, see also Brandon LaBelle, *Background Noise: Perspectives on Sound Art* (New York: Bloomsbury Academic, 2015), 35–46.

58. Nathaniel Mackey, Aldon Lynn Nielsen, Susan Weeber, Abram Foley, and Laura Vrana, "The Far Side of Mastery: An Interview with Nathaniel Mackey," *ASAP/Journal* 1, no. 2 (2016): 195.

59. On this, see Rafael Garcia and Francesca Wilmott, "Objects," in *Marcel Broodthaers*, ed. Christophe Cherix and Manuel Borja-Villel (New York: Museum of Modern Art, 2016), 76–79, quote at 77.

60. See Molly Donovan, "Wrapping Things Up: Finality in the Early Works of Christo and Jeanne-Claude," in *Christo and Jeanne-Claude*, ed. Rudy Chiappini (Milano: Skira, 2006), 25–31, quote at 25. On this early work, see David Bourdon, *Christo* (New York: H. N. Abrams, 1972); Burt Chernow, *Christo and Jeanne-Claude: A Biography* (New York: St. Martin's Press, 2002), 50–55; Christo, Jeanne-Claude, and

Matthias Koddenberg, *Christo and Jeanne-Claude: The Early Years: An Interview by Matthias Koddenberg* (Dortmund: Verlag Kettler, 2020); Matthias Koddenberg, ed., *Christo and Jeanne-Claude: Early Works 1958–64* (Bönen: Kettler, 2009).

61. On this history, see Thomas Hine, *The Total Package: The Evolution and Secret Meanings of Boxes, Bottles, Cans, and Tubes* (Boston: Little, Brown, 1995), 24–80.

62. Chernow, *Christo and Jeanne-Claude*, 81–82.

63. Hine, *The Total Package*, 14.

64. Jesse LeCavalier, *The Rule of Logistics: Walmart and the Architecture of Fulfillment* (Minneapolis: University of Minnesota Press, 2016), 63–70.

65. LeCavalier, *Rule of Logistics*, 68.

66. For an early account of this, see John F. Krafcik, "Triumph of the Lean Production System," *Sloan Management Review* 30, no. 1 (1988): 41–52.

67. Ohno, *Toyota Production System*, 103.

68. On this history, see Dara Orenstein, *Out of Stock: The Warehouse in the History of Capitalism* (Chicago: University of Chicago Press, 2019), 27–66.

69. Marx quoted in Orenstein, *Out of Stock*, 31, 45.

70. Hans Ulrich Obrist and Christo, "Christo in Conversation with Hans Ulrich Obrist," in *Christo and Jeanne-Claude: Barrels and the Mastaba, 1958–2018* (Cologne: Taschen, 2018), 9. For description of Christo's sculptures as "ready-made objects," see Lawrence Alloway, "Packages," in *Christo and Jeanne-Claude: Early Works 1958–1969*, ed. Lawrence Alloway (Cologne: Taschen, 2001), 58.

71. John Roberts, *The Intangibilities of Form: Skill and Deskilling in Art After the Readymade* (London: Verso, 2007), 25.

72. Bourdon, *Christo*, 14.

73. For these and other accounts of the exhibition, see Chernow, *Christo and Jeanne-Claude*, 99–101.

74. There is some discrepancy on what the pay actually was. Most critics and historians note that the workers were paid a set fee, while Bourdon describes it as a "generous tip." Bourdon, *Christo*, 22.

75. David Bourdon, "Barrels in Public Spaces," in Alloway, *Christo and Jeanne-Claude*, 205. See also Ellen Joosten, *Christo* (Otterlo: Rijksmuseum Kröller-Müller, 1978), n.p.

76. Pierre Restany, "Le Docker et Le Décor," in *Invitation Card for Le Rideau de Fer* (Paris: Galerie J, 1962). Translation adapted from Sophie Duplaix, "Christo's Gesture," in *Christo and Jeanne-Claude: Paris!*, ed. Sophie Duplaix (Munich: Sieveking Verlag, 2020), 14–32, at 16.

77. Restany quoted in Matthias Koddenberg, "Christo and Jeanne-Claude's Alternative Architecture," in *Christo and Jeanne-Claude: Urban Projects*, ed. Matthias Koddenberg (Dortmund: Verlag Kettler, 2017), 8–41, quote at 29.

78. Arman quoted in Chernow, *Christo and Jeanne-Claude*, 113.

79. See Helmut Deecke and Dieter Läpple, "German Seaports in a Period of Restructuring," *Tijdschrift Voor Economische En Sociale Geografie* 87, no. 4 (1996):

332–341; Iris Grossmann, "Perspectives for Hamburg as a Port City in the Context of a Changing Global Environment," *Geoforum* 39, no. 6 (2008): 2062–2072; Alexander Klose, *The Container Principle: How a Box Changes the Way We Think* (Cambridge, MA: MIT Press, 2015), 47–49.

80. Heribert Hall and Werner Baecker, eds., *Köln: Seine Bauten 1928–1988* (Cologne: J. P. Bachem, 1991), 455.

81. Marc Levinson, *The Box: How the Shipping Container Made the World Smaller and the World Economy Bigger* (Princeton, NJ: Princeton University Press, 2006), 137, 75. See also Chapter 3.

82. On the history of the MMA and the workplace conditions leading up to it and fallout from it, see Cole, *Dockworker Power*, 117–147; Lincoln Fairley, *Facing Mechanization: The West Coast Longshore Plan* (Los Angeles: University of California at Los Angeles Institute of Industrial Relations, 1979); Levinson, *The Box*, 100–126; Seonghee Lim, "Automation and San Francisco Class 'B' Longshoremen: Power, Race, and Workplace Democracy, 1958–1981" (PhD dissertation, Santa Barbara, UC Santa Barbara, 2015).

83. Quoted in Levinson, *The Box*, 115. The language of "unnecessary men" was formulated four years earlier in the joint principles agreed to by the International Longshore and Warehouse Union to start negotiations with employers.

84. Levinson, *The Box*, 116–117.

85. On this installation, see Chernow, *Christo and Jeanne-Claude*, 186–187; Stephen Prokopoff, *Monuments and Projects* (Philadelphia: Institute of Contemporary Art, 1968). Thanks to Kate Abercrombie, registrar at the Institute of Contemporary Art, for providing details on the exhibition over e-mail in April 2021.

86. Suzanne Delehanty, who worked on the exhibition, led on this with the ICA's director Stephen Prokopoff and Nathaniel Lieb, a board member with business stakes in the oil and gas industry. Delehanty's account is included in Chernow, *Christo and Jeanne-Claude*, 186–187.

87. Details on Christo and Jeanne-Claude's work with Janus Vaten draws primarily from my interview with the company executives, Ton Janus and Frits Janus, in April 2021. See also Chernow, *Christo and Jeanne-Claude*, 165–167. On these works specifically, see Joosten, *Christo*; Susanne Kensche, "Conservation of Christo's 56 Barrels: A Basis for Future Decision Making," in *Conserving Outdoor Painted Sculpture*, ed. Lydia Beerkens (Los Angeles: Getty Conservation Institute, 2014), 55–64.

88. See the "history" provided on the Janus Vaten website: https://www.janusvaten.nl/about-us/history/?lang=en; for details on their partnership with Mauser Packaging Solutions, see "Press Release: Mauser, NCG and Janus Vaten Open New Production Facilities at French Site of St Priest," March 29, 2017, https://www.prfire.co.uk/press_releases/mauser-ncg-and-janus-vaten-open-new-production-facilities-at-french-site-of-st-priest

89. See the invoice details included in Kensche, "Conservation of Christo's 56 Barrels," 64.

90. For documentation of these works, see Simone Philippi, ed., *Christo and Jeanne-Claude: Barrels and the Mastaba, 1958–2018* (Cologne: Taschen, 2018).

91. See the technical details available in Philippi, *Christo and Jeanne-Claude,* 150. See also Miranda Collinge, "Christo: The Artist Behind the Largest and Most Expensive Sculpture Ever Created," *Esquire,* June 27, 2018, https://www.esquire.com/uk/culture/a21965194/christo-the-artist-behind-the-largest-and-most-expensive-sculpture-ever-created/. Their largest oil barrel project—not created with Janus Vaten—opened in 1999, when Christo and Jeanne-Claude installed a 26-meter-high wall of 13,000 barrels inside a decommissioned gasometer in Oberhausen, Germany. See Wolfgang Volz, ed., *Christo and Jeanne-Claude: Gasometer, Oberhausen* (Cologne: Taschen, 1999).

92. On Christo and Jeanne-Claude's funding model, see Felda Hardymon, Josh Lerner, and Ann Leamon, "Christo and Jeanne-Claude: The Art of the Entrepreneur," Harvard Business School Case 806–014 (Cambridge, MA, February 2006).

93. Farah Nayeri, "Christo's Latest Work Weighs 650 Tons. And It Floats," *New York Times,* June 18, 2018, https://www.nytimes.com/2018/06/18/arts/design/uk-christo-london-mastaba.html.

94. Hettie Judah, "Christo at the Serpentine: A CGI Colourful Icon for a Greedy City," *The i,* June 19, 2018, https://inews.co.uk/culture/arts/christo-serpentine-london-mastaba-review-167081 (accessed July 7, 2020).

95. For the technical plan, see Philippi, *Christo and Jeanne-Claude,* 113. On the history of the project, see Chernow, *Christo and Jeanne-Claude,* 291–293.

96. See Marija Cetinić and Jeff Diamanti, "Oil Barrels: The Aesthetics of Saturation and the Blockage of Politics," in *Saturation: An Elemental Politics,* ed. Melody Jue and Rafico Ruiz (Durham, NC: Duke University Press, 2021), 264–282.

97. Christo quoted in Collinge, "Christo."

98. Chay Allen, "Experience, Chance and Change: Allan Kaprow and the Tension Between Art and Life, 1948–1976" (PhD dissertation, Oxford, University of Oxford, 2015), 130.

99. Jeff Kelley, *Childsplay: The Art of Allan Kaprow* (Berkeley: University of California Press, 2004), 61.

100. Among the key accounts of *Yard* that miss this includes Kelley, *Childsplay,* 58–62.

101. A partial list of Happenings with oil barrels includes *A Spring Happening* (1961), *A Service for the Dead* (1962), *Out* (1963), *Paper* (1964), and *Self-Service* (1967).

102. The most thorough account is in Joan Rothfuss, *Topless Cellist: The Improbable Life of Charlotte Moorman* (Cambridge, MA: MIT Press, 2014), 113–117. A film recording of one performance is available as part of the sculpture made by Paik called *Oil Drums, Hommáge a Charlotte Moorman* (1991).

103. For the fullest account of this, see Hiroko Ikegami, *The Great Migrator: Robert Rauschenberg and the Global Rise of American Art* (Cambridge, MA: MIT Press, 2014), 133–139. See also Branden W. Joseph, *Random Order: Robert Rauschenberg and the Neo-Avant-Garde* (Cambridge, MA: MIT Press, 2003), 224–225.

104. See Yuri Mitsuda, "Trauma and Deliverance: Portraits of Avant-Garde Artists in Japan, 1955–1970," in *Tokyo, 1955–1970: A New Avant-Garde*, ed. Doryun Chong (New York: Museum of Modern Art, 2012), 158–177; Midori Yoshimoto, "Off Museum! Performance Art That Turned the Street into 'Theatre,' Circa 1964 Tokyo," *Performance Paradigm* 2 (2006): 102–118. Mitsuda lists the performance as taking place in 1962, while most other accounts have it as 1961.

105. For details on *Transfer*, see Kelley, *Childsplay*, 130–132; Eric Padraic Morrill, "What Can We Learn from Photographs of Happenings? Allan Kaprow's *Transfer*," *MAP*, no. 5, June 2014, http://www.perfomap.de/map5/paradoxe-medien/what-can-we-learn-from-photographs-of-happenings-allan-kaprows-transfer/what-can-we-learn-from-photographs-of-happenings.pdf; for original documents on *Transfer* including photographs, see Boxes 14 and 15 available in "Series III. Project Files, 1946–1999" of the Allan Kaprow Papers, the Getty Research Institute, Los Angeles.

106. Richard Kostelanetz, *The Theatre of Mixed Means: An Introduction to Happenings, Kinetic Environments and Other Mixed-Means Performances* (London: Pitman, 1970), 7.

107. On *Gas*, see Kelley, *Childsplay*, 119.

108. For the De Maria's text that describes "Meaningless Work," see https://id3419.securedata.net/artnotart/fluxus/wdemaria-meaninglesswork.html; see also Jane McFadden, *Walter De Maria: Meaningless Work* (London: Reaktion Books, 2016).

109. Bourdon, *Christo*, 25.

110. Christo quoted in Bourdon, *Christo*, 25.

111. Chernow, *Christo and Jeanne-Claude*, 176.

112. Allan Kaprow, "The Education of the Un-Artist, Part II," in *Essays on the Blurring of Art and Life*, ed. Jeff Kelley (Berkeley: University of California Press, 1993), 110–126, quote at 112.

113. See the flyer for *Transfer* in Box 14 in "Series III. Project Files, 1946–1999" of the Allan Kaprow Papers, the Getty Research Institute, Los Angeles.

114. Robert Haywood, "Critique of Instrumental Labor: Meyer Schapiro's and Allan Kaprow's Theory of Avant-Garde Art," in *Experiments in the Everyday: Allan Kaprow and Robert Watts, Events, Objects, Documents*, ed. Benjamin H. D. Buchloh and Judith Rodenbeck (New York: Columbia University, 1999), 27–46.

115. Michael H. Belzer, *Sweatshops on Wheels: Winners and Losers in Trucking Deregulation* (Oxford: Oxford University Press, 2000).

116. Longshoremen quoted in Levinson, *The Box*, 126. See also Reg Theriault, *Longshoring on the San Francisco Waterfront* (San Pedro: Singlejack Books, 1980); Stan Weir, *Singlejack Solidarity*, ed. George Lipsitz (Minneapolis: University of Minnesota Press, 2004).

117. Michael C. Jackson, *Critical Systems Thinking and the Management of Complexity: Responsible Leadership for a Complex World* (Hoboken, NJ: Wiley Blackwell, 2019), 75.

118. Cowen, *Deadly Life of Logistics*, 34.

119. On the role of Bertalanffy's systems theory in shaping the total cost analysis in the logistics industry, see also Jackson, *Systems Approaches to Management*, 62–66. On systems theory in art, see Jack Burnham, *Beyond Modern Sculpture: The Effects of Science and Technology on the Sculpture of This Century* (New York: Braziller, 1968); Jack Burnham, "Systems Esthetics," *Artforum* 7, no. 1 (September 1968): 30–35; Jack Burnham and Melissa Ragain, *Dissolve into Comprehension: Writings and Interviews, 1964–2004* (Cambridge, MA: MIT Press, 2015). For a critical assessment, see Pamela M. Lee, *Chronophobia: On Time in the Art of the 1960's* (Cambridge, MA: MIT Press, 2004), 70–81; Luke Skrebowski, "Jack Burnham Redux: The Obsolete in Reverse?," *Grey Room*, no. 65 (2016): 88–113.

120. Jasper Bernes, *The Work of Art in the Age of Deindustrialization* (Stanford, CA: Stanford University Press, 2017), 90.

121. Davis and Brown, *Logistics Management*, 115.

122. Allan Kaprow, "The Education of the Un-Artist, Part I," in *Essays on the Blurring of Art and Life*, 97–109, quote at 106.

123. Davis and Brown, *Logistics Management*, 118.

124. Kaprow, "The Education of the Un-Artist, Part II," 116, 120.

125. Kaprow, "The Education of the Un-Artist, Part II," 122.

126. Kaprow, "The Education of the Un-Artist, Part II," 117.

127. Kaprow, "The Education of the Un-Artist, Part II," 116–117.

128. Kaprow, "The Education of the Un-Artist, Part II," 118.

129. *The Third Choir* was first shown at Goldsmiths in 2014, but Ourahmane premiered the performance at the John Jones Gallery in 2014 and at the Delfina Foundation in 2015 as part of the event *Repeat/Rehearse*. Details on *The Third Choir* are drawn in part from my interview with Lydia Ourahmane on August 23, 2020. Thanks to the artist for making available the archive and the performance script.

130. Clement M. Henry, "Algeria's Agonies: Oil Rent Effects in a Bunker State," *Journal of North African Studies* 9, no. 2 (2004): 68–81; Camilla Sandbakken, "The Limits to Democracy Posed by Oil Rentier States: The Cases of Algeria, Nigeria and Libya," *Democratization* 13, no. 1 (2006): 135–152.

131. For a critique of the resource curse theory, see Michael Watts, "Resource Curse? Governmentality, Oil and Power in the Niger Delta, Nigeria," *Geopolitics* 9, no. 1 (2004): 50–80.

132. Lydia Ourahmane, "The Third Choir Archives (Performance Documents)," courtesy of the artist.

133. As indicated in Ourahmane's archive, the exemption even required government officials to lightly amend Algeria's *Finance Act*.

134. Sianne Ngai, *Our Aesthetic Categories: Zany, Cute, Interesting* (Cambridge, MA: Harvard University Press, 2012), 157. See, for example, the 1966 exhibition *Working Drawings and Other Visible Things on Paper Not Necessarily Meant to Be Viewed as Art* curated by Mel Blocher at the New York School of Visual Arts. See also Alexander Alberro, *Conceptual Art and the Politics of Publicity* (Cambridge, MA: MIT Press, 2003).

135. Ngai, *Our Aesthetic Categories*, 145. On "the aesthetic of administration," see Benjamin H. D. Buchloh, "Conceptual Art 1962–1969: From the Aesthetic of Administration to the Critique of Institutions," *October* 55 (1990): 105–143.

136. Ben Blackmoore, "Lydia Ourahmane," *Bomb Magazine*, no. 143, March 15, 2018, https://bombmagazine.org/articles/lydia-ourahmane/

137. Adrian Lee, "Interview with Lydia Ourahmane," *Art Vehicle*, no. 67, 2014, http://www.artvehicle.com/interview/48

138. Susan Zieger, "'Shipped': Paper, Print, and the Atlantic Slave Trade," in *Assembly Codes: The Logistics of Media*, ed. Matthew Curtis Hockenberry, Nicole Starosielski, and Susan Zieger (Durham, NC: Duke University Press, 2021), 34–51, quote at 34.

139. Zieger, "'Shipped,'" 39.

140. Most of the details included in my account of *Wall of Oil Barrels—The Iron Curtain* draw from Chernow, *Christo and Jeanne-Claude*, 103–113.

141. In 1694, the *Dictionnaire de l'Académie française* defined a barricade as "usually made with barrels filled with earth for the purpose of defending oneself or finding cover from the enemy." Quoted in Mark Traugott, *The Insurgent Barricade* (Berkeley: University of California Press, 2010), 1. See also Éric Hazan, *A History of the Barricade*, trans. David Fernbach (London: Verso, 2015).

142. The invitation has been widely reprinted in English translation, including in Philippi, *Christo and Jeanne-Claude*, 40.

143. Chernow, *Christo and Jeanne-Claude*, 108.

144. Koddenberg, "Christo and Jeanne-Claude's Alternative Architecture," 28.

145. On these events, see Kristin Ross, *May '68 and Its Afterlives* (Chicago: University of Chicago Press, 2002), 40–64.

146. See, again, Koddenberg, "Christo and Jeanne-Claude's Alternative Architecture," 29.

147. See Giuliano Garavini, *The Rise and Fall of OPEC in the Twentieth Century* (Oxford: Oxford University Press, 2019), 163–166; Marta Musso, "'Oil Will Set Us Free': The Hydrocarbon Industry and the Algerian Decolonization Process," in *Britain, France and the Decolonization of Africa: Future Imperfect?*, ed. Andrew Smith and Chris Jeppesen (London: UCL Press, 2017), 62–84.

148. On these plans see, Chernow, *Christo and Jeanne-Claude*, 177, 173; Philippi, *Christo and Jeanne-Claude*, 46, 54.

149. Details on *Battle Bus* come primarily from my interview with Sokari Douglas Camp on May 5, 2021. See also Veronika Anna Molnár, "Art, Petro-Violence, and Neocolonialism in Nigeria: An Analysis of Sokari Douglas Camp's Battle Bus," *Assemblage*, no. 1, 2020, https://www.assemblagejournal.org/issue-1fall-2020/battle-bus; Susanna Rustin, "Ken Saro-Wiwa Memorial Art Bus Denied Entry to Nigeria," *The Guardian*, November 5, 2015, https://www.theguardian.com/environment/2015/nov/05/ken-saro-wiwa-memorial-art-bus-denied-entry-to-nigeria; Christiane Schlote, "Oil, Masquerades, and Memory: Sokari Douglas Camp's Memorial of Ken

Saro-Wiwa," in *Engaging with Literature of Commitment*, ed. Gordon Collier, Marc Delrez, Anne Fuchs, and Bénédicte Ledent (Leiden: Brill, 2012), 241–261.

150. On the events leading up to and resulting from the Ogoni Nine executions, see Apter, *The Pan-African Nation*, 258–277; Rob Nixon, *Slow Violence and the Environmentalism of the Poor* (Cambridge, MA: Harvard University Press, 2011), 103–127; Ike Okonta and Oronto Douglas, *Where Vultures Feast: Shell, Human Rights, and Oil in the Niger Delta* (London: Verso, 2003); Michael Watts, "Antinomies of Community: Some Thoughts on Geography, Resources and Empire," *Transactions of the Institute of British Geographers* 29, no. 2 (2004): 195–216.

151. On the campaign to free *Battle Bus*, see Celestine AkpoBari, "The Bus, Its Seizure and Our Story," *Platform*, May 14, 2018, https://platformlondon.org/2018/05/14/update-the-bus-its-seizure-and-our-story/

152. Liz Bolshaw, "Victor Ehikhamenor: Shaped by Memory and Tribal Tradition," *Financial Times*, March 27, 2015, https://www.ft.com/content/a3544b56-ce34-11e4-86fc-00144feab7de

153. Emmanuel Iduma, "The Wealth of Nations," *Guernica*, March 1, 2016, https://www.guernicamag.com/the-wealth-of-nations/

154. Fisher, *A Pipeline Runs Through It*, 258–265.

155. Christine Okoth, "Reconfiguring Resistance: Acts of Worldmaking and Aesthetics of Extractive Solidarity," *Berliner Gazette*, June 7, 2022, https://blogs.mediapart.fr/berliner-gazette/blog/070622/reconfiguring-resistance-acts-worldmaking-and-aesthetics-extractive-solidarity

156. The film is available here: https://vimeo.com/767000686; on *Karikpo Pipeline*, see Stephanie LeMenager, "Eden If We Dare," in *Zina Saro-Wiwa: Did You Know We Taught Them How to Dance?*, ed. Maria Bailey (Seattle: University of Washington Press, 2016), 39–45; Nomusa Makhubu, "The Poetics of Entanglement in Zina Saro-Wiwa's Food Interventions," *Third Text* 32, no. 2–3 (May 4, 2018): 176–199.

Chapter Three

1. I have in mind here the traveling performance *Origami* (2017) by Satchie Noro and Silvain Ohl, which involved Noro acrobatically performing atop a container whose sides and top had been engineered to move and fold like a piece of paper. See Laura Freeman, "Origami–Dance Umbrella Festival, Review: A Striking but Slow Spectacle," *Evening Standard*, November 14, 2017, https://www.standard.co.uk/culture/theatre/origami-dance-umbrella-festival-review-a-striking-but-slow-spectacle-a3683346.html

2. Luís F. A. Bernardo, Luiz A. P. Oliveira, Miguel C. S. Nepomuceno, and Jorge M. A. Andrade, "Use of Refurbished Shipping Containers for the Construction of Housing Building," *Journal of Civil Engineering and Management* 19, no. 5 (2013): 628–646, quote at 628. For a history of container architecture, see Mitchell Schwarzer, "The Emergence of Container Urbanism," *Places Journal*, February 2013, https://doi.org/10.22269/130212

3. See Lucy Holt, "Shipping Containers Are Not Housing," *Tribune Magazine*, February 11, 2021, https://tribunemag.co.uk/2021/02/shipping-containers-are-not-housing

4. On the history of the shipping container, see Alejandro Colás, "Infrastructures of the Global Economy: The Shipping Container as a Political Artefact," in *Technology and World Politics: An Introduction*, ed. Daniel R. McCarthy (New York: Routledge, 2018), 146–164; Alexander Klose, *The Container Principle: How a Box Changes the Way We Think* (Cambridge, MA: MIT Press, 2015); Marc Levinson, *The Box: How the Shipping Container Made the World Smaller and the World Economy Bigger* (Princeton, NJ: Princeton University Press, 2006); Craig Martin, *Shipping Container* (New York: Bloomsbury Academic, 2016).

5. Levinson, *The Box*, 15.

6. Charles Jencks and Nathan Silver, *Adhocism: The Case for Improvisation*, expanded and updated ed. (Cambridge, MA: MIT Press, 2013), 70.

7. Stewart Brand, *How Buildings Learn: What Happens After They're Built* (London: Phoenix, 1997).

8. J. Vijayalaxmi, "Towards Sustainable Architecture—A Case with Greentainer," *Local Environment* 15, no. 3 (2010): 245–259. For a primer on the unsustainability of shipping containers as housing, see Mark Hogan, "What's Wrong with Shipping Container Housing? Everything," *ArchDaily*, September 13, 2015, https://www.archdaily.com/773491/opinion-whats-wrong-with-shipping-container-housing-everything; among the most extreme visions for container architecture has come from the architecture firm LOT-EK, who embrace the entire containerization infrastructure, including its ships, cranes, and ports, as providing the scaffolding for newly nomadic lifestyles in which people live and travel along maritime routes in their personal "mobile dwelling units" made of shipping containers. See Jennifer Johung, *Replacing Home: From Primordial Hut to Digital Network in Contemporary Art* (Minneapolis: University of Minnesota Press, 2012), 68–87.

9. Consultants estimate that the "repositioning" of containers costs the shipping industry up to $20 billion each year, devouring 5 percent of an average carrier's operating budget. Ulrik Sanders, Lars Kloppsteck, Christian Roeloffs, Johannes Schlingmeier, and Jens Riedl, "Think Outside Your Boxes: Solving the Global Container-Repositioning Puzzle," *BCG*, November 17, 2015, https://www.bcg.com/publications/2015/transportation-travel-logistics-think-outside-your-boxes-solving-global-container-repositioning-puzzle

10. Costas Paris, "Old Containers Find Out-of-the-Box Second Lives," *Wall Street Journal*, May 16, 2017, https://www.wsj.com/articles/old-containers-find-out-of-the-box-second-lives-1494840601; see also John Churchill, "The Second Life of Containers," May 25, 2015, https://www1.maersk.com/stories/the-second-life-of-containers (accessed September 24, 2021). This corporate feature by Churchill is also available at https://www.cbn.co.za/industry-news/transport-logistics-freight-services/the-second-life-of-shipping-containers/

11. Allan Sekula, *Fish Story*, 2nd ed. (Düsseldorf: Richter, 2002 [1995]), 137.

12. David Harvey, *The New Imperialism* (Oxford: Oxford University Press, 2005), 137.

13. See chap. 26 of Karl Marx, *Capital: A Critique of Political Economy, Volume 1*, trans. Ben Fowkes (London: Penguin Classics, 1990). For important recent revisions and considerations of Marx's account, see Massimo de Angelis, "Marx and Primitive Accumulation: The Continuous Character of Capital's 'Enclosures,'" *The Commoner*, no. 2 (2001): 1–22; Silvia Federici, *Caliban and the Witch* (New York: Autonomedia, 2004); Harvey, *The New Imperialism*; Michael Perelman, *The Invention of Capitalism: Classical Political Economy and the Secret History of Primitive Accumulation* (Durham, NC: Duke University Press, 2000). On this expanded Marxist understanding of dispossession, see Zachary Levenson, *Delivery as Dispossession: Land Occupation and Eviction in the Post-Apartheid City* (Oxford: Oxford University Press, 2022), 52–59; Andrea Smith, *Conquest: Sexual Violence and American Indian Genocide* (Durham, NC: Duke University Press, 2015); Neil Smith, *The New Urban Frontier: Gentrification and the Revanchist City* (London: Routledge, 1996). For a critique of the range of what some say can be dispossessed in the service of capital accumulation, see Robert Brenner, "What Is, and What Is Not, Imperialism?," *Historical Materialism* 14, no. 4 (2006): 86.

14. Sandro Mezzadra and Brett Neilson, *The Politics of Operations: Excavating Contemporary Capitalism* (Durham, NC: Duke University Press, 2019), 203.

15. Glen Sean Coulthard, *Red Skin, White Masks: Rejecting the Colonial Politics of Recognition* (Minneapolis: University of Minnesota Press, 2014), 6–15.

16. Harvey, *The New Imperialism*, 176.

17. On how logistics has "intensified long-standing processes of dispossession and exploitation" rooted in the circuits of empire and colonization, see Charmaine Chua, Martin Danyluk, Deborah Cowen, and Laleh Khalili, "Turbulent Circulation: Building a Critical Engagement with Logistics," *Environment and Planning D: Society and Space* 36, no. 4 (2018): 617–629, quote at 619.

18. Levinson, *The Box*, 1.

19. Levinson, *The Box*, 33–35.

20. On the history of Sea-Land Service, see Marc Levinson, *Outside the Box: How Globalization Changed from Moving Stuff to Spreading Ideas* (Princeton, NJ: Princeton University Press, 2021), 59–66.

21. On the standardization of the shipping container and deregulation, see Deborah Cowen, *The Deadly Life of Logistics: Mapping Violence in Global Trade* (Minneapolis: University of Minnesota Press, 2014), 40–47; Keller Easterling, *Extrastatecraft: The Power of Infrastructure Space* (New York: Verso, 2016), 187–191; Levinson, *The Box*, 127–149; Craig Martin, "The Packaging of Efficiency in the Development of the Intermodal Shipping Container," *Mobilities* 9, no. 3 (July 2014): 432–451. On trucking deregulation in the United States specifically, see Michael H. Belzer, *Sweatshops on Wheels: Winners and Losers in Trucking Deregulation* (Oxford: Oxford University Press, 2000).

22. On the importance of war in establishing global shipping container services, see Colás, "Infrastructures of the Global Economy," 151–152; Cowen, *Deadly Life of Logistics*, 40–41; Levinson, *The Box*, 171–188.

23. Klose, *The Container Principle*, 126–27.

24. Estimates vary on the number of shipping containers in circulation; this figure has recently been cited in the financial press and is from Carl Bentzel, "Assessment of the People's Republic of China's Control of Container and Intermodal Chassis Manufacturing" (Washington, DC: Federal Maritime Commission, March 30, 2022), 9, https://www.fmc.gov/wp-content/uploads/2022/03/ContainerandChassisManufacturingFinalReport.pdf

25. Cowen, *Deadly Life of Logistics*, 31.

26. Alberto Toscano and Jeff Kinkle, *Cartographies of the Absolute* (Winchester, UK: Zero Books, 2015), 197.

27. Toscano and Kinkle, *Cartographies of the Absolute*, 197.

28. Toscano and Kinkle, *Cartographies of the Absolute*, 201.

29. Kiefer quoted in Michael Prodger, "Inside Anselm Kiefer's Astonishing 200-Acre Art Studio," *The Guardian*, September 12, 2014, https://www.theguardian.com/artanddesign/2014/sep/12/anselm-kiefer-royal-academy-retrospective-german-painter-sculptor; see the documentaries about Kiefer's La Ribaute project, *Over Your Cities Grass Will Grow* (dir. Sophie Fiennes, 2010) and *Anselm–Das Rauschen der Zeit* (dir. Wim Wenders, 2023).

30. See https://metisarts.co.uk/projects/3rd-ring-out

31. For Darkfield, the tight space of a shipping container trumps that of their portability. When Darkfield's installations tour internationally to countries like Australia, Mexico, and South Korea, the theater company finds it more cost effective to recreate their environments in shipping containers acquired locally rather than transport them (author interview with David Rosenberg, September 2021). Some artists, interested in the look of shipping containers, build their own instead of repurposing existing ones. An example is the set designed by Andrzej Goulding and built by Clockwork Scenery for Frantic Assembly's touring production *The Unreturning* (2018). The company considered adapting an existing container, but the number of modifications needed, which included being able to pack it flat for touring, led them to design and build their own (author e-mail with producer Peter Holland, September 8, 2021).

32. For an example of the latter, see the container complex that London's Arcola Theatre opened in 2021, called Arcola Outside (https://www.arcolatheatre.com/step-into-arcola-outside-as-part-of-open-house-2021/). See also the mobile chamber opera *Birds in the Moon* (https://birdsinthemoon.org/) and Requardt and Rosenberg's dance-drama *Future Cargo* (https://www.requardt-rosenberg.com/futurecargo-main), which began touring California and England respectively in the summer of 2021.

33. See https://www.thecontainerglobe.com/

34. Lizzie Crook, "Demountable Stadium Built with Shipping Containers Reaches Completion in Qatar," *Dezeen*, November 24, 2021, https://www.dezeen.com/2021/11/24/stadium-974-fenwick-iribarren-architects-qatar-world-cup/

35. See, for example, Christopher Balme, *The Theatrical Public Sphere* (Cambridge, UK: Cambridge University Press, 2014), 179–184; Claire Bishop, *Artificial Hells: Participatory Art and the Politics of Spectatorship* (London: Verso, 2012), 279–283.

36. Sekula, *Fish Story*, 49.

37. Charmaine Chua, "The Container: Stacking, Packing, and Moving the World," *Funambulist Magazine*, no. 6 (February 2016): 40–45, quote at 41.

38. Marco D'Eramo, "Dock Life," *New Left Review* 96 (December 2015): 85–99, quote at 89.

39. Levinson, *The Box*, 201.

40. On the struggles of the English ports in the 1960s, see Levinson, *The Box*, 201–207.

41. McKinsey & Company, *Containerization: The Key to Low-Cost Transport* (London: Report for British Transport Docks Board, 1967).

42. Levinson, *The Box*, 207.

43. Andrew Church, "Urban Regeneration in London Docklands: A Five-Year Policy Review," *Environment and Planning C: Government and Policy* 6, no. 2 (1988): 187–208, at 188. See also Adrian Smith, "Political Transformation, Urban Policy and the State in London's Docklands," *GeoJournal* 24, no. 3 (1991): 237–246.

44. See D'Eramo, "Dock Life"; Alice Mah, *Port Cities and Global Legacies: Urban Identity, Waterfront Work, and Radicalism* (Basingstoke, UK: Palgrave Macmillan, 2014).

45. *Raising the Titanic* was performed for ten nights, August 9–13 and August 16–20, 1983. A documentary, *Raising the Titanic* (dir. Allan Ravenscroft), was broadcast on Channel 4 on April 8, 1985. My discussion of the production draws from the documentary, archived files relating to the performance in the Welfare State International Collection available at the University of Bristol Theatre Collection (UBTC), author e-mail correspondence with the production's director John Fox in September 2021, and the following sources: Tony Coult and Baz Kershaw, eds., *Engineers of the Imagination: The Welfare State Handbook* (London: Methuen, 1999), 207–218; John Fox, *Eyes on Stalks* (London: Methuen, 2002), 76–80; Baz Kershaw, *The Radical in Performance: Between Brecht and Baudrillard* (London: Routledge, 1999), 8–12.

46. John Fox noted to me that WSI's production manager, Howard Steel, likely acquired the containers, but with Steel's death in 1989 knowledge of how the containers were acquired has been lost. Notes by Andy Plant, a sculptor and engineer working for WSI, include the only mention of containers in the archive. See "Notebook," in "Subfolder Background to Titanic" in Box 1.55 "Materials Relating to 'Raising the Titanic'" in UBTC.

47. Lyn Gardner, "Experimental Theatre to Spill into the Mainstream," *The Guardian*, April 1, 2009, https://www.theguardian.com/stage/2009/apr/01/experimental-theatre-spill-festival; on the history of WSI, see Coult and Kershaw, *Engineers of the*

Imagination; Gillian Whitely, "Welfare State International," in *British Theatre Companies: 1965–1979*, ed. John Bull and Graham Saunders (London: Bloomsbury, 2017), 223–249.

48. Fox, *Eyes on Stalks*, 196.

49. Fox, *Eyes on Stalks*, 79.

50. On the history and operations of the LDDC, see Church, "Urban Regeneration in London Docklands"; Mark Goodwin, "Replacing a Surplus Population: The Policies of the London Docklands Development Corporation," in *Housing and Labour Markets: Building the Connections*, ed. John Allen and Chris Hammet (London: Routledge, 1991), 254–276; Smith, "Political Transformation, Urban Policy and the State in London's Docklands"; Adrian Smith, "Gentrification and the Spatial Constitution of the State: The Restructuring of London's Docklands," *Antipode* 21, no. 3 (1989): 232–260.

51. Church, "Urban Regeneration in London Docklands," 191.

52. Church, "Urban Regeneration in London Docklands," 198.

53. "The Limehouse Area Development Strategy" was released by the LDDC in November 1982.

54. The fate of Riverside Mansions, first built in 1928, is the exemplary case of this. See Mike Brooke, "Riverside Mansions Marks Its First 80 Years," *East London Advertiser*, August 15, 2008, https://www.eastlondonadvertiser.co.uk/news/riverside-mansions-marks-its-first-80-years-1928-to-7648330; Smith, "Gentrification and the Spatial Constitution of the State," 245–247.

55. Jon Bird, "Dystopia on the Thames," in *Mapping the Futures: Local Cultures, Global Change*, ed. Jon Bird (London: Routledge, 1993), 121–137, at 127.

56. On gentrification as dispossession, see Nicholas K. Blomley, *Unsettling the City: Urban Land and the Politics of Property* (New York: Routledge, 2004); David Harvey, *Rebel Cities: From the Right to the City to the Urban Revolution* (New York: Verso, 2012), 75–77; Smith, *The New Urban Frontier*.

57. Michael Heseltine in 1981, quoted in Fiona Rule, *London's Docklands: A History of the Lost Quarter* (Hersham, UK: Ian Allen Publishing, 2009), 271.

58. Quoted in Deyan Sudjic, "Inside London's Docklands: 40 Years of Ambition, Politics and Financial Wrangling," *Financial Times*, June 11, 2021. On the advertising campaign, see Smith, "Gentrification and the Spatial Constitution of the State," 252.

59. Peter Dunn and Loraine Leeson, "The Art of Change in Docklands," in *Mapping the Futures: Local Cultures, Global Change*, 138–150, quote at 140, italics in the original.

60. For accounts of the organizing and arts activism that contended with the LDDC and the London Docklands in the 1980s, see Bird, "Dystopia on the Thames"; Dunn and Leeson, "The Art of Change in Docklands."

61. "Raising the Titanic: A Musical Event in Three Acts," n.p, in Box 5.4 "Old Brochure," in UBTC.

62. Debbie Mullins, quoted in the documentary *Raising the Titanic*.

63. LIFT publicity copy, Box 1.56 "Materials Relating to 'Raising the Titanic,'" in UBTC.

64. Coult and Kershaw, *Engineers of the Imagination*, 218. On the budget, see "Press Release" dated July 13, 1983, Box 1.56 "Materials Relating to 'Raising the Titanic,'" in UBTC.

65. Fox e-mail with author, October 2021.

66. See the project website: https://www.containercity.com/container-city-2; a fourth floor was added to Container City in 2003. For a time, LIFT, the festival that had commissioned *Raising the Titanic*, was headquartered in Container City. Thanks to Michael McKinnie for bringing this to my attention.

67. Eric Reynolds of USM, quoted in John Vidal, "Boxing Clever," *The Guardian*, January 14, 2004, https://www.theguardian.com/society/2004/jan/14/environment.environment

68. Schwarzer, "The Emergence of Container Urbanism." On the history of Trinity Buoy Wharf, see the short film *The Wharf* (dir. Rupert Murray, 2018).

69. For a partial list of the shipping container projects that the architects behind Container City have since created, see https://www.containercity.com/projects

70. "Shunt Jetty Proposal" (n.p.), submitted on April 25, 2014, to the Royal Borough of Greenwich as part of application 14/1099/F, "Temporary Performance Venue and Supporting Infrastructure (Portacabin-style Units) between 14th August and 27th September 2014," available at https://planning.royalgreenwich.gov.uk/online-applications/applicationDetails.do?activeTab=summary&keyVal=_GRNW_DCAPR_77306 / (accessed February 1, 2024).

71. Fredric Jameson, "Postmodernism, or the Cultural Logic of Late Capitalism," *New Left Review*, no. 146 (August 1984): 53–92.

72. On the history of Shunt, see Mischa Twitchin, "Shunt: A Performance Collective," in *The Twenty-First Century Performance Reader*, ed. Teresa Brayshaw, Anna Fenemore, and Noel Witts (London: Routledge, 2019), 468–473.

73. For Adaptainer's blog and video about *The Boy*, see "Mystery London Show Opens in Pop Up Shipping Containers," September 14, 2014, http://adaptainer.co.uk/container-conversion/pop-up-shipping-containers-the-boy-who-climbed-out-of-his-face-shunt/; a short film of the build for *The Boy*, created by Flora Azqueta (2014), is available at https://vimeo.com/104547227

74. Daniel Johnson, "Duke of Westminster No Longer UK's Richest Property Magnate," *Telegraph*, December 6, 2013, http://www.telegraph.co.uk/finance/newsbysector/constructionandproperty/10500634/Duke-of-Westminster-no-longer-UKs-richest-property-magnate.html

75. On the history of North Greenwich, see Mary Mills, *Greenwich Marsh: The 300 Years Before the Dome* (London: M. Wright, 1999); Imogen West-Knights, "Was the Millennium Dome Really So Bad? The Inside Story of a (Not So) Total Disaster," *The Guardian*, March 12, 2020, https://www.theguardian.com/uk-news/2020/mar/12/millennium-dome-experience-disaster-inside-story-new-labour

76. See Judith Evans, "Greenwich Urban Village Given Final Approval," *Financial Times*, November 20, 2015, http://www.ft.com/cms/s/0/970b8e1a-8eda-11e5-a549-b89a1dfede9b.html#axzz3sGBzsVlv; the commercial website for the redevelopment project is available at http://www.greenwichpeninsula.co.uk; for an update on the development, see Paul Norman, "Knight Dragon's Greenwich Design District Firing on All Cylinders," *CoStar UK*, January 23, 2023, https://www.costar.com/article/2086424002/knight-dragons-greenwich-design-district-firing-on-all-cylinders

77. Michael McKinnie, *City Stages: Theatre and Urban Space in a Global City* (Toronto: University of Toronto Press, 2007), 55.

78. McKinnie, *City Stages,* 89.

79. McKinnie, *City Stages,* 18.

80. Lindsey German and John Rees, *A People's History of London (London: Verso, 2012)*, 284–298.

81. This framing was formerly on The Jetty's website (http://thejettygreenwich.co.uk/), which has since been removed (accessed January 12, 2016).

82. In June 2015 Knight Dragon followed *The Boy* with another performance staged in the same containers on The Jetty. The Jetty was then converted into an urban garden offering everything from yoga classes to lectures on beekeeping. At the time of writing in 2023, The Jetty is closed to the public.

83. Dan Hancox, "Fuck Your Pop-Up Shops," *Vice*, February 21, 2014, http://www.vice.com/en_uk/read/shipping-container-elephant-park-dan-hancox

84. On the demolition of the Heygate Estate, see Andy Jones, "Every Flat in a New South London Development Has Been Sold to Foreign Investors," *Vice,* April 13, 2017, https://www.vice.com/en/article/qkq4bx/every-flat-in-a-new-south-london-development-has-been-sold-to-foreign-investors; Owen Hatherly, "After the Heygate Estate, a Grey Future Awaits," *The Guardian*, February 8, 2011, https://www.theguardian.com/commentisfree/2011/feb/08/heygate-estate-housing-gentrification; Ian Steadman, "Look to the Heygate Estate for What's Wrong with London's Housing," *New Statesman*, November 6, 2013, https://www.newstatesman.com/politics/2013/11/look-heygate-estate-whats-wrong-londons-housing

85. "Shunt Jetty Proposal."

86. Harry Mount, "London's Ultimate Village: Greenwich Peninsula," *Evening Standard*, October 9, 2014, https://www.standard.co.uk/lifestyle/londons-ultimate-village-greenwich-peninsula-9784838.html

87. UNCTAD (United Nations Conference on Trade and Development), *Review of Maritime Transport 2023* (Geneva: UNCTAD, 2023), 92, https://unctad.org/system/files/official-document/rmt2023_en.pdf

88. See David Barboza, "Shanghai Opens New Shipping Port," *New York Times*, December 11, 2005, https://www.nytimes.com/2005/12/11/business/worldbusiness/shanghai-opens-new-shipping-port.html; D'Eramo, "Dock Life," 96.

89. Phil Neel, *Hinterland: America's New Landscape of Class and Conflict* (London: Reaktion Books, 2018), 17.

90. Laleh Khalili, "Foreword to the 2018 Edition," in *Fish Story*, 3rd ed. (London: MACK, 2018), ii–ix, quote at ii.

91. Toscano and Kinkle, *Cartographies of the Absolute*, 204–205.

92. See Monumenta, "Exhibition Guide: Huang Yong Ping, Empires," 2016, n.p.; Kamel Mennour, "Press Release: Huang Yong Ping Exhibition," 2016, https://kamelmennour.com/exhibitions/huang-yong-ping-47; Emily Nathan, "At Monumenta 2016, a Giant Carcass and Shipping Containers Carry a Solemn Message," *ArtNet*, May 9, 2016, https://news.artnet.com/art-world/monumenta-paris-2016-huang-yong-ping-492374; Wilson Tarbox, "A Monumental Critique of Empire, from Napoleonic to Corporate Times," *Hyperallergic*, May 23, 2016, https://hyperallergic.com/300410/a-monumental-critique-of-empire-from-napoleon-to-corporate-times/

93. Tarbox, "A Monumental Critique of Empire, from Napoleonic to Corporate Times"; Jackie Wullschlager, "Huang Yong Ping's 'Empires' at Monumenta," *Financial Times*, May 7, 2016, https://www.ft.com/content/522afd5a-11dc-11e6-91da-096d89bd2173

94. De Loisy quoted in Nathan, "At Monumenta 2016."

95. "Exhibition Guide: Huang Yong Ping, *Empires*."

96. "2016 Financial Results: CMA CGM Maintains a Positive Core EBIT Margin Despite Historically Low Freight Rates," March 10, 2017, https://cmacgm-group.com/en/news-media/2016-financial-results-cma-cgm-maintains-positive-core-ebit-margin-despite-historically

97. For details on the project, see "Press Release: CMA CGM at the Heart of Huang Yong Ping's Monumenta 2016 Art Installation," April 27, 2016, https://cmacgm-group.com/en/news-media/cma-cgm-heart-huang-yong-pings-monumenta-2016-art-installation; see also Claudia Barbieri, "Huang Yong Ping Brings 'Empires' of Globalization to Paris," *Arts Beat, New York Times Blog*, May 6, 2016, https://artsbeat.blogs.nytimes.com/2016/05/06/huang-yong-ping-brings-empires-of-globalization-to-paris/

98. "CMA CGM at the Heart of Huang Yong Ping's Monumenta 2016 Art Installation."

99. See "CMA CGM: Highlights of 2016," December 23, 2016, https://cmacgm-group.com/en/news-media/cma-cgm-highlights-2016; Kentaro Iwamoto, "Asian Shipping Lines Navigate a War of Attrition," *Financial Times*, November 28, 2016, https://www.ft.com/content/f20b0ab0-b338-11e6-9c37-5787335499a0

100. De Loisy quoted in Tarbox, "A Monumental Critique of Empire."

101. "Exhibition Guide: Huang Yong Ping, Empires."

102. "CMA CGM at the Heart of Huang Yong Ping's Monumenta 2016 Art Installation."

103. Chua, "The Container," 41. On the shipping container as a synecdoche, see Toscano and Kinkle, *Cartographies of the Absolute*, 196.

104. See Nathan, "At Monumenta 2016."

105. See Qi Luo, *China's Industrial Reform and Open-Door Policy, 1980–1997: A Case Study from Xiamen* (Aldershot, UK: Ashgate, 2001).

106. "100 Ports 2020," *Lloyd's List,* 2020, https://lloydslist.maritimeintelligence.informa.com/one-hundred-container-ports-2020

107. Bentzel, "Assessment of the People's Republic of China's Control of Container and Intermodal Chassis Manufacturing," 8.

108. See "Belt and Road in the Great Game," *Chuang*, September 17, 2019, https://chuangcn.org/2019/09/belt-road-great-game/; Jonathan E. Hillman, *The Emperor's New Road: China and the Project of the Century* (New Haven, CT: Yale University Press, 2020); Laleh Khalili, "Growing Pains," *London Review of Books*, March 18, 2021, https://www.lrb.co.uk/the-paper/v43/n06/laleh-khalili/growing-pains

109. Cowen, *Deadly Life of Logistics*, 67.

110. Eli Friedman, "The Urbanization of the Chinese Working Class," *Jacobin*, October 3, 2014, https://www.jacobinmag.com/2014/10/the-urbanization-of-the-chinese-working-class; see also "The Changing Geography of Chinese Industry: Data Brief," *Chuang*, August 5, 2019, https://chuangcn.org/2019/08/the-changing-geography-of-chinese-industry-data-brief/; Eli Friedman, *The Urbanization of People: The Politics of Development, Labor Markets, and Schooling in the Chinese City* (New York: Columbia University Press, 2022).

111. Minhua Ling, "Container Housing: Formal Informality and Deterritorialised Home-Making amid Bulldozer Urbanism in Shanghai," *Urban Studies* 58, no. 6 (May 2021): 1141–1157.

112. Cowen, *Deadly Life of Logistics*, 8.

113. Chua, "The Container," 42.

114. Details about *Jonah's Whale* not footnoted are from my interview with Nida Sinnokrot on September 17, 2021, and subsequent e-mail correspondence.

115. Eyal Weizman, *Hollow Land: Israel's Architecture of Occupation* (London: Verso, 2017), 5. Thanks to Callie Maidhof for detailing to me the context for the use of shipping containers in settler outposts. On the history of settlements, including outposts, see Michael Feige, *Settling in the Hearts: Jewish Fundamentalism in the Occupied Territories* (Detroit: Wayne State University Press, 2009); Gershom Gorenberg, *The Accidental Empire: Israel and the Birth of Settlements, 1967–1977* (New York: Times Books, 2006); Ariel Handel, Marco Allegra, and Erez Maggor, eds., *Normalizing Occupation: The Politics of Everyday Life in the West Bank Settlements* (Bloomington: Indiana University Press, 2017); Samantha M. Shapiro, "The Unsettlers," *New York Times Magazine*, February 16, 2003, https://www.nytimes.com/2003/02/16/magazine/the-unsettlers.html

116. Dror Etkes quoted in Joel Greenberg, "Road Map Won't Succeed, Israeli Outpost Settlers Vow," *Chicago Tribune*, June 4, 2003, https://www.chicagotribune.com/news/ct-xpm-2003-06-04-0306040251-story.html

117. Weizman, *Hollow Land,* 5.

118. Weizman, *Hollow Land,* 8.

119. Weizman, *Hollow Land,* 5.

120. W. J. T. Mitchell, "Imperial Landscape," in *Landscape and Power,* 2nd ed., ed. W. J. T. Mitchell (Chicago: University of Chicago Press, 2002), 5–34, quote at 10. See also Denis E. Cosgrove, *Social Formation and Symbolic Landscape* (Madison: University of Wisconsin Press, 1998).

121. Iyko Day, *Alien Capital: Asian Racialization and the Logic of Settler Colonial Capitalism* (Durham, NC: Duke University Press, 2016), 73–114. See also Gary Fields, *Enclosure: Palestinian Landscapes in a Historical Mirror* (Oakland: University of California Press, 2017).

122. *Ka (Oslo)* received wide attention when it was featured on the cover of *Artforum* in August 2021. This was the third and largest iteration of the *Ka* series, which Sinnokrot started in 2009.

123. Nida Sinnokrot, "Sublime Pathos," May 11, 2012, https://www.nidasinnokrot.com/text/ka/

124. Kareem Rabie, *Palestine Is Throwing a Party and the Whole World Is Invited: Capital and State Building in the West Bank* (Durham, NC: Duke University Press, 2021), 20.

125. On Rawabi, see Ali Abunimah, "Role of Israeli Firms Raises Boycott Concerns about Rawabi," *Electronic Intifada*, December 30, 2010, https://electronicintifada.net/content/role-israeli-firms-raises-boycott-concerns-about-rawabi/9162; Palestinian BDS National Committee, "Palestinian Civil Society Denounces Bashar Masri's Normalization with Israel as Undermining the Struggle for Palestinian Rights," September 10, 2012, https://bdsmovement.net/news/palestinian-civil-society-denounces-bashar-masri%E2%80%99s-normalization-israel-undermining-struggle; Rabie, *Palestine Is Throwing a Party and the Whole World Is Invited.*

126. Nida Sinnokrot, "Jonah's Whale," 2014, https://www.nidasinnokrot.com/text/jonah-s-whale/

127. Nida Sinnokrot, "Caravans: Press Release," 2014, https://www.nidasinnokrot.com/text/caravans-exhibition/; themes of mortgage and debt run through much of Sinnokrot's recent work. See, for example, *Ya Ghanamati* (Billboard no. 02) (2014), which reuses a mechanical billboard like those that advertise mortgages in the West Bank. As Sinnokrot has explained to me, these billboards also connect to *Jonah's Whale* through their shared use of corrugated metal, a technology invented in the nineteenth century by the British engineer Henry Robinson Palmer, who is credited with developing an early theory of containerization.

Chapter Four

1. Ashutosh Dekhne, Greg Hastings, John Murnane, and Florian Neuhaus, "Automation in Logistics: Big Opportunity, Bigger Uncertainty," *McKinsey & Company*, April 24, 2019, https://www.mckinsey.com/industries/travel-logistics-and-infrastructure/our-insights/automation-in-logistics-big-opportunity-bigger-uncertainty

2. Aisha Chottani, Greg Hastings, John Murnane, and Florian Neuhaus, "Distraction or Disruption? Autonomous Trucks Gain Ground in US Logistics," *McKinsey &*

Company, December 10, 2018, https://www.mckinsey.com/industries/travel-logistics-and-infrastructure/our-insights/distraction-or-disruption-autonomous-trucks-gain-ground-in-us-logistics; on the current state of logistics automation technology, see Christopher Mims, *Arriving Today: From Factory to Front Door—Why Everything Has Changed About How and What We Buy* (New York: Harper Business, 2021), 67–86.

3. Alessandro Delfanti, *The Warehouse: Workers and Robots at Amazon* (London: Pluto Press, 2021), 117–118. On Amazon's drone patents specifically, see also Arthur Holland Michel, "Amazon's Drone Patents," Center for the Study of the Drone, September 2017, https://dronecenter.bard.edu/files/2017/09/CSD-Amazons-Drone-Patents-1.pdf

4. Delfanti, *The Warehouse*, 112–141.

5. Delfanti, *The Warehouse*, 118.

6. McKinsey & Company, *Containerization: The Key to Low-Cost Transport* (London: Report for British Transport Docks Board, 1967), 77.

7. Mims, *Arriving Today*, 79.

8. Sianne Ngai, *Theory of the Gimmick: Aesthetic Judgment and Capitalist Form* (Cambridge, MA: Harvard University Press, 2020), 2.

9. Ngai, *Theory of the Gimmick*, 8.

10. On this "law," see chap. 25 of Karl Marx, *Capital: A Critique of Political Economy, Volume 1*, trans. Ben Fowkes (London: Penguin Classics, 1990), 762–870.

11. Jason E. Smith, *Smart Machines and Service Work: Automation in an Age of Stagnation* (London: Reaktion Books, 2020), 11. See also Aaron Benanav, *Automation and the Future of Work* (London: Verso, 2020).

12. Leigh Phillips and Michal Rozworski, *The People's Republic of Walmart: How the World's Biggest Corporations Are Laying the Foundation for Socialism* (London: Verso, 2019), 77.

13. Christopher Fuller, "The CIA's Drone War and the Civilianization of Warfare," in *The Civilianization of War*, ed. Andrew Barros and Martin Thomas (Cambridge, UK: Cambridge University Press, 2018), 221–240; Mark Neocleous, "Air Power as Police Power," *Environment and Planning D: Society and Space* 31, no. 4 (2013): 578–593; Philip Olson and Christine Labuski, "'There's Always a [White] Man in the Loop': The Gendered and Racialized Politics of Civilian Drones," *Social Studies of Science* 48, no. 4 (2018): 540–563; Ian Shaw, "The Urbanization of Drone Warfare: Policing Surplus Populations in the Dronepolis," *Geographica Helvetica* 71, no. 1 (2016): 19–28. The literature on the history of drones is extensive. See, for example, Medea Benjamin, *Drone Warfare: Killing by Remote Control* (London: Verso, 2013); Grégoire Chamayou, *A Theory of the Drone*, trans. Janet Lloyd (New York: New Press, 2015); Katherine Chandler, *Unmanning: How Humans, Machines, and Media Perform Drone Warfare* (Newark, NJ: Rutgers University Press, 2020); Lisa Parks and Caren Kaplan, eds., *Life in the Age of Drone Warfare* (Durham, NC: Duke University Press, 2017); Adam Rothstein, *Drone* (New York: Bloomsbury Academic, 2015).

14. Rothstein, *Drone*, 135–36.

15. For the broadcast transcript and video, see "Amazon's Jeff Bezos Looks to the Future," *60 Minutes*, December 1, 2013, https://www.cbsnews.com/news/amazons-jeff-bezos-looks-to-the-future/ (accessed February 2, 2024).

16. For the first commercial, see Amazon, "Amazon Prime Air," YouTube, December 2, 2013, https://www.youtube.com/watch?v=98BIu9dpwHU

17. For the commercial featuring Jeremy Clarkson, see Amazon, "Amazon Prime Air," YouTube, November 29, 2015, https://www.youtube.com/watch?v=MXo_d6tNWuY

18. See Samira Shackle, "The Mystery of the Gatwick Drone," *The Guardian*, December 1, 2020, https://www.theguardian.com/uk-news/2020/dec/01/the-mystery-of-the-gatwick-drone

19. For Amazon's latest update on Prime Air at the time of writing, see Amazon Staff, "Amazon Is Launching Ultra-Fast Drone Deliveries in the UK, Italy, and a Third Location in the U.S.," *About Amazon*, October 18, 2023, https://www.aboutamazon.co.uk/news/operations/amazon-prime-air-drone-delivery-updates; see also Callum Jones, "Amazon Unveils Plan to Deliver Packages by Drone in UK and Italy," *The Guardian*, October 18, 2023, https://theguardian.com/technology/2023/oct/18/amazon-drone-delivery-uk-italy; on Amazon's drone rivals, see Jiayang Fan, "How E-Commerce Is Transforming Rural China," *New Yorker*, July 16, 2018, https://www.newyorker.com/magazine/2018/07/23/how-e-commerce-is-transforming-rural-china

20. See X, the moonshot factory, "Introducing Project Wing," YouTube, August 29, 2014, https://www.youtube.com/watch?v=cRTNvWcx9Oo

21. In 2022, Amazon's shipping costs were $83.5 billion. See Daniela Coppola, "Amazon's Shipping Costs from 2011 to 2022," *Statista*, February 15, 2023, https://www.statista.com/statistics/806498/amazon-shipping-costs/

22. On Amazon and the last mile, see Brad Stone, *Amazon Unbound: Jeff Bezos and the Invention of a Global Empire* (New York: Simon & Schuster, 2022), 213–243. On the history of Amazon and its shipping infrastructure, see Jake Alimahomed-Wilson and Ellen Reese, eds., *The Cost of Free Shipping: Amazon in the Global Economy* (London: Pluto Press, 2020); Delfanti, *The Warehouse*; Alec MacGillis, *Fulfillment: America in the Shadow of Amazon* (New York: Picador, 2022).

23. Stone, *Amazon Unbound*, 233.

24. Stone, *Amazon Unbound*, 194–196.

25. Brian Heater, "Amazon's Scout Robot Deliveries Expand to Additional Cities in Georgia and Tennessee," *TechCrunch*, July 21, 2020, https://techcrunch.com/2020/07/21/amazons-scout-robot-deliveries-expand-to-additional-cities-in-georgia-and-tennessee/; Amazon stopped public trials of Scout in late 2022, raising questions whether the project would be axed alongside others as the company tried to trim costs. See Brian Heater, "The Last Mile," *TechCrunch*, October 1, 2022, https://techcrunch.com/2022/10/13/the-last-mile/

26. Ngai, *Theory of the Gimmick*, 134.

27. Ngai, *Theory of the Gimmick*, 83.

28. Jeffrey Bezos, "2013 Letter to Shareholders," *About Amazon*, April 2014, https://s2.q4cdn.com/299287126/files/doc_financials/annual/2013-Letter-to-Shareholders.pdf; the letter is also available at https://ir.aboutamazon.com/annual-reports-proxies-and-shareholder-letters/default.aspx

29. Amazon Staff, "What You Can Expect to See on a Warehouse Tour," *About Amazon*, March 12, 2019, https://www.aboutamazon.com/news/operations/inside-amazons-fulfillment-centers-what-you-can-expect-to-see-on-a-warehouse-tour

30. Amazon Staff, "What You Can Expect to See on a Warehouse Tour."

31. On the Kiva bots, see Delfanti, *The Warehouse*, 49–52; Stone, *Amazon Unbound*, 223–224. For an overview of the organization and operations of Amazon's fulfillment centers, including the use of Kiva bots, see Mims, *Arriving Today*, 159–176.

32. On the Ford factory tour, see Dara Orenstein, *Out of Stock: The Warehouse in the History of Capitalism* (Chicago: University of Chicago Press, 2019), 16–18.

33. Sarah Miller, "Unfulfilled at the Amazon Tour," *The Outline*, August 26, 2019, https://theoutline.com/post/7879/amazon-fulfillment-center-tour

34. See *GigCo*, made by the Canadian artist collective SpekWork: https://gigco.app

35. Heike Geissler, *Seasonal Associate*, trans. Katy Derbyshire (South Pasadena, CA: Semiotext(e), 2018), 211.

36. André Spicer, "Amazon's 'Worker Cage' Has Been Dropped, but Its Staff Are Not Free," *The Guardian*, September 14, 2018, https://www.theguardian.com/commentisfree/2018/sep/14/amazon-worker-cage-staff; see also Kate Crawford and Vladan Joler, "Anatomy of an AI System: The Amazon Echo as an Anatomical Map of Human Labor, Data and Planetary Resources," *AI Now Lab/Share Institute*, September 7, 2018, https://anatomyof.ai/

37. Geissler, *Seasonal Associate*, 212. On work conditions at Amazon, see Delfanti, *The Warehouse*; Gabriel Mac, "I Was a Warehouse Wage Slave," *Mother Jones*, April 2012, https://www.motherjones.com/politics/2012/02/mac-mcclelland-free-online-shipping-warehouses-labor/; MacGillis, *Fulfillment*; Mims, *Arriving Today*, 197–220. On workers organizing at Amazon, see Charmaine Chua and Spencer Cox, "Battling the Behemoth: Amazon and the Rise of America's New Working Class," *Socialist Register* 59 (2023): 120–140.

38. About Amazon Team, "5 Facts to Know About Amazon Robotics," *About Amazon*, August 31, 2018, https://www.aboutamazon.eu/news/innovation/5-facts-to-know-about-amazon-robotics

39. About Amazon Team, "5 Facts to Know About Amazon Robotics."

40. Karen Weise, "Pushed by Pandemic, Amazon Goes on a Hiring Spree Without Equal," *New York Times*, November 27, 2020, https://www.nytimes.com/2020/11/27/technology/pushed-by-pandemic-amazon-goes-on-a-hiring-spree-without-equal.html

41. Weise, "Pushed by Pandemic, Amazon Goes on a Hiring Spree Without Equal."

42. Amazon Staff, "10 Years of Amazon Robotics: How Robots Help Sort Packages, Move Product, and Improve Safety," *About Amazon*, June 21, 2022,

https://www.aboutamazon.com/news/operations/10-years-of-amazon-robotics-how-robots-help-sort-packages-move-product-and-improve-safety; Scott Dresser, "Amazon Announces 2 New Ways It's Using Robots to Assist Employees and Deliver for Customers," *About Amazon,* October 18, 2023, https://www.aboutamazon.com/news/operations/amazon-introduces-new-robotics-solutions

43. Harry Braverman, *Labor and Monopoly Capital: The Degradation of Work in the Twentieth Century* (New York: Monthly Review Press, 1974).

44. Delfanti, *The Warehouse*, 52.

45. On employee turnover at Amazon, see Mims, *Arriving Today*, 209–211. Before the COVID-19 pandemic, Amazon was losing 150 percent of its workforce annually, a rate that was nearly double that of the logistics and retail industries. See Jodi Kantor, Karen Weise, and Grace Ashford, "The Amazon That Customers Don't See," *New York Times,* June 15, 2021, https://www.nytimes.com/interactive/2021/06/15/us/amazon-workers.html; an internal document leaked in 2022 suggested that this churn could be costing Amazon $8 billion annually; see Luciana Paulise, "Amazon's High Attrition Could Cost $8 Billion Annually," *Forbes,* October 27, 2022, https://www.forbes.com/sites/lucianapaulise/2022/10/27/amazons-high-attrition-could-cost-8-billion-annually/

46. Braverman, *Labor and Monopoly Capital*, 236–237.

47. Trip Gabriel, "Alone on the Open Road: Truckers Feel Like 'Throwaway People,'" *New York Times*, May 22, 2017, https://www.nytimes.com/2017/05/22/us/trucking-jobs.html

48. Delfanti, *The Warehouse*, 116.

49. Quoted in Delfanti, *The Warehouse,* 121. On the challenges to automating logistics work at Amazon, see Mims, *Arriving Today*, 177–196, 241–250.

50. In 2019, Amazon reported that only twenty-six, or 15 percent, of its fulfillment centers included robots. In total, Amazon is believed to have over 1,500 logistics hubs of some kind, like sortation centers and delivery stations. Mims, *Arriving Today*, 201.

51. Delfanti, *The Warehouse*, 38–41; Mims, *Arriving Today*, 173–187.

52. Phillips and Rozworski, *The People's Republic of Walmart*, 80.

53. On drones and art, see Ronak K. Kapadia, *Insurgent Aesthetics: Security and the Queer Life of the Forever War* (Durham, NC: Duke University Press, 2019), 44–75; Dominique Routhier, "Picasso's Drone," *b2o*, November 16, 2021, https://www.boundary2.org/2021/11/dominique-routhier-picassos-drone/; Thomas Stubblefield, *Drone Art: The Everywhere War as Medium* (Berkeley: University of California Press, 2020).

54. See Elise Morrison, *Discipline and Desire: Surveillance Technologies in Performance* (Ann Arbor: University of Michigan Press, 2016), 230–267.

55. Ian Frazier, "The Trippy, High-Speed World of Drone Racing," *New Yorker*, January 29, 2018, https://www.newyorker.com/magazine/2018/02/05/the-trippy-high-speed-world-of-drone-racing

56. Rothstein, *Drone*, 107.

57. Michael Paulson, "After Two New York Flops, Cirque du Soleil Bets Big on Broadway," *New York Times*, April 13, 2016, https://www.nytimes.com/2016/04/17/theater/cirque-du-soleils-broadwaybalancingact.html; Tyler Petersen, "Verity Studios Brings Drones to Broadway in Cirque du Soleil's Paramour," *Broadway World*, May 31, 2016, https://www.broadwayworld.com/article/Verity-Studios-Brings-Drones-to-Broadway-in-Cirque-du-Soleils-PARAMOUR-20160531

58. Gordon Cox, "Cirque du Soleil's 'Paramour' to Move Out When Theater Closes for Renovations," *Variety*, December 1, 2016, https://variety.com/2016/legit/news/paramour-moving-cirque-du-soleil-broadway-1201931474/; Staff, "Harry Potter and the Cursed Child Smashing Records Even Before Opening," *Sydney Morning Herald*, April 15, 2018, https://www.smh.com.au/entertainment/theatre/harry-potter-and-the-cursed-child-smashing-records-even-before-opening-20180415-hoyscc.html

59. Raffaello D'Andrea quoted in Gordon Cox, "Drones Make Theater, Not War in Broadway 'Paramour,'" *Variety*, May 25, 2016, https://variety.com/2016/legit/news/paramour-drones-cirque-du-soleil-broadway-1201782129/; Cirque previously collaborated with Verity Studios two years earlier on the short film *Sparked* (2014), which used the lampshade drones as magical accoutrement in a sorcerer's apprentice-like story. See Cirque du Soleil, "SPARKED: A Live Interaction Between Humans and Quadcopters," YouTube, September 22, 2014, https://www.youtube.com/watch?v=6C8OJsHfmpI

60. Mark Swed, "Epic, Extravagant: In Ka the Acrobatics and Dazzling Special Effects Are Stunning and Enchanting," *Los Angeles Times*, February 5, 2005, https://www.latimes.com/archives/la-xpm-2005-feb-05-et-ka5-story.html; see also Katie Lavers, "Cirque du Soleil and Its Roots in Illegitimate Circus," *M/C: A Journal of Media and Culture* 17, no. 5, 2014, https://doi.org/10.5204/mcj.882

61. Scott Zieger quoted in Cox, "Drones Make Theater, Not War in Broadway 'Paramour.'"

62. Erin Hurley, "The Multiple Bodies of Cirque du Soleil," in *Cirque Global: Quebec's Expanding Circus Boundaries*, ed. Louis Patrick Leroux and Charles R. Batson (Montreal: McGill-Queen's University Press, 2016), 122–139, quote at 123.

63. Jen Harvie and Erin Hurley, "States of Play: Locating Quebec in the Performances of Robert Lepage, Ex Machina, and the Cirque du Soleil," *Theatre Journal* 51, no. 3 (1999): 299–315, quote at 300.

64. Smith, *Smart Machines and Service Work*, 118; on skilled labor, see 123–124.

65. For a history of Kiva Systems, see Mims, *Arriving Today*, 163–170. On the history of Verity Studios, see Marianne Lucien, "Night at the Warehouse," *ETH Zürich*, August 11, 2021, https://ethz.ch/en/news-and-events/eth-news/news/2021/08/verity-drones-warehouse.html

66. On the Flying Machine Arena, see https://www.flyingmachinearena.ethz.ch/history/

67. "Verity Studios Obtains $18 Million for Drone Shows," *Wall Street Journal*, June 5, 2018, https://www.wsj.com/articles/verity-studios-obtains-18-million-for-drone-shows-1528232468

68. See Lucien, "Night at the Warehouse." During this time, D'Andrea also published on drone delivery. See Raffaello D'Andrea, "Can Drones Deliver?," *IEEE Transactions on Automation Science and Engineering* 11, no. 3 (2014): 647–648.

69. See https://verity.net/ (accessed November 10, 2023).

70. Lucien, "Night at the Warehouse."

71. Staff, "How Tech for Show Business Can Automate IKEA Warehouses," Ikea .com, November 19, 2020, https://www.ikea.com/global/en/stories/design/how-tech-for-show-business-can-automate-ikea-warehouses-201119/

72. Raffaello D'Andrea, "Meet the Dazzling Flying Machines of the Future," *TED Talks*, 2016, https://www.ted.com/talks/raffaello_d_andrea_meet_the_dazzling_flying_machines_of_the_future

73. Intel sold their drone business to Kimbal Musk in 2022, as part of a consolidation effort. See Dylan Martin, "Elon Musk's Brother Buys Intel's Fireworks-Replacing Drone Biz," *The Register*, July 5, 2022, https://www.theregister.com/2022/07/05/elon_musks_brother_buys_intels/

74. Recording available at Britain's Got Talent, "Flying Bebop and Their Drones Are Out of This World," YouTube, May 24, 2016, https://www.youtube.com/watch?v=cwNwdN2tpqY

75. See the company's website: https://www.dronisos.com/; corporate details based on information formerly available on BeTomorrow's website (https://www.betomorrow.com/en/our-projects/dronisos, accessed October 23, 2016) and my interview with then-managing director of BeTomorrow UK, John McKenna, in October 2016.

76. "Parrot + Dronisos: Imagining the Future of Drone Automation," *Parrot*, August 5, 2020, https://www.parrot.com/uk/newsroom/parrot-dronisos-future-of-drone-automation

77. Laura Cumming, "Anicka Yi's Turbine Hall," *The Guardian*, October 17, 2021, https://www.theguardian.com/artanddesign/2021/oct/17/anicka-yi-in-love-with-the-world-turbine-hall-tate-modern-hyundai-commission-review-sutapa-biswas-lumen-review; see also Tate Modern, "Exhibition Guide: Hyundai Commission: Anicka Yi, in Love with the World," n.d., https://www.tate.org.uk/whats-on/tate-modern/exhibition/hyundai-commission-anicka-yi/exhibition-guide

78. See the Pozyx company website at https://www.pozyx.io/ (accessed November 10, 2023).

79. Elly Schietse, "Pozyx Inspires Artist Anicka Yi in Tate Modern Museum," Pozyx.Io, October 13, 2021, https://www.pozyx.io/newsroom/pozyx-inspires-artist-anicka-yi-in-tate-modern-museum

80. Martin Ford, *The Rise of the Robots: Technology and the Threat of Mass Unemployment* (New York: Basic Books, 2015).

81. William J. Baumol and William G Bowen, *Performing Arts: The Economic Dilemma* (Cambridge, MA: MIT Press, 1966). For Baumol's influence on Marxist debates over automation today, see Smith, *Smart Machines and Service Work*, 72–91.

82. Cirque blamed its insolvency on the pandemic, but when the first cases of the novel coronavirus were recorded in December 2019, its ledgers showed a debt of nearly $1 billion, much of it saddled onto the company by TPG Capital, which had taken lead ownership over Cirque 2015. See Dan Bilefsky, "Will Cirque du Soleil Rise Again?," *New York Times*, May 17, 2020, https://www.nytimes.com/2020/05/17/world/canada/cirque-du-soleil-coronavirus-debt.html; Dan Bilefsky, "Cirque du Soleil's Return Could Be Its Most Challenging Feat Yet," *New York Times*, May 9, 2021, https://www.nytimes.com/2021/05/09/world/canada/cirque-du-soleil-returns.html; Andrew Hill, "Cirque du Soleil's Daniel Lamarre: From $1bn to Zero Revenues in 48 Hours," *Financial Times*, January 9, 2022, https://www.ft.com/content/c29d17f7-368f-457b-acc2-76f9aea7a812; Robin Wigglesworth, "Coronavirus: Is Investment Management the Weak Link?," *Financial Times*, April 13, 2020, https://www.ft.com/content/d9812fee-798a-11ea-9840-1b8019d9a987

83. Daniel Susskind, *A World Without Work: Technology, Automation, and How We Should Respond* (London: Allen Lane, 2020). On the "automation discourse" from this time, see Benanav, *Automation and the Future of Work*, 1–13.

84. Delfanti, *The Warehouse*, 11.

85. Gabriel Winant, *The Next Shift: The Fall of Industry and the Rise of Health Care in Rust Belt America* (Cambridge, MA: Harvard University Press, 2021), 261.

86. Robert Brenner, "Escalating Plunder," *New Left Review*, no. 123 (June 2020): 5–22. On Amazon's COVID-19 profits, see Dave Lee, "Amazon Reaps Rewards of Pandemic Shift Online," *Financial Times*, April 19, 2021, https://ft.com/content/a2b05040-3164-46f3-8bd5-399e6214ea74

87. Ngai, *Theory of the Gimmick*, 6. For Marx on the moving contradiction, see Karl Marx, *Grundrisse: Foundations of the Critique of Political Economy*, trans. Martin Nicolaus (London: Penguin Classics, 1993), 706.

88. Ngai, *Theory of the Gimmick*, 6.

89. Staff, "New Robots—Smarter and Faster—Are Taking over Warehouses," *Economist*, February 12, 2022, https://www.economist.com/science-and-technology/a-new-generation-of-smarter-and-faster-robots-are-taking-over-distribution-centres/21807595

90. Carey Dunne, "Norman Foster's High-Concept Drone Airport Will Bring Aid to Rwanda," *Hyperallergic*, June 7, 2016, https://hyperallergic.com/302295/norman-fosters-high-concept-drone-airport-will-bring-aid-to-rwanda/

91. Foster + Partners, "Press Release: Norman Foster's Droneport Prototype Goes on Show at the Venice Biennale 2016," May 27, 2016, https://www.fosterandpartners.com/news/norman-foster-s-droneport-prototype-goes-on-show-at-the-venice-biennale-2016; project details—including photographs, blueprints, and videos—are available on the websites of Foster + Partners (https://www.fosterandpartners.com/projects/droneport/) and the Norman Foster Foundation (https://normanfosterfoundation.org/?project=droneport).

92. Foster + Partners, "Press Release." See also Zoe Flood, "From Killing Machines to Agents of Hope: The Future of Drones in Africa," *The Guardian*, July 27, 2016, https://www.theguardian.com/world/2016/jul/27/africas-drone-rwanda-zipline-kenya-kruger

93. Adrian Anagnost, "Craft and Conquest: The 15th Venice Architecture Biennale, May 28–November 27, 2016," *Nonsite*, no. 20 (2017), https://nonsite.org/craft-and-conquest/; Rowan Moore, "Venice Architecture Biennale 2016: Ideas for Real World Problems," *The Guardian*, May 29, 2016, https://www.theguardian.com/artanddesign/2016/may/29/venice-architecture-biennale-2016-review-norman-foster

94. Anna Fixsen, "Interview with Norman Foster on Droneports and His New Foundation," *Architectural Record*, June 21, 2016, https://www.architecturalrecord.com/articles/11750-interview-with-norman-foster-on-droneports-and-his-new-foundation

95. Anagnost, "Craft and Conquest."

96. Jonathan Ledgard, "A Radical but Possible Plan to Connect African Nations with Cargo Drones," *Wired*, September 22, 2014, https://www.wired.com/2014/09/cargo-drones-in-africa/; early on, Ledgard referred to drones as donkeys, a choice he attributed to a Samburu elder in Kenya whom he claimed had drawn the comparison after Ledgard introduced him to the idea of drone delivery.

97. Jonathan Ledgard and Scott Macmillan, "Drones for Development," *Project Syndicate*, June 5, 2015, https://www.project-syndicate.org/commentary/drones-africa-development-by-j-m-ledgard-and-scott-macmillan-2015-06

98. See Andy Lockhart, Aidan While, Simon Marvin, Mateja Kovacic, Nancy Odendaal, and Christian Alexander, "Making Space for Drones: The Contested Reregulation of Airspace in Tanzania and Rwanda," *Transactions of the Institute of British Geographers* 46, no. 4 (December 2021): 850–865, at 859; Ben Taub, "Jonathan Ledgard Believes Imagination Could Save the World," *New Yorker*, September 23, 2019, https://www.newyorker.com/magazine/2019/09/23/jonathan-ledgard-believes-imagination-could-save-the-world

99. On Zipline, see Alex Konrad and Kenrick Cai, "Drone Delivery Startup Zipline Boosts Valuation To $4.2 Billion," *Forbes*, April 28, 2023, https://www.forbes.com/sites/alexkonrad/2023/04/28/drone-delivery-startup-zipline-boosts-valuation-to-4-billion/; Kirsten Korosec, "Zipline Is Now the National Drone Service Provider for Rwanda," *TechCrunch*, December 15, 2022, https://techcrunch.com/2022/12/15/zipline-is-now-the-national-drone-service-provider-for-rwanda/; Max Levy, "Drones Have Transformed Blood Delivery in Rwanda," *Wired*, April 21, 2022, https://www.wired.com/story/drones-have-transformed-blood-delivery-in-rwanda/; Rene Umlauf and Marian Burchardt, "Infrastructure-as-a-Service: Empty Skies, Bad Roads, and the Rise of Cargo Drones," *Environment and Planning A: Economy and Space* 54, no. 8 (2022): 1489–1509, https://doi.org/10.1177/0308518X221118915

100. Foster + Partners, "Press Release."

101. Ledgard, "A Radical but Possible Plan to Connect African Nations with Cargo Drones."

102. For an overview of the debates over delivery drones in Africa, focusing on Rwanda and Tanzania, see Andy Lockhart et al., "Making Space for Drones"; Umlauf and Burchardt, "Infrastructure-as-a-Service."

103. Foster + Partners, "Press Release."

104. Walter Rodney, *How Europe Underdeveloped Africa* (Washington, DC: Howard University Press, 1981), 209.

105. Rodney, *How Europe Underdeveloped Africa*, 209.

Epilogue

1. Nantina Vgontzas, "Toward Degrowth: Worker Power, Surveillance Abolition, and Climate Justice at Amazon," *New Global Studies* 16, no. 1 (May 3, 2022): 49–67. On degrowth and infrastructure, see also Jason Hickel, *Less Is More: How Degrowth Will Save the World* (London: Penguin Random House, 2020); Kōhei Saitō, *Marx in the Anthropocene: Towards the Idea of Degrowth Communism* (Cambridge, UK: Cambridge University Press, 2022), 216–244; Matthias Schmelzer, Aaron Vansintjan, and Andrea Vetter, *The Future Is Degrowth: A Guide to a World Beyond Capitalism* (London: Verso, 2022).

2. See Aaron Bastani, *Fully Automated Luxury Communism: A Manifesto* (London: Verso, 2019); Leigh Phillips and Michal Rozworski, *The People's Republic of Walmart: How the World's Biggest Corporations Are Laying the Foundation for Socialism* (London: Verso, 2019); Nick Srnicek and Alex Williams, *Inventing the Future: Postcapitalism and a World Without Work* (London: Verso, 2015).

3. Out of the Woods, "Disaster Communism Part 3—Logistics, Repurposing, Bricolage," *Libcom,* May 22, 2014, http://libcom.org/blog/disaster-communism-part-3-logistics-repurposing-bricolage-22052014

4. Andreas Malm, *How to Blow up a Pipeline: Learning to Fight in a World on Fire* (London: Verso, 2021).

5. Jason Burke, Kamal Ahmed, and Lars Bevanger, "Inquiry into Shooting of Protesters," *The Guardian,* June 17, 2001, https://theguardian.com/world/2001/jun/17/jasonburke.kamalahmed

6. Alberto Toscano, "Lineaments of the Logistical State," *Viewpoint Magazine,* no. 4, September 28, 2014, http://viewpointmag.com/2014/09/28/lineaments-of-the-logistical-state

7. For example, see the details for "Day-Tripping the Petrocapital" (2016–) on Borcilă's website: https://borcila.com/projects/day-tripping-the-petrocapital

8. For details—including images, video, and press of *Slave Rebellion Reenactment* (2019)—see the artist's website: https://www.dreadscott.net/portfolio_page/slave-rebellion-reenactment/

9. Deborah Cowen, *The Deadly Life of Logistics: Mapping Violence in Global Trade* (Minneapolis: University of Minnesota Press, 2014), 229.

10. See, for example, Martín Arboleda, *Planetary Mine: Territories of Extraction Under Late Capitalism* (London: Verso, 2020), 109; Katy Fox-Hodess, "How Dockworkers Are Fighting the Arms Trade," *The Nation,* July 16, 2019, https://www.thenation.com/article/archive/dockworkers-saudi-yemen-strike/

11. See Jake Alimahomed-Wilson and Immanuel Ness, eds., *Choke Points: Logistics Workers Disrupting the Global Supply Chain* (London: Pluto Press, 2018); The Invisible Committee, *The Coming Insurrection* (Cambridge, MA: Semiotext(e), 2009).

12. Charmaine Chua and Kai Bosworth, "Beyond the Chokepoint: Blockades as Social Struggles," *Antipode* 55, no. 5 (2023): 1301–1320, quote at 1306.

13. Chua and Bosworth, "Beyond the Chokepoint," 1303. For debates around the Port of Oakland blockade, see Jasper Bernes, "Logistics, Counterlogistics and the Communist Prospect," *Endnotes* 3, 2013, https://endnotes.org.uk/articles/logistics-counterlogistics-and-the-communist-prospect; Charmaine Chua, "Logistical Violence, Logistical Vulnerabilities," *Historical Materialism* 25, no. 4 (February 2017): 167–182, at 178; Rust Bunny Collective, "Under the Riot Gear," *SIC: International Journal for Communisation* 2, January 2014, https://www.sicjournal.org/311-2/index.html; Society of Enemies, "Blockading the Port Is Only the First of Many Last Resorts," *Libcom,* December 7, 2011, https://libcom.org/article/blockading-port-only-first-many-last-resorts; Toscano, "Lineaments of the Logistical State."

14. Søren Mau, *Mute Compulsion: A Marxist Theory of the Economic Power of Capital* (London: Verso, 2023), 290; italics in the original.

15. On these and other examples, see Alimahomed-Wilson and Ness, *Choke Points*; Sergio Bologna, "Inside Logistics: Organization, Work, Distinctions," *Viewpoint Magazine*, October 29, 2014, https://viewpointmag.com/2014/10/29/inside-logistics-organization-work-distinctions/; Edna Bonacich, "Pulling the Plug: Labor and the Global Supply Chain," *New Labor Forum* 12, no. 2 (2003): 41–48; Kim Moody, *On New Terrain: How Capital Is Reshaping the Battleground of Class War* (Chicago: Haymarket Books, 2017). For a critique of a tendency in the "chokepoints" discourse to assume the power of logistics workers is uniform across the globe, see the contributions of Katy Fox-Hodess here: Jake Alimahomed-Wilson, Katy Fox-Hodess, and Kim Moody, "Seizing the Chokepoints," *Jacobin*, October 9, 2018, https://jacobin.com/2018/10/choke-points-logistics-industry-organizing-unions

16. Martin Danyluk, "Seizing the Means of Circulation: Choke Points and Logistical Resistance in Coco Solo, Panama," *Antipode* 55, no. 5 (2023): 1368–1389, quote at 1372.

17. Joshua Clover, "Terminal Showdown," *Verso Books Blog*, January 29, 2017, https://www.versobooks.com/blogs/3073-terminal-showdown

18. Bernes, "Logistics, Counterlogistics, and the Communist Prospect." See also Joshua Clover, *Riot. Strike. Riot: The New Era of Uprisings* (London: Verso, 2016).

19. The video, *Person Obstructing a Line of Containers* (2009), is available online through the artist's website: https://www.santiago-sierra.com/200904_1024.php

20. See Claire Bishop, "Antagonism and Relational Aesthetics," *October* 110 (Autumn 2004): 51–79.

21. The video, *Obstruction of a Freeway with a Truck's Trailer* (1998), is available online on the artist's website: https://www.santiago-sierra.com/987_1024.php

22. Hans Ulrich Obrist and Santiago Sierra, "Santiago Sierra in Conversation with Hans Ulrich Obrist," in *Black Cone, Monument to Civil Disobedience* (Reykjavik: Reykjavik Art Museum, 2013), 33–51, quote at 43.

23. Santiago Sierra, "Obstruction of a Freeway with a Truck's Trailer (Artist Statement)," 1998, https://www.santiago-sierra.com/987_1024.php

24. Obrist and Sierra, "Santiago Sierra in Conversation," 43.

25. Obrist and Sierra, "Santiago Sierra in Conversation," 43.

26. Lisa Baertlein, "Truck Blockade of Major California Seaport Stretches into Day Three," *Reuters*, July 22, 2022, https://www.reuters.com/world/us/truck-blockade-major-california-seaport-stretches-into-day-three-2022-07-22/

27. See, respectively, Tracey Lindeman, "Maple Leaf Flags, Conspiracy Theories and The Matrix: Inside the Ottawa Truckers' Protest," *The Guardian*, February 11, 2022, https://www.theguardian.com/world/2022/feb/11/canada-ottawa-truckers-protest-covid-vaccine-mandates; Andrew Downie, "Pro-Bolsonaro Truck Drivers Threaten New Road Blockades in Brazil," *The Guardian*, November 18, 2022, https://www.theguardian.com/world/2022/nov/18/brazil-bolsonaro-truck-drivers-threaten-road-blockades

28. See, respectively, Joshua Clover, "The Roundabout Riots," *Verso Books Blog*, December 9, 2018, https://www.versobooks.com/blogs/4161-the-roundabout-riots; Jake Alimahomed-Wilson and Spencer Louis Potiker, "Decolonizing Logistics: Palestinian Truckers on the Occupied Supply Chain," in *Choke Points: Logistics Workers Disrupting the Global Supply Chain*, ed. Jake Alimahomed-Wilson and Immanuel Ness (London: Pluto Press, 2018), 110–125.

29. Chua and Bosworth, "Beyond the Chokepoint," 1303.

30. Joshua Clover, "The Political Economy of Tactics," *Verso Books Blog*, March 16, 2022, https://www.versobooks.com/blogs/5303-the-political-economy-of-tactics

31. Alberto Toscano, "Logistics and Opposition," *Mute Magazine* 3, no. 2, August 9, 2011, http://www.metamute.org/editorial/articles/logistics-and-opposition

32. Toscano, "Lineaments of the Logistical State."

33. The Invisible Committee, *To Our Friends*, trans. Robert Hurley (Cambridge, MA: Semiotext(e), 2015), 81.

34. Toscano, "Lineaments of the Logistical State." In this later essay, Toscano engaged specifically with Bernes, "Logistics, Counterlogistics, and the Communist Prospect."

35. Toscano, "Lineaments of the Logistical State."

36. Chua, "Logistical Violence, Logistical Vulnerabilities," 178.

37. Toscano, "Logistics and Opposition."

38. Cowen, *Deadly Life of Logistics*, 23.

39. Toscano, "Lineaments of the Logistical State."

40. Chua, "Logistical Violence, Logistical Vulnerabilities," 179.

41. The Invisible Committee, *The Coming Insurrection*, 112.

42. Degenerate Communism, "Choke Points: Mapping an Anticapitalist Counter-Logistics in California," *Libcom*, July 21, 2014, https://libcom.org/article/choke-points-mapping-anticapitalist-counter-logistics-california-degenerate-communism

43. Toscano, "Lineaments of the Logistical State."

44. Toscano, "Lineaments of the Logistical State."

45. Chua and Bosworth, "Beyond the Chokepoint," 1302, 1305.

46. Cowen, *Deadly Life of Logistics*, 222. See also Sam McBean, "Circulating Desire: Queer Logistical Aesthetics," *Feminist Media Studies*, August 11, 2022, 3369–3383, https://doi.org/10.1080/14680777.2022.2110606

47. Chua, "Logistical Violence, Logistical Vulnerabilities," 180.

48. Joshua Clover, "Riot, Strike, Commune: Gendering a Civil War," *New Global Studies* 14, no. 2 (August 2020): 121–131, quote at 131, https://doi.org/10.1515/ngs-2020-0014

49. Glen Sean Coulthard, *Red Skin, White Masks: Rejecting the Colonial Politics of Recognition* (Minneapolis: University of Minnesota Press, 2014), 169; italics in the original.

50. Nick Estes, *Our History Is the Future: Standing Rock Versus the Dakota Access Pipeline, and the Long Tradition of Indigenous Resistance* (London: Verso, 2019), 248; italics in the original.

51. Leanne Betasamosake Simpson, *A Short History of the Blockade: Giant Beavers, Diplomacy, and Regeneration in Nishnaabewin* (Edmonton, Alberta: University of Alberta Press, 2021), 10.

52. Simpson, *A Short History of the Blockade*, 56. See also Leanne Betasamosake Simpson, *As We Have Always Done: Indigenous Freedom Through Radical Resistance* (Minneapolis: University of Minnesota Press, 2017).

53. Simpson, *A Short History of the Blockade*, 10.

54. Kim Kelly, "The Next Target for Protests Against Israel: Ports," *In These Times*, November 6, 2023, https://inthesetimes.com/article/ports-protests-tacoma-oakland-orlando-israel-gaza

Index

Page numbers in *italics* refer to figures.

1957–58 American recession, 7
1997 Asian financial crisis, 73–74
2008 financial crisis, 41, 52, 149

Abramović, Marina, 200
Access Gallery, 227n131
Adaptainer, 147
Aivazovsky, Ivan, 75
Algeria: independence, 119–121; oil extraction, 117, 121
Ali, Hameed, 123
Amazon, 32, 36, 166, 168, 176; advertisements, 170–171, 173; Amazon Robotics, 176, 183; corporate performances, 36, 169; COVID-19 pandemic, 186; fulfillment centers, 171, 177, 179, 253n50; fulfillment center tours, 174–177; Kiva bots, 174–178; last-mile costs, 172, 174; patents, 172; Prime Air, 170–173; roboticized shelving methods, 179; Scout, 173; tracking tools, 179; workforce, 177–178, 179, 182, 253n45
Anderson Oil and Chemical Company, 109
Anishinaabe people, 205–206
Arman, 104
Arnold, Skip: *Freight*, 81–82
art: and global labor arbitrage, 15; and supply chain capitalism, 1, 14, 194–195. *See also* logistical mode of artistic production; reconfiguration thesis
art criticism and logistics, 32
Artist Placement Group, 77
Arts Council, 142
Artworks, The, 150
art world logistics, 12, 31–32
automation, 13–14, 113–114, 165, 168, 178, 185, 187

Bahamas: shipwrecks, 50–51
Bangladesh: shipbreaking, 53
barcodes, 18, 28–29, 100
barricades, 119, 238n141; as art, 120–122
Bathurst, Bella, 48
Baumol, William, 185
Bayley, Clare: *The Container*, 133–134
Bean, Anne, 59, 60, 64–65
Beb, Maryanto, 124

Becher, Bernd and Hilla, 161
Bernes, Jasper, 14, 15, 27–28, 30, 113
Bertalanffy, Ludwig von, 112
Beshty, Walead: *FedEx© Large Kraft Box*, 3; *FedEx* glass works, 2, 18–20, 31–32
BeTomorrow, 184
Beuys, Joseph, 81
Bezos, Jeff, 170–171, 173, 174, 175, 186
BGE (Bow Gamelan Ensemble). *See* Bow Gamelan Ensemble (BGE)
Bloch, Ernst, 65–66
blockades, xv, 36, 196–198, 201–202, 203–206; as art, 90, 200
Block the Boat campaign, 78
Blumenberg, Hans: *Shipwreck with Spectator*, 49
Borcilă, Rozalinda, 195
Bordiga, Amadeo, 52
Bosworth, Kai, 205
Bourdon, David, 103, 111
Bourriaud, Nicolas, 32
Bowen, William, 185
Bow Gamelan Ensemble (BGE), 34, 44, 58–67, 222n72, 223n74; *Concrete Barges*, 63–64, *63*; *The Navigators*, 60–62, *61*; *Offshore Rig*, 60–62, 64, 222n60; *Sunken Boat*, 223n74
Bowker, Geoffrey C., 23
BP, 117
Brand, Stewart, 127
Brant, Sebastian: *Ship of Fools*, 57
Braverman, Harry, 25, 177
Brecht, Bertolt, 93; functional transformation (*Umfunktionierung*), 30–31; *Rise and Fall of the City of Mahagonny*, 134
Brenner, Robert, 186
Breuer, Frank, 133, 153
British Transport Docks Board (BTDB), 137
Broodthaers, Marcel, 46, 97
Brooks (ship), 46, 218n21
Brown, Henry Box, 82
Brunel, Isambard, 66
Burden, Chris, 200
Burnham, Jack, 15, 113
Burtynsky, Edward, 133, 153
Burwell, Paul, 59, 61, 64–65, 223n84

Cai Guo-Qiang, 34, 44, 67–76; *Bonsai Ship*, 75; *Borrowing Your Enemy's Arrows*, 67–68, *68*, 73–74; *Bringing to Venice What Marco Polo Forgot*, 69; *To Build a Ship: Project for Nara Culture City of East Asia*, 75; *Cry Dragon/Cry Wolf: The Ark of Genghis Khan*, 74; *The Dragon Has Arrived!* 73; *Kaikou—The Keel (Returning Light—The Dragon Bone)*, 71–73; *The Ninth Wave*, 69–70, *70*, 75; *The Orient (San Jō Tower)*, 73; *Reflection—A Gift from Iwaki*, 74; *San Jō Tower*, 72–73
Camp, Sokari Douglas, 35, 90; *Battle Bus*, 122–123, 124
Campling, Liam, 20, 45–46
Cape Orlando (ship), 206
capital: accumulation, 86, 129, 163, 168, 187, 193; circulation, 10, 42, 47, 49, 204–205; global, 88
capitalism. *See* supply chain capitalism
Cast Away (film), 18–19, 20
César, 101
Cheng, Henry, 148
China, 69, 70–71, 73–74, 75, 157; dispossession, 157; Quanzhou, 68, 69; Shanghai, *70*, 158; Xiamen, 156–157
Christo, 97–98, 101, 107, 111, 120; *Inventory*, 99–100, *99*, 101–102; *The London Mastaba*, 106–107, *107*; *The Mastaba: Project for United Arab Emirates*, 107; *Packages*, 98; *Wrapped Objects*, 98. *See also* Christo and Jeanne-Claude

Christo and Jeanne-Claude, 34, 90, 200; collaboration with oil and logistic companies, 105–107; *Dockside Packages*, 13, *13*, 102–103, *103*, 104, 105, 111; *Stacked Oil Barrels*, 13, 102–103, *103*, 104, 105, 111; unrealized projects, 106–107, 121; *Wall of Oil Barrels—The Iron Curtain*, 119–120
Chua, Charmaine, 5, 42, 92, 136, 158, 205
circulation, 10–11, 204–205
circulation technologies, 23, 28. *See also* communication technologies; transport technologies
Cirque du Soleil, 181, 186, 256n82; *KÀ*, 181; *Paramour*, 36, 180–182, 185–186; performers replaceable, 181–182; *Sparked*, 254n59
Clarkson, Jeremy, 171, 173
Clockwork Scenery, 242n31
Clover, Joshua, 12, 198, 201, 211n30
CMA CGM, 35, 130, 152, 154–156
CMA CGM Bougainville (ship), 155
coal, 67, 90–91
cognitive mapping, 19, 146–147
Colás, Alejandro, 20, 45–46
Cold War, 9, 132
colonialism: British Empire, 45, 51, 66–67; Canada, 206; commodities of, 15; exploitation and dispossession, 129; France, 119; Israel, 160, 162–164; Netherlands, 124; Trinidad's anti-colonial struggle, 95–96; underdevelopment, 36, 169, 182, 191; United States, 205–206. *See also* neocolonialism
communication technologies, 21, 23
Conrad, Joseph: *Heart of Darkness*, 144, 146, 150
Container Artist Residency, 78
Container Globe, 135
containerization, xvi, 35, 45, 58, 104, 130–132, 158; and delocalization of industry, 136, 149; and logistical dislocation, 151
container ships, 41, 84, 126–127; art in, 77–78
Cosgrove, Denis, 162
Cotter, Holland, 68–69, 73–74
Coulthard, Glen Sean, 129, 205–206
COVID-19 pandemic: Amazon, 186; and global demand, 41; layoffs, 186; and outdoor container stages, 135; ship crews abandonment during, 54
Cowen, Deborah, 26, 112, 157, 158, 195, 205
Cresswell, Tim, 88
Cripps, Stephen, 222n72
CVJ Corporation, 106

Dakota Access Pipeline, 206
D'Andrea, Raffaello, 182–183, 184
Danyluk, Martin, 197
Darkfield, 135, 242n31
Day, Iyko, 74, 162
Dayan, Colin, 80
deindustrialization, 14, 15, 128, 130, 136, 149. *See also* industrialization
Delehanty, Suzanne, 234n86
Delfanti, Alessandro, 166, 178
Delfina Foundation, 237n129
delivery drones: Amazon, 36, 166, 171, 173; Google, 172; JD.com, 172; Walmart, 166, 172; Zipline, 166, 172
De Maria, Walter, 110–111
dematerialization, 11, 15, 16, 20
Denny, Simon: *Amazon Worker Cage*, 175–176
deregulation, 132
Devlin, Es, 134
dispossession, 28, 128–129, 151, 183; China, 157; Indigenous people, 129, 141; London, 150; Marx on, 129; Palestinian territories, 158, 164; and racialization, 33, 44, 157

distribution, 2, 5, 6, 7–8, 29, 88, 113, 118, 169
distribution centers, 151, 166, 172
dockside management, 165
dockworkers: injuries, 105; labor relations, 131, 197; paid to contribute to art, 102, 104, 111; working conditions, 13–14, 104–105; and xenophobia in England, 66. *See also* unions
drones, 36, 165, 167–168; in Africa, 187, 190–192; civilian drones, 179; civilianization, 169–170; performances, 36, 179–180, 185. *See also* delivery drones
Dronisos, 184
Drucker, Peter, 7
DuPont: *The Magic Barrel*, 94–95

Edinburgh Fringe Festival 2007, 134
Ehikhamenor, Victor, 35, 90; *Wealth of Nations*, 123–124; *Wealth of Nations—Ogoni Nine*, 124
Eliasson, Olafur, 189
Estes, Nick, 206
Ever Given (ship), 33, 39–43, *40*, 47, 50, 52, 202
exploitation and dispossession. *See* dispossession

Federal Aviation Administration (FAA), 171, 172
FedEx, 18–19
Festival of Great Britain, 95
financialization, 5, 8, 14, 15, 202; of art, 14
First Opium War, 70, 71
flags of convenience (FOC), 53–54
Flying BeBop, 36, 184
Flying Machine Arena, 183
Ford, Henry, 175
Fordism, 28, 101, 177
Forrester, Jay Wright: *Industrial Dynamics*, 88–89
fossil fuels, 93. *See also* coal; oil (petroleum)
Foster, Norman: *Droneport*, 36, 169, 187–192, *188*
Fox, John, 139, 142
Frantic Assembly: *The Unreturning*, 242n31
Friedman, Eli, 157

Galerie J. (Paris), 120
Gates Foundation, 189, 191
Geissler, Heike, 175–176
gentrification, 35, 128; London, 141–143, 150; Ramallah, 164
Géricault, Théodore: *The Raft of the Medusa*, 47–48
Ghana, 191–192
Gilmore, Ruth Wilson, 21–22
Gilroy, Paul, 80, 96
gimmicks, 166–168, 173–174, 184, 186–187
Glissant, Édouard, 81
global labor arbitrage, 2, 11, 15, 28, 128, 158
Global Mariner (ship), 53, 55–58, 195
Gogarty, Larne Abse, 19
Goldsmiths, University of London, 117
Google, 163, 172
Goulding, Andrzej, 242n31
Grand Palais (Paris), 130, 152, *152*, 153
Greenwich Peninsula, 148, 149; The Jetty, 149–150
Group Ongaku, 34, 96–97
GS1, 18
Guggenheim Museum (New York), *68*, 74
Gulf Oil Company, 106

Haiven, Max, 14
Hall, Stuart, 95
Hamburg Süd, 143
Hamera, Judith, 14
Hancox, Dan, 150

Hanjin, 76, 78, 143
Harney, Stefano, 9, 44–46, 81
Haro Lauhus Gallery, 14, 102, 104
Hartman, Saidiya, 77, 81, 82–83
Harvey, David, 129, 211n30
hauntology, 64–66
Hemsley, Alexandrina, 82, 84
Herbert, Simon, 60
Heseltine, Michael, 141
Hickson, Ella, 94
Hine, Thomas, 100
hinterlands, xvii, 130, 151, 165
Holcim Group, 188
hovercrafts, 167
Huang Yong Ping: *Empires*, 35, 130, 151–158, *152*
humanitarian architecture, 189
Hurley, Erin, 182
Hyperloop, 167

ice trade, 15
Ideal-X (ship), 126, 131
IKEA, 183
imperialism, 71, 158, 162
India, 53, 71
Indigenous people, 53; decolonization, 198; dispossession, 129, 141; land protection, xviii, 195, 197, 201; social struggles, 36, 205, 206
Indonesia, 76, 124
industrialization, 45, 66, 71, 91. *See also* deindustrialization
information technologies, 14, 29, 100
infrastructure: definition, 21–23; visibility thesis, 23–24. *See also* logistical infrastructure
Institute of Contemporary Art (Philadelphia), 105
Intel, 184, 255n73
intermodalism, 8, 10, 104, 127, 130–132
International Dockworkers Council (IDC), 56
International Organization for Standardization, 104, 132
International Transport Workers' Federation (ITF), 53–57
inventory management, 29, 100; computer systems, 175; drone systems, 183. *See also* just-in-time production system (JIT)
Invisible Committee, 202
Iron Man 3 (film), 4
Israel, 50, 78, 160–161, 163, 197, 206
Iwaki City Art Museum, 72

James, C. L. R., 95
Jameson, Frederic, 18, 27, 28, 29; cognitive mapping, 19, 146–147
Janus Vaten, 14, 106, 107
Japan, xvi, 7, 72–75, 94, 100, 132; Iwaki, 71–72, 74
JCB, 162
JD.com, 172
Jeanne-Claude, 98, 106. *See also* Christo and Jeanne-Claude
Jencks, Charles, 127
Jogja Biennale, 124
Jogja National Museum (Yogyakarta), 123
John Jones Gallery, 237n129
Johnson, Dominic, 82
Jones, Christopher F., 92
just-in-time production system (JIT), 8, 10, 88, 100–101, 132, 196

Kagame, Paul, 190
Kalabari people, 123
Kaprow, Allan, 34, 81, 90; *Fluids: A Happening*, 15–16, *16*; *Gas*, 110; *Overtime—A Happening (For Walter De Maria)*, 111; *Transfer—A Happening (For Christo)*, 109–110, *110*, 111, 112–114; *Yard*, 108
Kawara, On, 16

Kelley, Jeff, 108
Khalili, Laleh, 26, 89, 152
Kiefer, Anselm, 134
Kingsley, Charles: *The Water-Babies*, 144–145
Kinkle, Jeff, 18, 133–134, 152, 154
Kiva Systems, 174–175, 183
Klein, Yves, 101
Knight Dragon, 148, 149–150
Kojima, Nobuaki, 109
Kostelanetz, Richard, 110
Kröller-Müller Museum (Otterlo), 106

LafargeHolcim Foundation for Sustainable Construction, 188
last-mile costs, 172, 173, 174, 177
LDDC (London Docklands Development Corporation). *See* London Docklands Development Corporation (LDDC)
LeCavalier, Jesse, 29, 100
Ledgard, Jonathan, 190–191, 257n96
Lethal Weapon 2 (film), 17
Levantis, George, 77
Levinson, Marc, 127, 136
Liberate Tate, 94
Lieb, Nathaniel, 234n86
Limehouse Development Group, 141
Lin Yilin, 200
Liu, Petrus, 15
Lloyd's of London, 51
logistical infrastructure, xviii, xix, 8, 20, 21, 193, 194, 196, 197, 204, 211n30; capital investment, 9–12. *See also* blockades; reconfiguration thesis
logistical mode of artistic production, xviii, 2, 4, 5, 6, 12–13, 17. *See also* reconfiguration thesis
logistics: administrative work, 119; and colonization, 9; definition, xviii, 2, 5–6, 20, 44; and dispossession, 128–129, 151; etymology, 1, 24; and flow, 88; and friction, 86, 205; and global labor arbitrage, 11; and loss prevention, 42, 44–45; managers in, 8; and racism, 46, 87; and slave trade, 45–46; software, 25; as violence, 25–26; and warfare, 9
logistics revolution, 1, 6–12, 203–204
Loisy, Jean de, 154, 155
London: deindustrialization, 149; dispossession, 150; gentrification, 141–143, 150; Heygate housing estate (Elephant and Castle), 150; Limehouse Basin, 138, 140; Limehouse Link, 141; North Greenwich, 65, 143, 148, 150; real estate prices, 149; Shoreditch, 150; unemployment, 138
London Docklands, 60, 137, 138, 140; Canary Wharf, 140; Container City, 142–143; East India Docks, 138; gentrification, 142–143; Regent's Canal Dock, 140; Royal Docks, 138; Trinity Buoy Wharf, 142–143
London Docklands Development Corporation (LDDC), 140–141, 143
London International Festival of Theatre (LIFT), 142
Long Good Friday, The (film), 138
longshoremen. *See* dockworkers
LOT-EK, 240n8
Lovelace, Earl, 96
Lukoil, 106

Mackey, Nathaniel, 96
Maersk, 52–53, 128, 183
Magasin III (Stockholm), 199
Malm, Andreas, 91, 93
management, 25, 179. *See also* Fordism; inventory management; supply chain management; Taylorism
Managing Mayhem, 147

manufacturing, 1, 88–89, 114, 127; zero inventory, 88. *See also* just-in-time production system (JIT)
marine salvage, 47–52; as art, 34; legal aspects, 51
Martha Jackson Gallery (New York), 108
Marx, Karl, 9, 101; circuit of capital theory, 10; on dispossession and exploitation, 129; General Law of Capitalist Accumulation, 167; on transport labor, 21, 209n26, 210n27; value theory of labor, 209n26
Masri, Bashar, 163
material handling, 45
Mau, Søren, 6, 197
Mauser, 106
McClanahan, Annie, 8, 14
McKinnie, Michael, 148
McKinsey & Company, 89, 137, 165, 167, 187
McKittrick, Katherine, 82
McLean, Malcom, 131, 137
McQueen, Steve: *Drumroll*, 87–88
Mechanization and Modernization Agreement (MMA), 14, 104–105
Méduse (ship), 47
Menon, Jisha, 15
Metis: *3rd Ring Out*, 135
Metzger, Sean, 70
Mezzadra, Sandro, 129
Miller, Sarah, 175
Mitchell, Timothy, 89
Mitchell, W. J. T., 162
Moderna Museet (Stockholm), 109
Molesworth, Helen, 15
Monumenta, 152
Moorman, Charlotte, 34; *Variations on a Theme by Saint-Saëns*, 109
Morison, Ivan, 200
Moss, Rebecca: *International Waters*, 227n131
Moten, Fred, 9, 44–46, 81
MSC Napoli (ship), 48–49
Museum of Contemporary Art Tokyo, 72–73
Museum of Modern Art (MoMA) (New York), 121
Musk, Elon, 165
Musk, Kimbal, 255n73

Naftal, 115, 117
Naimou, Angela, 82
Narita, Miyako, 64
Nasser, Gamal Abdel, 50, 52
Neel, Phil, 151
Neilson, Brett, 43, 129
Nemser, Daniel, 23
neocolonialism, 187, 192. *See also* colonialism
Neptune Orient Lines, 155
Neue Flora Theater (Hamburg), 185
Newman, Michael, 87
Ngai, Sianne, 36, 118; *Theory of the Gimmick*, 167–168, 174, 186–187
Nigeria, 95, 122–125
Nijō Castle (Kyoto), 75
Nisbet, James, 32
Nixon, Rob, 26
Norman Foster Foundation (NFF), 189, 191
Nouveau Réalisme, 101, 104

Ocean Fleets, 226n129
Office of Naval Research, 89
offshoring, 9, 14, 114
Ogoni Nine, 122–123, 124
Ogoni people, xix, 122, 125
oil (petroleum), 90–91
oil barrels, 88, 92; as art, 34, 86, 89, 92; capacity, 230n30; cost, 91; transport, 91
oil consumption, 92
oil drilling: Algeria, 117, 121; Indonesia, 124; Nigeria, 122; Trinidad, 96; United States, 91

oilfield workers, 92
oil industry infrastructure, 94
oil tankers, 53, 72, 89, 90, 92, 131
Oil Wars (1860s–1870s), 91–92
Okoth, Christine, 124
Onassis, Aristotle, 54, 89
open registries. *See* flags of convenience (FOC)
Organisation for Economic Co-operation and Development (OECD), 88
Origami (Noro and Ohl), 239n1
Oslo Accords, 160, 162
Ostrale Biennale (Dresden) 2016, 124
Ourahmane, Lydia, 35, 90; *The Third Choir*, 115–119, *116*, 121, 237n129
Out of the Woods collective, 28

packaging, 98, 100, 102, 106
Paik, Nam June, 16–17, 34; *Variations on a Theme by Saint-Saëns*, 109
Palestine: dispossession, 158, 164; Gaza, 206; Ramallah, 164; Rawabi, 163; West Bank, *159*, 161, 162, 163, 164
Palestinian Museum (Birzeit), 162
Palestinian National Authority (PA), 163
Palmer, Henry Robinson, 249n127
Parrot, 184
patents, 102, 166
Peace Now, 160
Peak, Heather, 200
People's Armadas, 141
People's Republic of Walmart, The (Phillips and Rozworski), 27
Performance Arcade (Wellington), 135
personhood, 46, 79, 81–82
Philadelphia College of Art, 109
Philip, M. Nourbese, 82
Phillips, Leigh, 27, 179
Piggly Wiggly, 100
pipelines, 34, 36, 42, 89, 90, 92, 195, 197, 205
Platform, 122
Platoon Kunsthalle (Seoul), 135
Plato: *Republic*, 57
Polo, Marco, 69
Pope.L, 87
ports: Bremen, 137; Cologne, 13, *13*, 14, *103*, 104; Felixstowe, 137; London, 136–138; Oakland, xv–xvii, 196, 197, 198, 201, 202–203, 204, 206; Quanzhou, 69; Rotterdam, 137; Shanghai, 151; Stockholm, 198, *199*; Tilbury, 137, 146; Xiamen, 156–157. *See also* London Docklands
Posner, Miriam, 25, 29
Powell, Enoch, 66
Power Station of Art (Shanghai), 69–70
Pozyx, 184–185
Prebble, Lucy, 94
Prokopoff, Stephen, 234n86
PS1 Gallery, 67

Rabie, Kareem, 163
racialization: and dispossession, 34, 44, 157; and shipping crews, 54; and supply chain capitalism, 4, 9, 25; and workforces, 8, 50, 179, 198
racism, 46, 66, 78–80, 87
Rauschenberg, Robert: *Elgin Tie*, 109
real-time location systems (RTLS), 185
reconfiguration thesis, 26–32, 36–37, 58, 193–194, 204
Rediker, Marcus, 46, 79, 84
Restany, Pierre, 103–104, 120
Rise and Fall of the City of Mahagonny (Weill and Brecht), 134
Roberts, John, 101
robots, 165, 168, 173; and human workers, 175–176, 186. *See also* delivery drones; drones; Kiva Systems, warehouse automation
Rockefeller, John D., 7

Rodney, Walter: *How Europe Underdeveloped Africa*, 192
Rose, Charlie, 170–171
Rossiter, Ned, 43
Rothstein, Adam, 170
Rozworski, Michal, 27, 179
Rube Goldberg machine, 167, 174
Ruscha, Ed: *Twentysix Gasoline Stations*, 93
Rwanda, 36, 172, 189, 190, 191, 192

salvage, 33–34, 43–44, 46–47, 60; legal aspects, 51; and repurposing, 52. *See also* marine salvage
salvage spectacles, 39, 41, 51–52; shipwrecks, 47–48
Saro-Wiwa, Ken, 122, 123
Saro-Wiwa, Zina, 26, 35, 90; *Karikpo Pipeline*, 125, 195
Schlingensief, Christoph: *Bitte Liebt Österrich! (Please Leave Austria!)*, 135
Scott, Dread: *Slave Rebellion Reenactment*, 195
Seafarers Education Service, 226n129
Sea-Land Service, 104, 131, 137, 138
Sekula, Allan, 17, 26, 77–78, 84, 89, 128, 133, 135–136; *Ship of Fools*, *54*, *55*, 56–58
self-service retailing, 100
Serial Shipping Container Codes, 18
Sharpe, Christina, 81, 84
Shell, 35, 122, 125, 195
shipbreaking, 53
shipbuilding, 42–43, 67, 75, 140, 148
shipping, 25, 41, 66–67, 88; costs, 8; and exclusion, 76; rates, 76, 225n110
shipping container architecture, 127, 136, 143, 149, 158, 160, 240n8
shipping container art, 128, 133, 136, 143, 151
shipping containers, 35, 127–128, 130–131, 156, 240n8; in art, 126, 132–133; as barricades, 184; construction, 157; cranes, xvi; repurposing, 28, 126, 127–128, 129, 134–135, 136, 149; standardization, 131–132
shipping vessels: naval gigantism, 41, 42; production, 226n113; salvage, 49–50
ships, 24, 43, 53. *See also* oil tankers; slave ships
shipwrecks, 39, 47–52, 75
Shunt, 35, 129–130; *The Boy Who Climbed Out of His Face*, 143–150, *145*
Sierra, Santiago, 81, 202, 203; *Obstruction of a Freeway with a Truck's Trailer*, 199–200, 202; *Person Obstructing a Line of Containers*, 199–201, *199*, 202
Signer, Roman, 86–87, 88
Silver, Nathan, 127
Simpson, Leanne Betasamosake, 206
Sinnokrot, Nida, 26; *Caravans*, 161; *Jonah's Whale*, 35, 130, 158–164, *159*; *Ka (Oslo)*, 162; *Rawabi*, 163
Sinophobia, 69, 74
Six-Day War, 121, 132
slave ships, 23, 46, 77, 79–82, 84, 218n21
slave trade, 6, 9, 44, 45–46, 81, 82, 84, 85, 218n21
Smit, Fop, 50
SMIT International, 50–51
Smith, Jason, 168, 182
South Korea, 73
Spicer, André, 176
Srnicek, Nick, 27, 28
Stadium 974 (Doha), 135
Standard Oil Company, 96
Standing Rock Sioux Tribe, 206
Star, Susan Leigh, 23
steam, 66–67, 72; boats, 50, 71; engines, 45, 49, 50, 66–67, 91; shipping, 9, 67
Steel, Howard, 243n46
steel drums, 17, 95–96, 97
Steinmetz, Phel, 93
Stevenson, Robert Louis, 48

St. Paul (ship), 48
Suez Canal, 9, 39, 42, 47, 50, 52, 121, 132, 197
Suez Canal Authority (SCA), 42
supply chain capitalism, 1–2, 6, 11, 14, 127, 194–195, 207n1; exploitation and dispossession dynamics, 183
supply chain management, 24
supply chain techniques, 9
Susskind, Daniel: *A World Without Work*, 186
Suwandi, Intan, 11
Swiss Federal Institute of Technology, 183
systems esthetics, 113
systems theory, 112–113

Tanzania, 190
Tate Britain (London), *116*
Tate Modern (London), 184
Taylorism, 25
TechCrunch, 173
telegraph cables, 9, 66–67
Telford, Thomas, 66
Teller, Astro, 172
TEU (twenty-foot equivalent unit), 132, 220n41
Thames Steam Launch Company, 222n60
Thompson, Selina, 26, 34; *salt.*, 44, 76–85
Tinguely, Jean, 62, 222n72
Tokyo Bay (ship), 77
Toscano, Alberto: on blockades, 202–205; on reconfiguration thesis, 26–27, 30; on shipping container art, 133–134, 152, 154; on supply chain capitalism, 18, 194
total cost analysis, 7. *See also* systems theory
Toyota, 8, 100–101
TPG Capital, 256n82
transportation, 9, 20–21; costs, 11, 131, 172, 209n26; labor, 210n27; outlays, 209n26. *See also* shipping
transport technologies, 23; reconfiguration, 30–31. *See also* drones; hovercrafts; Hyperloop; oil barrels; pipelines; shipping containers; ships
Trinidad, 17, 95–96
Trinidad All-Steel Percussion Orchestra (TASPO), 95
Tsing, Anna Lowenhaupt, 51, 86, 207n1
twenty-foot equivalent unit (TEU), 132, 220n41
Twenty-Three Days at Sea Residency, 227n131

uncrewed aerial vehicles (UAVs). *See* drones
unions, 56, 105, 131, 137
United Kingdom: British Empire, 66–67, 96, 137; East India Company, 67; Navy, 67, 96
Universal Product Code. *See* barcodes
upcycling, 127
UPS, 24
Urban Space Management (USM), 143

value chain analysis, 218n16
Venice Biennale: 1995, 69; 1997, 73; 2017, 123, 227n131; of Architecture 2016, 36
Verity AG, 183
Verity Studios, 182–184, 254n59
Vietnam War, xvi, 132

Walmart, 27, 100, 166; and barcodes, 29; delivery drones, 166, 172
warehouse automation, 36, 165, 174–179, 183, 187
warehouses, 101
Warhol, Andy, 98

Weizman, Eyal, 160, 161
Welfare State International, 35, 129–130, 139; *Raising the Titanic*, 138–142, 243n45
Wells, Jamin, 48
Wenzel, Jennifer, 22
Wet'suwet'en, 206
Williams, Alex, 27, 28
Williams, Evan Calder, 51
Wilson, Richard, 59, 62, 64–65; *A Slice of Reality*, 65
Winant, Gabriel, 186
Wire, The (TV series), 133
workers: conditions, 8–9, 29, 54; deskilling, 177; disposable, 166; exploitation, 28, 128; and labor-saving devices, 167–168; migrant workers, 158; protests, 197; and robots, 175–176, 186. *See also* Amazon: workforce; dockworkers; oilfield workers; unions
World Bank, 190, 191; Logistics Performance Index, 88
World War II, xvi, 59, 63, 64, 72, 94, 137

Yi, Anicka: *In Love with the World*, 36, 184–185
Yomiuri Indépendent Exhibition (Japan), 109

Zemeckis, Robert, 19
Z'EV, 222n60
Zhuge Liang, 68
Zieger, Susan, 119
ZIM, 78
Zipline, 166, 172, 190–191
Zong massacre, 46, 218n21

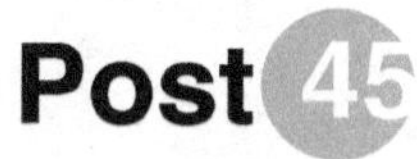

Adrienne Brown, *The Residential Is Racial: A Perceptual History of Mass Homeownership*

Patrick Whitmarsh, *Writing Our Extinction: Anthropocene Fiction and Vertical Science*

Rebecca B. Clark, *American Graphic: Disgust and Data in Contemporary Literature*

Palmer Rampell, *Genres of Privacy in Postwar America*

Joseph Darda, *The Strange Career of Racial Liberalism*

Jordan S. Carroll, *Reading the Obscene: Transgressive Editors and the Class Politics of US Literature*

Michael Dango, *Crisis Style: The Aesthetics of Repair*

Mary Esteve, *Incremental Realism: Postwar American Fiction, Happiness, and Welfare-State Liberalism*

Dorothy J. Hale, *The Novel and the New Ethics*

Christine Hong, *A Violent Peace: Race, U.S. Militarism, and Cultures of Democratization in Cold War Asia and the Pacific*

Sarah Brouillette, *UNESCO and the Fate of the Literary*

Sophie Seita, *Provisional Avant-Gardes: Little Magazine Communities from Dada to Digital*

Guy Davidson, *Categorically Famous: Literary Celebrity and Sexual Liberation in 1960s America*

Joseph Jonghyun Jeon, *Vicious Circuits: Korea's IMF Cinema and the End of the American Century*

Lytle Shaw, *Narrowcast: Poetry and Audio Research*

Stephen Schryer, *Maximum Feasible Participation: American Literature and the War on Poverty*

Margaret Ronda, *Remainders: American Poetry at Nature's End*

Jasper Bernes, *The Work of Art in the Age of Deindustrialization*

Annie McClanahan, *Dead Pledges: Debt, Crisis, and Twenty-First-Century Culture*

Amy Hungerford, *Making Literature Now*

J. D. Connor, *The Studios After the Studios: Neoclassical Hollywood (1970–2010)*

Michael Trask, *Camp Sites: Sex, Politics, and Academic Style in Postwar America*

Loren Glass, *Counterculture Colophon: Grove Press, the* Evergreen Review, *and the Incorporation of the Avant-Garde*

Michael Szalay, *Hip Figures: A Literary History of the Democratic Party*

Jared Gardner, *Projections: Comics and the History of Twenty-First-Century Storytelling*

Jerome Christensen, *America's Corporate Art: The Studio Authorship of Hollywood Motion Pictures*

The authorized representative in the EU for product safety and compliance is:
Mare Nostrum Group
B.V Doelen 72
4831 GR Breda
The Netherlands

www.ingramcontent.com/pod-product-compliance
Lightning Source LLC
LaVergne TN
LVHW091113080826
845145LV00008B/1899

* 9 7 8 1 5 0 3 6 4 0 4 3 6 *